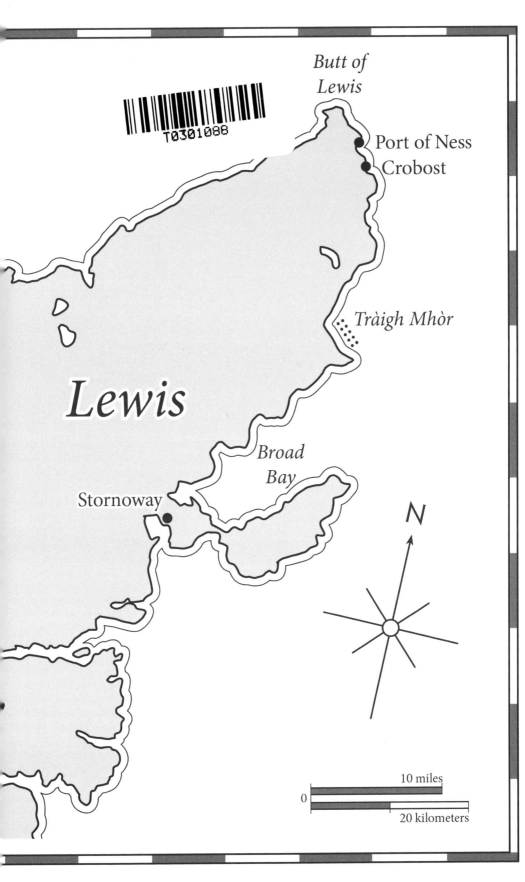

Butt of
Lewis

● Port of Ness
● Crobost

Tràigh Mhòr

Lewis

Broad
Bay

Stornoway ●

N

10 miles
0
20 kilometers

THE
BLACK
LOCH

Also by Peter May

PETER MAY

THE BLACK LOCH

riverrun

First published in Great Britain in 2024 by

r

riverrun
an imprint of
Quercus Editions Ltd
Carmelite House
50 Victoria Embankment
London EC4Y 0DZ

An Hachette UK company

The authorized representative in the EEA is Hachette Ireland,
8 Castlecourt Centre, Dublin 15, D15 XTP3, Ireland (email: info@hbgi.ie)

A CIP catalogue record for this book is available
from the British Library.

HB ISBN 978 1 52943 606 8
TPB ISBN 978 1 52943 607 5
EBOOK ISBN 978 1 52943 608 2

Endpaper map © 2024 Nick May

10 9

Typeset by CC Book Production
Printed and bound in Great Britain by Clays Ltd, Elcograf S.p.A.

Papers used by riverrun are from well-managed forests and other responsible sources.

For Ron Beard

When all desire at last and all regret
Go hand in hand to death, and all is vain,
What shall assuage the unforgotten pain
And teach the unforgetful to forget?

'The One Hope' – Dante Gabriel Rossetti

PROLOGUE

The sun set some time ago. Although it is not yet dark enough, somehow, for murder.

The east side of the island lies in dusky purple shadow, with the rising of the moon still hours away. But what little light remains in the sky is reflected pale and pink upon the unusually still waters of An Loch Dubh, making silhouettes of the man and woman as they run from the house. For more than an hour, only the single lit pane of a downstairs window has broken the twilight, seeming to flicker feebly, like a candle, in its fight against the smothering half-light.

It burns still as the figures flee the hulking shadow of the house that stands black against the sky. And the silence of the night is breached only by the sigh of the sea loch surging between headlands to drown the tiny sandy beach below at high tide.

Out across the clifftops they run, oblivious to the phosphorescence of salt water breaking white against the rocks thirty feet beneath them, the sound of it masking the shouted words exchanged. Until he reaches her with longer strides and catches her arm, turning her towards him. Then the shrillness of her voice rises into the night. Words lost, but meaning clear. He takes her other arm and shakes her. She tears it free and swings an open palm towards his face. The force of its impact is discernible in the sudden turn of his head.

There is a moment, then. A hiatus that might have lasted half a second or a whole lifetime. Before he lifts a hand to strike her back. She staggers away, caught either by surprise or by the strength of the blow, half turning and losing her footing as she does. It is almost possible to feel his panic as he lunges forward to try to catch her. But she escapes his grasp, as elusive as redemption, and topples sideways from the cliff, spinning into the night to vanish beyond an outcrop of black, Lewisian gneiss. The oldest rock on earth, witness to the snuffing out of a life, like the briefest flare of a match struck in the darkness of eternity.

CHAPTER ONE

I.

It was early. The exceptional spell of warm, still weather had brought tourists and midges in almost equal number to this island off an island on the north-west coast of the most north-westerly outpost of the European continent. The voices of children rang out in the bright, clear morning, tiny footprints left in wet sand. A shouted warning rose above the rush of the sea, as parents laden with folding chairs and rugs and a hamper hurried down the tiny single-track road towards the shore. But a solitary, sharp scream sent back fear like an arrow, and everything was dropped, sand flying in the wake of swift feet as they sprinted towards the water's edge.

The children were standing either side of a human shape lifting and falling only slightly on the ebb and flow of the sea, hair fanned out like seaweed in the sand. The young woman stared up into a sky reflected in the blue of her wide-open eyes. A pretty face, but bruised on the left side, the blood leached from a gash on her cheek by seawater. Her T-shirt was torn, ripped away at the neck, one breast exposed. She was barefoot, white panties shredded in bloodstained ribbons.

One of the children turned a pale face towards her parents, the death of innocence already apparent in dark eyes. And in a tiny voice said, 'Will she be alright?'

II.

George Gunn folded his jacket and laid it carefully on the driver's seat before swinging the door shut. It was not gone nine-thirty, and yet the morning sun was already hot. He clipped his Motorola Airwave to his belt and folded up each sleeve of his blue shirt to just a fraction below the elbow.

'It's going to be another hot one, George.' Detective Constable Louise McNish appeared pleased by the prospect.

Gunn grunted and glowered at her across the roof of the car. He preferred the wind blowing in off the sea, the sting of rain in his face. All a matter, he supposed, of what you were used to. McNish, a good twenty years his junior, was a mainlander. From the soft south. Sometimes known as Glasgow. They ran for cover at the first sign of real rain there. He turned his gaze towards the shore.

From the gravel parking area above the beach he saw the black rock exposed at low tide breaking through a skin of sand, high tide delineated by the seaweed it had left behind in wavy lines. The smell of it carried on the breeze, salty and familiar. Next to a white Nissan X-Trail, the ambulance was parked almost on the sand itself, the flashing of its blue light nearly lost in the brilliance of this late August sunshine. A woman crouched at the tideline, leaning over a figure that lay prone on the gentle shelving of the sand. A uniformed police officer and two ambulance men stood watching. Death seemed particularly inappropriate on such a morning.

Gunn picked his way across the beach, Louise following in his wake, black boots leaving deep treads in soft sand. The uniform nodded acknowledgement and stepped aside. The doctor looked up from the body. Fair hair dragged back and held out of her face by clasps. A strong face, pale, without make-up. She looked weary. 'Just a lassie,' she said.

Gunn let his eyes fall to the body and felt something turn over in his stomach. He knew this girl. Not personally. But her face was very familiar. A striking face, full lips that he had seen often parted in laughter. Her long silken chestnut hair lay tangled among the seaweed, blue eyes gazing up at him, almost in accusation. He knew, of course, that was just in his mind. The guilt he always felt when confronted by a death he had not been there to stop. He closed his eyes. What was her name again?

'Caitlin Black, Detective Sergeant,' the doctor said, as though she had overheard his thought.

Gunn nodded. Yes, he remembered now. He opened his eyes and ran them over the familiar contours of her face, taking in the bruising below her left eye and the gash on her right cheek. 'How did she die, Sam?'

Dr Samantha Blair had been on the island for a full year now, filling a vacancy at the GP practice in Stornoway, and bringing the invaluable expertise of three years working as a pathologist's assistant in Aberdeen. The powers that be in Church Street had immediately enlisted her services as police surgeon. In that capacity she had attended suicides and accidental deaths. But it seemed as though this might be her first murder. 'Violently,' she said. 'Much of the contusion you can see, the abrasions about her body and the wound on her face, occurred ante-mortem.' She pursed her lips. 'And she may well have been raped. Quite brutally.' She tugged at the girl's torn T-shirt, drying now in the sunshine. 'Ripped nearly off her. Panties torn. Vaginal damage.'

'Cause of death?'

Sam shrugged. 'Impossible to say. Could have been a blow to the head. She might have drowned. Her lungs are filled with water, though that doesn't mean anything. It'll take an autopsy to establish exactly how she died.' She stood up now, stretching stiffened muscles. 'I'll take a vaginal swab for DNA. If there's semen there it'll give us a clue to the identity of the rapist, who is probably also her killer.' She sighed. 'It'll be a few days, though, before we get results back from the lab.'

All Gunn could hear were the cries of gulls flying around the cliffs where they nested, the sound of the sea as the retreating tide sucked it out once more into the Black Loch. Sunlight fell, sparkling like jewels, on the surface of the water, and beyond the headland he saw a gannet diving for fish somewhere out

6

on East Loch Roag. Life continuing as it had since the beginning of time on this convergence of the Atlantic Ocean and the north-western fringe of the European landmass. But not for this poor dead girl at his feet.

And he knew that all this would still be here when he, too, was gone. He had been resisting retirement, despite the pleading of his wife, with the sense that it would only accelerate him towards an end he had resolutely refused to acknowledge all his life. An end that was becoming increasingly hard to ignore. He let his eyes fall again to the lifeless form of Caitlin Black at his feet and felt reproached for surviving this long when someone so young had not. Someone with everything to live for.

Sam dropped again to her hunkers, and her voice dragged him away from his reverie. 'You should look at this, George.'

He blinked and refocused, crouching beside her as she began carefully to part the girl's salt-crusted hair. The ends of a fine gold chain, irretrievably tangled among the individual hairs, caught the sunlight. The doctor turned the dead girl's head to one side and revealed a small shiny gold object nestled behind her left ear. It was still attached to the broken chain. Gunn frowned and peered at it more closely.

'What is it?'

'A pendant of some kind.' It was round, the same gold as the chain, and cut in the shape of an eye, with a virulent blue stone set at its centre like an iris. 'A sapphire, I think.'

Gunn looked at her, surprised. 'Real?'

She shrugged. 'Beyond my field of expertise. You'll need to ask a jeweller.'

'Hers, do you think?'

'Could be.'

Gunn reached around to the back pocket of his trousers for his Samsung phone. It was what they issued them now, a replacement for the traditional police officer's black notebook. Officially known, prosaically, as a Mobile Handheld Device. Unlike the old notebooks, you could take photographs with it, record statements, type in reports and send them wirelessly. Gunn hated it. He fumbled to activate its camera function. Louise leaned over and tapped the screen. 'Just swipe up now, George.'

He snatched it away from her in annoyance. 'I know how to use it!'

An image of the girl lying in the sand flickered on to his screen. He took several photographs before asking the doctor to part the hair again so that he could get a close-up of the pendant. He stood up, heard a crack in his knee and felt a twinge of pain in his lower back. 'Anyone know where she lives? How she got here?'

The uniform was eager to help. A young constable, not long out of probation. 'When I first arrived,' he said, 'there was a woman at that house over there.' He waved a hand vaguely towards the far side of the beach. 'She said there was a light on all night at the house on the cliffs.' And he turned to point almost directly overhead. Black rock rose twenty-five feet into the blue of the sky, and the gable ends and pointed dormers of a white-painted cottage with slate roof broke the skyline.

III.

Gunn was out of breath and trailing several paces behind his younger colleague by the time he and Louise had climbed the single-track road to the top of the cliffs. And he was glad of the stiffening breeze that blew in off the loch up here, cooling the heat in pink cheeks and providing much needed oxygen for toiling lungs.

The cottage was bigger than it appeared from below. An outbuilding attached itself at right angles to the far gable, creating a sheltered semi-courtyard behind the house. A vehicle gate stood open, but the pedestrian gate was jammed shut, and Gunn and Louise had to pick their way across a cattle grid.

The chippings that had once covered the courtyard were mostly lost in mud baked hard by the recent unaccustomed dry spell. The house itself had seen better days, whitewash peeling from roughcast walls, weeds growing in profusion around the step at the back door. A battered old lime green Ford Fiesta stood parked by the outbuilding.

Gunn stopped to take a photograph of it before approaching the vehicle. He pulled on latex gloves to open the driver's door. The interior of the car was faded and tashed, and Gunn was struck by the smell of damp fighting for ascendancy over the scent of stale perfume and the musty odour of wet dog.

He stooped to pick a lipstick holder from a mud-caked rubber mat on the floor. Fuchsia pink. He placed it carefully on the worn seat cover and glanced in the back. Half a dozen dog-eared fashion magazines were strewn across the back seat and liberally covered by muddy paw prints. He closed the door and rounded the car to the passenger side, where he sat in to open the glove box. Sweet wrappers and empty packs of chewing gum fell out, along with the other detritus of a teenage girl's life. A broken mascara brush. A dried-up bottle of pale blue nail varnish. Right at the back was an owner's manual, water-stained and tattered. Gunn leaned over to riffle through the stuff that had fallen out, and a short plastic wand about six inches long, pink at one end, white at the other, caught his attention. He picked it up. A small rectangular window at the white end displayed two short parallel red lines.

A shadow fell through the open door and he turned to see Louise leaning in for a closer look.

He said, 'Is this what I think it is?'

She bent down to retrieve an empty cardboard box from the floor and held it up. 'Well,' she said. 'It's not a Covid test.'

'Jesus!' The oath slipped from his lips in a pained whisper. Somehow, this only made it worse. He pulled himself together and photographed both items before slipping them into a clear plastic evidence bag and sealing it shut. He slid out into the warmth of the sun again. 'Check out the perimeter of the house, Louise. And follow that path out to the far end of the headland. If there's anything kicking about out there, we want to retrieve it before the wind gets up.' He turned to cast his eye over the back of the house, windows almost opaque with dirt and masking the gloom beyond. 'I'll take a look inside.'

The house was cool, thick stone walls defying the best efforts of the sun to penetrate its inner chill. There was a lingering hint of dampness in the air, and yet a sense of recent human presence. Something hard to define. Olfactory, perhaps. Bodies. Sweat. And something else. Alcohol, he realized, as he stepped from the gloom of a narrow hallway into the kitchen and saw a half-empty bottle of white wine catching the light of the sun that angled through a front window. Two glasses stood beside the bottle on a stained worktop. One still with an inch of wine in the bottom of it, a smudge of fuchsia pink on its rim.

There were crumbs on the worktop, and Gunn flipped open a pedal bin to look down on the remains of a half-eaten sandwich and its plastic wrapping among crumpled paper bags and napkins, and two empty wine bottles.

He crossed to the window and shaded his eyes from the sunlight to peer out. From here, the body and the little group of people attending to it down below were invisible. But he could see across to the far side of the bay where sunlight glinted off the bonnet of his car, and a woman was hanging up washing on a line outside a house on the hill above. He glanced at the ceiling and saw that the kitchen light was still on, although it would have been hard now to separate it from the wash of sunlight flooding the room. But it would surely have been visible at night from the house across the way, and he assumed that the woman hanging out the washing was probably the one who had reported it to the constable.

From the kitchen-diner, he wandered back into the hall. A door opened off it into a small living room with vintage nineteen-seventies wallpaper, faded and browned by years of peat smoke. The distinctive toasty odour of the peat lingered still, though who knew how long it was since a fire had burned in the grate?

Upstairs were two bedrooms, one either side of a small landing, separated by a tiny bathroom. In the room to his left, a lumpy old bed with wooden head- and footboards was covered with a frayed candlewick bedspread, dark blue, almost black, like a widow's modesty. In stark contrast, the bed in the other room lay shamelessly naked, exposed by sheets flung aside to reveal the chaos of what looked to have been frenzied activity, depressions left by heads pressed into soft pillows. The room smelled of sex. There were stains on the sheets, and the evidence of long chestnut hair shed on white pillowcases.

Something caught Gunn's eye on the floor, half hidden beneath the bed. He crouched down to see that it was a discarded credit card receipt. Standing up again, he crossed to the dormer. He tilted his head at an angle to see Louise coming back along the path from the headland, and took his Airwave from his belt to call her.

It was a couple of minutes before he heard her coming into the house and he shouted her up the stairs. She stepped into the bedroom and her eyes fell straight away on the bed. She turned to look at Gunn. He said, 'We're going to have to dust for prints, swab for DNA. And photograph everything here. Starting with this . . .' And he crouched once more, this time to photograph the credit card receipt before lifting it between latex fingers to examine it more closely.

'What is it?' Louise said.

Gunn dropped it into an evidence bag. 'Credit card receipt from the Co-op in Stornoway. Probably for that half-drunk bottle of wine sitting downstairs in the kitchen.'

Gunn left Louise on the beach watching as Caitlin Black was zipped carefully into a body bag, the impression she had left in the sand erased now by the incoming tide. Soon, any evidence that she had been there at all would be lost for ever, like her life itself.

The detective sergeant was perspiring freely by the time he had navigated the stony track that led from the road up to the bungalow on the far side of the bay, stopping and fumbling to find a handkerchief to wipe his forehead. The woman was still at the washing line. Had she been there the whole time? He saw that she was taking things in now. Sheets, shirts, socks. All dropped into a brown plastic basket. He could believe that she had hung them up and taken them down half a dozen times in the last hour. Giving her a fine excuse to be out in the garden with an uninterrupted view of activities on the beach.

She looked guilty as he approached.

Gunn said, 'Good morning, Mrs er . . .?'

'Caimbeul,' she said, and wiped both hands down the front of her apron. She was a woman in her fifties. Her shiny smooth-skinned face severely exposed by the silver-grey hair pulled back from it and held in a neat bun behind her head.

Gunn nodded towards the beach. 'Nice view.'

She glowered at him. 'It is.'

'That's a lot of washing you're doing today, Mrs Caimbeul.'

'Profiting from the good Lord's sunshine. Heaven knows, we don't see that much of it.'

Gunn managed a grim smile. 'Aye.' And took out his warrant card. 'Detective Sergeant George Gunn,' he said, holding it out towards her. 'You'll have seen the comings and goings down there, then.'

'I have. They came up here to phone the police.'

'Who did?'

'The folk that found her. Tourists. English, of course. Their schools are still on holiday.' She shook her head. 'There's no mobile signal down there.' And sighed. 'The children were in a terrible state. A young policewoman drove them back to Stornoway. To take statements.'

Gunn nodded. 'It was you that reported seeing a light on in the house over there all night?'

'It was.'

'Who owns it? The house.'

'Oh, I wouldn't know about that now. It used to be an elderly English gentleman. He came at Easter, and for a few weeks in the summer. But he died last year, so . . .'

Gunn waited for her to go on, and prompted her when she didn't. 'So . . .?'

'Anna Macpherson over at Breacleit used to clean for him. Before he came and after he left. So she's probably still got a key.' She folded her arms knowingly beneath ample bosoms. 'I've no doubt that's where they got it from.'

'Who?'

'Caitlin Black and her young man. They've been meeting there off and on all summer. No doubt they imagined that no one knew.' She blew derision through mean lips and shook her head. 'You can't do anything around here, Mr Gunn, without someone knowing.'

'Primarily you.'

If she thought to take offence, Gunn pre-empted the mounting of her high horse by producing his Samsung. 'Is this Caitlin?' he said, and swiped an image he had taken of the dead girl across its screen.

She glanced at it, and her eyes opened wide. A hand flew to cover her mouth. 'That's her down there?'

Gunn nodded.

'Oh, my God! The poor wee lassie.'

'Caitlin Black?' He didn't want there to be any dubiety.

Mrs Caimbeul nodded mutely. She appeared to have trouble catching her breath. 'Is she . . . is she dead?'

'I'm afraid so.'

To Gunn's discomfort, tears sprang unexpectedly to her eyes. 'Her poor mother'll be devastated.'

'You know the family, then?'

'There's not a lot of us left here on Great Bernera, Sergeant. Everyone knows everyone.'

He returned the Samsung to his back pocket. 'I don't suppose you'd know who her young man was?'

Indignation forced its way past her tears. 'Of course I do. I've seen him often enough at parent–teacher nights at the Nicolson.'

Gunn couldn't hide his surprise. 'He's a teacher?'

'Aye. And far too old for that lassie.' She returned teary eyes to the beach. 'That poor, poor girl.'

IV.

And still the good weather continued, as persistent as the summer rain that usually blew in off the Atlantic at the approach of autumn. All the way during the long drive up the west coast to Ness, Gunn sat silent in the passenger seat. Impervious to the sunshine. Wrapped in his own deep despond of gloom. He had been happy to let Louise drive, knowing that he would not be able to concentrate on the road.

For most of the forty-minute trek across the moor, he had gazed sightlessly through the windscreen, north and east, across its vast featureless expanse. The heather was already in bloom, an ocean of undulating purple that shimmered off into the uninhabited interior of the island, where at other times of the year blue flowering water forget-me-not would fill sodden hollows, and the yellow of marsh marigolds grew along roadside ditches.

Villages strung out like beads on a necklace lined the road north, fully exposed to the anger of the winter storms that blew across three thousand miles of ocean to vent their fury on a resolute coastline that reflected the character of those who lived there. Nothing grew, beyond a few stunted bushes, to offer any kind of protection. Trees here had an even more tenuous hold on the landscape than people. On the west side of the road, the land that stretched off to the shore was known as the blackland, the fertile machair that had drawn folk to settle here in the first place.

And each settlement had raised its own church, different denominations of the same religion, reflecting man's inability to agree on anything. The Church of Scotland. The Free Church of Scotland. The Free Church of Scotland Continuing. The Free Presbyterian Church of Scotland. Gunn had long ago given up counting. The things you saw as a police officer made it hard to have faith in anything.

They passed the dominating edifice of the Free Church at Cross, with its bell-free bell tower, and accelerated up the slope beyond. Then minutes later they began the gentle descent towards Port of Ness. At Crobost Stores, Louise turned right, and they climbed up to the village of Crobost itself, stretched out along the crest of the hill. An arc of golden sand opened out below them, sweeping around to the harbour at the port. Sunlight coruscating across the bay was blindingly bright, and

Gunn slipped on a pair of sunglasses, as much to hide behind as for protection.

On their right, a metalled turning crossed a cattle grid to Crobost Church, with its commanding view across the north of the island to the lighthouse at the Butt. A sprawling car park reflected the continuing influence of the church in the local community, and the manse that overlooked it stood proud against the blue, blue sky. The home at one time of Donald Murray, a man who had killed to save a life, and lost his own in consequence.

Which made Gunn think again of Fin Macleod.

It was many years ago now that he had first come to Ness with Fin to show him the place where Angel Macritchie had been murdered. In the boat shed just down there at the port. And it was almost as many years since he had last seen him. Not since he'd left the island following the shooting of Donald Murray outside the church court in Stornoway. He had liked Fin from the moment he met him. A troubled man, yes, but a cove with a good heart. He had deserved better than the things fate had flung at him in the past. And better, Gunn knew, than those that lay immediately ahead. He closed his eyes and felt despair in his soul.

'Is this it?' Louise's voice crashed into his darkness and he opened them again.

'Yes.'

She turned into a gravel parking area above a nineteen-fifties pebbledash bungalow that sat down below the road looking out across the bay.

'Do you want me to come with you?'

He nodded and they both stepped out of the car into a soft breeze blowing off the moor to the south. Gunn stood for a moment to gather himself, and took a deep breath.

Louise followed him down the path and they climbed to the door. Gunn rapped on it three times, then stood back to remove his sunglasses and slip them into a breast pocket. The knot of his tie felt uncomfortably tight.

It took an eternity for the door to open, and a slip of a girl stood there barefoot in T-shirt and baggy jog pants. It was years since Gunn had last seen Donna. He knew that she must be in her late twenties, or older, though she still gave the impression of a twelve-year-old. Small. Slight-built. Fragile. He was shocked, all the same, by her appearance. Sallow skin, almost translucent blue. Penumbrous shadows beneath her eyes. Shoulder-length hair was greasy, an almost indeterminate colour, and dragged back behind her ears. There was fear in her dark stare.

From somewhere Gunn dredged up his voice. 'Hello, Donna.' And even to himself it sounded unreal. He paused. 'Is Fionnlagh at home?'

CHAPTER TWO

The hum of the air conditioning was a distant accompaniment to his disillusion. Constant, if almost imperceptible. Awareness only ever perceived in the temperature management of this windowless room.

Fin blinked weary lids several times over gritty eyes in an attempt to clear them, before refocusing on the centre screen of three 27-inch computer monitors arranged on the desk in front of him. Beneath it he felt the heat of the computer terminal against his leg, and he moved his chair a little to the right. Both the computer itself, and the screens displaying the images it processed, issued their own distinctive hum, a chorus of discordance in jarring harmony with the air conditioning. He had long stopped hearing any of it. Aural sensitivity trumped by visual trauma.

He had been working this case for weeks now, investigating officers providing an endless supply of laptop computers, external drives, USB sticks. Desperate men had done their best to erase images downloaded from the dark web. It was Fin's job to recover them. Evidence against an extensive ring of men sharing what anyone else would regard as unthinkable.

He had done his best to tidy the cables of all the drives and peripherals that littered his desk, but still they resembled the leftovers in an Italian restaurant at close of service. With a flick of his mouse he launched a piece of file recovery software and sat back to watch the results of its processing power fill his screen with folders, and folders within folders, until it began to resemble a chequerboard of previously deleted data. The CPU whirred and growled beneath his desk, and he waited, and waited, until it had done its worst.

It was some minutes then before he could bring himself to select the first batch of recovered files and drop them into his preview software, which in quick succession opened dozens of jpeg images on his right-hand screen. There was hardly anything he hadn't seen by now, but still it repulsed him. Each fresh image like a fist in the gut.

He held out his hands and saw that they were trembling in the light of his monitors. His breath rapid and shallow. For a moment he wondered if he would be sick. There was a plastic bin beside his desk. It wouldn't be the first time he had used it. He made a conscious effort to breathe deeply, and remembered the description they had provided for this job on his application for it.

The successful candidate will be required, through robust digital forensic investigation, to direct technical aspects of computer investigations, by collecting, extracting, interpreting and presenting this evidence in a manner acceptable to the courts. The job will involve the viewing of distressing and disturbing images, and the Jobholder is required to attend sessions with a psychologist every six months, and where appropriate to engage with the occupational health section.

Ironically it had promised *all expenses incurred in attending these appointments will be met by the Force.* As if that might somehow ameliorate the experience.

Fin knew that however many sessions he had with the police psychologist, they could never erase from his mind the images that others had tried so hard to conceal. Their shame becoming his nightmare.

As a serving police officer, he had seen things that left him prostrate on the floor at night, shaking and inconsolable. Things he could never unsee. Perhaps naively, it had not occurred to him that as a civilian working in computer forensics he would be confronted by so much worse. Things he could never talk about, or share with anyone outside of the investigation. It had turned him in on himself, bottling up an explosive cocktail of emotions that he knew he couldn't contain for ever.

His next appointment with the psychologist was only two weeks away, but somehow he doubted he could survive that long.

With sudden determination he put his computer to sleep,

rolled back his chair and stood to lift his jacket from the back of it. He opened the door, stepping out into a corridor with windows all along one side, and was surprised to see that it was still light. In the dungeon, as he called it, you could never tell what time of day it was. Still, it was well after eight, and he would be late in getting home. The only consolation being that traffic at this time would be light as he tracked east across the south side of the city from Govan to Shawlands.

Outside, the night air was humid, still warm, and with the threat of rain from dark clouds gathering overhead. But it was good to breathe air that wasn't canned. Fin picked up his Honda from the car park and drove out into Helen Street. Cars were queuing at a McDonald's on the corner as he headed south to cross over the M8 and Paisley Road West, then skirt Pollok Country Park, past Crossmyloof, turning eventually into Moss-Side Road.

Here he slowed as he passed the two-storey red sandstone Shawlands Academy, and felt, as he always did, the pain of absence. His son, Fionnlagh, had taught here for nearly five years after graduating. He and Donna and little Eilidh had lived just ten minutes away from Fin and Marsaili, and the couple had seen their son and granddaughter almost every week.

For the first time in his life, Fin had felt part of a real family. He and Marsaili babysat Eilidh often. Sometimes they would all go out together for Sunday lunch. Christmas and New Year would be spent at one house or the other, and he had taken real pleasure in watching Eilidh open her presents. Her sheer naked delight in whatever concealed itself beyond the wrappings. Such a far cry from his own childhood Christmases with his aunt, huddled in front of a peat fire in a cold house, skin burning down one side, freezing on the other, while she watched mindless snow-screen TV shows and sipped on her favourite sherry. If she remembered to get him a present at all, it would not have been anything he might have asked for on his Christmas list to Santa.

Artair, on the other hand, was showered with gifts by doting parents, additional presents always to be found in the stocking beneath the tree. And he would take great delight in showing them to Fin when they met up between Christmas and New Year.

And so it had always been Fin's fervent desire to put the *festive* season behind him and get back to school.

At the traffic lights, he sat tapping the wheel impatiently. The news that Fionnlagh had secured a teaching post in the science department at the Nicolson Institute in Stornoway had come as a bolt from the blue. Donna was anxious to go back to the island, he had told them, somehow making it her fault, when both Fin and Marsaili knew that it was Fionnlagh who wanted to go *home*.

And that was it. Within three months they were gone. Flat sold, furniture loaded on to a van and sent to Ness, where the young couple intended to move back into the bungalow once shared by Artair and Marsaili. The Macinnes bungalow, where Fionnlagh had grown up, before learning that he was not Artair's son. It *was* his home, Fin supposed. But not a place that Fin had any desire to revisit. Too many bad memories still stalked there among the ghosts of his childhood, absorbed into the very fabric of the place. Fin could never cross its threshold without imagining that he smelled the pipe that Artair's dad had smoked. A sweet Dutch halfzware shag that lingered long after his death.

Eilidh was twelve now, and Fin and Marsaili had missed growing-up years that they would never see again. She called regularly on Skype or Messenger, but it wasn't the same thing, and Marsaili had gone into mourning, almost as if she had lost a daughter.

The departure of the *kids*, as they liked to call them, had left a hole in their lives, exposing an odd sense of failure as they drifted into middle age. A gnawing dissatisfaction with life. As well as each other.

So Fin had buried his head in a job that was sucking the life out of him, and Marsaili stayed home, nursing her disillusion. Before taking a waitressing job at the Ubiquitous Chip on Friday and Saturday nights – the only nights that they might have spent uninterrupted together.

Fin found a space to park his Honda near the foot of Bellwood Street, and walked wearily up to number forty-three. By the time he reached the second floor, his legs were leaden, and in his mind he wanted simply to turn around and head back out, find a pub where he wasn't known. Sit in a quiet corner, drink himself into oblivion.

His key had not even reached the lock when the door flew open and Marsaili stood there staring at him like a mad woman. She looked awful. Red-eyed. Tear-stained face.

He was shocked. 'Jesus, Marsaili, what's wrong?'

Her lower lip trembled as she tried to fill her lungs and speak. Eventually her voice came, punctuated by sobs that tore themselves free from somewhere deep inside. 'Fionnlagh . . .'

Fin felt the world fall away from beneath his feet. 'What about him?'

'He . . . he's been arrested.'

Which simply did not compute. 'What on earth for?'

'Murder.'

26

CHAPTER THREE

I.

It was overcast, a dull featureless morning, as Fin drove them north on Helen Street. Weather that reflected their mood. There had been little sleep. Fin wasn't sure that he had slept at all, and he was certain that Marsaili had not. He was up making coffee at five, unable to lie in bed any longer, and sat staring down into the back court until the faint light of dawn bloomed into the grey light of depression.

Hours spent on the phone the previous evening had established some cause for hope. Fionnlagh had not been arrested. He had gone voluntarily to the police station in Stornoway for questioning. But a teenage girl had been murdered, and the police felt that Fionnlagh was connected in some way with her death.

Seats on the first available flight to the island had been booked and checked in online. Overnight bags were packed and sat side by side on the back seat of the Honda. Marsaili had wanted him to phone his boss at Govan, but Fin felt the need to speak to him in person.

McDonald's was doing brisk breakfast business, open 24/7 and popular with officers on the night shift. Further on, vehicles were gathering on the forecourts of industrial redbrick sheds with corrugated asbestos roofs, and the sky spat its first drops of rain at Fin's windscreen as he turned into the police parking.

'Stay here,' Fin said and, without waiting for a response, got out and walked quickly towards the three-storey police headquarters.

Vaguely familiar faces nodded to him as he climbed the stairs to the second floor and strode along the east corridor. He had never felt at home here and had the sense now of it being an alien, even hostile environment.

The office of the Cyber Crime Forensics Coordinator was at the far end of the building. His door stood ajar. Fin knocked and entered. Ronnie Young looked up from his desk in surprise. He hadn't expected to see Fin for another couple of hours.

'Fin,' he said, as if somehow Fin might have forgotten his own name.

Young was not, as his name suggested, in the first flush of youth. He was a fifty-something grey man in a grey suit, who had lost his hair in his twenties. The dust of time had settled on him along with the acceptance that life was never going to fulfil its early promise.

'You're a bit previous.' His penchant for stating the obvious was famous among his team.

'I need some time off, sir.'

Young frowned and shuffled papers on his desk as if he might find a response hiding somewhere among them. 'You've had your full complement of leave for the year, Fin.'

'These are exceptional circumstances, Mr Young.'

Young looked up, a flicker of interest momentarily breaching his indifference. 'What are?'

'My son has been taken in for questioning in connection with a murder on the Isle of Lewis.'

Young frowned. 'I'm sorry to hear that.' He appeared to think it over. Then, 'We're short-staffed right now, Fin. I just don't have the people to be able to let you go.' And as if in mitigation, 'Anyway, there's nothing much you can do about things at this stage, is there? I mean, you're not a cop any more. And it doesn't sound like your son has been charged with anything yet.'

Fin's voice was tight with constraint. 'Is that a no?'

Young shrugged his apology with a smiling insincerity. 'I'm afraid it is.'

All the way back along the corridor, Fin was only vaguely aware of the rain now blowing against windows that looked out on to the scruffy retail park opposite. An Aldi, a Starbucks. But it wasn't until he stepped out again into the car park that he felt the full force of it. A warm summer squall, with big fat raindrops blowing almost horizontally across the roofs of cars. He was soaked by the time he reached the Honda and dropped into the driver's seat. Condensation formed almost immediately on the windscreen and side windows. He started the engine and turned on the blower. Marsaili looked at him anxiously. 'Everything alright?'

'Fine,' Fin said, and slipped into first gear. 'We'd better hurry if we're going to catch that flight.'

II.

They had long ago left behind the rain of the central belt as they flew north and west, scraping mountain tops bathed in sunlight that cut black shadows into deep valleys.

More sunshine lay like a shimmering skin across the Minch, before the jagged coastline of the island reached the first white-fringed fingers of rock into its sparkling blue water. Their Loganair Saab 340 twin-engine turboprop banked as it descended over Loch a Tuath, skimming the sandbank that lay to the west before finding the runway beyond the rocks. Inland, heather in dazzling purple bloom smothered a land-scape scarred by generations of peat-cutting, and Fin was reminded that the nickname of his island home was Eilean Fraoch. Heather Island.

George Gunn was waiting apprehensively in the arrivals area as passengers from the plane formed a straggling line across the tarmac to the terminal building. He had spent some time idly examining a partition wall subdivided into adverts for Harris Tweed and Lewis salmon, and the standing stones at Callanish. Anything to avoid thinking about the encounter to come. The giant wooden carving of a Lewis chessman that stood watch over the luggage carousel seemed to glare recrimination in his direction.

Fin was surprised to see him. Surprised, too, by the shirt-sleeves, and the tan that cast unaccustomed colour across Gunn's dimpled face beneath his widow's peak. He had put on weight, and Fin noticed the Motorola Airwave unit clipped to his belt where a white shirt appeared to be trying to free itself from the constraints of dark blue trousers. Did that mean he was here on official business?

Gunn stepped towards Fin and Marsaili, holding out an awkward hand. His smile was strained. 'Good to see you, sir.' He nodded towards Marsaili. 'I wish it could have been in happier circumstances.'

'Don't we all?' Fin said. 'What are you doing here, George? How did you know we'd be on this flight?'

'An educated guess, sir. We had word that you were on your way.'

Fin frowned. 'Did you?'

But George clearly wasn't going to elaborate. 'I thought I'd come and give you a lift into town. Unofficially, of course. Save you a taxi.'

They followed him out to the car park, and a soft south-westerly blew into their faces. There was a smell of the sea in the air, and a hint of peat smoke. Just enough to know that someone nearby had lit a fire, in spite of the good weather. Old habits died hard. Gunn lifted his folded jacket from the passenger seat to place in the boot beside their bags. And Marsaili stood on the tarmac staring at him, ignoring the door that Fin held open for her. It was the moment Gunn had been dreading.

'Are you going to tell us?' she said.

His face reddened. He sighed. 'It was me that brought him in, Marsaili.' And he added quickly, 'Though I've got very little to do with the investigation now.'

Fin said, 'You must know he didn't do it, George.'

Gunn braced himself, summoning all the diplomacy he could muster from his years of experience in the force. 'Much as I don't want to, sir, I have to confess that it very much looks like he did. There is so much evidence against him. And when the DNA comes back from the lab, it's likely to remove any lingering doubt.'

The silence blew about them like the wind. Finally, Marsaili said, 'I thought maybe you owed us a little more than that, George.' And her voice chilled the air.

Gunn looked from one to the other, but all he could manage was, 'I'm sorry.'

The drive to town passed in silence, Fin and Marsaili sitting in the back, Gunn alone up front like a disgraced chauffeur. It felt wrong somehow to be given a lift by an old friend who had just told them their son was a killer. And to be greeted by this unexpected sunshine, when they carried such darkness in their hearts.

Gunn sped along Oliver's Brae, sunlight glancing off rooftops and sparkling across a bay glimpsed fleetingly between houses. Down past the old yellow-painted Mackenzie's Mill, to Engebret's filling station at the roundabout. Then, as he drove up towards the Caladh Inn, he said, 'If you ever get down to the outer harbour, you'll see the new deep-water port they're building across at Arnish Point.' He knew they weren't interested, but he couldn't bear the silence any longer. 'They say it'll be operational soon, and take huge bloody cruise ships up to three hundred and sixty metres long.' He blew through pursed lips. 'Not that we have the infrastructure here to cope with five thousand folk at a time coming off these things and flooding the town.'

He glanced in his rearview mirror to see frozen faces staring blankly out of side windows. At the roundabout he turned into Matheson Road before taking a left into Church Street, down past the Bangla Spice Indian restaurant and the Peking Cuisine Chinese Takeaway to the parking area behind the police station.

They sat for some moments in further silence before he turned off the motor. Then Gunn twisted in his seat to look at them. 'Don't even think you can dig down into this one, sir. You're not in the police any more.'

'Then why do you keep calling me *sir*, George?'

'Force of habit, sir.' He made a face. A grimace. 'If you go talking to witnesses and the like, the powers that be will regard it as interference. The CIO will run you off the island.'

'CIO?' Marsaili said.

Fin glanced at her. 'Chief Investigating Officer.' And he turned back to Gunn. 'Who is it, George?'

'No one you would know, sir. From Inverness. One of those university graduates who're taking all the top jobs now, with their doctorates in criminal justice and their degrees in accounting.' His disapproval was patent. 'Like most CIOs, he's a bit of a bastard.' Bastards, apparently, could be measured now in increments. 'This one's a little different, though. He's a clever bastard.'

III.

The clever bastard was Detective Chief Inspector Douglas Maclaren. A sharp dresser with a footballer's haircut. He was a good fifteen years younger than Fin, who had recently crossed the half-century threshold, his once-blond curls thinning now and turning quietly silver. Fin recalled the old aphorism that you know you are getting old when the policemen start looking younger. This one looked like a boy, and possessed all the arrogance of youth. And his patronising attitude towards the father of the young man helping them with their inquiries irked Fin more than he wanted to admit.

He had left Marsaili in reception, sitting huddled on a hard plastic chair, as if by making herself smaller she could also reduce the size of the problem. He had told her it might be better if he spoke to the CIO on his own. Maclaren had given him a lukewarm greeting, waving him into a seat on the other side of a desk in an upstairs office. He regarded Fin curiously now and leaned back in his reclining office chair to interlace his fingers in his lap. His jacket, hanging on the back of the chair, trailed on the floor behind him. A dark pink shirt fell open at the neck, his cuffs neatly folded once above the wrists. Fin noticed that he was wearing an Apple Watch.

'So . . . Fin Macleod.'

'Well done. At least you got my name right, if nothing else.'

Maclaren's sardonic smile slowly faded. 'Aye, your reputation goes before you.'

'What reputation is that?'

Maclaren rocked forward to lean his elbows on the desk. 'Oh . . . where should I begin? Insolence? Insubordination?'

'Big words, Detective Chief Inspector. Did you learn those at university?'

Maclaren's jaw set now. 'You're not doing your son any favours, Macleod.'

'He shouldn't need them. The only thing that matters is the evidence.'

'And we've got plenty of that.'

'So, tell me.'

Maclaren couldn't contain his mirth. 'What? Are you his lawyer now? You should know better, Macleod. We don't share evidence with anyone at this stage of an investigation, least of all family.' He sat back again and his face hardened. 'I'll tell you this, though. We have forensic and witness evidence to put your boy at the scene of the murder. She was eighteen, you know that? Eighteen, for God's sake! And your son's what, thirty? Her fucking teacher! Literally.'

Fin felt his face stinging, as if he had been slapped. He didn't know if the shock showed, but behind the facade he was shaken to the core.

And Maclaren wasn't finished. 'He raped her, struck her on the head, and most likely threw her off the cliffs into the sea. They're fortunate here to have a police surgeon with experience in forensic pathology. She found semen in the girl and took DNA samples. When we get those back, I think your boy will be going down for a very long time.' He paused. 'So don't come waltzing in here telling me I've got it wrong.'

He reached for a sheet of paper on his desk and ran his eyes over some scribbled notes.

'I had a call from your boss at Govan. Seems you've gone AWOL. I suggest that if you want to keep your job, you go back to Glasgow and leave us to do ours.'

Fin let that slide and tried hard to keep focus. He said, 'Fionnlagh's still helping you with your inquiries, then?'

'No.' Maclaren shook his head. 'I arrested him an hour ago. Although he's not yet *officially accused*.'

'So you're holding him for twelve hours.'

'And another twelve if need be.'

'And the post-mortem?'

Maclaren sighed his frustration. 'I want them to do it here. I mean, I don't want anyone leaving the island until I nail this thing down. But the police surgeon's not qualified to do the PM, which means I've got to wait for a pathologist from the mainland. And it seems they're in short supply right now. So we have to put the lassie on ice at the morgue until they send us someone.'

Fin pushed clasped hands between his knees, finally at a loss for anything to say. He couldn't meet Maclaren's eye. The two men sat in silence for some moments before Maclaren finally relented. He reached into a drawer and pulled out an eight-by-ten colour photograph, and pushed it across the desk towards Fin. 'I'll share this much with you. No harm in it, since it'll be in all the papers tomorrow.'

Fin reached out to take it and gazed uncomprehendingly at a gold pendant in the shape of an eye, a fine gold chain broken at the clasp snaked around it on a pale grey background.

Maclaren said, 'It was found tangled in the girl's hair. Chain broken. Her mother says it's not hers. So . . .'

'Is it real gold?'

'Eighteen-carat. And that's a sapphire at its centre. We found it on an internet search. It's called "the Evil Eye". Worth around sixteen hundred quid.'

'Then it's not Fionnlagh's either.'

'That remains to be seen.'

Fin pushed it back towards Maclaren.

'Keep it. I've got plenty of copies. Maybe your boy's missus knows something about it.'

But Fin just shook his head. 'They don't have that kind of

money.' He stood up. 'My wife's waiting downstairs. Is there any chance we could see him?'

Maclaren pursed his lips and thought about it. 'You can have five minutes.' He stood up and lifted the phone. 'I'll get an officer to take you down to the cells.' Then he paused. 'Though there's something else it wouldn't hurt you to know, Macleod. We found a pregnancy testing kit in the girl's car. Used. And showing a positive result. The police surgeon tested both her blood and her urine. Just to be sure.' He let that sink in. 'She was pregnant. Which seems like a pretty good motive for a married man to get rid of the teenage girl he was having an affair with. Don't you think?'

IV.

The sergeant at the charge bar watched them with unabashed curiosity as his uniformed constable unlocked the gate to the cells and led Fin and Marsaili down the hall to the first door on the right. Fin had snatched a moment to fill Marsaili in on his interview with Maclaren.

This was the same cell in which they had kept Donald Murray overnight when the CIO leading the investigation into the murder of Angel Macritchie had decided, incorrectly, that he was a suspect. Nothing much had changed, except for the colour of the paint. The walls now were a pale blue, with dark blue doors. Gone was the deep red floor, replaced by a well-worn beige. Any blood spilled would be instantly visible.

The key scraped in the lock, and released the door with a dull clang. Fin felt sick.

As it swung open, he saw names scratched in the paint by local hard men who regarded a night spent in the cells as a badge of honour. Sunlight fell in through the cubed panes of a small, square window high up on the facing wall, and Fionnlagh sat on a slab of cold raised concrete beneath it, wrapped in a blue anti-suicide blanket. To the left of the door, a stainless steel toilet stood against the wall in the unforgiving glare of overhead lights that burned 24/7, and in full view of the CCTV camera set in the ceiling.

The uniform closed the door discreetly behind them, and Fin and Marsaili stood in silent despair at the sight of their son leaning forward on his elbows, staring at the floor, refusing to meet their eye. Both were shocked by his appearance. He had Fin's blond curls, and lean handsome features. But they were haunted now. Skin pale and taut, shadows around his eyes like bruising. Fin felt hope ebbing away. He had sat through countless interrogations during his time in the force, and figured he knew guilt when he saw it.

The silence in the cell was broken only by the distant hum of the overhead lights, and lasted for an inordinate length of time. Until finally Fin forced himself to speak. His voice sounded distant, disconnected, as if it came from someone else. He said, 'Well?'

Fionnlagh looked up. 'Welcome to my world,' he said. 'A cereal bar for breakfast. Pot noodle for lunch, served in a

paper bowl with a plastic spork. Lukewarm coffee, in case I
am tempted to throw it at someone. Can't take a shit without
someone watching me.' His eyes flickered upwards towards
the CCTV camera.

Marsaili said, 'Tell me you didn't do it, Fionnlagh.'

He responded by returning his stare to the floor. More
silence followed, before Fin spoke again. 'If you've got something to say, son, get it off your chest. Now. To us. You're not
incriminating yourself. We're not police officers, for God's
sake. We're your parents.'

'We're here to help.' Marsaili was almost pleading.

But Fionnlagh was unmoved, his fingers interlaced in front
of him to make a single fist. Fin saw that his knuckles were
white with tension.

Then Marsaili's voice turned suddenly harsh, unforgiving,
as she might have spoken to a child. 'Why, Fionnlagh?'

His eyes flickered briefly in her direction. 'Why what?'

'You were having an affair with that girl.'

The look he turned on her was sullen, intransigent. 'Is that
a question or a statement?'

'I'm asking you.' Her frustration broke through her distress.

He considered his response briefly. Then, 'Yes,' he said and
looked at the floor again.

'Why? For God's sake, why?'

Fin placed a hand gently on her arm, offering reassurance
and counselling restraint.

Fionnlagh drew a long, tremulous breath, as if summoning

courage or strength from the deep. He looked up, eyes filled now with both accusation and defiance. 'Because sometimes when you marry a girl that you got pregnant as a teenager, you grow apart as you grow up. You're not the same people any more. What you thought was love turns to disappointment, regret. And then resentment.'

Fin thought how articulate the boy was. How he must have thought this through. Turning it over and over again. In search, perhaps, of justification for his infidelity.

But he wasn't finished. 'We have nothing in common any more, me and Donna. Except maybe for a constant irritation with each other.'

Fin was aware of Marsaili's fleeting glance, as if their son had somehow touched a nerve that went beyond his own relationship. But he forced himself to focus on Fionnlagh. He said, 'And a daughter who needs you.'

Fionnlagh was suddenly scathing. 'And where were you when I needed you?'

Anger fuelled Fin's response, a clifftop scene on a rock in the Atlantic replaying vividly in his mind. 'Right where I needed to be, Fionnlagh.'

And as if that scene had replayed in his head, too, the fire left Fionnlagh and he hung his head, almost in shame. But Marsaili wasn't about to let the central issue drift. She said, 'This girl. She was just eighteen. A pupil in your class. What were you thinking? You were twelve years older than her, for God's sake! A grown man. She was just a child.'

And all Fionnlagh's vehemence returned. 'She was not a child, Mum! Caitlin was smart, and funny, and beautiful. I know that people will say the twelve years between us was wrong. But we knew it wasn't. And twenty years from now, no one would have thought twice about it.' Sudden tears filled his eyes with the realization that there would be no twenty years from now. At least, not for Caitlin.

His passion shocked both parents to silence for a moment, then Fin said, 'Are you going to tell us what happened or not?'

Once more Fionnlagh's defiance filled the room, sucking all the oxygen out of the confrontation. He shook his head and returned his gaze to the floor.

Fin said, 'I suppose you knew she was pregnant?'

Fionnlagh's head snapped up, and Fin felt Marsaili's eyes on him, too. Both caught by surprise. Then, 'Oh God.' Fionnlagh's voice escaped his lips in a whisper, and he dropped his face into his hands.

V.

They pushed through swing doors into reception, and then out into an unreal world where the sun shone, and other people who, if not always satisfied with their lives, were at least happy in the moment. For Fin and Marsaili, all happiness and hope had vanished.

They stood on the top step. The touching distance between

them felt like an unbridgeable gulf. And Marsaili said, 'So she was pregnant.'

Fin let his gaze drift down Church Street towards the pleasure craft lined up along pontoons in the inner harbour. 'Apparently.'

'Well, you saw Fionnlagh's reaction.'

Fin nodded.

'He didn't know.'

But Fin wasn't ready to commit to a consensus. 'Maybe not,' he said, then shook his head in shame and disbelief. 'She was his pupil, Marsaili. Just a kid. How could he . . .? ' He turned despairing eyes towards her, and she could barely bring hers to meet his. Their shame shared.

They heard the scrape of the swing doors behind them and turned as Gunn stepped tentatively out into the early afternoon. He was unable to hide his embarrassment. 'I don't know what your transport arrangements are,' he said. 'But I can have someone drive you up to Ness, if that would help. I take it that's where you're going?'

Dryly, Fin said, 'Don't do us any favours, George. We'll hire a car from one of the rental places in Bayhead.'

Gunn nodded. 'I got a bit of a bollocking in there, sir.'

Fin frowned. 'Who from?'

'The CIO. He didn't like it that I picked you up at the airport.'

Fin snorted. 'That figures.'

Gunn hesitated. 'He warned me to give you a wide berth. Not to fraternize, is how he put it.'

'Well, there's a surprise.'

Gunn shuffled uncomfortably. 'I told him you were my friends. He said a police officer has no friends. Particularly during a murder investigation.'

Fin's smile was sardonic. 'Aye, well, he's got that right, hasn't he?' And he took Marsaili's arm and steered her away, down towards the harbour and the sunlight glittering all the way across the bay to the castle grounds.

Gunn watched them go, and felt the weight of his heart in his chest like rocks in a sack.

CHAPTER FOUR

Neither spoke on the long drive up to Ness. Everything familiar to them appeared alien, as if they had returned only to haunt happier days and blight fond memories. Endless peat bog stretched away to uninhabited infinity. The Atlantic broke white against undifferentiated grey gneiss that lay in sedimentary seams along the shore. Villages with familiar names – Barvas, Shader, Galson, Cross – where childhood friends had lived and shared in the growing pains of adolescence spooled past like some scratchy old film documenting a past that no longer felt real.

It was painful, because there was such a sense of loss. Of innocence, of happiness. Of belonging. Made all the more surreal by this unaccustomed sunshine illuminating their bereavement. And it really did feel as if someone in the family had died, along with that poor girl. They almost expected that over the next rise they might come upon a funeral procession on the road. Men in black, coats flapping in the wind, bearing a coffin containing all their lost dreams towards its final resting place in the machair.

There was a sense, too, of dread. Of facing poor Donna, of sharing her grief and her house at the same time. It made sense that they would stay at the Macinnes bungalow. Though how else could they feel but guilty? Since Fionnlagh was *their* son. His infidelity somehow *their* responsibility. The death of a young girl weighing heavy on their shared conscience. Whether he had killed her or not, he'd been having sex with a teenage girl from his classroom. It was a homecoming neither could have imagined in their worst nightmares.

Fin turned off the main road at Crobost Stores and dropped down to second gear to pull up the hill. Neither of them wanted to reach their destination, and yet both were desperate to bring this awful journey of anticipation to an end. Fin couldn't even look at the church as they passed it on their right. Every landmark, every house, held memories that felt tainted now.

At the gravel parking area above the bungalow, Fin pulled in beside Donna's Fiat 500 and Fionnlagh's abandoned SUV. He and Marsaili stepped out into the warm afternoon sunshine. A brisk breeze blew in off the Minch, carrying on its leading edge the smells of remembered childhood. How many storms they had weathered here. At the lighthouse, just visible on the headland at Rubha Robhanais, he knew they recorded strong to gale-force winds nearly four months out of every year. Thirty-metre waves had been recorded just fifteen kilometres off the coast. Hard to believe on a day like this.

He took their overnight bags from the back of the car and they set off with trepidation down the path to the house.

Donna's appearance shocked them when she opened the door. Dressed only in a T-shirt and jeans with torn knees, she looked tiny and infinitely vulnerable, lank hair scraped back into a ponytail. Her pallor was almost painful, eyes red-rimmed and smudged in shadow. Immediately she saw them she burst into tears and fell into Marsaili's arms. Marsaili dropped her bag and held her close. Fin stood awkwardly as the mother of his granddaughter clung to his wife, and he realized that it had not even occurred to Donna to blame the sins of the son on his parents. She turned to Fin, then, and held him too. He placed a hand at the back of her head and drew her tiny frame closer, before stepping away to brush the tears from her face. 'I'm so sorry, Donna,' he said. 'I'm so, so sorry.'

Donna sat on the worn old leather settee that faced the window where Fin and Marsaili stood against the light. Dust hung in still motes, suspended in the sunshine that slanted through it. She held one of Eilidh's old teddies in her lap, threadbare and missing a limb, but it appeared to offer comfort of some sort. She toyed with it absently as she spoke.

'It didn't come as any surprise. Not really. I mean, things had been bad between us for some time. Since before we left Glasgow. I think that's why he wanted to come back here. Kind of like a fresh start. Back to the womb. But there was no rebirth. He came to bed hours after I did. Was always up before me. Left early with Eilidh every morning for the drive to Stornoway. Weekends he'd be out fishing, or meeting friends at the Social, or watching football. It's like . . .' she turned moist eyes towards them, 'like he just didn't want to be with me any more. Except for sex.'

Her voice cracked on that, and it was all she could do not to burst into tears again. When she regained control of her breathing, she raised a hand to sweep a stray strand of hair from her face.

'Then this summer he signed up to teach evening classes at a new adult community learning course being run at the Nicolson. Three nights a week. He said we needed the extra cash.' She snorted her derision. 'Of course, after they accused him of killing that girl, I learned he'd been having an affair with her. So I checked, didn't I? With the Nicolson.' She paused. 'No such thing as an adult community summer school. He was off meeting her somewhere. Fucking her!' And for the first time anger displaced grief.

Marsaili's interruption was hesitant. 'Did . . . did you know her?'

'Everyone knew her,' Donna said. 'Not personally. She was on the telly. Caitlin Black and her friend Iseabail. The two of them were champion swimmers, winning schools championships for the Nicolson all through secondary. Then last year, BBC Alba started airing a programme called *Canoe and Ocean – Canùdh agus Cuan*. Caitlin and Iseabail exploring the coastline of the islands from the sea. Canoeing into hidden coves, swimming above and below the water. They always filmed in good weather, so it made it look like we lived in the Caribbean. Fabulous blue and green seas, silver sands, and all the bird and sea life along the coast.' Donna sighed her frustration. 'I've got to admit, she was beautiful. Caitlin. And her friend.' Donna's voice cracked again. 'And look at me. How could I ever compete?'

Fin and Marsaili sat in troubled silence. Nothing they could say would take away her pain. All they could do was let her talk. Drain the boil.

'I even recorded the series. Of course, I had no idea.' She was building up a head of steam now. 'It's disgusting! She was just eighteen. From his science class. I mean, if they'd caught him he'd have lost his job. He'd never have taught again. I would say, what was he thinking? But I know what he was thinking. He was thinking if he was with her, he wouldn't have to be with me.'

She started sobbing, and Marsaili crossed the room to sit beside her, slipping an arm around her shoulder. 'It's okay,' she said feebly.

Donna barked back. 'It's not! It's really not. I hate him for what he's done to me and Eilidh.' She took a deep breath. 'But I know him.' She glanced from one to the other. 'There's no way he killed her. He couldn't have.'

Fin reached into his bag and took out the photograph that Maclaren had given him. He held it out to Donna. 'You ever seen this?'

She looked at it and frowned. 'No. What is it?'

'They found it caught up in the dead girl's hair, and her folks say it's not hers.'

'Well, it's not Fionnlagh's. It looks expensive.'

'A gift, maybe? Something he gave her?'

'Well, if he did, I've no idea where he'd get the money. Things are tight. You know?'

Fin nodded. 'They're saying he raped her.'

Donna's mouth fell open and she gazed at him in disbelief. 'Well, that doesn't make a blind bit of sense, does it? I mean, why would he rape her when he's been fucking her?' And then Fin saw the thought slowly coagulating in her mind. 'You think he did it, don't you? You think he killed her.' She looked at Marsaili, eyes afire with disbelief.

'Of course not,' Marsaili tried to reassure her.

But she turned her burgeoning anger back on Fin. 'You do, though.'

Fin drew a deep breath. 'She was pregnant, Donna. They found a testing kit in her car and confirmed it with blood tests.'

Tears filled the young woman's eyes. 'Well, there's irony for you,' she said in a tiny voice. 'I'm pregnant, too.'

CHAPTER FIVE

Fin was happy to escape the febrile atmosphere of the bungalow, and sensed, too, that Donna and Marsaili were glad to have the house to themselves, a chance to exchange inner thoughts that neither would want to share with Fin.

Eilidh would be home soon from school. And although he was anxious to see her, he was pleased to avoid an encounter with her grandmother – Donna's mother, Catriona. Donna told them she had been running Eilidh to and from school since Fionnlagh's arrest. Fin had never forgiven Catriona for abandoning Donald in his hour of need. Donald had been Fin's friend. For too short a lifetime. And although they'd had their differences over the years, had ended up sharing a granddaughter, and made their peace with each other in the final months before he died. Catriona, on the other hand, had wilted in the face of public opinion and failed to stand by him when the church court sat in Stornoway to determine his future as minister of Crobost Free Church.

Fin had reached the top of the hill before he saw Catriona's car pull up next to his, and watched as she got out to walk

Eilidh down the path to the door. From here, Eilidh looked like a skelf of a child, as frail and vulnerable as her mother. God only knew what hell she had suffered in silence as her family tore itself apart. When adults fought, it was the children who suffered.

The breeze was stiffer now that he stood at the crest of the hill, and he turned his gaze across the bay below, black rock rising thirty feet above the wide crescent of sand that swept around towards the harbour. An almost involuntary jump of focus brought his eyes to rest on the green- and black-streaked walls of the semi-derelict house that had been his home for the first eight years of his life.

He felt neither nostalgia nor pain. Just an aching emptiness. Sadness for the lost happiness of a little boy whose parents were taken from him too soon.

Earlier on the drive from Stornoway, crossing the moor to the west coast, he had avoided turning eyes towards the shieling with the green roof. He had always identified it with the spot on the road where his parents' car had gone into the ditch. A landmark seen every Monday and Friday from the bus that took him to and from Stornoway and the Gibson Hostel in Ripley Place where he lodged during his years at the Nicolson. A twice-weekly reminder of his status as *orphan boy*, which was what the bullies had called him.

Now as he surveyed what had been his family home in Crobost, he saw that the roof was completely gone. And with it the dormer window from which the young Fin had viewed the world, with all its infinite possibilities, including the little girl with pigtails called Marsaili who lived on the moor, beyond the rise, at Mealanais Farm. Having left the police, he had returned to the island with the idea of making his home there after nearly twenty years on the mainland. But the attempt to restore his parents' house, and recapture something of his lost childhood, had stalled. The place now was a sorry reflection of his own state of mind, and he didn't want to dwell upon it.

A little further on, as the land levelled off, he stopped outside an old white house on the west side of the road. Ironically, it had survived better than his childhood home. But still the windows and doors were boarded up. Tall grasses grew in a long-forgotten garden, among the footings of an old blackhouse.

This was a house that held happier memories for him than all the years he had spent living with his aunt above Crobost harbour. And yet, in truth, he had spent very little time in it. A decaying wooden gate hung off an old fencepost, and fell from its hinges as Fin tried to open it. He stepped over a scattering of stonework and bricks among the long grass to get to the front door. The oriented strand board that someone had used years ago to secure it was half rotten now, and pulled easily away from rusted nails.

It clattered to one side, and the old house breathed damp and fetid air into Fin's face. Inside, most of the floorboards had been lifted, and he stepped from joist to joist, moving deeper into darkness, only the faintest light seeping in around the edges of the boarded windows. And yet in his mind's eye he could furnish the place still, just as he remembered it, the old man sitting in his rocker gazing out on a life sacrificed to the sea, and the murder of its greatest inhabitants, a curl of blue pipe smoke dispersing in the draught of an ill-fitting window.

CHAPTER SIX

The man that death forgot. That's what my mother used to call him. Although, really, he couldn't have been that old. Early seventies, maybe. But he seemed ancient to me, and no doubt to my mum, who I knew never liked him. The dementia must have taken hold already, and maybe that coloured her view of him. But the old man always slipped a couple of coins into my palm whenever my dad sneaked me up the road for a visit. So that's what coloured *my* view of him.

My grandfather had a boyish look about him, in spite of his age. His hair had thinned, and was a cotton-wool white that always stood up on his head, as if he had just been out in the wind. And maybe he had. His voice had lost its depth, high-pitched and scraped thin by the years. But I never saw him without a pipe in his face, clenched easily between what was left of rotten brown teeth, as if he had been born with it there.

I never knew my paternal grandmother. She was dead long before I was born, and it had never occurred to me then to wonder why my father had been brought up by his uncle. His dad's brother. I just knew that he was.

When I was about seven I used to call in at my grandfather's house after school. I have vivid recollections of sitting with him in that front room. And it was there one day, peering through a fug of pipe smoke, with peats glowing in the hearth, that I learned why he had passed responsibility for his only son on to his brother.

It was a Saturday morning, a typically blowy November day, when I went running off up the road to Shen's house. Shen is the Gaelic for grampa, shortened from Seanair.

From his house at the top of the hill, you could see all the way across to the Butt and down along the west coast. I could smell the peat burning in Shen's hearth as I skipped up the path to his door. It was never locked, of course. No one locked their doors then. I remember years afterwards, a fella telling me that he'd bought a house on the Cross–Skigersta road, and only when he sold it sixteen years later did he realize he'd never got the key from the previous owner.

Shen was sitting in his habitual chair by the window and appeared glad to see me.

'Did I ever tell you about the whaling, boy?'

He never had.

'You know what a whale is, Fin?'

'Of course!'

'Well, there was a time when we killed them all over the planet. Hundreds of thousands of them.'

'Why?'

'Hah! Good question, lad. People wanted what whales could

provide. Mostly whale oil. They got that from the blubber. Rendered it down in huge boilers on factory ships, and used the oil for lamps, and lubricants, and to make soap and candles.'

'Ugh!' It sounded horrible to me.

'Then they made women's corsets and umbrella ribs from the whalebone. And used all manner of intestinal stuff for cosmetics and perfumes.'

'Is that what *you* did?' I asked. 'Make umbrellas and cosmetics?'

'No, Fin,' he said. 'I just killed the whales.' And he sighed. 'Thousands of them.'

I had trouble picturing this. I remembered the previous year there'd been a whale beached on the east coast. A minke, they called it. My dad, and some of the men from the village, made the trip across the island in someone's van to go and see it, and he took me with them.

It had washed up on what they called Tràigh Mhòr, the big beach, and it was enormous. Some men had tried to refloat it, but failed, and it just lay there in the sand dying. In great pain, as I later learned. We went right down on to the beach, which was the first time I'd had any real sense of how big a whale was. And minkes are not the biggest. Thirty-five feet long, my father estimated. And someone else said it probably weighed about twenty thousand pounds. And I could only imagine how many two-pound bags of sugar it would take to make up that weight.

'So where did you kill them?' I asked Shen. 'Out there in the Minch?'

'No, no, no, laddie. It was down in the South Atlantic. We

were based on a wee group of islands called South Georgia and the Sandwich Islands. Just about as close to the Antarctic as it's possible to get. It was full of international whaling stations in those days.' He straightened up. 'That's where I spent half my life, Fin, killing whales. As far away from home as I could be. I went down to there for the first time in the *Southern Harvester*. Took bloody weeks. We played crib, and darts and dominoes and stuff like that, to pass the hours. And when we got to the tropics, well, it was suntan time. Laying out on the deck, toasting in the sunshine. Unheard of for a laddie from Ness.' He chuckled. 'The few times I came home, folk thought I'd been away on holiday.' His smile faded. 'Though I didn't come home nearly often enough.'

He pulled on his pipe again, but it had gone out. Though he hardly noticed.

'You should have seen it, Fin. Firing harpoons at the poor unsuspecting things. Water turning red with their blood, right there among the white and blue of the ice floes.'

I was shocked to see tears trickling down his cheeks.

'Don't know how many I killed, Fin. I really don't. But if I had my time over, I'd not kill a living thing. It stays with you, death. We only have one life, all of us. And we don't realize just how precious it is till it's almost gone. Then there's no going back. No undoing all those you've taken.' He paused in painful reflection. 'Or the ones you've ruined.'

He wiped the tears away from his face with bony, bruised and shaking hands.

PETER MAY

'I still have the bad dreams. Drowning in a sea of blood, with
the whales just circling, watching me die. And I pray every
night that God will forgive me. For every whale I hunted down,
every life I took.' He looked at me very directly. 'And for the
wrong I did your father. And his mother.'

I had no idea what he was talking about. 'What do you
mean, Shen?'

He took the pipe from his mouth to relight it. 'There were a
few of us back then, Fin, who went from Ness to the whaling
in South Georgia. Most came back at the end of each season.
The cold and the ice made it near impossible to catch whales
in the Antarctic winter. But one or two stayed over, including
me. We spent winters there, at Leith Harbour, or Grytviken,
doing maintenance on the factory ships. There was something
compelling about it. I'm not sure what. A strange beauty about
that place in winter, with the mountains ringed around it and
capped by snow.'

And suddenly, as if shutters had fallen on his unseen window
into the past, he returned to the present and looked at me with
his pale, watery blue eyes. His gnarled old hand clutched the
bowl of his pipe, and he stabbed the stem of it at me through
the smoke.

'But I'll tell you why I stayed. Because I was a bloody coward,
Fin. Some folk are frightened of ghosts. Others of God. Me? I
was afraid of the responsibility. A wife and a wee laddie that
relied on me. For everything. Everything! And, really, I didn't
want that. I told myself I was doing right by them, sending

59

back money every month. They never wanted for anything. That's what I told myself.' He returned the pipe to his mouth, and his voice fell away. 'Except for a husband. And a father.'

Shen turned his face towards the light again, staring once more through the window of recollection.

'I came home one year after getting a letter from my brother. God knows how long it took to reach me, all that way across the world. He had written to tell me that my Morag was ill.' He shook his head. 'I didn't want to come back, and delayed it until I couldn't wait any longer. Then by the time I got here she was dead. Long buried in the machair down there at Crobost cemetery. And whatever tears I cried came far too late.'

He fussed with his pipe. Once more relighting the remaining tobacco and tamping it with a callused fingertip.

'Your father must have been about twelve then. Do you know, I wouldn't have recognized him if I'd met him in the street. I told my brother I'd have to go back to South Georgia to collect my stuff. Got the first steamer down to the Southern Ocean and didn't come back till the whaling finished some-time in the mid-sixties. By which time your father was a man. My brother, who'd looked after him all these years, was dead from cancer. And I've spent the rest of my life haunted by the whales I killed, and the guilt of failing my own family.'

Tears, like glass beads, gathered on his lower lids, and when he blinked, they rolled down his cheeks, following in the tracks of their predecessors.

'There's nothing more important than family. I know that

now. Way too late. You bring someone into this world, Fin, you have to be there for them. No matter what.'

It left an impression on me, that Saturday morning at Shen's, when he confessed to me his sins and his failings. He went downhill quite rapidly after that. As if unburdening himself to his grandson had somehow released him from the shackles of life. The dementia ran its course, and, when he could no longer be cared for in his own home, they took him to a place in Stornoway where old folk went to die.

CHAPTER SEVEN

The sun was lower in the sky as Fin stepped out from the claustrophobia of Shen's house and the memories it had evoked. A crumpled blanket of golden sunlight lay across the moor, casting shadows in every hollow and setting the purple of the heather alight. The Minch glowed with an inner luminescence, and frothed all along the shore. The sound of it carried on the breeze, and Fin was reminded of peat-cutting when he was a boy. On still, damp spring days, with the midges driving you insane, you could hear the voices of other families out at the peats, half a mile away or more. Conversations conducted at a distance with folk you could barely see.

The land fell away again towards the sea, and the single-track road led Fin down to Crobost harbour, where all his childhood memories lay in wait. But it wasn't the pain of recollection that ambushed him. It was the sight of his aunt's house, where he had lived alone with her through all his growing years, restored now to a former glory he had never known, glowing pristine white in the late afternoon sun.

She had left it in her will to some animal charity, which in turn must have sold it to someone with money to spend. It sat in splendid isolation here on the clifftops, looking out over the sheltered shingle bay that he had known so well, transformed from a tired and decaying old edifice into a beautiful modern home with a view. New windows, new doors, new roof. A new life that somehow erased all the years of his that he had spent there.

He wondered how his aunt would have felt about it. She had never cared much for the place, just as she had never had any great fondness for Fin. Inside she had disguised the decay by painting it over with the lurid colours of the sixties, a decade from which she seemed never to have moved on. Dressing it up like some old whore. Too much rouge on raddled cheeks, virulent red on too thin lips, turquoise blue on the lids of sunken eyes. Crude and colourful pottery, paper flowers, chiffon drapes of blue and yellow. While on the outside the walls were blackened by the rain, gutters leaking, rusted window frames giving free entry to the winter gales.

A car sat on the tarmac apron in front of it. Someone else was living there now. It was a home. As it had never really been for Fin. He imagined the burden he must have been to his aunt, who had never wanted him. And yet had taken him in, clothed him, fed him, put a roof over his head. Sacrificed the remaining years of what must have been a lonely life to steer her sister's boy through childhood and adolescence. Caring for him, while never loving him. In some ways she had been as cold as the house. But like the house itself, had offered him protection.

63

He dragged his eyes away from it and wandered down the concrete ramp towards the tiny harbour itself. The winch hut stood with its door ajar, and steel cables left rust lines on the runway. Boats lay at odd angles on the slope. Peeling blue and red paint on an old wooden fishing boat, the white-painted letters of its hull identification number barely visible. A white plastic dinghy canted towards the cliff, its name, *Caitlin*, partially hidden by an orange fender dangling on a blue rope. And Fin thought of the girl his son was accused of murdering, not for the first time disturbed by the knowledge that, whatever else he had done, Fionnlagh had taken advantage of his role as her teacher.

At the side of the winch hut, the carcass of an old rowing boat lay in skeletal decay, barely a flake of its original purple paint still visible. The name of it, carefully traced in white on its bow by his father, was long gone. *Eilidh*. The name of his mother, and now his granddaughter. Fin recalled his father's disappointment in having to launch her without Fin. They had spent most of the summer working on her together, and on the day they were to have put her in the water, Fin had snuck off for a clandestine meeting with Marsaili. He remembered, too, the day many years later that he had knelt by the remains of the *Eilidh* and wept, all the regrets of his life welling up from somewhere deep inside to choke him.

Strangely, he felt nothing now, as if remembered sadness had a sell-by date that had long since passed.

He sensed her presence before he heard her footfall, and

half turned to find Marsaili approaching. She wore jeans and trainers and a white blouse that gave just a hint of the bra beneath it. Her hair was drawn back severely from a face without a trace of make-up. Tiredness and stress etched themselves into a pale complexion, eyes shadowed with lack of sleep. And yet still he saw the fine-looking woman with whom he had fallen in love again as a grown man. Was it really possible to fall in love with someone twice, he wondered. Even three times. The answer seemed obvious. Only if you had fallen out of love with them. In which case, had it ever really been love in the first place? But he knew that it had.

He had fallen in love with Marsaili on his very first day at school, when she had volunteered to translate for him because he was the only pupil in class who couldn't speak English. He recalled her walking him up the road to Crobost Stores on that blustery September day, and how she had shortened Finlay to Fin, the name that stuck with him for the rest of his life. Then again as a teenager, when she had taken his virginity, and he'd discovered too late that hers was already gone. And once more when Fionnlagh had been revealed to him as his son and they had rediscovered the passion of their teenage years.

All of that was so long ago now that he no longer knew whether what he felt for her was really love, or just an echo of it.

'Hi,' she said, and slipped an arm easily through his, and they walked slowly together down to the little jetty. The deep blue of the sky reflecting in the water was broken only by the ochres and greens of the cliffs that rose to a house at their summit. There were no boats here, or creels, or buoys. It just felt abandoned.

He said, 'You saw Catriona?'

She nodded.

'How was she?'

'Difficult. There was so much I wanted to say to her, but Eilidh was there. And Catriona was being on her best behaviour. Still, there was a lot of ice in the air. And it was clear that somehow she blames us for whatever it is that Fionnlagh has done. We are his parents, after all, so it must be our fault.' She sighed and turned her face towards him. 'Fin, what are we going to do?'

'I don't know, Marsaili. I really don't.'

'You were a detective, Fin. You've investigated lots of murders.'

'I'm not a policeman any more.'

'No, you're a father. With a better motive for getting to the truth of this than any cop.'

And he remembered his grandfather's words from all those years before. *You bring someone into this world, Fin, you have to be there for them. No matter what.* He turned towards her and rested a gentle hand on her cheek. 'I'll try,' he said.

CHAPTER EIGHT

Fin sat on a wooden bench outside the police station in Church Street. He wondered how many lost souls had sat here over the years waiting for good news or bad from the inner sanctum.

A flurry of phone calls the previous evening had established contact with a lawyer in Stornoway who'd been at school with Fin. Derek Macrae. A soft boy, as Fin recalled. But bright. And subject to relentless bullying, as the clever ones and the soft ones usually were. Macrae was now the go-to legal aid solicitor appointed to represent accused persons without the financial means to defend themselves.

He had been reluctant when Fin first called. 'It's really outside the realms of my experience, Fin,' he'd said. 'Murder. I mean, do you know what the average murder rate is on this island?' And answered his own question before Fin could respond. 'It's about one a century. Two, if we're lucky. Which makes me rather unsuited to represent the legal interests of anyone accused of it.'

'Derek, he needs legal representation.' Fin was not going to give up. 'He'll plead not guilty, of course, and they'll remand him to Inverness to appear at the High Court. And when they do I'll get him some hotshot lawyer who knows his way around a murder charge. But right now, at the very least, he needs someone to protect him from himself. And I want to know what the police are going to throw at him.'

The sound of morning traffic drifted up from Cromwell Street, sunlight striking the masts of yachts as they tilted gently back and forth on the spangled waters of the inner harbour. There was a regular coming and going at the charity shop on the corner, and someone out of sight in the scruffy yard opposite was intermittently employing a power tool.

Fin fidgeted impatiently. He had barely slept again. And struggled now to shake off the cloud of pessimism that had descended on him with darkness the night before, in a house filled only with morbid recollection.

He heard the scrape of the door to reception as it swung open, and got quickly to his feet. Macrae hurried down the four steps from the entrance to the police station. He was a thin man, tall, with a crown of jet-black hair fringed by silver, and Fin wondered if he was dyeing it, and had left the grey around the edges to pretend that he wasn't. He appeared agitated. 'Let's get a coffee,' he said.

They walked down to the harbour in silence, and then along to the Kopi Java coffee shop, whose window looked out on all the pleasure craft berthed at the pontoons. Fin could barely contain his impatience. A large choice of coffees was chalked up on a blackboard behind the counter. He ignored it and bought them two cappuccinos that he carried to a table in the window. The wall opposite was draped with empty coffee sacks stencilled with descriptors and countries of origin. `Clean Coffee - Product of Guatemala. Union hand-roasted coffee. Arabica coffee, triple hand-picked.` There were few customers at this time, but still the old schoolmates kept their voices low.

'It's a mess, Fin. I don't know what to tell you. Except that it really doesn't look good.'

'How was Fionnlagh?'

'Hard to tell. He wouldn't say much.'

Fin nodded. 'What about the police? What do they have?'

'A ton of evidence. Fionnlagh's fingerprints are all over the house above the cliffs where the girl was washed up. A credit card receipt from a purchase Fionnlagh made at the Co-op was found on the bedroom floor. Witnesses will testify that Fionnlagh and the girl were regular, clandestine visitors to the house. One in particular saw them arrive together earlier on the night she was murdered.' He paused to draw breath, then sighed deeply and shook his head. 'They've taken DNA swabs from the bed, and around the house. As well as from the girl's vagina. You know they think she was raped?'

Fin nodded, despair rising like acid in his throat. 'Yes.'

'Obviously they've taken DNA samples from Fionnlagh. When they get the results back, they expect a match.'

'What about the girl? What do we know about her exactly?'

'She was something of a local celebrity, Fin. A TV show that she co-hosted on BBC Alba. Her name was Caitlin Black, or Nic

Ille Dhuibh, depending on whether you want the English or the Gaelic. Her parents are divorced. Niall and Ailsa. Caitlin lived with her mother at Tobson on Great Bernera.'

'Jesus!' The curse escaped Fin's lips in a breath. 'Niall and Ailsa Black?'

Macrae frowned. 'You know them?'

Fin found it hard to breathe. He nodded. 'I do. Both of them. We grew up together in Ness.' He closed his eyes. With every fresh revelation, the whole thing only got worse.

The drive south and west to Bernera took around forty minutes. The island of Great Bernera and her little sister Bernera Beag were like flames in the mouth of the dragon. An illusion created by the deep bites that West and East Loch Roag took out of the west coast of Lewis. Separated from the main island by a narrow strait of water linking the two sea lochs, Great Bernera was reached by a tiny bridge that spanned it. The Bridge over the Atlantic, they called it.

As he headed west on the Achmore road to Garynahine, a vast expanse of peat bog stretched away to the mountains of Harris in the south. Myriad tiny lochans caught and reflected the sunlight, as if someone had scattered a handful of shredded tinfoil across the land. But Fin's thoughts were elsewhere. With Niall Black, and Ailsa, and that fateful summer before he left for university. A summer both idyllic and cataclysmic. The summer that he lost his virginity, and Iain Murray lost his life at the cages. The summer that he went to An Sgeir to kill guga, and watched Artair's father fall to his death from the cliffs.

At Garynahine he turned south, skirting the ragged southern shore of Loch Ceann Hùlabhaig and the Linshader estate, before leaving the main road to head north across undulating wilderness peppered with dark stretches of pine plantation. As the road carried him down, then, towards the Bridge over the Atlantic, he saw mussel lines stretching east in the water, where once Niall's father, Hamish, had established the first salmon farm on the island. Fin felt a chill run through him, even though the cages were long gone. And despite this brilliant spell of late summer weather sending sunlight to shimmer across the cut-glass blue of the loch, a dark cloud of sadness and regret fell upon Fin to snuff it out.

The handful of houses at Tobson clustered around a small bay on the west coast of the island, and were reached by a single-track that left the main road north to Bosta. Set on cliffs looking towards the scattered islets of Fuaigh Mòr, Bhàcasaigh and Pabaigh Mòr, the house that Niall Black had built for his family boasted one of the most breathtaking sunset views on the island.

Its architecture owed nothing to Hebridean cultural heritage, uncompromising in its geometric lines, and its acres of triple-glazed west-facing walls that mirrored the long stretch of golden sands on Reef Beach opposite. White and slate-grey walls gave it angular form that stood in defiant resistance to the storms that Fin knew would drive in off the Atlantic to

assault it during the winter months. A house built as a statement of wealth and power, only to become a broken home.

Fin pulled in at the opening to the drive that led up to
the house, apprehensive about the encounter that lay ahead,
almost overwhelmed by the memories that flooded back.

CHAPTER NINE

I never did know who organized the party that day on Eilean Beag. It was one of those events where word just gets around. And it had got around as far north as Ness. I don't recall now who first told me about it, but I do remember that Artair couldn't come. His father was away on the mainland, and his mother wasn't well. Chest pains and high blood pressure. We all thought she was a bit of a hypochondriac, Artair's mother. Her spells of illness always seemed tactical, designed to keep her husband and son in line.

And then, of course, she had a stroke, and spent the rest of her days in a wheelchair.

But in truth, I was quite pleased to be free of Artair for a while. Although he was my best pal, he had turned into a right gloom merchant. Depressed by poor exam results and condemned to the prospect of a future daily commute to a dead-end job at the oil fabrication yard at Arnish Point. So escape to Great Bernera with Iain Murray and Seonaidh in Donald's open-topped red Peugeot was a welcome relief. We were all off to one university or another come the end of the summer, and these were our last months of freedom before spreading our wings and escaping the island for pastures new.

It was stunning weather, like now. And I remember the drive down the west coast like it was yesterday. The wind in our hair, blowing soft in our faces, sunshine dazzling on an ocean that breathed its benevolence from the deep, breaking in gentle cadences all along the western shore.

Children waved at us in every village, while older folk shook their heads in quizzical disbelief at the folly of anyone on this island buying a car without a roof.

At the north end of Great Bernera, Donald found a space to park the Peugeot among the dozens backed up along the tiny road that ran down to the jetty. He was a good-looking boy, Donald. Tall and rangy, with a mop of sandy hair that had a life of its own. When he rang the bell, a rowing boat came across the narrow strait to fetch us.

Eilean Beag was just a couple of hundred yards from the shore. A narrow strip of an island that they used as summer grazing for the sheep. Half a mile long and only a few hundred yards wide, it had a fine sandy beach along its southern shore, and a shingle margin on its north-west flank. There must have been a hundred or more teenagers on the island that day. Fires burned at intervals all along the beach, and kids gathered around them, fish and lamb roasting on skewers laid across the embers. Barbecue smoke rose to hang in a wonderful-smelling pall across the island. A shieling near the jetty was being employed as a repository for the beer that everyone had brought, and we dumped ours there, too, before setting off to find friends and food.

Donald went his own way, an appointment with a quarter-ounce of dope, he said. Iain and Seonaidh chummed up with a couple of friends from the Nicolson, and I found myself wandering happily along the shoreline, pleased to be on my own, pulling on a can of lager, and soaking up the atmosphere.

I turned at a tug on my elbow and found Ailsa Maclean falling into step alongside me. My heart sank as she slipped her hand around my arm and I felt the warmth of her body pressing against mine. She smiled her best smile. 'Hi Fin.'

I had spent most of the last year dodging Ailsa at school, and at weekend parties and dances. But no matter where I turned, she always seemed to be there, smiling at me from across the room, or the dancefloor. And I would grab someone, anyone, to dance with, just so I wouldn't have to be with her.

We had been out together a few times, but always in a crowd, and with one or two exceptions I'd usually managed to avoid being left alone with her. Not that she wasn't a good-looking girl. Quite the opposite, in fact. But somehow, when someone is that needy, it puts you off. I tried being rude to her, making jokes in company at her expense, but nothing worked. She would just laugh along with the rest. And no matter how brusque I was, she always came back for more.

I sighed a weary acceptance, not wanting to spoil the mood of the day. 'Hi Ailsa,' I said. 'How's it going?'

'Great,' she said. 'Was that Donald you arrived with?'

I nodded.

'Good. He always manages to get the best dope.'

I looked at her, surprised. 'You smoke?'

She shrugged coyly. 'Sometimes. Why? Don't you?'

'Of course.'

Of course, I didn't. My first encounter with a joint was still an hour or two away.

She said, 'I heard that you and Artair got caught spying on the girls sunbathing topless on the beach at Port of Ness.' Ailsa lived at Fivepenny, and I supposed that everyone in Ness had probably heard the story by now.

But I was irritated. 'We weren't spying on them! We were already there when they came along. It was Artair's idea to drop the crabs off the cliff and give them a fright. I just slipped, that's all.'

Ailsa laughed. 'And got your face slapped by Marsaili for your trouble. That must have been hilarious.'

I pulled a fake smile. 'Yeah, really funny.'

Which shut her up for a few minutes. Not long enough, though. Because after a bit she said, 'So have you two still got a thing going?'

'Who?'

'You and Marsaili.'

'No!' My denial was probably too quick.

She smiled. 'That's not what I heard.'

'Yeah, well, you heard wrong.' And to my relief I spotted Seonaidh and Iain with a group of classmates sitting round a fire a little further along the beach. Iain raised an arm to wave me over and I pulled mine free of Ailsa's grasp. 'Ah, there they are. The boys have been looking for me. See you around, Ailsa.' And I hurried off to plank myself down in the sand with my friends and grab another can from a cold box. When I risked a glance back along the water's edge, I saw her still standing there, watching me. She looked good in skin-tight jeans and a T-shirt with the legend *Stones* stretched across her chest. No accident. Long blond hair fell in silken ropes around her shoulders, and I wondered why I wasn't interested in such an attractive girl. But looks weren't everything, and I thought she was quite pathetic standing there, as if somehow I had jilted her. I might even have felt sorry for her, but I didn't, and quickly averted my gaze.

Darkness fell almost unexpectedly. I hadn't realized how late it was when we arrived, and after a few beers you don't really notice time passing. Faces glowed red around the fire. The sky overhead was free of the light pollution you would get on the mainland, and was almost painfully clear, stars set like precious stones in black velvet. I remember conversations about space, infinity, God, the future. Things that kids talk about when their lives lie ahead of them, and the ways of the world and the universe are still mysteries they think they can solve.

At some point, I left Seonaidh and Iain to wander off along the shore, watching the Milky Way drift across the night sky like smoke. Which was when I spotted Donald and Marsaili together, gathered with others around the embers of another fire. I was shocked to see that he was snogging her, and reluctant to join them when they called me over. It's all a bit hazy now, but I remember that's when I smoked my first joint. I hadn't even noticed Donald slipping off into the night when Marsaili kissed me, bold and provocative as she always was in those days. A long, lingering kiss that sent blood rushing to my loins. And as we broke apart, beyond the ring of firelight, I saw Ailsa watching us, pale-faced in the dark, big doe eyes reflecting the glow of the dying flames.

I felt her eyes on us again when Marsaili took me by the hand a little later and led me off to the room at the back of the shieling where we made love for the very first time.

Afterwards we found a spot on our own, butts smooshed into the sand, and just talked. As we had never talked before. About everything that we thought mattered, and much that we didn't. Marsaili's arm around my waist, her head resting on my shoulder. And over the top of her head, by the light of the nearest fire, I saw Niall Black and Ailsa Maclean, hand in hand heading for the shieling and the tiny room in the back, with its travelling rugs and cushions. The couple whose future child would be found dead on a beach not far from here, our future child accused of her murder.

Just before they stepped inside, Ailsa glanced pointedly back in my direction, making sure that she caught my eye. Wanting me to know that she was giving herself to Niall. Wanting me to be jealous.

*

It must have been about a week later that Marsaili and I bumped into Niall at the Crobost Social. We were standing at the bar, me with a pint and Marsaili with a glass of Niersteiner. It was quiet, and we had been thinking about heading down to the beach at the port. If he'd come five minutes later we'd have missed him. He saw us and grinned and joined us at the bar.

'Halò. How are you guys?'

He was a likeable sort, Niall. A good-looking boy. Tall, with tar-black hair and the deepest of blue eyes. He had an engaging smile, and dimples that burrowed deep into each cheek. His father, Hamish, had been in the *Stornoway Gazette* the previous week, winning an industry award for his salmon. The island's first fish farmer, he had been raising salmon from smolts since the late seventies in cages he had installed in East Loch Roag.

Niall ordered a pint and turned to me. 'Been meaning to talk to you, Fin. A wee proposition. A chance to make a few quid before we head off to the glitz and glamour of the big city.' He grinned and glanced at Marsaili. 'But that's for another time.' His pint arrived and he took a long pull at it, wiping the residue of its foaming head from his upper lip with the back of his hand. 'Hey, you guys up for a wee night out in our very own metropolis?'

'If you mean Stornoway,' Marsaili said, 'who can afford that?'

Niall winked. 'I can. My treat. Just the four of us.'

'The four of who?' I said, already suspicious.

'You and Marsaili, me and Ailsa.'

I shook my head. 'I don't think so, Niall—'

But Marsaili cut me off. 'If you're paying, we'd love to.'

'Great!' He grinned from ear to ear. 'Ailsa'll be delighted. She really likes you guys.'

I glared at Marsaili, but she didn't seem to notice. 'When?' she said.

It ended up being that Friday night. At the Crown Hotel. Niall borrowed his dad's van. He and Ailsa sat up front, with Marsaili and me squeezed into the back among empty poly-styrene boxes that smelled of fish and squeaked, one against the other, at every turn and bump in the road. Marsaili and I had argued about going out to dinner with them. I told her that Ailsa had a thing for me, and she just laughed and said she could have sworn she was the only idiot with a crush for the bastard from Crobost. I took scant satisfaction from the fact that she was clearly regretting it by the time we got to Stornoway.

They gave us a table in the window with a view out over the inner harbour. In those days there were dozens of fishing boats berthed there for the weekend, and they sat high now on a full tide, towering over the quayside. We were served by an elderly waitress in a black pinny with a white apron, and ordered prawn cocktail, and squat lobster, which were delicious, but hardly worth the trouble it took to shell them. Never mind that they shredded your fingers. Niall and I had a pint apiece, and the girls shared a half bottle of Riesling.

Ailsa, I thought, was unusually quiet, stealing secret looks in my direction when she thought no one else was watching. The others didn't appear to notice.

Niall was nothing if not loquacious, and he could be very entertaining. At least, Marsaili thought so. She did a lot of laughing, and I found myself becoming increasingly irritated.

Finally, I dropped my napkin on the table and excused myself. I needed to take a breath or two and calm down. The toilet was at the end of a short hallway, and, after I'd relieved myself of the beer, I stayed in there as long as I thought I could, preening my curls in the mirror. But I knew they'd start to wonder what had happened to me, so I stepped out again into the hall. Only to find Ailsa waiting there, leaning against the wall beside the door to the Ladies. I was caught off-guard and stopped in my tracks. She pushed herself off the wall and faced me down. Very close. And confrontational in a way that she'd never been before.

'What's Marsaili got that I don't?' Her voice dropped to barely a whisper.

I summoned all the contempt for her that I felt and said, 'Me.'

It took her a moment. Then she pulled back her hand to take it off the side of my face before I even saw it coming. A stinging slap that carried more weight in it than I'd have thought her capable of. I took a step back and felt my cheek burning. And then she was on me before I could move. Arms around my neck, pushing herself up on tiptoes, trying to kiss me.

I pushed her away with a violence that surprised even

myself, and she banged against the wall. I shoved my face into hers. 'Stay the fuck away from me, Ailsa!' And I hurried off down the hall, wondering if her handprint would be visible on my face.

Of course, the others knew that something had happened, and it ruined the rest of the meal. Even Niall found himself short of his usual crack. And when finally he paid the bill, we passed the forty-five-minute drive back to Ness in frigid silence among the squeaking boxes and the stink of fish.

Niall and I had further dealings that summer, though neither of us mentioned that night at the Crown. And I never did see Ailsa again. Not after I left the island.

CHAPTER TEN

I.

The house stood L-shaped at the top of the drive, a metalled parking area protected on each side from the prevailing weather. There were two cars there. A Toyota RAV four-by-four, and a scraped and battered lime green Ford Fiesta with a large tortoiseshell cat sunning itself on the bonnet.

A tiled awning sat above a fully glazed back door, although Fin could barely see beyond it into the house for reflections. When he rang the bell he heard the muffled barking of a dog, which then appeared, jumping up at the glass, breath exploding in condensation on the far side. A red setter, its rich rust coat shining in sunlight that fell through floor-to-ceiling windows all along the front of the house behind it.

Ailsa appeared then, catching the setter by its collar and pulling it back as she swung the door open. She was so concerned with the dog that she didn't immediately look up, and Fin had a moment to take stock of her. Gone were the long blond locks, cropped now to platinum spikes that elaborated the fine shape of her head. She was thinner than when he had last seen her, almost painfully so. She wore jeans, and what looked like a man's pale blue baggy shirt over them. Her white leather trainers were scuffed and discoloured.

When finally she looked up, he saw that she was still a handsome woman. But grief had taken its toll. Deep lines cut shadows beneath her eyes, and her mouth was set in sadness. The same doe eyes that had gazed at him across the fires on Eilean Beag scanned him now without recognition. The dog was still barking, and fighting to free itself from her grip. 'Can I help you?' she said.

Fin said, 'You can let the dog go. Usually they like me.'

She frowned and stood up, her head tilted a little to one side. The setter slipped from her grasp and jumped up on Fin, who made a great fuss of it, ruffling its ears and averting his face from a tongue desperate to slather him with saliva.

It was her turn to assess him, and it didn't take long for recognition to turn to recrimination. 'What do *you* want?' Her tone was uncompromising. But she was distracted by the dog. 'Down, Bella, down!' And reluctantly Bella dropped back to all fours.

'Nice to see you, too, Ailsa.'

She snapped at him. 'Don't give me that shit, Fin. Last time we were together, you told me to stay the fuck away from you. I think I kept my side of the bargain.'

Fin lowered his head a touch. Regret for the cruelty of intemperate youth welling up inside him. 'I'm sorry,' he said, and felt the inadequacy of the apology even as he uttered it.

'Sorry, too, no doubt, that your son murdered my daughter. Why are you even here?'

'Ailsa, I want to bring Caitlin's killer to justice as much as you do. I just don't believe that Fionnlagh did it.' He wondered how convincing he appeared, when behind the facade he was still tortured by uncertainty.

Her stare was unrelenting. 'The police think he did.'

'The police aren't always right.'

'You used to be one, didn't you?'

He nodded.

'So you have evidence to the contrary? Is that what you're saying?' She paused. 'Or maybe you're just biased.'

He had no response to that.

'You realize he was fucking her, right? Him thirty and her just eighteen. A pupil in his class!'

Fin couldn't meet her eye. He shook his head. 'And that's unforgivable,' he said. 'I can't defend him in that.'

There was a long moment between them then when she might have slammed the door in his face. He half expected that she would. But in the end she stepped back, holding it open, and said, 'Well, if you have something to say you'd better come in.'

He stepped inside, and a marble floor stretched away to the outer limits of a sprawling space that encompassed an open-plan kitchen, dining and living area. The entire far wall comprised huge sliding glass doors that looked west on to a paved terrace that was more wishful thinking than of practical use. Even when weather allowed, the midges would, Fin knew, put it off-limits. Still, the view made it all worthwhile. Beyond the islands that broke the green of the water, and the beach behind them, the mountains of Uig cut purple against the clearest of blue skies.

At one end of the room, a red leather settee and reclining armchairs gathered themselves around a long glass coffee table facing an enormous wall-mounted TV. At the other, a vast oak table beyond the kitchen counter seated ten with ease, twelve at a push. Sheepskin rugs softened the marble underfoot, and somewhere in the background a soft radio voice was punctuated by the squawking of a parrot in a bamboo cage that hung from a looping chrome stand. Sunlight heightened the vivid blues and reds of its feathers as it told them repeatedly to *Mind the gap!*

Ailsa said, 'Caitlin taught him that. She heard it on the Underground during a trip to London and thought it would be funny. The bloody thing never stops. But in a way I don't want it to. I hear her voice every time.' She bit her lip, controlling an urge to spill tears. 'The traces people leave when they're gone.' She took a deep breath. 'They're all hers. The animals. Bella. And there are three cats around somewhere.' She nodded in the direction of the parrot. 'And Oscar, of course. We've even got sheep somewhere out the back. I mean, who keeps pet sheep? I'm giving them to the crofter on the other side of the bay. They'll probably end up on someone's plate. Caitlin would have hated that. But *I* can't keep them.' She stopped

86

then. Nervous small talk exhausted. She looked at Fin. 'And what if he did?'

Fin frowned. 'I don't . . .'

'Fionnlagh. What if he did kill my Caitlin?'

It was not a thought that Fin had yet brought himself to confront head-on. He shrugged despondently. 'He'll probably spend the rest of his days in prison.'

'And that's supposed to make me feel sorry for him?'

'No, of course not.' Fin was starting to think that coming here was a mistake. He could neither account for, nor defend, anything Fionnlagh might have done.

But from somewhere in the depths of her grief and anger she found, perhaps for the first time, a spark of sympathy. Not for Fionnlagh. But for his father. The shared experience of a parent losing a child. She said frostily, 'Take a seat. I'll put the kettle on.'

She crossed to the kitchen as Fin slipped uncomfortably on to one of the armchairs, perching on the edge of it and turning his head to look beyond the glass and take in God's work of art that the architect had framed with his windows. Bella curled up on the rug at his feet. The room was warm, but the air was icy.

Ailsa called across the room as she filled the kettle, 'I'd have sold this place years ago if it wasn't for Caitlin. She loved it. Even though the two of us were like peas rattling about in an empty can. I could have done with the money. And I could have done without the commute.'

She came back across the room and sank into the settee.

'I knew him, you know.'

Fin frowned.

'Your son.' She spat that out, like a criticism. 'I've been teaching Gaelic at the Nicolson since Niall and I divorced. When . . .' and she clearly had trouble saying his name, 'when Fionnlagh first joined the science department, I thought there was something familiar about him. And then I knew. From the moment I spoke to him. He's so like you, Fin. Just not such a bastard.' She paused. 'At least, that's what I thought. But if I'd known he was fucking my daughter . . .'

Fin's embarrassment was acute. He couldn't meet her eye.

She said, almost sarcastically, 'Oh, don't worry. I don't blame you. Lots of other things I can blame you for, Fin, but not that. After all, she was fucking him, too.'

They sat in silence for some moments until he said, 'What other things do you blame me for?'

She said, 'I'd never have married Niall if it wasn't for you.'

'Why?'

'Because I only ever went with him to make you jealous.' She cast accusatory eyes in his direction. 'But you never were, were you?'

'I was with Marsaili.'

'And still are, apparently.'

He nodded.

'Lost a kid, too, I heard.'

'You seem to hear a lot of things.'

'It's the island, Fin Macleod. No one has any secrets here. You should know that.' She hesitated, but clearly felt that her own grief gave her the right to ask. 'What happened?'

The shaking of his head was almost imperceptible. 'A hit-and-run. In Edinburgh. He was just eight, Ailsa.'

'But not Marsaili's boy.'

'No. Mona and I . . . well . . . it wasn't the kind of marriage that was ever going to survive a loss like that. And then I was sent up here on a murder investigation.'

'Angel Macritchie.'

He nodded. 'And I reconnected with Marsaili. Discovered that Fionnlagh was really my son, not Artair's. Not that it compensated for the loss of Robbie. It just brought a different kind of responsibility. A commitment I hadn't expected.'

'For which he rewards you by going and killing my girl.'

Fin winced at the sudden vindictiveness of her words. Then got defensive. 'Or not.'

'We'll see.' She heaved herself out of the settee as the kettle boiled on the kitchen counter. 'You want tea or coffee? I've only got instant.'

'Tea.'

She returned carrying a tray with cups, saucers and a teapot, a milk jug and sugar bowl, which she placed on the coffee table. 'Help yourself.'

As she sank back into the settee, he said, 'That pendant. The one they found caught in Caitlin's hair. I suppose the police let you see it?'

She nodded. 'It wasn't hers.'

'Or Fionnlagh's.'

'We don't know that, do we?'

'We don't know that he didn't give it to Caitlin. A gift. Not something either of them was going to advertise.'

A slight shrug of Ailsa's shoulders conceded the possibility. 'Expensive,' she said.

'People do crazy things when they're in love.'

'Oh, so that's why he killed her? For love?'

Fin's head dropped, and his gaze fell on Caitlin's dog, still curled up on the rug. Almost as if she sensed his eyes on her, she turned her head to look at him. Bella would be missing Caitlin, too. He said, 'I don't suppose her father might have given her the pendant, and she didn't want to tell you.'

Ailsa scoffed. 'Hah! Not a chance. They didn't have that kind of relationship.'

He turned curious eyes in her direction. 'What happened between you and Niall?'

'What do you care?' And when he didn't respond, she shrugged. 'Just didn't work out, did it? Turned out he was even more of a bastard than you.' She leaned forward to fill her cup and add a splash of milk. 'When you all went to Glasgow, he went to Stirling. Took a degree in marine biology at the Institute of Aquaculture at Stirling University. I went with him. Trained as a teacher. But we came back to the island when his father died suddenly, and Niall took over the fish farm. I even encouraged him.' She sighed. 'Biggest mistake I ever made.'

'Why?'

'It was really the end of that era. Of the little man with his own small fish farm. All the independents were getting hoovered up by the big boys. A hell of a lot of money in it. I mean, *big* bucks. A Norwegian company called Stor Laks made Niall an offer he couldn't refuse. But he held out for more. He wanted a job with the firm. Figured he had something to offer.'

'And they said yes?'

'They did. And he spent the next ten years, most of them in Norway, climbing their internal career ladder. All the way. And by the time he was CEO, they were the third largest salmon farming concern in the world. Turning over, literally, billions. That's when he renamed the company Bradan Mor and built this place. It was supposed to be a home for his family. Me and Eòghann, and later Caitlin. Only it was never a home. Because he was never here. They were buying up fish farms all over the world, and wherever there was a fish farm for sale that's where he would be.' She pressed her lips together, containing her emotion, before sipping at her tea. 'In the end, there's no amount of money that can sustain a relationship like that.'

'So you split.'

She nodded. 'The surprise was that he insisted on having custody of Eòghann.'

'Your son?'

'Yes. He didn't give a shit about Caitlin, and he was happy to leave us the house, but he wanted that boy.' Bitterness laced her words. 'And, you know, what Niall wants, Niall gets. Especially with billions to back him up.'

Fin resisted the temptation to express his surprise at how easily Ailsa had given up her son. He said, 'How did the kids take it?'

'Caitlin was pretty upset. Eòghann was too. I mean, he doted on his dad, but he couldn't understand why I would be prepared to let him go. He's never forgiven me for that.' Sudden tears punctured a brave front. 'And I've never forgiven myself either. He won't even speak to me now.'

Fin had no idea what to say.

She fought to regain control. 'He lives with his dad on Cyprus. Tax exiles, the pair of them. They even took Cypriot nationality, so that they've still got European citizenship post-Brexit.' She glanced at the tray on the coffee table. 'You haven't poured your tea.'

'I won't bother, thanks.' Fin stood up. 'It's a sad story, Ailsa.'

She nodded her agreement and wiped the tears away. 'With a tragic ending. Thanks to your son.' She got to her feet. 'They're on the island just now, you know?'

Fin was surprised. 'What, Niall and Eòghann?'

'Niall bought that big white house that sits up on the cliff overlooking Port of Ness. A few years back now. He wanted a base on the island. He's restored and extended it. You wouldn't recognize the place these days.'

'Why would he want a place here?'

'Because they've invested a fortune on state-of-the-art cages in East Loch Roag, out near the mouth of the loch. Scottish salmon is still the brand that sells the product, Fin. Hence the Scots Gaelic, Bradan Mor. Big Salmon. It was a direct translation from the Norwegian.'

With Bella trotting at her heels, she followed him to the door and held it open. Fin paused on the step. 'I'm sorry, Ailsa,' he said. 'For everything.'

She looked at him with the tears of loss welling up again in her eyes, and the ache of regret in her voice. 'So am I.'

II.

At Garynahine he turned left on to the road that would take him all the way up the west coast to Ness. A long drive with time to think. Past the standing stones at Callanish, the tweed mill at Shawbost, the abandoned church at Barvas, transformed now into a stylish home. And all the tiny settlements with their mini-marts and filling stations, potteries and art galleries established by incomers. The museum and café run by Ness Historical Society – Comunn Eachdraidh Nis – in the old Cross Primary School at North Dell. The Cross Inn, where once the only tree of note on the west coast had spread its boughs, only to be brought down sometime during his years of absence. His old friends Roddy and Whistler had fought there one night in the car park after an Amran gig. They were both long gone, like the tree itself, a landmark that had survived generations. All things, Fin thought, must pass. The only constant in life was change.

At Crobost Stores he carried on down the gentle slope to the port, the coastline vanishing in a heat haze that shimmered away to his right. Vehicles stood in a row outside a light grey roughcast building behind a white picket fence. A blue and white sign on the wall identified it as the Breakwater, and through its back windows, Fin could see folk sitting at tables, eating and drinking, enjoying views out across the inner harbour and the beach beyond. A couple emerged carrying a pile of takeout pizzas in boxes, and got into a car. This was new since Fin's last sojourn on the island, and was clearly popular with tourists.

He drove slowly past it in second gear, and glanced down towards the boat shed where Angel Macritchie had been found disembowelled and strung up from the rafters. A dark chapter in so many lives.

And now he turned his attention to the house that sat proud on the cliffs ahead of him. Its harled walls were painted white, bay windows incorporated into a conservatory that wrapped around the front and the far side. On the near chimney, gulls sat on clay pots screeching at the sky. An extension at the rear of the property had been extended again. But tastefully. Nothing seemed out of character, although Fin thought that the house must virtually have doubled in size.

What had not changed was its exposure to the elements. Fin had witnessed waves breaking sixty or seventy feet into the air over the harbour wall below. There was no shelter for what was now Niall Black's island home, no hiding place for the house they had all known so well as children playing on the beach or the inner harbour when the tide was out. And yet it had stood resolute and strong against whatever weather the winter storms might have thrown at it.

Fin had never known who lived there, but had the impression that it might have been a holiday home, lived in or rented out for just a handful of weeks in the year.

He freewheeled along to iron gates that stood open, and passed through them into a large asphalt parking area at the rear of the property. There were three randomly parked vehicles. A dark green Range Rover, a Nissan pickup and a silver Mercedes saloon. He pulled in beside the pickup and stepped out to feel the heat of the sun on his face and the wind in his hair. And he remembered the day that Niall Black told them of his grand plan to steal his father's fish.

CHAPTER ELEVEN

I.

I feel privileged to have grown up on the island.

Of course, it has its downsides. A high rate of unemployment, alcoholism. And when you're a teenager, you can feel trapped here, watching through a distant lens as the rest of the world conducts its affairs. But there's very little crime. And as a kid you were free to roam the highways and byways, bathed in one moment by watery sunshine, and lashed the next by stinging rain. The moor was ever-changing. Winter brown morphing to green. Spring flowers growing in colourful profusion. Bog cotton dipping and diving like snowflakes in the wind. All giving way, finally, to the blanket of purple laid down by the fraoch. We would spend hours on the beach, clambering among the rock pools in search of crabs left behind by the outgoing tide.

During many years living on the mainland, I've lost count of how often folk would tell me that this place where I grew up was the middle of nowhere. But I've always thought of it as being the middle of everywhere, the centre of everything.

That summer, though, before we left for university, I was ready to go. A black cloud hung over my immediate future. Artair and I had been selected to join the guga hunters on their annual August trip to An Sgeir, a rock way out in the Atlantic where we were to slaughter two thousand young gannets. Guga is the Gaelic word for a juvenile gannet, and once plucked and salted, they are considered a delicacy back here on the island.

Twelve men from Crobost had been making the trip every summer for four hundred years. What had begun as a desperate search for food had grown into a tradition, a rite of passage for young men. But neither Artair nor I wanted to spend two weeks on that bleak and inhospitable rock, scrambling among the blood and shit that covered the cliffs, slaughtering defenceless birds. It was not an activity that either of us believed was likely to make men of us. But it had been arranged by Artair's dad, and there was no way we could avoid it.

It was the cloud that lurked always on my horizon, looming ever larger as the time drew near. So it came as a relief, a welcome distraction, when Niall described his plan to us that fine July day on Traigh Shanndaigh, the beach at Eòropaidh. Hardly anyone, other than locals, knew about that beach back then. Fine golden sands gathered in an arc at the head of a narrow inlet cutting deep into the profile of the north-west coast, just about a mile south of the lighthouse at the Butt. The lighthouse itself was built in the mid-eighteen-hundreds by the Stevenson brothers, one of whom was the father of Robert

Louis Stevenson. I didn't read his books until much later, and probably only because of the connection to the island. Reading was far from our minds then.

I had been to the beach often with my father when I was young, combing for the treasures washed up by winter storms. But that day we were just passing the time, sitting smoking, barefoot in soft golden sand, and basking bare-chested in the unaccustomed warmth of the sun, hoping for tans, but mostly just being burned red.

There were five of us, all looking forward to escaping the island and going to university in the autumn. Except for Artair, who was still in a blue funk about being the only one left behind. He had never made it to the Nicolson, poor grades at Crobost sending him instead to the vocational Lews Castle College, which in those days was still in the castle itself. While the rest of us talked excitedly about student accommodation and grants, Artair sat with his heels pressed into the sand, depressed and sucking intermittently on his inhaler, his puffer as we all called it.

Artair had suffered from asthma since childhood, and I'd never known him to be without his puffer. The other kids called him Wheezy, because of the breath that always seemed to whistle in his chest. We all had nicknames, of course. That was the way of it on the island then. Still is. I was just known as Fin, short for Finlay, my English name. Niall was called Niall Dubh, because his surname was Black, the same as the colour of his hair. Iain Murray was a cousin of Donald's, whose father was the minister at Crobost Church and also called Iain. So young Iain was known as The Rev. Alasdair Fraser had a shock of carrot-coloured wiry hair, and naturally everyone called him Ally Ruadh – ruadh being the Gaelic word for red.

If your nickname was Mickey Mouse, an envelope addressed to Mickey Mouse, Ness, Isle of Lewis, would reach you from anywhere in the world.

Iain was a quiet boy. He would sit without a word at parties and drink beer until he fell asleep, and someone would invariably have to take him home. But he was smart. Dux several years running at the Nicolson, and got six straight As in his Highers, so had the choice of almost any university he wanted. He picked Glasgow, because he'd heard there were lots of parties and a never-ending supply of beer.

I never cared much for Ally Ruadh. There was something sleekit about Alasdair, untrustworthy. You would never let him in on a secret, which is why I was surprised that day when Niall included him in his plans.

We were all sharing the one cigarette. Niall passed it to me and winked, as if I were already in on the scheme he was about to unveil. 'You guys fancy making a wee bit of cash before we leave the island?'

Artair growled, 'Aye, just rub it in.'

Niall ignored him, and everyone else turned interested heads in his direction. After all, who wouldn't want to make a little money? He said, 'You know how my dad's got a fish farm?'

'Who doesn't?' Alasdair said.

Niall pulled a face. 'Well, you know where his cages are.'

'Down by the Bridge over the Atlantic.' I wondered where on earth this was leading.

'That's right. On the East Loch Roag side. Six of them. A good few thousand salmon in each.' He grinned. 'I figure he's not going to miss a few.'

Stupidly, none of us realized what he was getting at. 'Why would he miss any?' Iain said.

Niall shrugged casually and smiled. He'd never been short on self-confidence. 'Well, maybe if we were to go and lift one or two . . .'

Ally Ruadh frowned. 'Why would we do that?'

Niall leaned in confidentially. 'Because,' he said, 'I just happen to know a fella that works on the Linshader estate. A ghillie, who knows folk that'll pay good money for wild.' Even then there were restrictions on the catching of wild salmon.

'But they're not wild fish in your dad's cages,' Artair said. 'They're farmed salmon, and there's no great value in those. You can buy the fillets in the supermarket.'

Niall said, 'And *you* can tell the difference, can you?'

Artair shrugged, defensive. 'Well, maybe not me. But there are folk who would know. Especially if they're paying top dollar, supposedly for the real thing.'

'Aye, well, maybe with some farmed salmon you could tell. But not my dad's.' The cigarette had made its way round to Niall again, and he took a long pull at it. 'See, where he's put his cages, there's these really powerful currents that flow through that narrow strait between the two Loch Roags. So strong that my dad has to put weights on the nets that hang down from the rafts, otherwise the tide would lift them to the surface and the fish would escape.'

'What's that got to do with anything?' Alasdair said.

Niall pulled a face that reflected his disdain. 'Think about it, Ruadh. When the tides are at their strongest, even with the weights, the nets are forced to an angle of forty-five to sixty degrees. Which means that the fish are all swimming in one direction. Against the tide. Rather than just mooning about in the cages, getting fat, like they do at other fish farms. It makes them sleek and firm, well-toned the way wild salmon are. They're like Ferraris, my dad says. He defies anyone to tell the difference between his fish and the wild ones they pull out of the Grimersta River.'

'All of which means what?' I said.

'It means, Fin, that any salmon we take from my dad's cages can easily be passed off as wild. And wild salmon fetches big money these days. Restaurants, exporters, just ordinary punters who want a taste of the real thing. My dad's got tens of thousands of the bloody things. He's not going to miss a few, and we can all make ourselves a nice wee addition to the shitty grants the government's giving us to go to university.'

Silence fell among us then, as the implications of Niall's plan sank in. I remember listening to the incoming tide breaking along the beach, just feet away from where we sat, and I watched the foam bubble up and disperse among the fine grains of wet sand.

'How would we do it?' Alasdair asked.

Niall said, 'I've got a friend at Tabost who'll lend me his van.' Then he qualified himself. 'Well, we'll have to pay him a bit out of the proceeds, and deduct the cost of the petrol. But it'll do the job. We'll rendezvous at the end of the Cross–Skigersta road at about, say, one in the morning. It'll take us an hour, hour and a quarter, to get down there. Same back again. That'll give us about an hour at the cages, and we'll be back by half four.'

More silence as we digested this.

'How do we get out to the cages?' It was Iain this time.

'There's a wee harbour at Baile na Mara on the east side of Great Bernera that my dad uses to service the cages. The place is deserted at night. He keeps a couple of working boats there, so we'll borrow one of those, and it'll take no time to motor round to the bridge.'

'What if someone sees us?' Artair pulled on his puffer, anxiety at the prospect tightening his chest.

'It'll be dark. Mostly,' Niall said. 'And nobody lives along the coast there. There'll be no one around at that time.'

I was excited by the idea, all thoughts of the upcoming guga hunt banished from my mind. And I think Artair was, too, in spite of his nervous disposition.

'Well?' Niall demanded.

'I'm in,' I said.

'Me, too.' That from Iain. And then Artair and Alasdair both threw in their lot, and Niall beamed with delight.

I don't know why none of us thought it was a bad, or immoral, thing to do. Stealing from Niall's dad. But a few fish out of a good few thousand didn't seem like that big a crime. He'd never miss them.

I had a word of caution, though. 'Just one thing,' I said. And I cast a meaningful look in Alasdair's direction. 'Not a word of this to anyone, okay? No one. If the Macritchie brothers, Angel or Murdo, got to hear about it, you can bet your life they'd want a piece of the action. And when the Macritchies get involved in anything, it always ends in disaster.' The debacle of our futile attempt to steal an old tractor tyre for Bonfire Night loomed large in my memory, even although it was years ago now. And the guilt of what had happened to poor Calum up on the roof of the castle still haunted me. The Macritchies had been at the heart of both.

II.

Just as we had five years earlier, embarking on the great Bonfire Night tyre theft, Artair and I shared a bike ride to the rendezvous. There was no climbing out of my window at dead of night this time. I was seventeen, going on eighteen, and I came and went as I pleased. My aunt couldn't have cared less.

It still never got fully dark at that time of year, but dark enough that we wouldn't be seen easily. I had arranged to meet

Artair at the Crobost end of the Cross–Skigersta road, and as usual he was late. A full ten minutes. I was nervous enough as it was, but waiting for Artair set me on edge. I was stiff with tension as I sat there on the angle of my bike watching the moon lay its silver across the Minch. Artair's folks were more strict, and I had no doubt he'd had to sneak out when he was sure everyone was asleep. Still, I was none too happy.

I heard him before I saw him, wheezing up the road, moonlight throwing his shadow across the moor. 'About bloody time!' I told him. But he just stood there gasping, and sucking on his puffer until he had recovered his breath.

'My dad was sitting up reading late. I had to wait till he'd gone to bed and put the light out. Even so, I'm not sure he was asleep when I left. He might have heard me go out the back.'

'Time you stood up to him, Artair. You're not a kid any more.'

But Artair was withering. 'Aye, like you stood up to him about having to go out to An Sgeir with the guga hunters.'

I had no response to that, and we shared a silent, unhappy moment. A million and one things understood between us, but left unspoken. 'Come on,' I said, and he hopped on to the saddle and put his hands on my shoulders. I stood on the pedals to get the chain turning the back wheel.

The night was warm, and as still as it ever gets on the island. Which meant there were midges. We were alright as long as we kept moving, the breeze of our own momentum sending the little bastards flying off in our wake. But it made me think of that old joke: how can you tell a happy motorcyclist? Answer: from the flies embedded between his teeth.

The road was about two and a half miles long, and I knew it would take us anything up to fifteen minutes. Because Artair had been late, we were both late. But still I felt compelled to stop when I heard it. I jammed on the brakes so suddenly Artair nearly came off the saddle. 'Jesus Christ, Fin, what are you doing?'

I shushed him, putting a finger to my lips, and told him to listen.

He glared at me. 'What am I listening for?' Then he heard it, too. That distinctive *crex, crex* drifting across the moor in the dark. And he frowned. 'What is it?'

'It's a corncrake.'

'Jesus, Fin!' And he waved his hands around his head to fend off the flies. 'You stopped us here to get eaten alive by midges, just to listen to some bloody bird?'

'It's not just *some* bird,' I said. 'My shen told me it was one of the rarest sounds you'll ever hear on the islands. Most of the corncrakes left in the world breed in eastern Siberia. And you'll hardly find them anywhere else in the British Isles. "Ràc an fheòir" was what Shen used to say when he heard one. Croaker of the grass.'

Artair was alternatively slapping his face and running frantic hands through his hair. 'I don't give a shit, Fin. You'll be croaking in the grass if you don't get moving!'

And reluctantly I set off again.

When eventually we came out opposite the Cross Inn, the van was sitting idling at the side of the road. An angry voice hissed through the open window. 'Where the hell have you been?' It was Niall, leaning across from the driver's side.

'Fin wanted to stop and listen to a corncrake,' Artair said, his voice laden with sarcasm, ignoring the fact that he'd been a full ten minutes late meeting me in the first place.

'For God's sake, get in! We haven't got time to go listening to bloody birds in the night.' A door slid open, I leaned my bike against the fence, and we climbed into the back of the van. Alasdair was sitting up front with Niall, and Iain was sitting opposite the door with his back pressed against the side of the van, knees pulled up to his chest. When the door slid shut and the van juddered off into the dark, Iain leaned across and said, 'Was it really a corncrake?'

'It was,' I said.

A brief blink of light from a streetlamp momentarily illuminated his pale face. And I saw awe in his bright, shining eyes. 'I've never heard one,' he said, and, for the first time in all the years I'd known him, I felt an odd kinship with The Rev.

In the end we made up for lost time, and got down to the Bridge over the Atlantic in just under an hour. We saw Niall's dad's cages basking in moonlight. But it took another ten minutes on winding single-track roads before we drove down through a dark copse of pine trees to emerge into brilliant moonshine at Baile na Mara. Deep shadows fell across the water from a pier that reached out on concrete stilts into the loch.

Deserted buildings huddled around the harbour, dark shapes in the night. A seafood processing factory, huts with tin roofs that housed offices or stored equipment. A sign, mounted on a railing next to the ramp, languished in the shadow of rusting blue barrels. COMHAIRLE NAN EILEAN SIAR Baile na Mara. This pier is owned by the Local authority. All users must report their presence to the Harbour Master. Even had there been one, we certainly wouldn't have been reporting our presence to him.

We parked up beside a concrete hut and scampered across the ramp, pursued by our own shadows. Past untidy heaps of crab and lobster creels. On to the pier, where a rusting crane stood ready to load and unload supplies from fishing and service boats. More creels, and plastic boxes, fenders and buoys whose multifarious colours, brilliant in daylight, were lost in the colourless light of the moon.

There was an assortment of boats tied up around the pier. Motorboats for laying and collecting creels, sailing dinghies, smaller service craft with outboard motors. At high tide they would be easily accessible. But the tide was out, and you could only get to them down flimsy, rusted ladders.

Across the loch, you could see the streetlights of Breascleit strung out along the far coast. We had brought torches with us, but so bright was the moon we had no need of them. Which made life a little easier, though it made us more visible. I felt very exposed as, one by one, we slithered down the ladder to drop into one of Hamish Black's service boats. It was a sixteen-foot aluminium ex-army assault craft with a large outboard motor. Niall said his dad had bought two from a man who'd brought a job lot of them to the island. It made quite a racket when we jumped down into it, and the thing lurched dangerously.

'What about lifejackets?' I whispered. None of us, I knew, could swim. Which was how it was on the island back then. Parents discouraged their children from ever going near the water, never mind into it. So very few ever learned to swim.

Niall cast me a withering look. 'Get real, Macleod!'

He yanked on the pull cord, engaging the starter mechanism, and the motor burst into life. The noise of it thundered in the still of the night, and I knew just how far sound travelled on water. We were all so jumpy we barely noticed the midges, and I lost my footing, falling back into the belly of the boat, as Niall accelerated out from the harbour and into the loch proper.

He pulled back on the throttle then, and we cut almost silently through black water, leaving a luminous trail in our wake, hugging the shore as close as we dared. There was always a danger of striking hidden rock, especially in the dark, but Niall said he had done the journey many times with his dad, and was confident of the course he carved out in the night.

It took nearly fifteen minutes to get to the cages. We rounded the headland and saw them from the water for the first time, six interlinked square structures sitting very low in the loch, the profile of the bridge beyond them standing dark against the sky.

We tied up at the nearest and clambered clumsily on to a walkway of layered larchwood planks that sandwiched deep polystyrene blocks for buoyancy. Threaded rods between the inner and outer planks were set at regular intervals to clamp them tight, and the walkways fed into heavy galvanised steel corners with tying eyes for mooring the cages, or bolting them together. I was amazed at how big they were once you were on them. Nine square metres, Niall said. I was struck, too, by just how makeshift it all appeared. Old tyres lashed between the cages to stop them from bumping together, and a sea of polystyrene beads floating in the water around them.

The net to contain the salmon was hung from a crude wooden handrail on the interior of the structure, but there was another net draped along the outside that caught my foot as I tried to leave the boat.

'For Christ's sake, Fin, be careful,' Niall hissed. He was a silhouette against the moon, stretching out a hand to help me on to the cage.

'Why the hell are there nets on the outside?' I said, annoyed with myself for needing assistance to get out of the boat.

'Predator nets,' Niall said. 'To stop seals and the like getting at the salmon. Bloody useless things!'

Now we were all on the walkway, except for Iain, who was to stay in the boat and pack the fish into the insulated blue plastic containers of ice we had brought with us. Niall unclipped a long pole with a net attached to a triangular frame at one end.

'There's another pole on the rail at the far side, Fin. You go round and get it. We'll net the fish, and Alasdair and Artair can carry them to the boat. Half an hour at the most. We'll try and get as many as we can.'

The first problem arose when I couldn't find the net on the other side of the cage. Niall cursed at me across the water, then ran round to look for himself. This time he cursed his father. 'There should be two. Fuck knows why there aren't.' He leapt across to the adjoining cage, but couldn't find any there either.

We went back around to where Artair and Alasdair stood waiting nervously.

'We'll just have to make do with the one,' Niall said. 'Next time we'll bring our own!' And he thrust his pole over the rail and into the water, stirring up a flurry of activity among the salmon. I saw them writhing around, either in panic or perhaps the belief that food was on the way. At any rate, the surface of the water itself came alive. Niall guided his net through the turbulence, before lifting it out to raise above the level of the rail. Two salmon in it squirmed and leapt around, and, as he swung it across the rail for us to grab them, both slipped free of the mesh and fell back into the water.

'What the hell?' Niall thrust his net in once more, lifting three fish clear this time. But before he could swing it towards us, they had fallen out again, landing with a splash. 'Fuck! Fuck! Fuck!' His language was deteriorating as rapidly as the fish were escaping. 'How's that possible?' He slid the pole back through his hands to examine the net. Exasperation exploded from between his lips. 'It's got a fucking hole in it. What the hell's he playing at?'

'Who?' said Alasdair.

'My dad. One fucking net, and there's a bloody hole in it!' He hurled the pole down on to the walkway. 'We'll have to guddle for them.'

'What's that?' Artair said.

'Catch them by hand,' I told him.

Niall said. 'It should be easy enough. The water's hoaching with the buggers.' He got down on to his hands and knees and squeezed himself through the spars of the handrail so that he could reach down into the water. Within seconds he had pulled a squirming fish out of the depths and held it up for one of us to grab. I grasped the thing and felt it slithering about through my fingers, passing it on to Artair before I lost it. He gave it to Alasdair, who ran to the boat and threw it to Iain.

'Jees!' Artair said. 'This'll take for ever.'

In fact, over the next fifteen minutes, with both Niall and me reaching into the water, we only managed to pass something approaching a dozen fish to waiting hands, dropping several in the process. Before finally Niall said, 'Let's call it a night. We'll come better prepared next time.'

I passed a final fish up to Alasdair, who didn't really get a proper hold of it. And as it squirmed and wriggled out of his grasp, he reached further over the rail and virtually

somersaulted across it as his feet slipped from beneath him
on the wet larch.

We all watched in abject horror as Alasdair was swallowed
by the water, the surface of it still boiling with the fevered
activity of the fish. He never uttered a sound, but the splash
as he fell in was like an explosion in the still of the night.
We stood then for an eternity waiting for him to resurface.
Although I've no idea now what we thought we could do to
help him.

Iain called from the boat. 'What's happening?'

We all ignored him, still holding our collective breath. Until
suddenly Alasdair broke the surface, arms flailing. The sound
of his panicked gasping for air filled the night. But he was a
long way out in the cage, and there was nothing for him to
grab on to.

It was Niall's quick thinking that saved the day. He snatched
the pole he had earlier flung in a temper on to the walkway, and
thrust it out across the water towards the frantically splashing
Alasdair. After two unsuccessful attempts, Ally Ruadh finally
managed to catch hold of it, and everyone lent a hand to pull
him in and drag him, gasping, over the rail.

We clustered around him, standing watching as he lay on his
back fighting for breath, eyes wide, but panic finally starting to
subside. Before, inexplicably, he began shouting and writhing
at our feet.

'What in God's name's wrong with him?' Artair's panic mirrored Alasdair's.

And then a huge, wriggling salmon squeezed itself out from the neck of Alasdair's shirt, to lie thrashing beside him on the walkway, and we all burst out laughing, as much from relief as anything else.

'Well caught,' Niall said, between peals of laughter.

'That's not even funny!' Alasdair bellowed, almost in tears, his red hair smeared wet across his face. But that only sent us off into further paroxysms of laughter.

We laughed and made jokes at Ally Ruadh's expense for most of the way back to Baile na Mara, while he sat shivering in silence in the bow of the boat, glaring back at us resentfully.

Niall counted the fish in the blue plastic container. Thirteen, including Alasdair's whopper. 'Not as many as I'd have liked. We'll have to do better next time.'

'Lucky for some, though.' Iain grinned.

'Aye, but not for Ally Ruadh,' I said, and we all laughed heartily again at the look on Alasdair's face.

By the time we got back to the pier, Alasdair's red hair had dried sufficiently to restore some of the curl to it, as well as a little of his sense of humour. He allowed himself a grudging smile as we joked about him swimming the Atlantic to land the biggest salmon ever pulled out of the ocean.

His clothes were dry, too, after the hour-long drive back to Ness. And as the van headed off up the road, Artair and I got back on my bike for the final leg of the return journey over the Cross–Skigersta road.

I felt his hands on my shoulders and his breath on my

neck as he said, 'And no stopping this time to listen to bloody corncrakes!'

III.

It seemed to me that I had just drifted off to sleep when my aunt's voice came crashing into distant dreams. I surfaced from a warm sea of gentle oblivion to an awareness of sunlight slanting in through the dormer and lying hot across my bed. It had been dark when I closed my eyes, or at least the sun had not yet risen over the horizon, and it was somehow shocking to realize how far the day had progressed in what felt like such a short time.

'Finlay?' she shouted again from the foot of the stairs, and I swung my legs out of bed to plant them on cool linoleum. I rubbed the sleep from my eyes.

'What is it?'

'Your friend's here. He says you're expecting him.'

I frowned. I wasn't expecting anyone. Reluctantly I dragged on some clothes and a pair of trainers, and stumbled down the stairs to the tiny hall below, running fingers back through my hair. My aunt was standing by the open door wearing some kind of tie-dyed lilac smock, pale powdered face like a death mask cut across by the two slashes of scarlet that were her lips. Beyond, silhouetted against a backdrop of sunlight on sea, stood the tall figure of Niall Dubh.

'I don't know what sort of hour you got in last night, Finlay, but you're too young to be wasting your life lying in bed half the day.' And she headed off into the kitchen, leaving Niall standing on the doorstep.

'What is it?' I was not best pleased at being awakened so rudely.

He flicked his head to indicate that I should follow him outside, and I shut the door behind me. We walked a few paces towards the harbour, and I clocked his father's van sitting there. 'I want you to come with me,' he said.

I frowned. 'Where?'

'To Linshader. I don't feel like facing Coinneach Smith on my own. I promised him more than just eleven fish.'

'I thought we caught thirteen?'

He shrugged. 'I gave one each to the other boys.'

'But not to me and Artair?'

'Like you could have carried two fish with you on the bike!'

I had to concede that might have been tricky.

'I just need some moral support, Fin. He's a prickly character, Coinneach. Not a fella you'd want to rub up the wrong way.'

I sighed. 'I'll just get some toast then to keep me going.'

On the drive down to the Linshader estate, Niall explained to me the mystery of the missing nets. I sat munching on toast, with honey dripping down my T-shirt, and sipped from the flask of tea my aunt had insisted on giving me. 'They're being replaced,' he said. 'The one that we found with the hole in it

shouldn't even have been there. Someone forgot to take it.'
He laughed, and I thought, aye, you weren't laughing at three
o'clock this morning. He said, 'The good news is that we'll have
plenty of nets to work with next time we go.'

'When'll that be?'

He darkened a little. 'As soon as possible, Fin. We're going
to have to keep Coinneach happy.'

Coinneach, I discovered soon after, was a bad-tempered bastard, on whose wrong side you definitely did not want to get.

The Linshader estate extends south from the headland at
Rudha Linsiadair, directly across the water from the Callanish
standing stones. It takes in Loch Ceann Hùlabhaig, really
just an extension of East Loch Roag, and the mouth of the
Grimersta River, which it follows all the way into a marshy
hinterland peppered with large and small lochs. In fact, it's
quite possible that there's more water on the estate than there
is land. Fishing and hunting are conducted from the lodge,
and provide most of its income. There's a gamekeeper and
water bailiff, and varying numbers of ghillies and watchers,
depending on the season.

Coinneach Smith was a full-time ghillie, and his family lived
with him on the estate. Niall had arranged to meet him at a
rocky outcrop near Lundale where we were unlikely to be
seen together. It was a bleak spot, accessed by a potholed dirt
track that came to an abrupt end at a tiny crescent of shingle
beach. Coinneach was standing in silhouette at the top of a
peat-covered promontory from which he could see us coming.

He strode down the hill to greet us as we pulled up on the shingle next to his battered old Land Rover. A big man, in his forties, with green wellington boots and a military green pullover with leather at the shoulders and elbows. He wore a flat cap pulled low over his brow, and there was a nasty scar on his upper lip. Niall jumped out and rounded the van to throw open the back doors. He dragged out the blue plastic container with the fish, and it dropped on to the stones with a clatter.

Coinneach scowled at me. 'Who's this?'

'Fin Macleod,' Niall said. 'One of the boys.'

Coinneach curled his upper lip as if I gave off a bad smell, and stooped to pull the lid off the container. He looked at the eleven fish lying higgledy-piggledy in the bottom of it and his head snapped up. 'What the hell's this?'

'It's all we could get, Coinneach. There weren't any nets and we had to guddle them.'

Coinneach kicked the container to send it skiting off across the shingle. 'That's no bloody use to me. I've got customers all lined up and waiting. You promised me fifty good-sized salmon. I'm only going to net about thirty quid for a sliced side D cut. Sixty quid a fish. What's in that box? Ten, eleven? Six hundred quid tops. I need four or five times that much to make it worth my while. And yours.' He reached into his jacket and pulled out a leather wallet. He drew a fifty from it and threw the note at Niall. It fluttered to the shore. Then he strode off to pick up the blue container and slide it into the back of his Land Rover.

'That's not fair,' I called after him. 'We're the ones who risked our necks to get the bloody things.'

He spun around, dark eyes blazing, and reached me in three strides. A hand thrust into my chest forced me to take a step back. I lost my footing and sat down heavily in the shingle. He stabbed a finger at me. 'You, sonny, are risking bugger all! I'm the one at the point of sale who'll get lifted if the cops get wind of this. So don't give me any of your shite.'

Niall stooped quickly to retrieve the fifty note and hurried to help me to my feet. 'He didn't mean anything by it, Coinneach. We'll have nets next time, and you'll have your fifty fish.'

'Just make sure I do!' Spittle gathering around his mouth passed from the upper to the lower lip and he turned his head to gob into the incoming tide. 'Or there'll be trouble, son.'

IV.

Over the next couple of weeks we risked six trips out to the cages, netting between forty and fifty fish each time. We divided the taking of the salmon between the different cages, moving from one to the other each time, hoping that would make the loss of the fish less noticeable to Niall's dad, or his workers. Financially we were all doing very nicely out of it, but knew it couldn't last.

Niall in particular was starting to get the jitters. 'My dad's going to cotton on,' he said. 'Sooner or later. We can't keep this up for much longer.'

The problem was that Coinneach Smith didn't want us to stop. If we were doing well out of the enterprise, he was doing even better. He figured we could keep going right through the month of August.

Of course, Artair and I knew that was impossible. At least for us. We had an appointment with two thousand gannets out on An Sgeir. And Iain and Alasdair didn't want to do it if we weren't there. So we all met up one Monday towards the end of July to try to reach a consensus on what to do. But there was no decision to make. Niall had already taken it for us.

We gathered down at the jetty at Port of Ness, just by the boat shed, and wandered along the breakwater to climb the rock that separated the inner and outer harbours. There we sat among the tussocks at its grassy summit. The spell of fine weather looked to be coming to an end. Gone were the clear skies. Dark clouds gathered ominously in the west, the wind strong enough now to drive in waves that broke over the far wall, throwing spray fifteen or twenty feet in the air. We felt it in our faces.

'Tonight,' Niall said. 'Last time.'

'What about Coinneach?' I asked.

'Fuck Coinneach. There's a limit. And we've reached it.'

I don't think there was one of us who disagreed, and a certain amount of relief did the rounds among us. But none of the others had met Coinneach, and Niall and I exchanged glances. I had no desire to be there when Niall told him it was over.

On previous trips to the cages, Artair and I had travelled the Cross–Skigersta road in about fifteen minutes. That night it took us more than twenty because of the wind. One person presents a formidable amount of resistance, two made it all the more difficult. And by the time we reached the Cross Inn, the muscles of my legs were on fire.

The atmosphere in the van was tense. We were already late, and the weather was deteriorating. Big fat drops of rain hit the windscreen like pebbles, and by the time we got down to Barvas, the windscreen wipers were working overtime. And still we could barely see out.

I made my way up to the front of the van and shouted above the roar of the motor and the pounding of the rain. 'Maybe we should just forget it, Niall. It's not a night for going out to the cages.'

Niall's face was a study of concentration, his eyes fixed on the short stretch of road ahead made visible by the headlamps. He shook his head. 'I promised Coinneach.'

'It's not bloody worth it,' I shouted.

'Too late to turn back now.'

I glanced round at the others. I couldn't tell if they had fully heard our exchange or not, but I'm sure they had guessed the gist of it. Iain shrugged. 'We've come this far. Might as well see it through.' I slumped back into the coil of rope I had been using as a seat and drew my knees up to my chin. I had such a bad feeling about this.

It took us longer than usual to reach the pier at Baile na

Mara, and, while on previous outings we'd had the light of the moon to see by, it was pitch-black that night. We had our torches, of course, but they didn't penetrate far through the rain and the darkness. Enough, though, to see the whitetops coursing across the loch. The boats tied up at the pier rose and fell violently on the swell, the whine of cables vibrating against masts, fenders smacking off concrete stanchions.

And this was the east side of Great Bernera, relatively sheltered from the incoming storm. I made one final pitch in favour of abandoning the whole thing, but was shouted down. 'Stupid to go back now,' Alasdair said.

Niall shouted, 'The cages'll be protected from the worst of the weather. Half an hour, that's all we need! If we work fast, we'll get enough to keep Coinneach happy.'

'You know he's not going to be happy,' I shouted back at him. 'Not when you tell him it's finished.'

But Niall just slipped over the edge of the pier and shimmied down the ladder to the boat. He looked up through the rain at the rest of us peering down at him. 'Come on, hurry up.' And against my better judgement, I followed the others down the ladder and into a boat that was lurching wildly beneath our feet. Niall started the motor, which you could barely hear above the roar of the wind, and cast off.

We fought our way out into the loch, taking waves side on, before Niall started hugging the shoreline for shelter. A spotlight mounted in the prow of the boat cut through the rain and the dark, providing a limited arc of visibility. Enough and no more to circumvent the jagged black rocks that would appear out of nowhere, our only warning being the water that broke white all around them.

But it wasn't until we rounded the point at Rudha Glas that we felt the full force of the wind. Gale force now, I was pretty certain. It whipped the breath from your mouth, and I found myself gasping for air.

Ironically, the boat itself felt more stable as we ploughed head-on into the storm. But progress was slow, and it was much longer than on previous trips before we saw the cages ahead of us, rising and falling on the swell, tugging at their anchors. The nets, I knew, would be at an angle of sixty degrees or more, the salmon they contained all facing west and swimming hard against the tide and the swell. Waves breaking against the furthest cages threw spume up through the light of our spot lamp to vanish into darkness, before lashing our faces like myriad burning sparks from a fire. We tied up and four of us jumped out on to the heaving walkway.

For the first time I felt real fear. One slip and any one of us could be in the water. Gone. Beyond rescue, beyond hope. Even if we'd had lifejackets.

Despite two of us netting fish, getting them back to the boat was almost impossible. You had to hang on to the wooden barrier, and try to restrain a writhing salmon with one free hand, clutching it to you as you made your way along the walkway. We were losing almost as many as we netted, and after about twenty minutes we had fewer than five in the boat.

'Enough!' I bellowed at Niall, but if he heard he didn't react, his focus entirely on the pole and his net, pulling fish out of turbulent water. His expression was grim, his face shining wet. Then a shrill shout cut above everything else, and I turned to see Alasdair, his freckles standing out against white skin like they'd been painted on. His green eyes so dilated they looked black. He was staring past us towards the Bridge over the Atlantic. I spun around and saw a line of white in the distant night. It almost appeared to glow in the dark, growing in size as it approached, breaking in luminous phosphorescence over the Bernera bridge. The biggest wave I have ever seen come ashore. As it drove between the two points of land, it rose up into the night, and the wind that preceded it nearly knocked me off my feet.

I grabbed the wooden handrail with both hands and crouched on my hunkers as low as I could get, my back to the approaching wave. The roar of it was frightening, deafening. And I felt it break over me with hurricane force, very nearly breaking my grasp on the handrail. My feet went skiting from under me, water dragging me at full stretch along the larch planking. I have no idea how I managed to hang on. I saw our boat rise up into the air, clearing the water completely at the end of its rope, before crashing back into the loch. I caught a fleeting glimpse of Artair's face inside it as he hung on for dear life.

As the force and roar of the water subsided, I looked back to see Niall staring at me along the length of the walkway. I could see the fear in his eyes. And I felt Alastair's hand pulling me to my feet. His panicked voice. 'We've got to go, for Christ's sake, we've got to go!'

We got to the boat, and Niall slithered along behind us. The look of abject terror on Artair's face stood out like a beacon of smudged white light in the raging darkness of the storm. He was shouting. But I couldn't make out a word. Then Alasdair turned to bellow in my face. 'Where's Iain?'

Fear stabbed me with such force I felt the pain of it, just as if someone had slammed a blade into my chest. All eyes turned back along the walkway, but he wasn't to be seen. He had been right there, on the far side of the cage, with one of the nets. I pulled myself to my feet. Hands that had lost almost all feeling clung to the handrail, scanning the water in the cage. I hooked my arm around the rail and fumbled with my free hand to get the torch from my pocket. When finally I managed to retrieve it, the light it gave made little impression. I could see fish in long undulating shoals fighting against the force of the water just beneath the surface. Then suddenly there was Iain's net and pole being tossed around well out in the cage. But no sign of Iain.

We divided up, then, Niall, Alasdair and I, to fight our way along each side of the square, scanning the water, searching in vain for some glimpse of our friend. Perhaps he was clinging to the net, or the foot of the barrier, hanging on for dear life in the hope that his friends would come and rescue him. But there was no trace of him. And it was clear he could just as easily have been swept off into the loch.

By the time we met up again at the boat, still lashed by the gale and the sting of rain on its leading edge, we knew he was gone. Niall shouted, 'We've got to get out of here.'

'We can't just leave without Iain!' I screamed at him.

And Niall grabbed my collar with both hands. He shook me with the force of a madman. 'There's nothing we can do, Fin. He's gone. Dead.'

And I knew he was right.

I allowed myself to be bundled, then, into the boat, and heard the motor starting up. And once free of its tether, the aluminium ex-army assault craft lurched away from the cages, propelled east at much greater speed than the journey out. Niall sat up at the stern, steering us back the way we had come, huddled against the storm behind him, while the rest of us crouched in the belly of the boat, miserable and desperately trying to come to terms with unimaginable loss. I heard Artair sobbing and gasping behind me. I turned to see the panic in his eyes. 'Can't . . . can't breathe,' he wheezed.

'Where's your puffer?' I shouted at him.

He shook his head in desperation. 'Don't know. Lost it.'

I put my arm around him and drew him close. I could feel every attempted breath convulsing through his body, and knew that without his puffer the best I could offer was reassurance.

I'm not sure how Niall managed to get us back to Baile na Mara in one piece, but we were a sorry group that climbed the ladder to stand desolate among the creels and fenders blowing around the pier. Nothing seemed quite real. Iain was gone. Iain was dead. No one was to blame, but it was still our fault. All of us. Stupid, greedy boys!

In the van on the way back, I closed my eyes to relive that fleeting moment just a couple of weeks earlier when Iain had been awestruck at the thought of hearing a corncrake on the moor. Bright eyes, clever and sensitive, full of wonder. He would never attend those student parties in Glasgow, or drink too much beer, ever again. He would never graduate and make his parents proud. He would never be the doctor, or lawyer, or whatever it was he had aspired to be in life. He had never said, and I had never asked. I had such a sense of loss, it was painful even to contemplate it.

Ironically, by the time we got to Cross, the worst of the storm had passed, although the rain had not stopped. Artair had recovered a little of his breath, but was still labouring. I could hear it, curdling thick in his chest.

Niall cut the engine, and only the sound of rain on metal broke the silence until Niall did. 'We can't breathe a word about this,' he said. 'To anyone. We can't! We absolutely can't. Iain's gone, and there's nothing we can do about that now. If anyone finds out what we were doing out there . . .' He didn't need to finish the sentence. We all knew what it would mean. Whatever future any of us had dreamt for ourselves would be gone. Iain's life lost, the rest of ours ruined. No one said anything.

I slid open the door and jumped out into the rain. Artair followed, and we stood there for some time until finally I banged it shut and heard the engine cough life into the night. The van lumbered away up the road towards the port.

My bike had blown over. I picked it up and ran a wet sleeve over the saddle. But Artair brushed my arm aside. 'It doesn't matter.'

I swung a leg over the bar and he slipped on to the saddle behind me. This time I felt his arms around me, and his face pressed into my back. And I set off with tears for Iain coursing with the rain down my face.

V.

I'm pretty sure I didn't sleep that night. Certain that I didn't drift off, even for a moment. I remember weeping. Tears that seared my cheeks. Sobs that tore themselves from my chest to be muffled by my pillow.

By the time I heard my aunt in the kitchen downstairs, I was lying with burning eyes staring at the ceiling, a feeling of such aching emptiness inside me that I could barely move. When life has dealt you the most devastating and irreversible hand, it is almost impossible to grasp. I can remember thinking that, if only I had been able to sleep, I would wake up to realize it had all been a bad dream. I would cycle down to the port to find Iain sitting up on that rock in the harbour with a can of beer in his hand and a cigarette burning between his fingers. 'Heard a corncrake last night,' he would tell me. 'At the back of the croft. Clear as day. *Crex, crex.*'

'Finlay!' My aunt's voice. 'Are you awake yet?'

I didn't have the energy to respond.

'Finlay!' she shouted again. 'Finlay, you need to hear this. Come down.'

It was only when I stood up that I realized I hadn't undressed, and that my clothes were still residually damp from the night before. At least I had kicked off my trainers. I pulled them on now and went carefully down the stairs on shaking legs, hands braced on the walls either side of me.

My aunt looked up from the kitchen table and her jaw fell open. 'For God's sake, Finlay, what have you been up to? You look dreadful.'

I caught my reflection in the window as I rounded the kitchen table. She was right. I looked like death. Eyes mired in shadow, skin chalk-white and stretched over gaunt features. The transistor radio that sat on the fireplace was playing the morning news in Gaelic from Radio nan Gàidheal. It barely penetrated my consciousness. Just meaningless background. Wallpaper. I didn't even hear it.

'They'll give a resumé of the headlines in a minute,' my aunt was saying. 'He was one of your friends, wasn't he?'

'Who?' I said, suddenly alert.

'Iain Murray. His body's been recovered from one of the fish farm cages down by Great Bernera. Workers went out to check on damage after the storm and found him floating face down in the water. No one knows what he was doing out there in the middle of a storm in the middle of the night, or how he even got there. Apparently there's to be a police investigation.'

I got out of the house as fast as I could. My aunt wanted to cook me breakfast, but I knew I wouldn't be able to keep it down. I followed the path down to the shore, buffeted by the wind. But at least it was dry.

In a daze, I drifted past the remains of what had once been a fish processing factory, just a collection of stones now in the grass. I climbed the hill on to the promontory, and followed the cliffs out to where men returning from war had built cairns in memory of those who had not. I sat among them now, hair blown free of my face by the remnants of the storm, and thought about Iain. It was the first time I had lost a contemporary. A friend. And those thoughts of death that you bury deep in your subconscious, to be faced only in some indeterminate and unimaginable future, were suddenly front and centre in my mind. My own mortality looming large.

I stood up then, and started collecting the stones that lay around me, to build a cairn for Iain. A repository for his soul. A place he would always be remembered.

I saw Niall coming from a long way off, hands thrust deep in his pockets, skirting the cliffs to make his way out to the point. I carried on building the cairn, and without a word, Niall, when he reached me, began collecting stones to add to the pile. Nothing passed between us except for a silent understanding. When finally we were finished, we sat side by side looking out across the Minch. Sunlight fell in scattered fragments through broken clouds, constantly on the move, as if God himself were trying to calm the seas with light. Niall cupped his hands around a cigarette that he then passed to me. We smoked in silence before finally I said, 'We need to tell people what happened. His folks deserve to know.'

His head snapped round. 'No!' He took the cigarette off me for one final puff before flicking it away into the wind. 'Nothing's going to bring him back, Fin. And we still have our whole lives ahead of us.' I felt his eyes on me, without turning to look at him. 'I want you to come with me.'

Now it was me turning my head. 'To see Coinneach?'

'I don't want to go alone.'

I closed my eyes, and a long sigh released itself from deep inside. The last thing I wanted was a face to face with Coinneach. I felt an unreasonable anger towards him, as if Iain's death were somehow his fault. And in a way it was. But no more than ours. Or Iain's. I wanted to tell Niall to do it himself, but I didn't. My head fell a little and I nodded acqui-escence. 'Okay.'

Coinneach was waiting for us at the usual spot. I saw him standing on the headland, watching as we bumped down the dirt track towards the shingle beach. By the time we reached the shore he was already there, standing by his Land Rover, glaring at us from beneath the peak of his cloth cap. He was clearly agitated.

We were barely out of the van before his voice flung itself

at us on the edge of the wind. 'What the fuck happened? Jesus Christ! It's all over the news. How fucking stupid are you going out in a bloody storm?'

Niall cast a sullen gaze at the big ghillie. 'You wanted your fish, Coinneach. Turns out the price we've paid for it is much higher than any of us expected. Iain most of all.'

'No one said you had to go out to the cages in weather like that.'

'Oh yeah? And if we'd turned up this morning empty-handed, you'd have been biting our heads off for being scared of a bit of rain.'

He stared at us, wild-eyed, seething inside. 'So you've got something for me?'

The words were out of my mouth before I could stop them. Shouted into the wind. 'No, we bloody haven't! What kind of a monster are you?'

Fire flamed in Coinneach's eyes and he took a threatening step towards me. But Niall pushed the flat of one hand into his chest to stop him and said quietly, 'It's over, Coinneach.'

The big man's head whipped around. 'No, it's not.'

'We're not going out there again,' Niall said.

'Aye, you are. A few days, a week at the most, it'll all die down. The police'll figure the boy was out at the cages trying to steal fish, his boat sunk by the storm. Death by misadventure. And I've got enough orders for another whole month.'

Niall shook his head. 'It's finished.' He glanced at me. 'Come on, Fin.' And we turned back towards the van.

Coinneach's voice pursued us, laden with menace. 'You boys stop bringing me fish, there's a good chance folk might learn the truth about what Iain Murray was doing out there last night, and who was with him.'

Niall opened the driver's door, holding it wide as he turned back to face Coinneach. 'You won't shop us, because you'd be shopping yourself.'

But Coinneach just grinned. A nasty grin that made me want to punch him. 'Nothing to connect me to a bunch of stupid boys stealing salmon from Hamish Black. That's on you. And there's a hundred and one ways I can get that information out there without implicating myself. Not least to the police, who I'm sure would be very interested in the whole sorry tale. An anonymous tip. A wee call from a concerned citizen.'

'Fuck you!' Niall slid into the driver's seat and banged the door shut.

As we drove back up the track towards the road, I looked at him across the van, oscillating between the desire to tell the truth and fear of what it would mean. 'If he breathes a word about any of this, Niall . . .'

But Niall just shook his head, the grim set of his jaw betraying a stubborn determination. 'He won't.' And he paused. 'I'll make sure he doesn't.'

It was about a week later that I came downstairs to breakfast in the kitchen to find cold eggs, sausage and bacon set in a plate of congealed fat waiting for me on the table. My aunt was

dismissive. 'You spend half the day in bed, Finlay, you have to
expect that your breakfast will go cold. If you don't want it, I'll
feed it to the cats.' She flounced off to the living room, and I
sat staring at a yolk set solid in a pool of white turned grey. I
pushed it away. I'd lost my appetite both for food and for life
this past week, and lying in my bed felt as good a way as any
to avoid facing the reality of Iain's death, and my upcoming
trip to An Sgeir.

I was only vaguely aware of the transistor radio on the fireplace. It was turned down low. A background commentary on
my misery. But suddenly it penetrated my indifference and I
found myself sitting upright, heart pounding.

A ghillie on the Linshader estate in south-west Lewis was found
dead this morning on the southern shore of East Loch Roag near
Lundale. Coinneach Smith, or Mac a'Ghobhainn, a 44-year-old
estate worker, married with one young son, is believed to have
fallen from cliffs above a shingle beach on the western edge
of the estate. Police do not believe there are any suspicious
circumstances.

Niall's family lived in a tiny settlement called Knockaird,
near the Butt. His father was away at the fish farm, but his
mother was home, and she told me that Niall had taken a
walk out to Dùn Èistean. Said he'd wanted to clear his head.
There was disapproval in her voice. 'He was out far too late
again at the Social last night. Though from the look of you,

Fin Macleod, you probably know all about that. You boys think you're immortal. But it'll catch up with you in the end, you know.'

Dùn Èistean was a site of archaeological interest. The ruins of what was once the stronghold of the Clan Morrison, built on an intertidal sea stack connected now to the main part of the island by a flimsy green tubular steel bridge. I found Niall on the far side of it, sitting closer to the edge of the stack than felt safe. The sea had cut deep into the rock all around, and several smaller stacks rose out of its turbulence fifty feet below, water frothing angrily and foaming around their feet. The sound of the ocean venting its fury on the rocks, and the sucking sound of water being dragged out again by the retreating tide, fought for dominance against the howling of the wind that I could see tugging at his clothes, and dragging dark hair back from a pallid face.

He didn't turn as I planked myself down beside him. For several long minutes we sat without a word, a cacophony of sound breaking all around us. Then finally I said – well, shouted – 'Tell me you didn't do it.'

His face was set, as if in stone, not a hint of emotion anywhere on frozen features. His lips moved, but I couldn't hear what he said.

'What?'

He turned to look at me and shouted to make himself heard, 'No, Fin, I didn't do it.' No impassioned denial. Just a plain statement of fact, as he saw it. But I remained unconvinced.

'So what happened to him?'

Niall shrugged. 'No idea. They say he fell. I've heard the police think it might have been suicide.'

I scoffed. 'Coinneach? Suicide? You really believe that?'

He shook his head. 'Seems unlikely.'

And that was it. He didn't want to discuss it further. In fact, he made it clear he didn't want to talk to me at all, turning his face back to the ocean and casting his gaze on some faraway place that only he could see.

I walked back to the road to fetch my bike and made the return journey to Crobost, my mind seething with dark thoughts and uncertainty. When I got back to my aunt's house, I could hear the sound of loud music coming from inside. I recognized it immediately. *Sgt. Pepper's Lonely Hearts Club Band*. My aunt played it all the time, stuck for ever in a decade when she had been young and glamorous and in demand, a Mod girl of London's swinging sixties. Before some tragedy, I never knew what, brought her back to the island to live out the rest of her days in exile, and a splendid isolation that I had spoiled for her by becoming an orphan.

She played the Kinks, and the Stones, too, and an early Who album that she loved. Songs about heatwaves, and Boris the spider.

The last thing I wanted was another dose of my aunt's nostalgia. Neither did I relish the fug of cannabis smoke that doubtless hung in the sunlight angling into the living room. Perhaps she had always smoked, but been more discreet about it. Nowadays, it seemed to me that she was semi-permanently high.

I walked instead down towards the jetty. The sound of McCartney singing of things getting better all the time receded behind me until it was lost in the wind. And all I could think was that things were getting worse all the time. It was only as I reached the ramp that I saw Artair sitting at the end of the jetty, legs dangling above the water. It was sheltered here in the lee of cliffs, and the protective walls of the tiny harbour, and the wind seemed a distant roar. Artair turned as I sat down beside him, and scrutinised my face for several moments without speaking. I could hear the crackle of his breath in his chest.

Eventually I said, 'I suppose you've heard?'

He nodded and looked away. 'What does Niall say?'

'That he has no idea what happened.' I breathed out hard. 'What are we going to do?'

He seemed surprised. 'What do you mean?'

'I can't keep this to myself any longer, Artair.' My pendulum of accountability had swung towards confession. 'Apart from anything else, Iain's people have a right to know what happened to him. And why.' I spat into the water. 'And then there's Niall. Okay, he says he had nothing to do with Coinneach's death, but . . .' My voice trailed away, reluctant to put words to dark thoughts.

Artair was silent for a long time, almost as if he had gone into a trance, gazing out beyond the cliffs. Then suddenly he focused, and looked at me. 'So here's the thing, Fin. His folks knowing what happened isn't going to bring Iain back. Nothing can. All you want to do is offload your own guilt. And if you do that, chances are you're going to screw up the rest of your life. Mine, too. So my advice is to shut up and live with it.' He shook his head. 'You're not going to make anything better by confessing to . . . well, what? Stealing a few fish?'

'What about Coinneach?'

'What about him? The police think he fell. Niall says it was nothing to do with him. So it's none of our business.' He put an arm around my shoulder. 'Get a perspective, Fin. You'll feel better for it.'

But I knew I wouldn't.

When I got back to the house, I realized the music inside had stopped. I went in the front door and through to the living room. My aunt was taking another album from its sleeve to put on the Dansette. She turned as I came in and I could see how black her pupils were. Still, she seemed to see right through me.

'You're always so miserable these days, Finlay.'

'Am I?'

She straightened up and sighed. 'It's time you found the fun in your life. Because it'll all be gone before you know it. You'll be twenty soon enough, then forty, then sixty. And you'll end up old and lonely, and living in some dilapidated house on a clifftop au bout du monde.' Which I knew from my French classes meant the end of the world. By which I knew she meant the middle of nowhere. Here.

I said, with a hint of bitterness, 'Why would you be lonely? You have me.'

The look she turned on me was withering, and I shrank away from its implication.

'Anyway,' I said, trying to lighten things. 'You're not that old. You'll probably live to be a hundred.'

She turned to gaze wistfully at the album sleeve she was holding in her hands. *Face to Face* by the Kinks, a colourful example of sixties psychedelia. And she said quietly, 'I'm not likely to live a hundred days, Finlay. They tell me I have terminal cancer.'

CHAPTER TWELVE

Much of the new extension at the back of the house was glass, though most of it faced away from the prevailing weather. Beyond the cars and the reflections, Fin could see a large living room. The floor was tiled and littered with rugs. White leather furniture. There was a bar, a line of beer taps below optics attached to bottles in varying states of emptiness, sunlight catching the gold and ambers of single malts, and the deeper hue, almost red, of a fine old cognac.

A figure passed through sunshine that angled into the room from a window at the far side of it, and a large glass door slid open. A big man stood framed in the opening. He had the kind of face that was difficult to put an age to, but Fin reckoned he was younger than he looked. Thirty, perhaps. His head was cropped to a fine, dark stubble, but his fleshy face was shaved to a shine, and Fin could almost smell the aftershave from where he stood. He wore a white T-shirt stretched over a muscular frame, and dark blue jog pants. His sneakers were outsized and garishly coloured, LEDs in his heels lighting up as he walked. Fin revised the estimate of his age, and reduced it by around ten.

The man lifted his head a little, glaring at Fin with the palest of blue eyes, the smallest upward movement of his jaw asking the question that he couldn't be bothered putting into words. *Who the fuck are you?*

Fin responded as if he had actually asked. 'Fin Macleod. An old friend of Niall's. Is he around?'

But before the man could even reply, Niall appeared at his side, much heavier than the skinny teenager Fin remembered. Once-dark hair had thinned, reduced to an indeterminate grey, a belly lurking obtrusively beneath his open shirt. He appeared not to have shaved for several days, a rough silver bristle growing along his jawline.

'Fin fucking Macleod,' he said without any enthusiasm. He stepped barefoot on to the tarmac, placing his hands on his hips, and cast critical eyes over his old friend. 'Well, you haven't changed much in, what, must be thirty years? More?'

Fin nodded tentatively. 'Something like that.'

Niall half turned towards the man still lurking at the opening to the room beyond. 'That's okay, Jack. I got this.'

Jack nodded and moved back into the shadows, only the intermittent light generated by his trainers betraying the path he took to the far side of the room, where he slumped into an armchair. Niall lowered his voice, speaking Gaelic now. 'Jack's an acquired taste,' he said. 'And I acquired him as protection for me and Eòghann. You make a bit of money, Fin, there's aye someone wants a piece of you. And Jack's the man to keep them at bay. Dempsey. You maybe heard of him? They call him The Ripper.'

Fin shook his head.

'Briefly a media darling a few years back, when he stymied a terrorist attack on a train between Glasgow and Edinburgh. Complete disregard for his own safety. Or anyone else's. It got big press coverage. So I did a wee bit of background research. Seems he used to run with one of the gangs in the east end of Glasgow. He has no empathy, Fin. But no fear either. And there are times when you need someone like that on your side.'

He rubbed his jaw with an open palm and Fin heard the scratch of his bristles.

He said sarcastically, 'If I'd known you were coming, I might have had a shave.' He turned back towards the house. 'Let me get a pair of shoes and we'll walk down on the beach. And you can tell me why I should keep a civil tongue in my head when the man whose son killed my daughter comes calling.'

There were tourists on the beach. A couple with a dog bounding playfully in and out of the water. A family of five trailing barefoot along the tideline. A young couple on a travelling rug at the foot of the cliffs, delving into a picnic hamper. All of which would have been alien when Fin was a boy. Island tourism was a relatively recent phenomenon.

Even so, it could hardly be described as crowded, and Fin and Niall were able to talk freely as they walked the length of the sands. The gentle wash of the sea, the scattered calls of nesting gulls, the occasional shriek of children running in and out of the water, were the only accompaniments to their conversation.

Niall had buttoned up his shirt and slipped on a pair of sunglasses. His suntan, Fin was sure, owed more to the Cyprus sun than this present spell of fine Hebridean weather. 'I'll be honest with you, Fin,' he said. 'I don't know how to be with you. My head says none of this is your fault. My instinct is to kick the shit out of you. Turning up at my house when your son has raped and murdered my daughter. I mean, what do you expect me to say?'

Fin shrugged helplessly. 'I don't know what to tell you, Niall. I'm really sorry. Marsaili and I were as shocked as anyone to find out Fionnlagh had been having an affair with her. One of his pupils. Then I learn she's your daughter. Jesus, I can only imagine how you feel about that. And there's nothing I can say to defend him. Wouldn't want to.' He breathed deeply. 'I just find it impossible to believe that he killed her.'

Niall said, 'It was a shock, Fin. A real fucking shock. Me and Eòghann only arrived on the island a few days ago. I hadn't even had a chance to see her. Not that her mother takes kindly to me coming to the house.'

Fin nodded. 'She was pretty hostile when I saw her.'

Niall cast him a withering glance. 'Ailsa? What did you expect?' He snorted. 'Mind you, knowing Ailsa, she'll be making the most of it. Everything's always about her.'

He scuffed the toe of his shoe in the sand, propelling a pebble towards the water.

'Maybe it's not fair to hold you responsible for something your boy's done, Fin, but you can hardly blame us if we do.'

Fin said, 'When we were kids and got into trouble, it was always our folks that got the blame for it. Bad parenting, they said.'

Niall laughed for the first time. 'Aye, that's how it was.' But his smile faded just as quickly. 'So how *is* Ailsa taking it?'

'Badly.'

Niall nodded, and his gaze grew distant. 'I'll have to pay a visit. She was a beautiful-looking lassie, Caitlin. Got her looks from her mother.' He turned to Fin, then. 'If I'd known your boy was fucking her, I'd have killed him myself.'

Fin's shame stopped him from meeting Niall's eye.

Niall said, 'I always thought Fionnlagh was Artair's boy.'

'So did I. Till I found out different.' Fin didn't want to get into it. 'Long story.' He quickly changed the subject. 'Ailsa says you're a billionaire now.'

Which elicited a guffaw of ironic laughter. 'Ailsa always was prone to exaggeration. But I've done alright.'

Fin looked at him. 'Tax exile in Cyprus. CEO of the third largest salmon farming concern in the world. I'd say you'd done a bit better than alright.'

Niall shrugged his modesty. And it was his turn now to change the subject. 'You used to be a cop, didn't you?'

'I was. But it screwed up my life in too many ways. I quit the force a good few years ago.'

'What do you do now?'

'Computer forensics. Took an Open University degree in IT. Still working with the police, but it's a civilian job.'

'Enjoying it?'

Fin gazed off along the beach, wondering how to frame his response. But Niall just laughed derisively.

'Man, if you have to think about it, the answer's got to be a no.'

Fin's smile was rueful. 'That transparent, am I?'

They had almost reached the rocks that lay in slabs like toppled dominoes at the far end of the beach when Niall said, 'So you've come to investigate her murder?'

Fin shook his head. 'Not exactly. Though I would like to prove that it wasn't Fionnlagh who did it.'

Niall tipped his head one way then the other, pursing his lips reflectively. 'I'd probably do the same in your shoes. Just don't expect any sympathy, or help, from me.'

Fin felt his face colouring. 'I can understand that, Niall.' He paused. 'So what are you doing on the island, you and Eòghann?'

'Bit of trouble-shooting. Out at the cages we installed in East Loch Roag. There's twelve of them. Giant things. State of the art. We're having a wee problem, and it seemed like a good excuse to come back to the island and deal with it myself. Didn't expect this, though.' He was struck by a sudden thought. 'Look, I was just about to head down there. I need a quick word with my manager. Come with me. It'll give us a chance to talk this thing through.' He glanced at his watch. 'Three hours tops.'

Fin checked the time and thought about it. He had no sense of what else it was he might do today. He took out his mobile phone. 'I'll just call Marsaili to let her know what I'm doing.' Then shook his head in frustration. 'Of course. No bloody signal. Nothing changes.'

'Nothing does,' Niall said. His pause was almost imperceptible. 'So you and Marsaili are still together?' And he cocked an eyebrow. 'Well, apart from the God knows how many years she was married to Artair.'

'Yes. Yes, we are.' Though in his heart of hearts, Fin wondered if their relationship could survive Fionnlagh's conviction for murder.

CHAPTER THIRTEEN

Marsaili came out of the bathroom and looked down the hall. It was dark, as it always had been. There were no windows that opened directly on to it, and daylight would spill across it only from doors that opened into bedrooms on the right, or the dining room on the left – a room they had never used.

At the end of the hall, the door to Artair's mother's room was shut. It had been her bedroom for all the years that Marsaili was married to Artair. A room that represented the little box of horrors that Marsaili had found herself living with every day for all of that time. The smell of urine, the changing of the sheets, feeding the poor woman with a spoon, physically manoeuvring her in and out of bed, on and off the toilet.

The sad thing was that, although the stroke had robbed the old lady of many of her physical functions, it had left her mentally acute. So that she was only too aware of those things that Marsaili was having to do for her. And embarrassed by it. Ironically, she had proved better company than Artair, and the two had grown close over the years. But neither Marsaili nor Artair had been able to bring themselves to tell her the truth about her husband, and she had gone to her grave believing that Mr Macinnes had fallen to his death from the cliffs of An Sgeir as the result of an accident.

The short flight of steep, narrow stairs that led up to the teenage Fionnlagh's attic room simmered, too, in darkness. Almost like a reproach. The mother of a child who grew up to kill must surely be to blame. Marsaili closed her eyes and took a deep breath. She had promised not to let herself succumb to the fear that Fionnlagh really had murdered that girl. And, so, how could she be to blame? But that he'd had an affair with her was undeniable. A girl from his science class. She felt a mix of shame and disgust. It just didn't seem like the Fionnlagh she had raised. That good-looking, happy-go-lucky kid who'd always had the knack for making them laugh. The father who doted on his daughter. The Fionnlagh they'd seen in that police cell was barely even recognizable to her.

She drifted through to the kitchen and put the kettle on. It was as if this house was haunted. Not by ghosts, but by memories. Hers, and Fin's before her. She had never allowed herself even to speculate what Fin might have suffered in the room at the back of the house that opened off the living room. Mr Macinnes's study, where the boys had passed so many child-hood hours being tutored in English and maths.

'Make me a cup, too?'

Marsaili turned, startled, to see Donna standing in the doorway. And her heart went out to her. Always a tiny creature, she was further diminished somehow by all of this. Childlike and lost. Her hoodie and jog pants appeared several sizes too big, drowning her. At the age of just twelve, her daughter Eilidh was already taller. 'Sure.' She dropped a teabag into a second cup. 'How are you holding up?'

Donna just shrugged. 'Oh, you know . . .'

Marsaili didn't. But she could imagine.

'What about you and Fin?'

Now Marsaili was evasive. 'It's not easy.'

'You mean because of Fionnlagh, or between the two of you?'

Marsaili was shocked, both by her perception and her bluntness. 'Is it that obvious?'

'It was obvious before we ever left Glasgow, Marsaili. Fionnlagh and I used to talk about it. I mean, you two seemed destined for each other. But . . . something's not right. That was clear.'

Marsaili had no idea how to frame a response to her daughter-in-law's candour. This was something she didn't really want to address, had been avoiding for years. And here was a girl almost half her age forcing her to confront it for the first time. Colour rose on her cheeks.

She said, 'I remember once, at school, our English teacher asked us what we all wanted out of life. And almost everyone in the class said their ambition was to be happy.' Her tiny laugh was full of irony. 'Well, it seems that's an ambition I failed to achieve.' She looked at the girl. 'I'm not happy, Donna. Not sure when I became fully aware of that. Unhappiness is like pain. You just get used to it. Or take palliatives. Like alcohol. I suppose I've known it for a while now, though I never wanted to admit it. I always remember something Artair's mother said to me all those years ago. *No one should expect to be happy, Marsaili.* Which I guess was just a reflection of her own sad life. But I kind of understand it now.'

'What about Fin?'

Marsaili shook her head. 'My unhappiness is not his fault, Donna. He's unhappy, too. Probably more than me. He made such a mistake taking that job. It's doing him harm. In ways that neither of us could ever have imagined.'

'So you still love him?'

'I do.' The affirmation came quickly, easily. Before doubt followed. 'It's just . . . sometimes I wonder if the love I have for him now is more about remembering how we were than how we are.'

The kettle boiled and Marsaili filled both their cups, handing one to Donna, who leaned against the architrave and cradled it in both hands as if she were cold. She said, 'I'm not sure I can even remember what it felt like to be in love. It's been so long since we did anything except annoy each other.' Then quickly, 'I'm not saying it's all his fault. I mean, I can be a sulky bitch.' Her laugh was humourless. 'I guess I get that from my mum.'

And Marsaili wondered, as she had many times before, whether Donald's genes had somehow bypassed his daughter. She wondered, too, what Donna would think if she knew that it was her father who had taken her mother-in-law's virginity.

'But I've known for a long time that he'd lost interest in me. Never commenting on my appearance, or asking about my day. Spending more time with,' she made quotation marks with her fingers, '*the boys* than with his own family.'

She tried a sip of her tea but it was too hot still and her lips recoiled from the rim. She blew across the surface of the liquid.

'When I saw what was happening, I tried hard to keep him engaged. I really did. We hardly ever had sex, and when it happened it was nearly always my idea. Though he never said no. I thought . . . I thought if maybe I got pregnant, it might be the glue that would stick us back together. I stopped taking precautions. One last attempt to try and rescue my marriage. And then I missed a period and took the test.' She gazed into her cup as if somewhere in it she might find the words to express her pain. 'But when I told him, he was furious. Accused me of trying to trap him. Said I had no right to get pregnant without his agreement. It would be my baby, not his.' She shook her head despondently. 'I don't know whether that was guilt, because he was having a relationship with her. Or if it was what he really felt.' Her head fell a little. 'I used to adore Fionnlagh, Marsaili. He was so straight, so honest. Supported me in everything I ever wanted to do.' She paused, and then there was a catch in her voice. 'But in the end, when your partner loses interest in you, you start to lose interest in yourself.'

The outside door swung open and Eilidh stepped in, dropping

her schoolbag by the fridge door, which she opened to take out a small carton of fresh orange juice. Marsaili turned to look out the window as she heard car tyres skidding on gravel, and saw Catriona driving off down the road. Eilidh's other grandmother clearly wasn't coming in today following her frosty reception yesterday. Eilidh looked wan and tired.

'Hi,' she said to her mother, before crossing the kitchen to give her grandmother a perfunctory hug. They had always been close in Glasgow, but present circumstances had driven a wedge between them all. Eilidh poked a straw into the carton and took a pull at it. Then said, 'I've got homework.'

She stooped to retrieve her schoolbag and brushed past her mother in the doorway, heading to her room at the top of the stairs. Her father's old bedroom. Marsaili placed her cup, untouched, on the kitchen counter and said, 'I've got some admin to do on the laptop. Bills to pay. Life goes on, even when your own is on pause.'

Donna nodded and stood aside to let Marsaili past.

The laptop sat on the dresser by the window. This had been the spare bedroom when Marsaili lived here with Artair. But there had hardly ever been guests. She lifted the lid of the laptop, and waited while it read her face. There were no bills to pay. The conversation with Donna had been painful. She needed an excuse to escape. As she waited for the Finder to open, she glanced from the window beyond. It gave on to the machair that dropped to the cliffs above the beach, and the sand that swept away towards the port.

A family was splashing about in the shallows, a large dog haring along the water's edge, and she saw two figures walking back towards the boathouse. One of them was Fin. She recognized his distinctive gait immediately, even from behind. But who was he with?

A pair of old binoculars that had belonged to Artair's dad sat on the mantelpiece. She fetched them and focused through the glass on the figures below. It wasn't until the other man half turned to look back at something that she saw his face for the first time. It was oddly familiar. And yet, not. She frowned. Who was it? The two men stopped, standing face to face, deep in conversation. And then the other man laughed, and she realized who he was. Niall Dubh. She knew that Niall had gone into fish farming and made a great success of it. So much so that he'd gone into tax exile in Cyprus. But what was he doing back on the island? And in a sudden, heart-stopping moment, she knew why. The dead girl. Her name had been Black. Niall's daughter? And yet he was laughing. If she'd been Marsaili's daughter, Marsaili doubted that she could ever have brought herself to laugh again.

The men continued walking until they reached the far end of the beach and climbed the steps to the parking. From there they vanished round the bend of the tiny road that wound its way up to the village, exiting opposite Ocean Villa.

CHAPTER FOURTEEN

The drive down to Great Bernera in Niall's Mercedes passed more quickly and in greater comfort than any of the journeys they'd made in the dark in their borrowed van all those years before. Niall had suggested that the drive would give them a chance to address things. Caitlin's death. Fionnlagh's involvement in it, or not. In fact, they drove in icy silence, retracing the steps of their teenage years in the company of ghosts. The phantoms of distant childhood, and a life lost almost before it had begun.

A scattering of sunlight sparkled on still waters where Niall's father's cages had been, replaced now by mussel lines. But neither of them chose to look as they crossed the Bernera bridge. The first words spoken came as they drove past a turnoff heading east towards an inlet from East Loch Roag. Niall said, 'That's the road to the Black Loch. It's where Caitlin's body was found.' And Fin thought he should probably go there tomorrow. If only to get a sense of the place. And the house where the ill-fated lovers had met in secret across the summer.

Just a few minutes later they passed through the shadow of the pine trees on the curve of the road leading down to the harbour at Baile na Mara. It was the first time Fin had been back since the night Iain drowned.

At a glance, nothing much had changed. A gangway led to a new pontoon at the right side of the pier. Untidy piles of crab and lobster creels accumulated around the harbour like detritus washed up after a storm. Barrels and buoys, fenders and fish nets. A large, rusting orange skip with a heavy lid stood to one side of the ramp, white plastic containers loosely stacked beyond it. Umpteen fishing boats lined up along the pontoon bobbed gently on the swell. A larger service vessel was tethered to the pier, along with several workboats. Long gone were the aluminium ex-army assault craft used by Niall's father, replaced now by sleek 7-metre Polarcirkel workboats with inboard diesel engines.

Niall stood on the pier and looked down on one of them. 'My father could only have dreamt of a boat like this,' he said. 'Rigid buoyancy boats, they call them. RBBs. Self-bailing. Rigid pontoons filled with polystyrene. Combine that with the V-shaped hull, and this baby is virtually unsinkable. Unbreakable, too. They take a lot of punishment, these boats, operating in some pretty treacherous conditions.' He turned a sadly knowing look on Fin. 'Well, we know all about that.'

He nodded towards the disused fish processing plant. 'We use that place as offices now, but most of the time the men are at the cages. Come on, let's take a spin out.'

Fin stood beside Niall, who sat behind the wheel at the back of the boat, a windscreen raised from a white engine cowling to protect them from the spray. He held on to a grab bar and felt the wind blow through his hair, still soft in the sunshine. The motor was remarkably quiet, and they skimmed at high speed across the still waters, beyond the low-lying island that sheltered the harbour, and out into the deep, brooding body of the loch.

As they rounded the headland, the Bradan Mor cages came into view. Huge circular constructs in two parallel rows of six. A large red and white service ship was anchored at one of the far cages, enormous flexi-tubes feeding down into the water, where the fish were nearing full size. Drawing closer, Fin saw that the two banks of six cages were separated by around a hundred metres of water, in the middle of which sat a small raft. What looked like a network of either cables or trunking snaked off on either side to the cages themselves.

'That's the feed silo,' Niall shouted, following Fin's gaze. 'Feeding tubes go to each of the cages. The whole process is automated these days. A far cry from when we used to go out with buckets of the stuff and shovel it into the water.'

'What's the ship?'

'The *Bradan Harvester*. She comes down from Norway to wash the fish in fresh water and make sure they're free of sea lice. A hydrolyzer, sometimes known as a wellboat.'

Niall pulled the RBB into a docking site at the nearest cage and jumped out with a rope. He extended a hand to help Fin up on to a grilled metal walkway that ran the full circumference of the cage. Containment nets were tethered to a sturdy handrail, and Fin could see thousands of fish swimming in languid circles beneath the surface of the water.

'A hundred metres circumference, thirty in diameter,' Niall said. 'Both the nets and the structure itself are anchored by a mooring system that ensures stability, even in the worst weather. It means we can maintain net volume and improve water and oxygen flow, which enhances fish welfare and growth.'

He sounded to Fin like a PR man rhyming off his company's response to accusations in the media of unsustainable industrial fish farming practices. Aquaculture, as they called it, was getting plenty of bad press these days. Claims of disease, pollution and waste, as well as poor treatment of the salmon themselves. The papers were full of horror stories of fish half eaten by lice, and high mortality rates in the cages. Almost as if he read Fin's thoughts, Niall added, 'It's one of the things I've worked hard to achieve here. Sustainability, welfare, pollution control. We want to deliver the highest quality product.'

Fin nodded. 'How many salmon does this place produce?'

'There's about a hundred thousand per cage. So about 1.2 million in total.' He waved an expansive hand vaguely towards the east. 'And we have cages like these all over Scotland. Of course, we're not the only operators out here on Loch Roag. You know, back in the day, there were so many fish farms on this loch they were producing more tonnage than the whole of North America. Not so many now. It's quality we aim for rather than quantity.' He glanced across the nets to where another workboat was tethered and two men were working to attach a feeder tube. 'Back in a minute.' He headed off around the circumference of the structure. Fin watched him go, and a quick calculation brought home to him for the first time just how much money there was in aquaculture.

He gazed off across the loch towards Tolsta Chaolais and Loch Carloway in the distance. The low profile of the land, purple and green and broken through by grey gneiss, cut treeless against the deep blue of a cloudless sky. It was hard to believe on a day like this that such placid waters could turn so quickly malevolent and take a young life in less time than it took to blink.

His thoughts turned then to Niall and Ailsa, and the poor dead girl they'd found washed up on the beach at the Black Loch, and he wondered whether it was worse to lose your daughter or have your son accused of her murder.

Niall was gone about ten minutes, and Fin turned as he heard him coming back around the cage. Niall tilted his head and looked curiously at Fin. 'Penny for them,' he said.

But a million pennies wouldn't have persuaded Fin to share his thoughts with Niall. He said, 'I was just wondering what it was that went wrong between you and Ailsa.'

Niall's skin darkened visibly. 'What did *she* say?'

'I didn't ask,' Fin lied.

Niall shook his head. 'Too sordid,' he said. 'You wouldn't

want to know. Besides, it's none of your business.' He jumped down into the boat. 'Come on, let's get you home.'

They cruised most of the way back to Baile na Mara in silence, before, out of the blue, Fin said, 'What really happened, Niall?' He had been wanting to ask ever since Port of Ness.

Niall's head swung around, eyes wary. 'What do you mean?'

'With Coinneach Smith. That summer. You and I both know he didn't fall. And I don't believe it was suicide. Not for a minute.'

Niall looked at him for a long time, as if deciding what he should or shouldn't say. Before he sighed and turned his attention back to the loch ahead of them. 'It's all so long ago now, Fin. Everyone involved is dead. So what does it matter?'

When they got back to the house on the cliffs at Port of Ness, the dark green Range Rover was gone. But the Nissan pickup still sat next to the spot where Fin had parked his rental. Niall stepped out of the Mercedes and glanced at his watch. He said, 'I know it's getting late, but it might be best if you came in and met Eòghann. Get it over with.' His mouth set in a grim line. 'He's taken his sister's death pretty badly.'

Fin said, 'Then he's hardly going to want to shake my hand.'

'Just give him a little latitude. Come on.' Niall beckoned him into the house, and Fin reluctantly followed him through the rear sun lounge, which extended into what must have been one of the original front rooms. French windows opened from here into the wraparound conservatory. But they were closed, and shutters reduced ambient light in the room to a few stray spokes of late sunshine leaking in around the edges.

The main source of illumination was an enormous large-screen TV in the corner. From a surround-sound system, the crackle of automatic gunfire and distant explosions filled the room. Soldiers in uniform stole across the screen through the smoking remains of a bombed-out building.

Eòghann half sat, half lay, sprawling in an armchair in front of the TV, studiously working a controller with both hands. He wore jeans with the knees slashed across, his bare feet buried in the shagpile of a rug. A multicoloured designer shirt was unbuttoned and lay open revealing a ripped torso, the muscles of his six-pack cutting deep shadows across his midriff.

Niall said, 'He's addicted to video games. This one in particular. *Call of Duty: Modern Warfare III.* I think he has every previous version of it.'

Eòghann paused the game and twisted in his chair to see who his father was talking to. Fin saw that he was a good-looking boy. Then revised that thought. Not so much a boy as a young man. About twenty-three or twenty-four. His hair was dark with blond highlights, shaved at the sides but growing thickly on top and falling across his brow. 'Who's this?' he said.

'An old friend,' his father told him. 'Fin Macleod. We were at school together.'

Eòghann frowned. 'Macleod? Not Fionnlagh Macleod's father?'

Niall glanced cautiously at Fin. 'He is.'

Eòghann looked at his father with incredulity. 'You don't expect me to be civil to him, do you?' As if Fin wasn't in the room. 'His fucking boy killed my sister.' He looked at Fin directly for the first time, and Fin saw the anger in his eyes.

Niall said, 'Innocent until proven guilty, Eòghann.' Then turned to Fin. 'The boy's upset, that's all.' His eyes darkened. 'And who can blame him?' Then quickly, as if to steer the conversation on to safer ground, 'I'm grooming him to take over from me sometime in the future. When I figure it's time to retire. But right now he's more obsessed with his career as a male model – oh, and all his techie stuff. Obsessed with his gadgets is our Eòghann. Phones, watches, iPads, HomePods, VR headsets, you name it. He's been on the covers of all the leading male magazines both sides of the Atlantic. But the one he's most proud of is *Computerworld* magazine, would you believe?' He smiled. 'Good-looking boy, too. Has the women falling at his feet.'

Eòghann tutted his irritation, turning away to hide his embarrassment and resume *Call of Duty*. 'You're interrupting my fucking game,' he said pointedly, raising his voice above the sound of mortar fire. And Fin thought that whatever else he might have inherited from his father, Eòghann's propensity for swearing was clearly high on the list of genetic hand-me-downs.

CHAPTER FIFTEEN

They sat around the kitchen table in an awkward silence punctuated only by the scrape of cutlery on china. Boil-in-the-bag duck leg and mashed cauliflower. For which none of them had any real appetite. Donna had prepared the meal while Fin briefed Marsaili in the living room on everything he had done and learned that day. Which, in the summing up, he realized, amounted to very little.

Donna had called them through when the food was ready, and shouted Eilidh down from upstairs. The girl barely touched her food, staring in sullen silence at the duck fat congealing on her plate. Fin stole several glances at her, and felt a part of him dying inside. Growing up in Glasgow, she had been close to her grandfather. When Fin and Marsaili babysat, she would curl up with him on the couch to watch TV, often falling asleep with her head on his shoulder. He loved that little girl, unreservedly. Perhaps, he thought, because he saw so much of Marsaili in her. At any rate, she didn't deserve any of this. None of them did, but she was the least well equipped to deal with it.

Finally, Eilidh pushed her chair back from the table and stood up. 'I haven't finished my homework yet.'

'You haven't finished your dinner,' Donna said.

'Not hungry.' She turned and fled through to the hall, her footsteps on the stairs resounding around the house.

Donna called after her, but Fin leaned over to put a hand on Donna's arm. 'Leave her,' he said. 'She'll eat when she's hungry, and she'll open up when she's ready.'

The trill of Fin's iPhone set everyone on edge. He answered it quickly. 'Fin Macleod.'

He heard George Gunn's voice in his ear. 'Mr Macleod, I shouldn't be calling you. But I thought you deserved to know.'

'George, I have Donna and Marsaili here. Can I put the phone on speaker?'

Gunn hesitated, and there was reluctance in his voice. 'I suppose . . .'

Fin laid the phone on the table. 'Go ahead, George.'

'The DNA results came in late today from the lab.' He hesitated again. 'It was Fionnlagh's sperm in the dead girl.'

Fin saw all the muscles tighten around Donna's mouth and he understood Gunn's hesitation. But she had to know the truth. They all did. 'And?'

'The CIO has formally charged him with her murder.'

Fin felt the bottom falling out of his world. 'So he'll make a first appearance at the Sheriff Court in the morning?'

'Well, he should have, sir. But GEOAmey have got staffing

problems. They can't send anyone in time. Then it's the weekend. So it'll be Monday before the plea hearing.'

Fin closed his eyes and took a deep slow breath. It was a reprieve of sorts. And would give him another three days. But he was going to have to make more progress than he had today.

'Thanks, George,' he said. 'I appreciate that.'

He hung up and slipped the phone into his pocket and found the two women looking at him. Marsaili said, 'GEOAmey?'

'I don't know what it stands for,' Fin said. 'Some kind of joint venture to provide prisoner escort and custody services. All privatized these days. Fionnlagh will make his first appearance here at Stornoway Sheriff Court, to have the charges read to him. It's usual for the accused to make no plea or declaration. He would then be remanded in custody, and the whole thing gets passed on to a higher authority. In this case, the High Court in Inverness, where he'll be tried.' He caught a glimpse of silent tears rolling down Donna's cheeks and tried to stay focused. 'After his appearance at the Sheriff Court, he'll be escorted to Inverness and held in remand at the prison there. But they need qualified staff to do that, which they don't have. So that first court appearance is going to be held over till Monday.' He paused. 'Which is the only good news in all of this. It means we're going to have more time.'

'To do what?' Donna demanded. 'He was sleeping with that girl. The DNA proves it. So . . . what? Someone else appears from thin air, rapes her without leaving his sperm and kills her? And somehow Fionnlagh doesn't notice? It doesn't make any sense. None of it does.'

Marsaili put a hand over hers. 'You don't think he did it, Donna?'

'I don't want to. I really don't. But I'm running out of excuses for him. I'm wondering now if I ever knew him at all.' She gazed at each of them in turn through tear-glazed eyes. 'If any of us did.'

She pulled her hand away from Marsaili's, stood up abruptly and left the room. They heard her sobbing as she ran down the hall to her bedroom. The room she had shared with Fionnlagh. The room where their unborn baby had been conceived. The door banged shut, leaving Fin and Marsaili sitting in a miserable silence that neither of them had any idea how to fill.

Fin lingered for a long time in the dark of the sitting room. The still of the night was very nearly palpable. It felt like hours ago that Marsaili and Donna had gone to bed. But Fin wasn't tired. He sat replaying his day. Over and over. Looking for something he had missed. Something that had slipped by him, significance lost in a tsunami of information, emotion and memories. His early meeting with the solicitor, the evidence accumulated against his son by investigating officers. Ailsa's hostility, and her sad tale of marriage breakdown and divided custody. A son who felt abandoned by her. A daughter murdered. Niall's ambivalence, Eòghann's anger. The hulking presence of their psychopathic minder, Jack Dempsey.

Then there had been Niall's refusal to cast any light on the death of Coinneach Smith all those years before. Indifference or concealment? Fin recalled his apparent emotional disconnect at the time over what happened to Iain. Niall's focus had been on whether or not they would be found out. Which still left Fin wondering if his childhood friend really had taken the ultimate step to ensure that they weren't?

And finally there was the DNA confirmation that it was Fionnlagh's sperm they had recovered from the dead girl. But why would he rape her when their relationship had always been consensual? And what possible reason might he have had for killing her? Of course, she was pregnant. But did he even know that? His reaction when Fin had broken the news to him suggested not.

Fin rubbed his face in frustration and sighed deeply, sitting back to let the softness of the settee engulf him. From somewhere outside, in the long grass behind the bungalow, came the faint but distinctive *crex, crex* that he and Artair had heard that night on the Cross–Skigersta road. His grandfather's ràc an fheòir, croaker of the grass. A corncrake. And the image returned to him of Iain's face, caught so briefly in that passing streetlight, awed by the very thought of it.

His own thoughts turned to Caitlin. The murdered girl. He knew almost nothing about her. And yet, surely she must be the key? Someone had a reason to murder her. A motive. If Fin could find that, he would find who killed her. Even if it meant accepting that it was Fionnlagh.

He turned on a lamp that sat on the bookcase below the window, and picked up the remote control for the TV. Donna said she had recorded – what was it called? He fought to bring the title of the programme to mind. *Canùdh agus Cuan. Canoe and Ocean.* He turned on the TV, and scrolled through the menu of the satellite box to bring up a list of recordings. There were films and episodes of TV shows. Football matches and box sets. And there, on a fourth row of thumbnail images, the thirteen broadcast episodes of BBC Alba's *Canùdh agus Cuan*. Each thirty minutes in duration. Below a still taken from every episode, a blue line confirmed that it had been viewed. Fin selected one at random and pressed play, then fast-forwarded through sunshine shots of sea stacks and cliffs and beaches, the turquoise waters of the Atlantic Ocean washing gently over silver sands. It might have been a travelogue for somewhere in the tropics. Except that there were no palm trees. No trees of any kind.

When the show's presenters appeared, he returned play to normal speed. Two attractive teenage girls in one-piece swimsuits, one black, one white, carrying a canoe across the sands at what Fin recognized to be Uig Beach. The tide was out, so they had a long way to walk. Captions appeared identifying one as Caitlin Nic Ille Dhuibh and the other as Iseabail Nic a' Phearsain, the girls' Gaelic names. The camera tracked backwards ahead of them and they spoke animatedly to the lens, appearing to communicate directly with the viewer, as well as each other. Fin barely listened to what they were saying, ignoring the captions in English and focusing his attention on Caitlin herself.

He saw immediately why anyone would have been drawn to her. She was wonderfully vivacious, with an easy smile and a compelling charisma. Long chestnut hair verging on red tumbled across a swimmer's shoulders, blue eyes dancing in the sunlight. If her words were scripted, it didn't feel that way. They appeared spontaneous, directed not just at some anonymous viewer, but specifically at *you*. As if she sensed *you* watching her and wanted to talk to you. He recalled the words that Fionnlagh had used to describe her. *Smart, and funny, and beautiful.* But Fionnlagh had still been twelve years her senior. And, regardless of the view that his son had expressed, Fin knew it was wrong.

Iseabail was equally attractive, but lacked the magnetic personality of her co-presenter, although their obvious friendship made for good onscreen chemistry.

A sound from the hall made him pause the recording, and Caitlin's face was frozen in close-up, laughing without inhibition. It was hard to believe that all that life and laughter had been snuffed out so brutally by his own son.

The door opened and he turned as Eilidh padded into the room, barefoot in a cotton nightie that reached down below her calves. Mousy fair hair tangled about her head and shoulders, face blanched, eyes wide and staring from the shadows that surrounded them. Fin was on his feet immediately, tears springing to his eyes. 'Darling, what are you doing up at this time? You should be sleeping.'

She ran the short distance from the door to the settee and threw her arms around him. He cupped the back of her head, drawing it to his chest. He would have done anything to protect her from all of this. Anything. 'Can't,' she said. Then drew away and looked up at him earnestly. 'Did my dad really kill Caitlin?'

Fin took her back in his arms and held her tightly, fighting to keep the tears at bay. He had to stay strong. It was the very least he owed her. This child with his mother's name. But he barely trusted his own voice. 'Of course not.'

'All the kids at school are saying he did.' Her voice came muffled from his chest.

'What?' He held her at arm's length, staring at her in dismay. He and Marsaili had been so concerned about how Fionnlagh's arrest was affecting them and Donna, it had never occurred to them that Eilidh might suffer the cruelty of children at school.

He sat her down on the settee and slipped an arm around her shoulders, drawing her to him. She clasped her hands on her knees, staring at them, and without turning her head, said in a very small voice, 'There's this rhyme they keep chanting in the playground. *Eilidh, Eilidh, quite contrary, who did your daddy kill?*' She tilted her head up towards him and his heart broke as the tears trickled down her face.

He brushed them away with his thumbs. 'Kids are awful, darling. You mustn't listen to them.' Words that felt wholly inadequate as soon as they left his mouth.

She said, 'I knew Caitlin at school. Not well, because . . .' she shrugged, 'well, because she was in sixth year and I was only in first. But everyone knew her. Her and Iseabail. They were kind of famous, because of the TV series.' She glanced up at the image of Caitlin frozen on the screen. '*Canùdh agus Cuan*. They were always together, the two of them. They even looked alike. The same hair, the same make-up, the same clothes. Everyone called them The Twins.' She paused. 'I really liked her.'

Fin said, 'I thought you didn't know her well.'

'I didn't. But . . .'

'But what?'

Eilidh blushed. 'I've never told my mum and dad this, but I get bullied at school.'

Fin felt a cauldron of mixed emotions bubbling up inside him. Anger, sadness, sympathy, regret. He knew what it was to be bullied when you were young. It had happened to him. He had watched it happen to others. He hated bullies with a passion, but felt powerless now to protect Eilidh from their cruelty.

'There's this bunch of older girls. Usually the same ones. They're always picking on me. Stealing my packed lunch. Emptying my schoolbag out in the playground and laughing when I try to stop the wind from blowing everything away.'

'Don't the teachers do anything to stop that?'

Eilidh scoffed. 'Teachers are never around when it's happening.'

Fin saw that she was wringing her hands now.

'Anyway, there was this day they were teasing me. Trying to grab my schoolbag and I wasn't letting go, and in the end I fell and hit my head on the pavement. The next thing I know, this girl is helping me to my feet. It's Caitlin. And she's raging. The other girls have got my bag, and she shouts at them to give it back. Which they do. Cos, it's Caitlin Black. She's older, and she's famous, and they're all in awe of her. So she tells them what a pathetic bunch of little shits they are and that they'd better just fuck off and leave me alone.' Eilidh sneaked a glance at her grandfather to see if he was shocked by her language. But it hadn't even registered. 'So then she wanted to know if I was okay, and told me that the only way to deal with bullies was to stand up to them. She said that your fear was their fuel, and if you showed them you weren't afraid, they wouldn't be energized to bully you, and they would leave you alone.'

Fin almost smiled. If only it was that easy. But the fact that Caitlin had rescued his granddaughter from the school bullies made her real for him, flesh and blood, perhaps for the first time. With which came the realization that he wanted to find her killer, no matter who it was. The least she deserved was justice. He said, 'I suppose she knew who you were? I mean, that you were Fionnlagh Macleod's daughter?'

Eilidh shrugged. 'Probably.' She sat quiet for some time, and Fin knew she was turning over a million questions in her head. Then she turned and asked again, 'He didn't really kill her, Grampa, did he?'

170

'No. No, he didn't, Eilidh,' Fin said, and hoped that the doubt in his heart was not apparent in his words. 'And I'm going to do my best to prove it.'

CHAPTER SIXTEEN

Fin awoke to an empty bed. He ran his hand over the sheets beside him. Cold. Marsaili must have risen some time ago. A glance at the clock told him it was 6 a.m., though it was already daylight. He lay listening, but there were no sounds of movement in the house.

He slipped out of bed to dress hurriedly and make his way quietly through to the kitchen. There was no one here, no smell of cooking, save for the stale odour of last night's uneaten meal. He touched the kettle with the back of his fingers. Stone cold. He went through to the sitting room and was shocked to see Caitlin's image still on the screen. He must have forgotten to turn it off when finally he went to bed. Only to be haunted in his dreams, through all the tortuous hours of half sleep, by the radiance of her smile and the laughter in her eyes. It was almost painful to look at her again now. And he realized that Marsaili, when she got up, must have seen her, too.

He turned the television off and went to the window. The sun had not yet risen clear of the faraway mainland mountains, but still the horizon glowed amber across the Minch, announcing its imminent appearance. In the distance he saw a solitary figure walking south along the clifftops towards Skigersta. Marsaili. She cut a sharp silhouette against the light scattered across the sea beyond her. Hands thrust deep in jacket pockets, her stride slow and pensive.

He thought about that time when there was nothing they would not have shared. All their inner fears, every insecurity. Their hopes and heartaches. How long was it since they had really talked, beyond the transactional necessities of everyday life for two people who lived together? He couldn't remember. And for a moment he contemplated going after her, to slip his arm through hers and walk with her side by side along the cliffs. To let out all the demons he'd kept hidden, in the hope that one day, when he summoned the courage to face them, they might simply have withered and died.

He hesitated for several long moments before deciding against it. By the time he got down to Great Bernera, the day would already be under way, and time was precious. He grabbed his jacket and headed up the path to where he had parked his rental car next to Donna's Fiat and Fionnlagh's SUV. The air was cool beneath a clear sky, and he felt the wind run wavy fingers through his hair. Marsaili was disappearing over the far horizon. Fin slid into his car and started the engine. He would call her later to let her know where he was.

*

It was after seven by the time he crossed the Bernera bridge, and, after taking two wrong turns that led to dead ends, he finally reached the Black Loch just before seven-thirty.

He parked above the beach as sunlight fanned out towards him across cut-crystal water, revealing the secret colours that concealed themselves on the shore, among rocks and boulders and the seaweed washed up to dry along the high-tide mark.

To his right, cliffs of Lewisian gneiss rose steeply out of the water, and he could just see the gables and chimneys of the house that stood above them overlooking the bay. He cast his eyes down again, to the water's edge, and left footprints in wet sand as he followed the curve of the bay towards the looming black of the cliffs. Somewhere here, Caitlin's body had been washed ashore. Cause of death as yet unknown. But someone had done unspeakable things to her, and Fin could not get that image of the girl frozen on the television screen out of his mind. Wind blowing in her hair, laughing with unselfconscious happiness. It filled him with an immeasurable sadness.

He stood for a long time with his hands in his pockets, gazing out across the Black Loch trying to summon the courage to go up to the house. Beyond narrow headlands, East Loch Roag opened out into the dragon's mouth. He and Iain, with Alasdair, Artair and Niall, had motored many times past that opening on their way to and from the cages by the Bernera bridge. And here, all these years later, his own son would keep secret trysts with a girl twelve years his junior, whom he was now accused of murdering. Fin couldn't help but wonder what his young self might have done differently that would have led to another place, another outcome. Where Caitlin Black would still be alive, her whole life ahead of her, and his own son would not be languishing in a police cell in Stornoway. Had he made different choices at any one of the crossroads he'd encountered along the way, perhaps he wouldn't be standing here now. But, then, who knew? Perhaps he would. Maybe all paths taken would have led here anyway.

He turned away from the shore and walked up to the tarmac apron above the beach. The road to the house branched off to his left. A steep climb, and he was breathless by the time he got to the cattle grid and crossed it. Weeds poked through cracks in beaten earth where cars would have parked in a courtyard bounded on two sides by the house and its outbuilding. Police crime-scene tape fluttered in the breeze, pinned across the rear door of the house. He freed one side of it and watched it stream out into the courtyard. The scenes of crime people would have finished with the place long ago. Still, old habits died hard, and he took out the pair of latex gloves he had found in a box under the sink at the bungalow, and snapped them on.

The back rooms of the house languished in gloom, while early sun spilled through front-facing windows to light up the kitchen and the sitting room. The prevailing smell was one of dampness. It lingered pervasively. Apparently the house had lain empty after the death of its owner. And it seemed like a sad place for the young lovers to have pursued their illicit affair. Secret sex snatched in the shadows.

Fin wandered through the kitchen, opening and closing cupboards and drawers. All empty. The police had found a half-finished bottle of wine and two glasses on the worktop. Not enough for alcohol to have played a role in whatever unravelled here on the night Caitlin died.

His footsteps creaked on carpeted stairs like wet snow. Sunlight spilled down from a skylight on the landing, and he turned in to the bedroom on his right, where Fionnlagh had made love to Caitlin on the three nights a week they had met here across the summer. Sheets and a duvet were thrown back to reveal a mattress cover creased by passion. The lovers' heads had left their impressions in soft pillows. And all Fin could feel was anger at Fionnlagh.

He crossed to the window and looked out along the headland. There was a path that led from the house all the way to the point. Caitlin's body had been washed up somewhere on the beach below. So the chances were she had fallen from the cliffs. Or been pushed. Or thrown. What had happened here in the house? Had Fionnlagh really raped her? Had she fled then along the path towards the point, Fionnlagh giving chase? If she had gone over the edge at any point along there, the chances were the fall would have killed her.

Fin turned away from the window in despair, and immediately froze at the sound of someone moving about downstairs. He stood perfectly still, holding his breath, listening intently as footsteps passed softly from room to room. He heard drawers opening and closing. The creak of cupboard doors. Someone following in Fin's footsteps, just minutes behind him. He moved carefully out on to the landing and winced as the floorboards creaked beneath his weight. Whoever was downstairs heard it too, and a silence laden with tension filled the house.

Fin decided to take the initiative, and charged down the stairs two at a time, balancing himself with hands on either wall. A figure flashed through the light of the open door. Long chestnut hair, a pale face half turned in panic. For a moment he thought it was Caitlin, and the shock almost robbed him of breath. He caught her arm as she tried to escape through the door, and she spun around, fear writ large on her face.

'Don't you touch me!' she screamed at him in English, fear and bravado and defiance in wide eyes. And she yanked her arm free of his grasp.

'Iseabail Macpherson,' he said, relieved by the passing of that fleeting moment when bizarrely he had believed she was somehow Caitlin's ghost.

She was still scared, but standing her ground. 'Who are you?'

'I'm Fionnlagh Macleod's father.' He spoke in Gaelic now.

And all her alarm at being caught in the house by this stranger dissipated. 'My God!' she said. 'You look like him.' Then, 'What are you doing here?'

'I used to be a cop, Iseabail. What are *you* doing here?' But before she could reply, he said, 'And don't lie to me. Your best friend is dead, and my son is accused of killing her. The least we owe one another is the truth.'

The fight went out of her, replaced by an odd embarrassment.

She found it hard to meet his eye. 'My mother cleans the place from time to time. She still has the key.' And guilt replaced embarrassment in the flicker of her eyes towards him. 'I let Caitlin have it so that she and Fionnlagh could meet here. The police have been at the house asking my mum about it. But she couldn't find it. I knew that Caitlin left it under that pot there at the back door.' She half turned towards a flower pot with a long-dead plant sitting on the outside step. 'I thought if I came and got it, and hid it somewhere in our place where Mum would find it . . .' She paused. 'But it's not here. And there's no sign of it anywhere inside.'

Fin said, 'Then the chances are the police have already found it. Either here, or among Caitlin's belongings.'

Iseabail deflated visibly. 'I'm going to be in the shit, then.'

They stepped outside into the sunshine and Fin said, 'Have you seen the photograph of the chain and pendant they found tangled in Caitlin's hair?'

She nodded. 'The police showed it to me. If it was Caitlin's, I've never seen it. And she'd have shown it to me if it was. We shared everything.' Grief welled up to manifest in sudden tears. She turned quickly away. 'Sorry.' Her breath trembled as she filled her lungs. 'Still can't believe she's gone. I've known her since we were kids. We started primary school together.'

And Fin thought of himself and Artair. And Marsaili. All starting together in the same class on the same day.

Iseabail turned towards him as the tears spilled. 'I loved that girl. She was like my sister, you know? Almost twins.' She wiped away the tears. 'That's what they called us at school. The Twins.'

'I know. Eilidh told me.' He saw her frown. 'My grand-daughter. Fionnlagh's kid. Apparently Caitlin stopped her from getting bullied.'

Iseabail nodded. 'Yes. That was typical of her. Caitlin was the kindest, most generous person I've ever known, Mr Macleod. She looked out for people, you know? Cared about them. Used to have me standing out on street corners in Stornoway on wet Saturday afternoons, collecting for this charity or that. Kids, or animals. Or old folk.' She laughed through her tears. 'Could charm anyone, you know? We always finished up with full collection tins.'

Fin shut the door of the house and lifted the trailing end of the crime-scene tape to reaffix it to the other architrave. He peeled off his latex gloves. 'We probably shouldn't be seen here at the house,' he said. 'It's still a crime scene. And you're a witness. I could get into trouble just for talking to you.'

'Well, that's stupid,' she said.

He nodded towards the distant headland. 'Walk with me out to the point. Tell me about Caitlin's relationship with Fionnlagh.'

The wind had stiffened with the rising of the sun, and blew through their hair and clothes as they followed the path out along the cliffs. The far shore was lost in heat haze. Iseabail wore jeans, and trainers, and a pale lemon blouse tucked loosely in around the waist. Her hair flew out behind her like a flag of freedom, but Fin had a sense of her being diminished by the loss of Caitlin, as if she had lost a piece of herself. As if they really had been twins.

'She was besotted with Fionnlagh,' Iseabail said, and Fin wondered if she had been jealous. 'We had him in fifth year. But, you know, in sixth you spend much more time with your teachers. God, how she flirted with him.' She turned to look at Fin. 'He never stood a chance, your son,' she said. 'If Caitlin set her mind on something, she usually got it. Eventually they ended up having sex in a walk-in stationery cupboard off his classroom. And that's when it all started. About six months ago, when we were still at school.'

Fin did not want to break into her flow of recollection, no matter how painful it was to him, and they walked in silence for some time.

Finally, she said, 'I know people probably think there was something wrong with it. I mean, him being married, and that much older. But they were in love, Mr Macleod, those two. They really were. Fionnlagh . . . he was a one-off, you know. Well, you would, you're his dad. He was kind, and considerate. And funny. Always making us laugh. If Caitlin hadn't got him first, I'd have fancied him myself.'

And Fin thought how much of her description of his son he recognized. Which made it even harder, somehow, to reconcile with the sullen young man who had faced them in his police cell.

'Do *you* think he killed her?'

Her head snapped around. 'No,' she said, without hesitation. 'Then who did?'

'I have no idea.'

'But there was something not right, yes? Had they fallen out?'

She pressed her lips together and stared straight ahead as they walked. Then stole a glance at him. 'Caitlin and me were sort of helping to expose stuff that's going on at Bradan Mor's fish cages in the loch.' From where they stood now, almost at the point, they could see north up East Loch Roag, all the way to the first of those cages.

Fin frowned. 'You mean Caitlin's dad's fish farm?'

She looked away, avoiding his eye. 'I suppose you could say that.'

'What's that supposed to mean?'

She just shrugged.

But he wasn't going to let her off the hook. 'What stuff going on at the cages?'

'Shit that people should know about,' she said. 'Half the fish in them are dead or dying.' She sat suddenly, cross-legged, among the tufts of heather at the cliff edge, gazing out across the water and chewing at the end of a long stem of grass.

Fin remained standing. 'Care to explain?'

She said, 'It started in the early summer. We'd just begun shooting the first video sequences for the new series of *Canùdh agus Cuan*. We were down near Mangersta, you know, off the south-west coast. In among all those sea stacks. A beautiful day.

The sea was like glass, and you could see all the way across to St Kilda. We had two canoes with us and we were working in turns off the support boat. There was the producer, a camera-oblique-sound man, and big Danny.' She laughed. 'Big Danny's not the brightest, but he's the strongest swimmer I know. Ripped, like Adonis. He's our safety guy. Either of us gets into difficulty, he's there to pull us out of the water.' She paused briefly to stifle the emotion of realizing suddenly that she was talking about herself and Caitlin in the present tense.

Fin sat down beside her. 'What happened?'

'We had both the canoes out, and we were going to explore this inlet, a kind of opening in the cliffs. You know how everything is down there, all kind of fractured and broken up. There was some sort of geodha that cut right into the rock, and the sea was boiling around the entrance, you know, like the water was alive just below the surface. Only way into it was from the sea. I mean, I guess you could probably abseil down from the top of the cliffs, but you'd probably have to walk five miles over rough ground to get there.

'Anyway, we steered the canoes through the gap. Caitlin first, me right behind her, the cliffs rising sheer on either side of us. It was kind of spooky. And then we smelled it. Before we even saw it.'

'Smelled what?'

'Fish, Mr Macleod. Rotten fish. Jesus, I'd never smelled anything like it. You know, the stink of dead decaying fish, only multiplied a thousand times. We were just about gagging on it as we passed into a little hidden creek with a wee sandy beach at the foot of the cliffs. It was dead calm in there, hardly any movement of air, which I suppose is why the smell never really dispersed. Anyway, that little beach was piled high with dead salmon. And I'm not talking a few. I'm talking thousands. Tens of thousands. A mountain of the fucking things.' She glanced at him self-consciously. 'Excuse my French.'

'They'd been dumped there?'

'Well, Mr Macleod, I very much doubt that they'd jumped off the cliff.'

But Fin didn't smile. 'You had no idea who dumped them, then?'

'Not then, no. But when we got back to base, Donnie – that's our producer – got on to this guy he knew. Someone he'd done interviews with. An anti-fish farm activist. A guy called Colm Hendry.' She hesitated then.

'Go on,' Fin said.

She glanced at him and sighed. 'He came and set up camp in a disused crofthouse on Loch Riosaigh near the old Norse Mill. Basically, within striking distance of the cages themselves, but hidden from view by Aird Mhòr. He's got all sorts of equipment up there. Including drones that were able to follow boats making the journey down to Mangersta with the dead fish they were dredging from the bottom of the cages.'

Fin shook his head in consternation. 'Why are there so many dead fish in the cages?'

'Pollution. An epidemic of sea lice. And Colm says that

there's been jellyfish blooms as well, caused by increased sea temperatures.'

'Colm,' Fin said. 'Obviously you're on first name terms with him.'

She blushed. 'Like I said. Me and Caitlin were helping him out.'

'How?'

But she clammed up, then, drawing her knees up to her chin and folding her arms around her shins. 'You'll have to ask Colm that.'

He thought for a moment. 'Do the police know any of this?'

She glanced round sharply. 'Of course not. It's got nothing to do with what happened to Caitlin.'

'So why would it have caused friction between Caitlin and Fionnlagh?'

'Because he was dead set against her having anything to do with Colm.'

'Why?'

'You'd better ask Fionnlagh.'

He sighed and they sat on in silence for several long minutes before he got stiffly to his feet. 'Okay, tell me exactly where I can find this Colm Hendry.'

She looked up at him. 'Why should I?'

'Because,' he said, 'I'm sure you wouldn't want the police, or your mother, finding out who gave Fionnlagh and Caitlin the key to that house.'

CHAPTER SEVENTEEN

I.

The old Norse Mill was one of more than two hundred scattered at one time about the island. It dated back to the twelfth century. Restored now, it sat at the mouth of a stream that flowed from a tiny freshwater loch above to the sea loch below. A turf roof on a two-tier stone structure, wooden paddles in the lower half turned by running water for the millstones to grind the grain.

Fin skirted the mill, following a pitted dirt track through the heather, down towards the shore at the Aird Mhòr side of Loch Riosaigh. He was grateful that it had not rained for weeks, or the path would have been impassable in his two-wheel-drive rental car. As it was, he tensed each time the vehicle lurched into a pothole, fearing that it would rip away the sump.

Finally he saw the old crofthouse that Iseabail had described. It sat right down on the shingle shore at the far side of the loch, once-white walls streaked black by the weather. There was a broken concrete platform on the loch side of the house, from which a ridged slipway angled down into the water. An inflatable dinghy, its outboard motor tipped into the body of it, was pulled up on to the shingle, and Fin could see figures squatting among the concrete and weeds outside the house. He lost sight of them as he rounded the head of the tiny loch, and the house itself was almost obscured by blasted rowans laden with clusters of orange berries turning virulent red. A sure sign of a cold winter to come.

A battered old grey Land Rover stood on a levelled area at the front of the house, weeds and moss almost obscuring the chippings laid in some distant past to provide a hard-core base for parking. Windows at the front of the property were boarded up, and a ragged green curtain hung across an entrance that was missing a door. There was not a breath of wind here as Fin stepped out into the midge-infested morning. The tiny flies were instantly in his hair, on his face, under his collar, myriad little biting bastards, and he hurried out of the sunshine, pulling the door curtain aside and moving from bright light into impenetrable gloom. The old crofthouse exhaled damp in his face, and he stood for a moment, letting his eyes adjust.

He could hear the thump, thump of distant music, and he called out into the shadows, 'Hello?' But there was no response. As his pupils dilated and the wreck of this abandoned house took shape around him, Fin stepped carefully through a hallway of half-rotted floorboards that moaned and complained underfoot. A doorway on his right opened into

186

a room devoid of furniture, save for a scattering of sleeping bags and pillows that lay about the floor. Nineteen-fifties sepia wallpaper hung in strips from pitted plaster, and the place smelled of stale tobacco. And something else. Musky and vaguely familiar.

Further down the hall, a door to his left led to a room where sunlight leaked in around all sides of a window sealed with strips of cardboard. Two computer screens on a table filled the room with an eerie light, and the air whirred and hummed with the sounds of a computer processing digital information. The floor was a snakepit of cables coiling among open packing cases, video equipment, a camera on a tripod, and a couple of drones piled one on top of the other. Fin wondered where the electricity came from. He had seen no power or telephone lines leading to the house.

At the end of the hall, a door opened into a lean-to kitchen with a ceiling that sloped down to a back door. Black mould mottled damp plaster. All the kitchen fittings, including the sink, had been removed. A fold-up table stood beneath the only window, and a kettle, toaster and microwave were all plugged into a bar of sockets powered by a cable that wound its way out through the back door.

The music, coming from outside, was much louder here, and Fin heard the purr of a diesel generator, and the chatter of voices. He held aside the beaded curtain that hung in the doorway and stepped out on to the broken concrete patio. The generator stood on a plinth away to his left. To his right a group of teenagers and an older man sat in a circle, on mats and makeshift chairs. Three girls, around the same age as Caitlin and Iseabail, and a boy with a shaven head. They were passing around a joint. A fug of scented smoke hung in the air, joss sticks arranged like a fan in a glass jar in the centre of the circle. To keep the midges at bay, Fin assumed. He swiped the air around his head to stop them from eating his face.

The older man had his back to the door, but turned as Fin stepped out. He looked like a throwback to the punk era of the nineteen-seventies, a face full of studs and other piercings. His tanned and naked torso was well sculpted, a riot of tattoos. Each arm adorned by a tattoo sleeve. He wore shorts and open sandals, his black hair gelled into spikes. His lean face was unshaven, just the first hint of silver among the bristles, and Fin thought he was a good-looking man in a seedy sort of way. He was, perhaps, forty. But could have been younger. Or older.

The music came from an ancient ghetto blaster at his feet, and it appeared he was holding court at the centre of a circle of adoration, apparently exerting some kind of Svengali-like influence on his teenage followers. Abruptly he turned off the music and jumped to his feet. 'What the hell do you want, mate?' The soft Irish cadence of his voice belied the aggressive nature of his query.

Fin said, 'Colm Hendry, I presume.'

'Which doesn't answer me question.'

'I'm Fionnlagh Macleod's father.'

There was a momentary hiatus. Then one of the girls said,

'His dad's a cop.' And the boy holding the joint threw it quickly away into the loch, where it fizzled briefly.

'Used to be,' Fin said, and there was a collective groan around the circle.

Hendry shook his head and smiled wryly. 'Well, that was a waste of good dope,' he said. Then his face darkened. 'So you're the father of the boy that killed our girl.'

'I don't believe he did.' Fin paused. 'Do you?'

'I wouldn't know, mate.'

'But you knew Caitlin?'

'Of course I did. Great girl. Total gem. Why anyone would want to do her harm is beyond me.'

'And Iseabail?'

'Well, you never got one without the other, did you?'

'So they both spent time here?'

Hendry shrugged non-committally. 'Maybe.'

'And you knew Fionnlagh, too?'

He scratched his bristles. 'Knew him wouldn't exactly describe it.'

'How would you describe it, then?'

'The only thing I know about him is that he didn't like me very much.'

'Why is that?'

'You'd have to ask him. I only met him the once, Mr Macleod. Turned up here one day and threatened to punch me lights out if I didn't stay away from his girl.'

'Meaning Caitlin?'

'That's right.'

'Why?'

Hendry laughed. 'I don't know. Maybe he was jealous.' He turned towards his acolytes. 'Jenny, put the kettle on, would you, love?' Then to the others, 'Maybe you guys would give us a wee bit of privacy, eh?'

Jenny was on her feet first, and disappeared into the house. The others dispersed more slowly, wandering off around the far side of the building.

Fin looked at Hendry. 'Your little coterie of followers?' His voice laced with more than a little sarcasm.

Hendry was unperturbed. 'They're just killing time till they leave for university. Giving me a wee hand while they wait.'

'Doing what?'

Hendry gazed at him thoughtfully before appearing finally to make a decision. 'Come inside and I'll show you.' He pushed past Fin and into the house with a rattle of wooden beads.

Fin followed him through the kitchen and into the room with the computer. Hendry leaned over the desk, and a swipe of his mouse banished screensavers from both monitors to reveal rows of files.

As he searched among them, Hendry said, 'Got a call last June from a guy I knew. Young producer of a Gaelic-language TV show. He and his presenters had found this huge quantity of dead salmon dumped illegally down at Mangersta. I set myself up here, and got secret drone footage of one of those huge Norwegian hydrolyzer ships scooping thousands of dead salmon out of the cages. They loaded them into big plastic containers and ferried them down the coast to Mangersta where they'd found this wee hidden geodha in the cliffs. They were taking the containers in and out of there in smaller boats and dumping the fish on the beach.'

He stood up and sighed. 'I couldn't follow them all the way with the drones.' He grinned. 'So camped myself out on the cliffs down at Mangersta for a week, and caught them red-handed. Footage of them dumping the fish. And they had no idea I was even there.' He turned back to the computer. 'I've edited together a wee sequence.' Two mouse clicks opened a video file and one of the screens filled with the footage. It was clearly shot from some considerable height above the cages in East Loch Roag. A large hydrolyzer, like the boat Niall had pointed out to him yesterday, was hoovering dead fish from the bottom of the cages through a wide flexi-tube, sorting them into big blue plastic containers that were then swung by crane on to hovering support boats. When the deck of one was fully loaded, it set off for the mouth of the loch, and another took its place.

The clarity of the images was remarkable, the camera zooming in and out, focusing on different elements of the operation. Men in orange overalls could be seen moving about on the decks of the various boats, hooking up crates to cranes and guiding them to safe landing spots on other vessels.

The sequence cut then to grainy distant shots from shore of a fully laden service boat heading south along the coast.

Then more aerial images, at Mangersta this time, of a smaller crane offloading crates one at a time from the service boat to a smaller craft that shuttled back and forth, in and out of the geodha, where the contents of each crate were tipped out on to the vast and growing pile of dead salmon on the beach.

Fin said, 'But surely this was bound to be discovered?'

Hendry shook his head. 'Not really. In time, nature will dispose of the evidence. The fish'll biodegrade. Then when the winter storms come, and the sea gets driven in at force, it'll all be washed away. It was pure bloody chance that Donnie and the girls were filming down there.'

'Iseabail told me it was sea lice and jellyfish that were killing the salmon.'

Hendry nodded. 'There've been several jellyfish blooms around the coast this year. And there's only going to be more of them as water temperatures rise. But the cages are infested with sea lice, Mr Macleod. There's far too high a concentration of fish, and the lice literally eat them alive. I'll show you.'

He leaned over the desk again, and Fin saw a thin line of red abrasion around the back of his neck, as if something had cut into it. 'What happened to your neck?' he said, and Hendry absently raised a hand to run soothing fingers over it.

'Damned light meter,' he said, still focused on his screens. 'I keep it on a leather thong around my neck. Bloody thing caught on something and broke. Just about cut me head off, too.' He opened another video file. 'Here.' And he stood back. 'This is inside the cages themselves.'

These shots were taken underwater. With audio. Seawater bubbling around dozens of grey-looking salmon with great chunks eaten out of them by the lice. Fin watched in horror as the fish swam lethargically about the camera lens like zombies, half-alive, half-dead, staring through murky water with large, sad eyes.

'How did you get footage like this?' Fin said.

Hendry tapped his nose and smiled. 'Been in this game a long time, mate.' He dropped into a wheely chair, folding his hands across his belly in a gesture of self-satisfaction, and stretched his legs out in front of him. 'Bradan Mor have been panicking,' he said. 'Trying to spin this. Putting wrasses into the cages.'

'Wrasses?' Fin frowned.

'Smaller fish that actually eat the lice off the salmon. Scavengers. But that's just a PR exercise. There are too many salmon in these cages. You know, modern cages can be up to twenty metres deep and some of the bigger ones can have anything from a hundred thousand to half a million fish in them.'

'So what do the jellyfish do?'

'Micro jellyfish, really. They kill the salmon by blocking and stinging their gills. But the real problem is just overcrowding. Profit above welfare. In the past, that kind of concentration of fish led to all sorts of diseases. Furunculosis, fibrosis, stuff like that. The early fish farmers basically used to chuck antibiotics into a cement mixer with the feed, then throw it into the cages. These days it's more scientific. The smolts from the hatcheries are being vaccinated against lots of different diseases before they even go into the sea.'

He took a tin of roll-ups from his pocket and held it out to Fin, who shook his head. Hendry selected one, lit it, and sat back to blow smoke through the arrows of light that fired themselves into the room from where the cardboard failed to meet the window frame.

He said, 'You know that lovely pink colour of the salmon we buy in the supermarket? Fake. Like Donald Trump and his phoney tan. Completely artificial. They add a pigment called astaxanthin to the feed, which wild salmon get from eating prawns and krill. And sometimes they use the fermentation of a microorganism that does the same job. Without that, the flesh of farmed salmon would be a very unappetising grey, and no one would want to buy it.'

He leaned over to run his mouse across the desktop and activate a screensaver that wiped the images of zombie salmon from his screens.

'So now Bradan Mor are resorting to pretty extreme measures to get rid of the lice.'

'Extreme how?'

'By flooding the cages with formaldehyde. Well, maybe flooding would be a wee exaggeration. But they're using it as a treatment. Formaldehyde! A highly toxic, fucking systemic poison.' He jumped to his feet, suddenly energized. 'But don't take my word for it. Let me show you.'

II.

It look less than ten minutes, after negotiating the access track in Hendry's Land Rover, to reach the harbour at Baile na Mara. The place was deserted.

Hendry parked where Niall had left his Mercedes the day before, and the two men strolled down to the pier. A slight breeze kept the worst of the midges at bay, the rest burning off in the sun as it rose higher in the most painfully blue of skies. Without the wind and the rain, Fin had the impression of being somewhere foreign, a trip abroad. Only the smell spoiled the illusion.

He had been aware of it yesterday, though it didn't seem as powerful then. The stink of rotting fish. Hendry went straight to a rusted orange skip and climbed the rungs attached to its far side. He gestured for Fin to follow. 'Come on up.'

Reluctantly Fin climbed to the top of the sealed skip, the stink of decaying fish growing more pungent with every rung. Hendry threw open a large hatch and the odour that struck them was like a physical assault. Fin could see the thousands of dead, diseased and half-eaten salmon inside, filling it almost to the roof, and he retched several times. Had he eaten breakfast, he was certain he would have reintroduced it to the world, right there on top of the skip. The interior of it was alive with flies and maggots.

Hendry closed the lid again with a clang, and stood up. 'This site is RSPCA and ASC assured,' he said. 'You'll see that label on salmon in the supermarket. It's supposed to reassure you about the quality of the fish and the responsible and sustainable environment in which they were raised.' He cocked an eyebrow and shrugged his shoulders. 'No comment necessary, eh?'

'But what are these fish doing here in a skip?' Fin said.

'They've been trucking these disposal skips in and out for months. I don't know where they take them, but clearly they couldn't get rid of the morts fast enough. Which is why they started dumping them down at Mangersta. I figure mortality in the cages must be around twenty-five percent.'

Fin whistled silently through pursed lips. If Niall's figure of one hundred thousand fish a cage was right, that meant somewhere around three hundred thousand salmon would die before harvesting at this farm alone. He climbed down the rungs after Hendry and followed him around to the far side of the skip, where white plastic 1,000-litre containers were stacked two high. Hendry jabbed a finger at the label on one of them. 'Formaldehyde Solution,' he read. Then ran his finger down a list of warnings opposite a skull and crossbones in a red diamond. 'May cause cancer. Do not breathe in. Causes damage to organs.' He glanced at Fin. 'Employees have to use special protective clothing when they work with this stuff.'

He started walking towards the former fish processing plant that Niall had told Fin was now used as offices. Fin went after him.

'With freedom of information, I got figures from the Scottish

Environment Protection Agency. More than fifty tons of for-maldehyde have been used here and elsewhere in Scotland.' He paused at the steps leading up to the offices. 'And the UK Health and Safety Executive have ruled that chemical levels in the fish don't pose a health risk.' He shook his head slowly. 'Mr Macleod, would you want to eat salmon that have been pumped full of vaccines, half eaten by sea lice and drowned in toxic chemicals?'

They heard the sound of an approaching vehicle. Hendry glanced back along the road, and they saw sunlight reflecting from the roof of a car. 'Better make ourselves scarce.'

Fin was perplexed. 'Why?'

'Because I don't want to be seen here.' He took the steps two at a time up to the door and disappeared inside. Fin sighed. He had no desire to be found hiding in the offices of Bradan Mor like some thief in the night. But he seemed left with little choice, so he ran up the steps to vanish inside just as the approaching car pulled in next to Hendry's Land Rover. Hendry was lurking in a corridor hanging with protective white plastic suits.

Fin whispered, 'What about your vehicle?'

'Could be anyone's,' Hendry's voice came back at him out of the gloom. There was a dartboard on the wall behind him, half a dozen darts clustered together in the cork. 'There's fish-ermen use the pier all the time.' He turned and opened a door marked **Health Room**. 'In here.'

With a dreadful sinking feeling, Fin knew that, if the

occupants of the vehicle came into the building, he and Hendry would be trapped in this room and almost certainly discovered. Hendry, by contrast, was hyped up with excitement, and Fin realized he was enjoying this. The activist closed the door softly behind them and went to crouch by the window. The room itself was lined with shelves groaning with paperwork and blue and white cardboard boxes. A large noticeboard was pinned with memos and instructions on jellyfish surveillance and the sampling of sea lice.

Hendry was sneaking glances out of the window. 'They're not coming in.'

Fin breathed a sigh of relief.

'They're taking one of the RBBs. Probably going out to the *Bradan Harvester*.'

'That's the boat that washes off the sea lice?'

'A hydrolyzer, yeah.'

'How does it do that?'

'It's got a reservoir of fresh water aboard, Mr Macleod. They suck the fish out of the cages, sluice them through the fresh water, then put them back.'

'The fresh water kills the sea lice?'

'No, just washes them off. Every so often they have to sail out of the loch to dump the lice at sea. They've got their own desalination plant on board, so they make more fresh water, and come back to rinse more fish.' Hendry sat on the floor now, with his back to the wall beneath the window. 'They're pulling out all the stops, because government inspectors'll be here soon to visit the cages.' He snorted his derision. 'Of course, the Marine Directorate never arrive unannounced. So there's always time to clean up or cover up.'

And Fin realized now exactly why Niall and his son were on the island.

They heard the inboard motor of the RBB starting up at the pier. Hendry had relaxed. He took out his tin and lit another roll-up. 'There's a lot of people pissed off at what's going on out there, you know. Not least the Linshader estate.'

Fin scowled. 'How does it affect them?'

'This plague of sea lice, Mr Macleod, it's not entirely confined to the cages. It spills over into the surrounding loch and affects wild salmon returning to spawn upriver. And selling beats on the Grimersta River used to be a lucrative source of income for the estate. Not any more.' He stood up and looked out of the window to see the black RBB leaving a deep green trail in its wake as it headed out beyond the near island.

'How would the estate even know what's happening at the cages?'

Hendry grinned. 'They read my blog, Mr Macleod. Same as everyone else. Including Bradan Mor. Which makes me a marked man as far as the company is concerned. But they're not going to be able to stop me posting my documentary on YouTube in a few weeks. And then everyone's going to know what they've been up to.'

Fin shook his head. 'They're not going to be very happy about that.'

'They are not,' Hendry agreed. 'The stakes are huge, Mr Macleod. Farmed salmon is Britain's biggest food export. Sales of Scottish salmon bring in nearly 1.5 billion pounds annually. But the problems they encounter farming them are creating huge mortality rates – about fifteen million fish every year. And folk could very easily lose their appetite for salmon if they knew exactly what it was they were eating.'

III.

Hendry's Land Rover lurched and lumbered down the track towards the head of the loch. But it wasn't until they cleared the stunted rowans that they saw the green Range Rover parked next to Fin's pale blue rental.

'Uh-oh!' Hendry was immediately on his guard. 'Who the hell's that?'

But Fin knew. He had seen that same green Range Rover parked at the back of Niall Dubh's house on the cliffs at Port of Ness.

Hendry pulled up beside it, and both men got cautiously out of the vehicle. There was a little breeze now, though the midges were still in evidence. Sunlight glittered all across the water beyond the abandoned crofthouse. On a cluster of rocks, a group of shags, wings outstretched to dry their feathers, stood in silhouette against the shimmering loch.

Hendry strode boldly through the curtained door, shouting names as he went. 'Alasdair! Jenny!' But there was no reply.

Fin followed at a distance, and, when he passed from sunlight into the tenebrous damp of the house, heard Hendry cursing from the far end of the hall. He made his way cautiously along to the computer room, and found Hendry ripping the cardboard from the window, allowing sunlight to stream in, casting shadows among the chaos. Someone had systematically smashed everything in the room. Computer, monitors, video and still cameras, tripods. An orgy of calculated destruction.

Hendry was dismayed. 'Fuck, fuck, fuck,' he kept saying as he strode among the remains of his equipment. 'This stuff cost a fucking fortune.' He looked despairingly at Fin standing in the doorway. 'How am I ever going to replace it?' A pause, then, 'Fuck!' at the top of his voice. It resounded around the room. He cast frantic eyes about the wreckage. 'The drones are gone.' And he pushed past Fin, through the kitchen and out on to the broken concrete patio. By the time Fin had parted the bead curtains on the back door, Hendry was picking up the shattered remains of the two drones from among the woody tendrils of heather where someone had thrown them.

Off to the left, it looked as if that same person might have taken a sledgehammer to the generator. It was smashed beyond repair.

Hendry appeared to be on the verge of tears. He dropped the broken pieces of his drones back into the heather and stared disconsolately at Fin, as if somehow Fin might be able to fix all this. 'Jesus Christ, Mr Macleod,' he said.

Fin had not particularly warmed to the man in the last

couple of hours, but he felt sorry for him now. 'Does this mean you've lost everything? All your video files?'

Hendry shook his head. 'All backed up to the cloud.' Though in this moment that seemed to offer him little comfort.

A voice startled them both. 'Bit of a mess all this, eh?' They turned to see Jack Dempsey step out from beyond the far gable. There was an ersatz attempt at sympathy somewhere behind a grin that faded as his gaze fell on Fin standing in the doorway. 'Mr Macleod,' he said, nodding his acknowledgement.

'Mr Dempsey,' Fin said, and stepped out on to the remains of the patio. Joss sticks still stood fanned around the jar, but had long since burned out.

Dempsey turned back to Hendry. 'Nice place you have here, Mr Hendry. I was just passing, know what I mean, and it seems I scared off some kids.' He glanced towards the shattered drones. 'Looks like they might have been vandalising your stuff. Maybe you should check if anything's been stolen.'

'You bastard!' Hendry almost spat at him.

Fin said, 'Does Niall know you're here?'

Dempsey swung around. 'What do you think, Mr Macleod? Though he'll be surprised to know that you are.'

The smile wrote itself all over his face again and he turned back to Hendry. 'It might be an idea, Mr Hendry, if you were to leave the island. For your own safety, I mean. No telling if those kids might be back.' He nodded at Fin and then turned and vanished around the side of the house.

Fin and Hendry stood in silence, listening as the Range

Rover's engine coughed into life on the far side of the building. And they heard the whine of its gears as it set off on the long trek back to the road. Fin found Hendry staring at him. 'You know who that guy is.' Not a question, but a clear accusation.

'He's Niall Black's minder,' Fin said. 'A thug from Glasgow.'

'And it would seem you're a friend of the said Mr Black.'

'We were at school together.' Fin thought about it. 'But that doesn't make us friends.'

'Then how the hell did he know where to find me? There's only a handful of folk know I'm here.'

CHAPTER EIGHTEEN

It was on an impulse that Fin left the Stornoway road less than half an hour later, prompted by the sight of Linshader Lodge out on the point. It nestled among pines planted by the island's nineteenth-century owner, James Matheson, a long green and white painted building that stood down at the water's edge opposite the standing stones, clearly visible from the main road.

Fin took the single-track turn-off, losing sight of the lodge only briefly as the land fell away. Then, as he crested the rise, there it was again, basking in the unaccustomed sunshine. He drove through its gate, across a bone-shaking cattle grid, and up the short stony drive to the parking area bordering the loch in front of the house.

The lodge had been expanded several times over the years since its construction in the early 1870s, and a long green-roofed extension built against the north gable housed the ghillies and the seasonal watchers.

Fin drew up outside the extension, and saw the estate's owner leaving by the front door of the lodge, striding across the parking area in shirt sleeves and moleskin trousers to where his Land Rover was parked beside a short slipway that angled off into deep green water. Fin jumped out of the car and chased after him. 'Jamie!' he shouted. 'Jamie!' And Jamie stopped mid-stride, turning to see who was calling him.

Fin caught up and smiled at Jamie's frown of confusion. 'Do I know you?'

Fin held out his hand. 'It's been a long time, Jamie. We used to play on the beach when your father sent you up to Ness for the summer during the school holidays.'

And the veil of uncertainty lifted from his eyes as recognition returned. He shook Fin's hand. 'Fin Macleod,' he said. 'My God, we were just children.'

Fin grinned. 'Well, if your father hadn't sent you off to that fancy school down south, we might have been friends, too.'

'We were!' Jamie protested.

'Summer acquaintances, Jamie. But I always liked you.'

'Likewise.' He shook his head in fond recollection. 'What brings you to Linshader?'

'Caitlin Black.'

And Jamie's face clouded instantly. 'I heard about that poor lass. What a tragedy. Such a lovely girl.'

'You knew her?'

'Oh, yes. She used to work summers here at the lodge. An absolute one-off. We welcomed her back with open arms every summer, and returning guests were always disappointed if for some reason she wasn't here. Folk just fell in love with her,

Fin.' He paused. 'What's your connection to her?' And even as he asked the question, realized he knew the answer. 'Fionnlagh Macleod. Oh my God, Fin, don't tell me he's related?'

Fin nodded solemnly. 'My son.' He paused. 'I don't think he did it, Jamie.'

'You were in the police, weren't you?'

Fin nodded.

'Are you still?'

'Not any longer. But I'm trying to find out a bit more about Fionnlagh's relationship with Caitlin.'

Jamie shrugged sympathetically. 'I'm afraid there's nothing really that I can tell you about that.'

'No, but you might know something about the reason they were arguing.'

The estate owner frowned. 'I don't see how.'

Fin said, 'I'm told they had a difference of opinion about her involvement with an anti-fish farm activist who's currently on Great Bernera collecting evidence of malpractice by Bradan Mor.'

Jamie breathed his disdain into the midday heat. 'Colm Hendry.'

'You know him, then?'

'Not personally, no. I read his blog. But only because I'm indirectly affected.'

'Sea lice?'

He nodded and glanced at his watch. 'Walk to the vehicle with me, Fin. I don't have much time.' And as the two men sauntered towards the Land Rover sitting at the water's edge, he said, 'Look, I don't hold much store by Hendry, but I'm no advocate for Bradan Mor. And if he manages to get those cages removed from the loch, I'll be more than happy. It's ruining the wild salmon fishing on the Grimersta River. And that's always been an important part of the estate's income.'

Fin said, 'I thought that lice just fell off the fish in fresh water.'

'Oh, it's more than just lice. The wild salmon don't have the strength or the energy to swim upriver any more. When I was a young boy growing up here, you could stop by the mouth of the Grimersta, and you would see hundreds of fish waiting for the tide to turn so they could swim upriver. You go down there now, you'll see hardly any.'

'Because of fish farming?'

'Not just that. There's no doubt that the wild salmon are being overfished in international waters. I mean, there's nothing to regulate the catching of fish out there. But the fish farms do have a lot to answer for. They discharge waste, and pesticides and other chemicals directly into what are ecologically fragile coastal waters. Do you know that a two-acre salmon farm produces as much waste as a town of ten thousand people?'

Fin whistled his surprise.

Jamie was on a roll. 'The pollution's bad. You go out there sometimes, and you'll see huge blankets of green slime on the surface of the water. Which kills oxygen, and much of the sea life below it. When I was a kid, we used to go along the shore collecting mussels. You could just scrape them off the rock with a small shovel and have a couple of buckets full in no time. Now . . .' he shook his head, 'you go down on to the rocks and you can't find any mussels at all.'

'The mussel farms seem to be doing alright.'

'Oh, aye, it's not that the mussels have died off. It's just that most of the shellfish are gone from the coastline.' He hesitated. 'I have my own theory about that.'

'Which is?'

Jamie opened the driver's door of his Land Rover. 'They put oil in the fish feed, Fin. To make it more buoyant and absorb water less easily. It makes the pellet float longer. But if you look around the cages, you often see what looks like an oil slick coming off them. The oil of course is organic, not a pollutant in itself. But over the years it's been settling on the rocks, like Teflon, so the shellfish can't attach to them properly, and they just get washed off in the winter storms.' Another glance at his watch. 'Got to go, Fin. Late already for a meeting in town.' He slipped into the driver's seat. 'Good luck with your boy.'

Fin watched the Land Rover lumber off down the drive. He stood for several thoughtful moments looking out on the water. A wasted diversion, he thought. He turned towards his car and saw a figure approaching across the car park. A stout man in green overalls and olive-green Hunter wellies. Younger than himself, Fin thought, but losing his fine sandy hair and growing it long to cover up. He remembered, when he was very young, his father saying, *never trust a man with a combover.*

This one stopped several paces short of Fin and regarded him with a look that hovered somewhere between contempt and malice. 'Fin Macleod,' he said.

Fin was immediately on his guard. 'And you are?'

'Oh, you wouldn't know me. We were at the Nicolson at the same time, but I was about three years behind you. Calum Smith.' He paused, his stare unwavering. 'It was you and Niall Dubh that sold stolen salmon to my father thirty-odd years ago. Farmed fish nicked from Dubh's father's cages out by the bridge.'

Fin was aware of his face reddening. It was not something he could deny, and he felt a sick sensation settling in his stomach. He said, 'Coinneach Smith was your father?'

'Aye. And taken from us far too soon. But you'd know all about that.'

'I remember hearing about it at the time.'

'Must have been a blow, eh? Losing your middleman.'

'What do you mean?'

'Aw, come on! We all knew that you and a bunch of your pals were using my father to pass off farmed salmon for wild.'

'Who's *we*?'

'Just about everyone on the estate. It was an open bloody secret.'

Fin shifted uncomfortably. 'Well, you should know that the whole thing was Coinneach's idea. He was the one insisting that we had to keep the fish coming. Even after . . .' His voice trailed away.

'Aye, after that lad drowned in the cages. Funny how the

supply just dried up after that, and less than a week later, my father's found dead at the foot of the cliffs along the shore there.' He howked phlegm into his mouth and spat on the ground. 'An accident, they said. Or suicide.' And he scoffed. 'My dad was as sure-footed as a mountain goat. And he never had a day's depression in his life.' Calum set his legs apart and folded his arms. 'Nah. If you ask me, someone shut him up so he wouldn't spill the beans about a bunch of stupid boys stealing salmon and leaving one of their own to drown.'

Niall Dubh's words came back to Fin from the previous day. *It's all so long ago now, Fin. Everyone involved is dead. So what does it matter?*

Calum said, 'My father took a phone call that night and went out shortly afterwards to meet someone. I think it was you and Niall Dubh.'

Fin bristled. 'I can't speak for Niall, but it certainly wasn't me. And I don't believe for a minute that Niall would or could have killed your father.' And he wondered if he really did believe that.

A sick smile slid across Calum's face. 'Just like you probably don't believe it was your son who killed Niall Dubh's daughter.' The smile transitioned from sick to ugly. 'Maybe some kind of justice in that, eh? The sins of the fathers visited upon both of their children.' He stood a moment longer. 'Have a nice day.' And he turned and walked briskly back towards the extension with the green roof.

CHAPTER NINETEEN

I.

Stornoway was enjoying a holiday mood brought on by the extended spell of fine weather, waterproofs and winter jackets abandoned in favour of open-necked shirts and rolled-up sleeves. Tourists in shorts and Jesus sandals roamed the lunchtime streets. Chattering schoolkids wandered around with blazers slung over shoulders. Old ladies perspired beneath summer hats. Flower baskets hanging from shop and pub doorways swayed gently in the warmest of August breezes.

Fin did not share in this festive spirit as he trudged wearily up Church Street, frustrated and depressed by his lack of progress. What he had learned about Bradan Mor's fish farm could not compensate for his failure to cast light on his son's guilt or innocence. In fact, he was far from convinced that anything Colm Hendry had told him was even relevant. He needed to talk to Fionnlagh.

The CIO was out to lunch, and the sergeant at the charge bar was initially reluctant to let Fin into the cells. It was only the appearance of George Gunn that settled the issue. 'Let him in, Tam,' he told the sergeant. 'I'll take responsibility if there's any kickback.'

Fin nodded his silent thanks, and the uniformed sergeant unlocked the gate giving them access to the cells. Circular overhead lights cast their shadows on a scarred floor, and the rattle of the officer's keys was accompanied by the unappetising smell of lukewarm food coming from the cell.

The door swung open to reveal Fionnlagh squatting on his blue blanket, which was folded beneath him on the concrete plinth below the window. He was forking tepid pot noodle from a paper bowl into his mouth without any great enthusiasm. He appeared surprised to see Fin, and used his arrival as an excuse to abandon his lunch. He laid it on the concrete beside him and said, 'The least you could have done is bring me a Chinese carryout. I'm going to go insane eating this shit.'

The door clanged shut, and Fin stood looking at his son, almost drowning in a sea of silent mixed emotions. He had no experience of Fionnlagh as a child. He had already reached the age of sixteen when Fin first met him. And now he was a grown man. But somehow, sitting there, with the sunlight falling across him in small squares from the window above, he looked to Fin like a little boy. Six, seven, eight years old, and as lost as Fin had been when his aunt took him from his parents' home to live with her in that lonely house above Crobost harbour.

Fionnlagh found his father's gaze unsettling. 'What?' he said.

'I want you to tell me about Caitlin and Colm Hendry.'

Fionnlagh broke eye contact and cast his eyes towards the floor. 'Still playing the cop?'

Fin felt anger spike through him. 'It's a role I played for years, Fionnlagh. And I can still remember my lines.'

Fionnlagh shook his head. 'What's the point?'

'Just tell me about Caitlin and Colm Hendry.'

Fionnlagh sighed and leaned forward. 'Hendry thinks he's God's gift to women.'

'How do you know that? You only met him once.'

Fionnlagh looked up sharply. 'You've been speaking to him?'

Fin nodded.

'I heard enough about him from Caitlin.'

'How was she involved with him?'

'He didn't tell you?'

'No.'

Fionnlagh shook his head in frustrated recollection. 'You know he's trying to discredit Bradan Mor? That's why he's here.' When Fin made no response, he said, 'Caitlin and Iseabail were swimming out to the cages at night and getting underwater shots for him of the fish inside. Gross stuff. Salmon half eaten alive by sea lice.'

Fin nodded slowly. That made sense now. He said, 'I've seen the footage.'

Fionnlagh looked up, surprised. 'You know it was Iseabail

and Caitlin that found all the illegally dumped fish down at Mangersta?'

'I do.'

'Well, it was Iseabail that talked Caitlin into swimming out to the cages with her.' Fionnlagh gasped his exasperation, and it reverberated around the walls of the cell. 'Not that she took much persuasion. She was so into the environment. Animal rights. All that stuff. It was her passion.' He paused. 'It was one of the things I loved about her.' He looked very directly at his father. 'And I did love her.'

Fin saw the painful truth of that in his son's eyes.

'But I hated her doing what she was doing. It wasn't just dangerous, it was stupid. She was allowing herself to be used by that guy. They both were.'

'So you went and told him to sling his hook.'

'I did. I didn't trust him. The girls were spending way too much time up at that old crofthouse. Two attractive young teenage girls, and him ten years older even than me. I figured he was looking for more from them than just swimming out to the cages.'

Fin said, 'That's a bit rich coming from someone who was having sex with one of them.' Which drew a look from his son. 'So tell me about the night she was killed. Did you two fall out?'

Remembered anger flashed then across Fionnlagh's eyes. 'I didn't want her to go.'

'Out to the cages?'

He nodded.

'And?'

'She told me I didn't own her. If she wanted to swim out to the fish farm, that's what she would do.'

'And?'

But Fionnlagh just shook his head.

'What happened, Fionnlagh?'

Fin's insistence provoked an angry response from his son. 'What does it matter now? She's dead. And nothing I can say, and nothing you can do, is going to change that.' His voice cracked, and he dropped his face into despondent hands. 'Fucked it up for everyone, didn't I? Donna didn't deserve this. And, God knows, poor little Eilidh didn't. And Caitlin . . . If I could turn back the clock, undo it all, I would. But I can't.' He drew a despairing breath. 'I wish to God I was dead, too.'

II.

Fin felt battered as he stepped from the police station. His own son had just wished himself dead. *I did love her*, Fionnlagh had said to his father. And the death of someone you love, Fin knew, was a loss from which some people never recovered. No matter how wrong that relationship had been, he didn't doubt his son's feelings.

Depression descended on him like the heat of the day as he walked down Church Street, sunlight playing on the inner harbour in direct contrast to the darkness in his heart.

'Mr Macleod. Mr Macleod.' The voice calling his name barely

penetrated his introspection. 'Mr Macleod!' Finally Fin turned
to see George Gunn hurrying down the street. He stopped, and
Gunn caught up with him outside An Taigh Cèilidh. He was
breathing hard, and glanced back towards the police station.
'I need to talk to you, sir, but not here. It's a bit public. Have
you had lunch yet?'

Fin shook his head. 'No.'

'Well, what about we meet at the Harris and Lewis
Smokehouse in, say . . .' he looked at his watch, 'fifteen minutes?' He paused. 'Well, maybe it's called Beckett and Sons,
or something like that, now. Anyway, if we sit upstairs, we'll
likely not be seen by anyone from the station.'

Beckett and Sons served coffee and brunch in a modern
building of glass and wood set back from Sandwick Road on
the outskirts of the town centre. It stood directly opposite
the Nicolson Institute, where Fin had received most of his
secondary school education. Gone were the old familiar school
buildings, replaced now by two- and three-storey blocks of glass
and stone, although the old Italianate clock tower remained, a
familiar landmark through all his formative years.

Chalkboard menus in the restaurant were set on a wall next
to a counter where orders were placed. But Fin climbed the
stairs to the mezzanine and found a table in the far corner.
He couldn't bring himself to call Marsaili, and sent her a text
instead. He would go down to Bernera again after his meeting
with Gunn, and suggested that he could pick Eilidh up from

school on his way back. It would give Marsaili some fleeting pleasure to tell Catriona that her services were not required today.

Gunn was late, and arrived sweating and apologising profusely. 'Sorry to keep you waiting, Mr Macleod. The CIO heard about your visit to the cells. He wasn't best pleased.' He sat opposite Fin and picked up a menu. 'The smoked salmon's very good.'

Fin could not see past images of half-eaten zombie salmon swimming around in Bradan Mor's cages. He shook his head. 'I'm not hungry, George. A coffee'll do me.'

Gunn went downstairs to order a salad and Fin's coffee. When eventually they arrived, he regarded his salad without enthusiasm and said, 'My wife will be happy to hear that I had rabbit food for lunch. She's trying to persuade me to lose weight.' He picked up a fork, but made no attempt to eat. He looked at Fin. 'I've not been able to sleep, Mr Macleod, since speaking with you and Marsaili the other day. When you first arrived.' He lowered his head to stare at his salad. 'You know I can't tell you things about an ongoing investigation.'

'George, I do. I understand. And I'm sorry if we were brusque. You can't even begin to imagine what kind of stress we were under. And still are. Your own son being accused of murder is not something they teach you how to deal with at the academy.'

'You're right, Mr Macleod. I've no idea what you must be going through. I just wanted to apologise.'

'You've got nothing to apologise for, George. I'd have been bound by the same constraints as you.'

'Still,' he said, toying now with his salad, but not yet eating it. 'You'll tell Marsaili?'

Fin smiled. 'I'll tell Marsaili, George.'

Which encouraged him to push a forkful of salad into his mouth. He munched on it thoughtfully for a few moments. Then, 'One thing I can tell you,' he said. 'The pathologist is arriving first thing tomorrow. So the post-mortem on the girl will likely take place later in the morning.'

Fin was surprised. 'On a Saturday?'

Gunn had returned to pushing the constituent parts of his salad around the plate. 'The service is so short-staffed these days, sir. We're lucky to get anyone to come over here at all.'

'Any idea who it is?'

Gunn allowed himself a wry smile, reflecting on a first encounter that had taken place more than a decade before. 'I do, Mr Macleod. It's your old pal. Professor Angus Wilson.'

CHAPTER TWENTY

I.

Fin parked above the pier at Baile na Mara. It was his third time here in two days. As on previous visits, it was completely deserted. When he and the boys had been making their clandestine outings to steal salmon from Hamish Black's fish farm more than thirty years before, there were half a dozen fish farms out on the loch, all serviced from Baile na Mara. Fishermen went out regularly to harvest crabs and lobsters from creels. There was the fish processing plant. The harbour had sustained, perhaps, a hundred and twenty full-time jobs. It was likely that there were more people commuting to work every morning *to* the island of Great Bernera than there were leaving it to work elsewhere.

Now the only folk working out of the harbour were a handful of Bradan Mor employees, and most of their time seemed spent out at the cages. There was a sense of neglect and decay about the place, a tiny corner of the island whose time had come, and gone.

Fin walked around the bay, past empty and derelict buildings, to a crumbling slipway at the point. The carcasses of old fishing boats lay canted at odd angles in the seaweed, next to a ramshackle pontoon draped with ropes and fenders and a solitary orange lifebelt. He turned north then, leaving the path, unhooking a gate and climbing through the heather to the top of the promontory.

From here, he had an unobstructed view across coruscating waters to the twin banks of circular salmon cages to which Niall had taken him yesterday in the RBB. The hydrolyzer was still there, and men working at the barge that distributed food to the fish. A power boat left the farthest of the cages, accelerating across the unbroken surface of the loch. Heading, Fin thought, for the tiny harbour at Breascleit, which appeared to service most of the other operators on the loch.

The breeze was cooling and kept the midges away, and Fin stood for some time gazing out across the water. Somehow, following his encounter with Fionnlagh, he had come to believe that these cages might, after all, hold some clue as to what had happened that night. And it seemed to him that the person closest to the centre of it all, apart from Fionnlagh, was Iseabail Macpherson. He needed to talk to her again. Only this time, he would beard the lioness in her own den.

II.

Breacleit was the largest settlement on Great Bernera, not to be confused with Breascleit over on the main island. It had been home to the primary school, now closed due to lack of pupils, the place where both Caitlin and Iseabail would have received their primary education, and where doubtless they first met and forged the friendship that would see them through schools swimming championships, TV celebrity, and finally tragedy.

Fin drove up from the south, Loch Geal to the west, Loch Breacleit on the east. Past a children's play park, and the austere little building that housed the Church of Scotland. Beyond the church, Fin saw the school, moss breaking through asphalt in a playground where the girls must once have played together, fenced and gated off now from the outside world.

He turned right into a narrow road that curved away towards the loch that gave the village its name. A war monument that sat up on the left cast a short shadow to the north. And a couple of hundred yards further on, Fin pulled in at the gate of the house where Iseabail had grown up. There were two other vehicles parked there, each facing in a different direction. An old Nissan Micra and a silver Peugeot.

The Macpherson home was a pebbledash bungalow that presented a low profile to the prevailing weather but commanded an impressive view over the loch. Discarded farm machinery lay scattered about an unkempt garden, and a woman stood hanging out washing on a line strung between two crooked posts. She turned as she heard Fin's car, and watched him climb out of the vehicle and come through the gate. As he approached, she said warily, 'Can I help you?' She was about Fin's age. A handsome woman treated unkindly by the years. But still it was evident where Iseabail had got her looks.

'I was looking for Iseabail,' Fin said. 'I take it you're her mother?'

'I am. And what would you be wanting with my daughter?' She frowned at him. 'You're not the police again, are you?'

'Used to be,' Fin said. 'Is she at home?'

'You haven't told me what it is you want with her.'

'I was hoping to ask her about Caitlin.'

Mrs Macpherson took the plastic basket of wet clothes she had been holding and laid it at her feet. She straightened up, shaking her head sadly. 'Poor, poor Caitlin. An absolute tragedy, Mr . . .' She squinted at him suspiciously. 'You didn't tell me your name.'

'Macleod. Fin Macleod.'

Suspicion turned to a scowl. 'You're not related to that one they've charged with her murder, are you?'

'I'm his father.'

She absorbed this like blotting paper. 'Well, you've got a damned cheek showing up here,' she said. 'You ought to be ashamed of yourself, raising a monster like that. If I'd known the half of what was going on, I would have grounded our Iseabail months ago. Poor Caitlin. Groomed by her own teacher, for God's sake, and made to have sex with him at that house on the Black Loch.'

'That's not how Iseabail tells it, Mrs Macpherson.'

She bridled with indignation. 'What do you mean?'

'It's alright, Mum.' Iseabail came hurrying anxiously from the house to thread an arm through Fin's and pull him away towards the loch. 'I'll take it from here.' Over her shoulder, she called, 'And I'm too old to be grounded!'

'You be careful, girl!' her mother shouted after her. 'I'll be watching. God knows, it might run in his family.'

Iseabail turned her face towards Fin and lifted eyebrows to the heavens. Then hissed, 'Why did you have to come here?'

Fin said, 'Because you weren't entirely frank with me this morning.'

Iseabail glanced nervously back at her mother and hurried Fin further from the house towards the shore. 'I didn't lie to you,' she said. Then reluctantly, 'There was just some stuff I didn't tell you.'

'Lying by omission is still lying,' Fin said.

They arrived at the water's edge and stopped. The loch reflected the blue of the sky, but Fin saw now that there were clouds bubbling up along the western horizon. White, fluffy cumulus that in themselves carried no threat of rain, but were often a precursor, he knew from long experience, to a change in the weather. Perhaps this long hot August was about to end in tears.

'I didn't lie to you!' Iseabail stood with her hands on her hips and dared him to contradict her.

'You and Caitlin were swimming out to Bradan Mor's cages to take video of diseased and damaged fish for Colm Hendry.'

Her self-certainty wavered and she glanced back towards the house, where her mother was taking her time hanging out the remaining washing, and keeping an unambiguous eye on them. 'For God's sake, don't tell anyone that!'

'Why not?'

'Because I could get into serious trouble.'

'Maybe you should have thought of that before you got involved.'

He heard Iseabail's breath trembling in her chest as she turned away towards the water. She folded her arms defensively, and there was a crack in her voice. 'It's all my fault.'

'What is?'

'It was me that talked Caitlin into going out to the cages. She was always the sensible one. Said it was too dangerous.'

Fin said, 'I thought it was Caitlin who was passionate about the environment, and animal welfare.'

'She was. Totally. That was the degree she was going to take at Glasgow. A BSc in environmental science and sustainability.'

'So what was your motivation?'

Iseabail flicked a guilty glance in his direction. 'It was obvious to me that Colm was infatuated with Caitlin. I mean, she wasn't interested. She had Fionnlagh. But . . .'

Fin finished for her. 'You'd fallen for Hendry.'

Iseabail kept her gaze fixed on some imaginary point on the distant horizon, avoiding eye contact. 'I didn't want to swim out there on my own. I thought if I could persuade Caitlin to come with me . . .'

'You'd somehow get into his good books?'

She shook her head despondently. 'Stupid, I know. You can't make people like you. I mean, not that he didn't like me. But just not in that way.'

Fin gave vent to his exasperation. 'Iseabail, he must be old enough to be your father. What would your dad say?'

She turned now to look at him very directly. 'My dad died nearly fifteen years ago. I was only three. Never really knew him.'

Fin closed his eyes, and knew that he should have seen that coming. 'I'm sorry,' he said.

She shrugged. 'Doesn't matter.' A pause. 'So, anyway, I played the animal welfare card big. To Caitlin, I mean. Persuaded her that getting the evidence was the right thing to do.' She sucked in and bit her lower lip. 'I wish to hell I hadn't.'

'So what happened on the night she was murdered? You were going out to the cages again?'

She nodded. 'A lot of the earlier stuff we'd got was unusable. Not enough light. Colm had got us lightweight LED strips that we were to strap around our heads to use with the GoPro cameras he provided. He said they would give more than enough light to get good clear footage underwater.'

'So you went out that night?'

'No.' Iseabail sighed. 'We were going to. I was supposed to meet her on the shore at the far side of Aird Mhòr. It was the closest point to the cages. We always took a canoe out with us when we went, swimming one either side of it. For safety if anything went wrong.' She shook her head. 'But Caitlin never showed up. It really wasn't like her. I mean, I waited a whole hour, and in the end I just gave up and went home.'

'Did Hendry know the two of you planned to go out that night?'

'Of course.'

'And where was he?'

'I don't know. Back at the croft, I suppose.' She looked at Fin with sudden fire blazing in her eyes. 'It wasn't him! Colm didn't kill Caitlin.'

'How can you be sure?'

'Because he was in love with her.' Saying it out loud visibly had a sudden sobering effect on her, as if framing it in words made it real in a way that it hadn't been before.

Fin said, 'Most murder victims are killed by people who claim to have loved them. Family members. Partners.'

'It wasn't Colm!' She turned her defiance towards the water. 'I mean, what possible reason could he have had to kill her?'

'Maybe she turned him down. Some people can't take rejection.'

'No!' She waggled her head with certainty. 'It wasn't Colm. I know him.' Then turned back to Fin. 'I know I told you I didn't think Fionnlagh did it. And I don't. But by your logic, he could have. They were lovers, after all.'

Which came back at him like a slap in the face. Iseabail was nothing if not smart. But she relented.

'I'm sorry, Mr Macleod. I really don't think he did. But you're looking in the wrong place.'

'Where should I be looking?'

'I wish I knew.'

They stood for a long time, then, without speaking. And as the cloud thickened from the west, so the wind grew stronger, sending the water of the loch rippling towards them. Fin glanced back and saw that Mrs Macpherson had finished hanging out her washing and returned to the house. Sheets and blouses and socks lifted on the edge of the stiffening breeze.

Eventually he said, 'Something you said this morning's been troubling me.'

She scowled at him. 'What?'

'When I talked about those cages out on East Loch Roag being Caitlin's dad's fish farm, you said something odd.'

She tilted her head into the oncoming wind, evasive now. 'Did I?'

'You said, *I suppose you could say that.*'

She shook her head as if caught in some misdemeanour. 'Nothing much gets by you, does it? You can tell you were a cop.'

'What did you mean?'

She folded her arms and sighed deeply. 'I suppose it doesn't matter now. I mean, she's dead. So I'm not really bound by things she told me in confidence.'

'Such as?'

She turned eyes towards Fin that were filled with regret and resignation. 'Maybe Niall Black wasn't her dad.'

CHAPTER TWENTY-ONE

I.

Fin approached Stornoway along Bayhead and on to Cromwell Street. The surface of the water in the inner harbour was ruffled now by the wind, and reflected the gathering accumulation of cloud overhead. Lews Castle still basked in late afternoon sunshine, but the clouds were pursuing their shadows down the hillside towards the harbour and skimming across dark blue water to cast the town in intermittent shade. The heat of the day, however, had not abated. It was, if anything, warmer. Almost suffocating. And Fin was glad of the air conditioning in his rental car.

As he drove across the spit of land that separated the inner and outer harbours, past the Crown Hotel, he saw the deep-water port across the bay. The one-time oil fabrication yard at Arnish now provided berths for cruise ships bringing tens of thousands of tourists to swamp the island every summer. To his left, The Narrows, where he and generations of island teenagers before and since had gathered on Friday and Saturday nights in search of drink and sex and an escape from joyless Calvinism. Right now it was full of tourists and shoppers enjoying the sunshine. But Fin could remember winter nights in the rain and the cold, huddling in the shelter of doorways, sharing illicit roll-ups and hoping for word of a party that might provide warmth and beer and relief from boredom.

It was as if the whole history of his life was here on the island, and all the years he had spent away from it since offered only phantom memories, wraithlike and insubstantial. The only one of those that stayed with him, and real, was the most painful and the one he least wished to dwell on. The death of the son he'd had with Mona. Robbie would have been nearly twenty now, the growing pains of adolescence behind him, all his adult years lying ahead.

Fin nearly choked on the thought, and blinked furiously to keep the tears from his eyes. South Beach floated past on a sea of unwanted memories, sun glancing off the roofs of all the cars parked along the water's edge, and he drove up James Street to the roundabout at the top of the hill.

Schoolkids were already streaming out of the Nicolson, holding up traffic at the crossings on Sandwick Road. Fin pulled in at double gates that opened into the staff car park. Eilidh stood just inside the gate, a gathering of a dozen or more children on the grass behind her, mostly girls. To his shock, Fin saw tears streaming down her face, shoulders slumped, her schoolbag clutched to her chest. As he wound down the window to call to her, he heard the gleeful chant of the kids behind her. *Eilidh, Eilidh, quite contrary, who did your daddy kill?*

Anger spiked up his spine like an electric shock. He yanked on the handbrake and jumped out. 'What do you think you're doing, you stupid little bastards?!' And he was almost shocked by his own voice reverberating around the angle of the school buildings.

The chanting faded away to stunned silence, shock and fear in the faces of the children.

'It's alright, it's alright,' Eilidh said quickly, anxious to stop any further outbursts, and she hurried towards the car.

Fin was about to get back into the driver's side when one of the few boys in the group shouted, 'Who are you, then, the killer's daddy?' His voice treacly with sarcasm. Fin slammed the door shut again and strode towards the group on the grass.

Somewhere in his peripheral hearing, he was aware of Eilidh calling after him, 'Don't, Grampa, don't!'

The children collectively shrank from his angry approach. And Fin stabbed an accusatory finger towards the boy who had called out. 'You. What's your name?'

The boy stood his ground. 'None of your business.'

'Grampaaaa!' Eilidh was wailing behind him.

'What's going on?' A sharp voice cut through it all, and Fin looked up to see a young male teacher marching towards him. 'You can't talk to the children like that.'

'Oh, can't I? What kind of school do you run here?' Fin shouted at him. 'A bunch of kids ganging up on a little girl.

Reducing her to tears.' He waved a hand vaguely behind him in Eilidh's direction.

'I don't know who you are, or what you think you're doing,' the teacher said. 'But if you don't leave now, I'm calling the police.'

Fin drew a deep breath and closed his eyes, pulse racing. He used to *be* the police. What was he doing? He turned abruptly and walked back to the car. Eilidh got in as he slid into the driver's seat. She sat staring straight ahead of her, tears trickling down pink cheeks. She said, 'I have to come here every day, Grampa. You don't.'

He clutched the steering wheel and breathed his frustration. Angry with himself for losing control. 'I'm sorry, Eilidh, I'm sorry.'

She said simply, 'Can we go. Please.'

Fin glanced at the group of schoolkids and their teacher standing watching him. He banged the car into first gear, and took off into Sandwick Road with a squeal of tyres. A chorus of car horns sounded from traffic in the road behind him, and he gritted his teeth, accelerating towards the Engebret's roundabout.

He took a back road out of town, and he and Eilidh drove all the way to Ness in a brittle silence. Inside, Fin was seething with anger and regret. He glanced at his granddaughter a couple of times, but she sat with her hands folded in her lap, gazing passively out across the machair, at an ocean transitioning from blue to pewter as darker clouds approached.

When he pulled in outside the bungalow, she got out without a word and ran down the path. By the time Fin had climbed the steps to the kitchen, both Marsaili and Donna were pacing anxiously inside.

Marsaili said, 'What on earth happened?'

'She came in without a word,' Donna said, 'and ran straight up to her room.'

'We didn't want to go after her until we knew why.' Marsaili's glare was accusatory.

Fin's head dropped. Partially in despair, partially in shame. 'The kids at school were chanting horrible things,' he said. 'I'm afraid I lost it.'

'What do you mean *lost it*?' Marsaili's tone was unforgiving.

'I shouted at them. Well, swore at them.'

Both women were shocked.

'A teacher threatened to call the police.'

'Jesus, Fin!' Marsaili ran a hand back through her hair in exasperation.

Donna shook her head, staring at her father-in-law in disbelief. 'Fucking stupid . . .' She turned and slammed out of the kitchen, and they heard her footsteps on the stairs up to Eilidh's room.

After several moments of silence, Marsaili said, 'What were you thinking?'

'I wasn't thinking. That's the problem. I just reacted.'

'What were they chanting?'

He told her.

And her hand flew to her mouth. 'Dear God!' Then, 'I hope you told that teacher he could go fuck himself.'

Which brought a reluctant smile to Fin's face. 'That's what you'd have said?'

'Probably worse.' And they shared a moment before their smiles faded and she said, 'Where have you been all day, Fin? You've been gone for hours.'

Fin glanced from the window. 'I think the weather's going to break later tonight. Why don't we go down to the beach after we've had something to eat and I'll tell you everything?' He cast eyes towards the door to the hall. 'There's probably stuff it might be better that Donna didn't hear.'

II.

It was still warm. Abnormally so. Darkening clouds gathered in the north and west, masking the sun and bringing premature twilight. Sunset was arriving increasingly early each night as the earth turned on its axis and the sun headed inexorably towards the equator. Tonight, it would be gone before ten.

Fin and Marsaili walked across the machair to the steep path they had taken many times in their youth from the cliffs down to the beach below. As soon as they reached the sand, they kicked off their shoes and felt the fine, cool grains pushing up between their toes. The tide was on the way out, and they ran over wet, compacted sand, both hopping to pull up the legs of their jeans. They splashed into the water, and despite weeks of sunshine, it still felt cold. But good. And Fin knew that Marsaili's squeals were a release of tension. She nearly fell, and he caught her arm, and in an instant she had fallen into both of his, pulling him to her, pressing her head into his shoulder, and he felt the sobs that racked her body. He folded her into his arms and held her close, resting his cheek against the softness of her hair, and let his own silent tears fall into the gathering gloom.

They stood like that for some time, the sea washing up against bare calves before sucking sand away from beneath their feet. Further along the beach, Fin saw a man with a black Labrador heading for the port. The only other souls on the otherwise deserted sands. Eventually they broke apart, letting the wind dry salt tears on streaked cheeks, and hand in hand, they sauntered slowly along the tideline, following at a distance in the footsteps of the man and his dog. By the time they reached the port, the dog walker and his Lab were nowhere to be seen, and they turned to wander back along the water's edge, foam washing sand from their feet and obliterating footsteps in their wake.

'So,' Marsaili said at length. 'Tell me.'

And he told her about his encounter at the house with Iseabail, and making his way to the abandoned crofthouse where the anti-fish farm activist Colm Hendry had set up his base of operations. He described to her in detail the activist's aerial shots exposing the illegal dumping of dead fish, and the zombie salmon, half eaten by sea lice, swimming listlessly around in cages where anything up to twenty-five percent of the fish were already dead.

She listened in horror as he conjured up an image of the stinking maggot-ridden morts, as Hendry had called them, in the skip at the harbour, and the 1,000-litre containers of formaldehyde that a desperate Bradan Mor was using to try to kill the sea lice.

'God, Fin! Are we ever going to be able to eat salmon again?'

Fin shook his head gravely. 'Unless it's pulled fresh out of a river, I think I might have lost my appetite for it.'

Away on the horizon they saw distant flashes of lightning, and a long time later the faintest rumble of thunder.

'Let's hope it doesn't come ashore,' Fin said.

They walked slowly as the light faded, and the sea breaking along the sand glowed as if lit.

At length Fin said, 'There's something I've never told anyone.' And immediately corrected himself. 'Apart from Artair. And that was more than thirty years ago. He told me to shut up about it, and I did.' He could feel Marsaili turning curious eyes towards him. 'But, you know, when you keep something inside like that, something unpleasant, it festers. Turns toxic.'

'For heaven's sake, Fin!' Marsaili's exasperation at his procrastination rose above the sound of the sea breaking along the beach.

He smiled ruefully. 'Sorry.' And so he told her, all about those clandestine night-time drives down to Great Bernera the summer before they left for university, to steal salmon from Hamish Black's fish farm.

Marsaili expressed her surprise. 'And Niall was okay with stealing from his own father?'

'It was his idea, Marsaili.'

He told her about the night of the storm, and Iain being lost. And how his body had been found in one of the cages the following morning. She listened in silence. Rapt. Shocked. He told her about Coinneach Smith passing off the farmed fish they had stolen as wild salmon, and how he had insisted they continue to supply him even after Iain's drowning. Threatening to expose them if they didn't.

'What did you do?'

'We stopped, of course. There's no way we could have gone out to those cages again.'

'And Coinneach Smith?'

Fin hesitated. 'You probably don't remember. But it was in the news at the time. His body was found at the foot of cliffs on the Linshader estate. They figured he'd fallen. Or committed suicide.'

He felt her grip on his arm tighten. 'And you thought Niall had done it?'

'I didn't know, Marsaili. I confronted him, and he denied it.' He turned to look at her. 'I asked him again yesterday, when he took me down to Loch Roag.'

'And?'

'Classic evasion. He neither admitted nor denied it. Just said it didn't matter now because everyone involved was dead.'

He stopped and took her by the shoulders. 'But it matters to Calum Smith. Coinneach's son. I met him today at Linshader. He thinks we did it, Marsaili. Me and Niall. And that Caitlin's murder, and Fionnlagh's arrest, are the sins of the fathers being visited on their own children.'

'Oh, Fin, that's awful.' She took his hand, and they continued their slow progress towards the rocks at the far end of the beach. 'I can't believe you never told me any of this.'

'What would you have said if I had?'

She shrugged. 'I don't know. But it would have been a burden halved.' And he realized the truth of that. He felt better already for having shared it with her. She said, 'I saw you and Niall walking on the beach yesterday, and I did some research on the laptop today. Just out of interest.'

'Research on what?'

'Niall.'

'And?'

'There's a ton of stuff about him on the internet. He's even got his own page on Wikipedia. All about his meteoric rise to CEO of the company he rebranded as Bradan Mor. Moving to Cyprus as a tax exile, though it's not exactly a tax haven. But you pay less tax in the sunshine. You know, they say he's worth £780 million.'

Fin exhaled sharply.

'There's even stuff about the break-up of his marriage to Ailsa, and how they each got custody of one of the kids. The boy went with his dad. Ailsa got Caitlin.'

'Yes, she told me.'

'The son's a male model, apparently. A bit of a jet-setter from all accounts.'

'He's here, you know.'

'On the island?'

'His father's grooming him to take over the business when he retires. But he didn't seem to me like someone who'd be much interested in running a company.'

'You met him, then?'

'Briefly. He was pretty hostile. I am, after all, the father of the man accused of murdering his sister.' He paused for reflection. 'I heard something else interesting today.'

'What?'

'Apparently Caitlin told Iseabail that Niall wasn't her father.'

Marsaili stopped dead in the sand, and the sea washed over their feet. 'Really?' She thought about it. 'That would explain the split custody. Assuming Niall knew that Caitlin wasn't his.' Then, 'It wouldn't surprise me.'

'What wouldn't?'

'Years ago, long after you'd left the island, and Niall was spending months at a time away in Norway, we used to meet Ailsa occasionally at parties or dances and social events.'

'You and Artair?'

Marsaili avoided his eye and just nodded. 'She – this is going to sound coarse – but, well, for want of a better expression, she put it about a bit. Dressed up to the nines. Always drinking too much. Like she was looking for a man, and finding the courage in alcohol to do it.' She sighed, relenting a little on her harsh assessment. 'I guess she was just lonely.' Then reflected some more. 'If it's true, who do you think Caitlin's real father is?'

Fin shrugged. 'You're more likely to be able to make a guess at that than me.'

They started walking again. 'Not really. I mean, I can't say that I ever saw her with anyone in particular. But I suppose there must have been someone. How do you think Niall found out?'

'Who knows. What's maybe more interesting is how Caitlin found out.'

'Iseabail didn't tell you?'

'No.'

'And she didn't know who the real father was?'

'I think she'd have said if she did.'

More lightning flashed along the far horizon, black cloud gathering overhead. And yet it was oddly still. No breeze to speak of. The air humid with lingering warmth.

The shadows of the rocks at the end of the beach lay in simmering darkness, the occasional blink of moonlight peeking through torn cloud to cast silver reflections on rock pools where stranded crabs scuttled through seaweed. There was still just enough light to see by as Fin and Marsaili clambered over canted slabs of gneiss to find the tiny hidden patch of sand where they had made love more than thirty years before, naked under the moon.

They squatted now in the sand, backs to the rock, and

Marsaili said, 'You don't really think that Niall killed that ghillie, do you?'

Fin pondered the question for a long time before he said, 'I find it as hard to believe as him being worth £780 million. But one of those things is true.'

A thought that both found sobering. They sat wordless for a long time, listening to the gentle breath of the sea as it washed up on the slope of the beach before being drawn out again by the tidal undertow.

Fin slipped an arm around her shoulder to draw her close. 'Do you remember that night—?'

She cut him off. 'That we made love right here after going skinny-dipping?'

'No, I meant the time I had food poisoning, and couldn't keep anything down for twenty-four hours.'

She punched his shoulder, and a laugh broke free from his pursed lips. 'You bastard!' she said. And as his grin faded, 'When was the last time we had sex, Fin?'

He cast his thoughts back over the preceding months.

'See? If you have to think about it, it was far too long.'

He nodded his sober agreement. 'It was.'

And she stood up suddenly, peeling off her top, and then her bra, and casting them on to the rocks.

'What are you doing?'

'What do you think?' She pulled down her jeans to step out of each leg, and threw white panties away into the darkness.

'It's far too cold to be going into the sea,' he said.

'Speak for yourself, old man.' And she went running off into the brine, splashing and shrieking as she went, until she fell forward, toppling into a gentle swell to submerge herself completely.

Fin stood up, briefly hesitant, then whispered at the night, 'Fuck it!' And quickly stripped off T-shirt and jeans to go chasing after her. The shock of the cold water very nearly took his breath away as he dived into its deep dusky chill, and found the warmth of Marsaili's body as she struggled to get to her feet. He pulled her down again, and they crashed into the water, clutched in each other's arms. Anyone on the beach, even as far away as the port, might have been alarmed to hear raised voices shrieking in the falling darkness, almost in sync with the lightning that flashed and flickered soundlessly now on the far horizon.

As they emerged dripping from the ocean, the warm night air caressed them, like the arms they slid around each other. Lips finding lips, passion unhindered by the cold. Quickly they laid out their clothes on the damp, compacted sand and fell on to the makeshift mattress, surrendering themselves to a lust they had not felt in a very long time.

And when finally it was over, they lay on their backs, side by side, breathing hard and gazing up at a sky pregnant with coming storm. A sky laden, somehow, with disapproval. While their son slept on a hard concrete plinth in a police cell, they were making love on the beach as if all was well with the world.

Smiles faded. Guilt displacing passion. And the longer they lay there, naked in the sand, the more they felt rebuked by the night. Fin found a break in the clouds through which he could see a part of the Milky Way smudging the cosmos. He stared at it for a long time, trying to find the words to frame his thoughts. Finally he said, 'We should brace ourselves, Marsaili, for the likelihood that, if this goes to trial at the High Court in Inverness, Fionnlagh's going to be found guilty of murder, and they're going to put him away for a long time.'

Marsaili gave voice to her consternation. 'Why would you even say that?'

'Because we have to be realistic. The evidence against him is pretty damning. And he's not helping himself by his behaviour, refusing to talk about it, to us or anyone. The pathologist arrives tomorrow for the post-mortem. If that goes against him, there's really very little we can do about it.'

She lifted herself on to one elbow and looked at him. Fin kept his eyes firmly fixed on the Milky Way. 'You really think he did it, don't you.' It wasn't a question.

'I think we're going to have to come to terms with that possibility. Particularly since Fionnlagh refuses to deny it.' He rolled his head to one side, meeting her eyes for the first time, and saw the pain and disappointment in them.

'For God's sake, Fin! If his own father doesn't believe in him, what chance does he have?'

She was chittering as she got to her feet and searched about in the dark for her things. Fin sighed his despair and stood up to recover his own clothes and get dressed. They were damp, and did little to banish the chill that had set in. 'Marsaili—'

But she put a finger to her lips and shooshed him, still-wet hair falling in ropes over her shoulders. 'What's that?'

He frowned and listened to the still of the night, and the soft cadences of the sea. 'I don't hear anything.'

'No, listen,' she insisted. And he focused again. This time he heard it. Like the very distant call of seagulls.

'Gulls?'

'Not at this time of night. They're sleeping.'

'What is it, then?'

'I don't know.'

And there came, suddenly, a strange crackling sound reverberating faintly through the night air, almost as if it were washing ashore with the sea. 'It sounds like a badly tuned radio station,' Fin said. 'Like the old BBC World Service.' And once more the far cries of distant voices cut through thick, warm air, and raised goosebumps on Fin's neck and arms. 'What *is* that?'

Marsaili was mystified. 'Dolphins?'

But Fin shook his head dismissively. 'Dolphins must sleep, too, surely?'

CHAPTER TWENTY-TWO

I.

Marsaili awoke in the half-light. She had spent most of the night hovering somewhere between sleep and consciousness, watching the painful passage of time on the bedside clock. One o'clock, three o'clock, four-thirty. Now she was startled awake from an unexpected slumber to blink in the grey light that filled the bedroom and wonder what it was that had wakened her. It was five-fifteen. Twenty minutes or more before the official start of civil twilight, and yet darker than usual.

She swung her legs out of bed and sat with hands pressed into the mattress on either side of her thighs, breathing deeply, trying to clear a mind fogged by lack of sleep. Fin lay on his back, mouth slightly open, purring gently. At least he was sleeping now. She had been aware through all her waking hours of him tossing and turning in the bed next to her, tortured no doubt by the same thoughts that prevented her, too, from succumbing to sleep.

She stood up and padded to the window, drawing the

curtains on the faintest of light washing across the Minch, and saw immediately why it was so dark. Great bruising clumps of black cloud blew across the island from the north-west, scraping the hills and shedding tears to run down window-panes, distorting the world beyond. From the chill in the room, she could tell that the outside temperature must have dropped steeply, and she hugged her arms around herself for warmth. A flimsy nightie had been all that was required during the preceding nights, but was wholly inadequate now.

A gust of wind rattled the window frame, and she thought that perhaps this was what had wakened her. But then another sound carried from somewhere out in the bay, blown up from the cliffs on the edge of the wind. A disquieting noise, like breath exploding through pursed lips. A sound of distress.

She dressed quickly, dragging a woollen pullover on over a chequered shirt that she only half tucked into her jeans. From her bag she took a pair of thick socks and pulled on a sturdy pair of walking shoes. Her waterproof jacket hung on the rack in the hall. She slipped it on, and tucked her hair up beneath a baseball cap that she pulled low over her brow.

She went through to the back room, Artair's dad's old study, and crossed to the window, from where she knew she would have a better view out across the machair to the beach. She pressed her face to the windowpane, cupping her hands around the brim of her cap to shut out any internal light. It was hard to see anything clearly beyond the rain. And yet there was some-thing odd down there on the beach. Dark shapes huddled in the sand. Dozens of them, spread around the curve of the bay. She screwed up her eyes, trying to see more clearly. And still she was unable to determine what it was she was looking at.

That sound came again, like muted bugling, and she was filled suddenly with a dread sense of foreboding.

She hurried back through the house and out of the kitchen door, closing it softly, so as not to waken anyone. Down the steps and out across the machair. In spite of the rain, it was still rock-hard underfoot following weeks of drought. From here she couldn't see the beach, the near horizon at the cliff edge obscuring it.

She heard that noise again. Louder now. And she broke into a run, stumbling across tussocks, almost twisting her ankle in a deep dried rut. She reached the path to the beach, wind driving into her face, and kept her focus on each step as she picked her way carefully downwards. It was only when she stepped out on to the sand that she looked up from beneath the brim of her baseball cap, and frowned in complete incomprehension. The beach was littered with huge black and grey shapes, shining in the rain, and spread randomly across two hundred yards of sand above a retreating tideline.

At first nothing would compute. What on earth was she looking at? Before it dawned. With a sudden, awful clarity. They were whales. Like giant dolphins. And she remembered that fifty or more of them had beached on the east coast a couple of years back, attracting international media coverage.

She started running among them. Some appeared to be dead

already. Others were exhaling through blowholes, trumpeting their despair. She began to count them, but gave up after twenty. Her sense of urgency was acute. She felt helpless, and had no idea what to do. But understood that it was imperative she alerted someone who would.

II.

Fin awoke to the sound of doors banging, and raised voices. He had no idea how long he had been asleep, but figured he must have woken from somewhere in the middle of a deep sleep cycle. His thinking was sluggish, and he was unable to make sense of what he heard. The overhead light came on and nearly blinded him as he sat up in bed.

'Fin! Fin!' Marsaili's pale face swam into view. She was wearing a baseball cap, wet hair falling from it in a chaos of flyaway strands, and for a fleeting moment he thought how attractive she still was. But he could feel his heart trying to break through ribs with what felt like a sledgehammer.

'What is it?'

'There are whales on the beach. Dozens of them.'

If he had hoped for clarity, neither of these statements provided it. 'I don't understand . . .'

'They're pilot whales, I think. They must have come ashore during the night at high tide. And now they're stranded on the beach.'

He tried to blink the sleep from his eyes, and threw back the

248

covers to plant his feet on the carpet beside the bed. Beyond Marsaili, he could see Donna and Eilidh standing watching wide-eyed from the hall, both still in their nighties. 'How? Why?'

'I have no idea. But it must have been the whales we heard last night out in the bay. I don't know what we're supposed to do, but if the ones who're still alive can't be refloated fast, they'll die.' Her face reflected her despair. 'I think quite a few of them are already gone. Fin, we need help.'

He ran his hands back through his curls, trying to focus. 'Okay, okay. First thing we need to do is alert the police.' He reached for his mobile, which was charging on the bed-side table. He quickly searched for and found the number of Stornoway police station. It rang twice before a sleepy-sounding duty officer picked up.

Marsaili stood listening impatiently as Fin relayed everything she had just told him. He gave them his name and address and listened for a good thirty seconds before hanging up.

'Well?' Marsaili looked at him expectantly.

He stood up. 'They'll despatch a couple of uniformed officers and inform the coastguard. And whoever else needs to know.'

'A couple of uniformed officers?' Marsaili was incredulous. 'Well, that'll really help.'

Fin put a hand on her arm. 'Marsaili, everything begins with a first step. The coastguard will be key in this. He'll know what needs to be done, who needs to be mobilised.'

Marsaili pulled her arm free. 'Fin, it was raining when I

first found them, but the rain's stopped now. I don't know much, but I know this. If these animals aren't kept wet and cool, they'll overheat and their skin will crack up.' She turned towards mother and daughter still standing in the hall. 'Donna, we're going to need blankets and towels. As many as possible. And buckets. Spades, shovels. Anything you have.'

Donna nodded and vanished from view. Eilidh looked alarmed. 'What can I do?'

'You can get dressed and help carry stuff down to the beach, Eilidh.' Marsaili turned back to Fin. Her initial panic was giving way to clarity. She was taking charge of the situation. Fin very nearly smiled. This was the Marsaili he knew and loved. 'But you can't get involved, Fin. Fionnlagh has to remain your priority. There are only two days left before they take him off to Inverness and we'll lose him into the system.' She hurried out into the hall, and he heard her calling instructions to the girls. He reflected that one of those two remaining days was a Sunday. The Lewis Sabbath. And nothing much would happen on that day, save for the singing of Gaelic psalms, and the spouting of righteous sermons on God and hellfire. Which effectively left only today.

Fin began to get dressed. He had, at least, a notion of where to begin, and amid the clatter and clamour of activity elsewhere in the house, he sat on the bed and lifted his phone to search its browser for today's schedule of incoming flights.

III.

Fin stood in the departure lounge gazing through floor-to-ceiling windows, out across the apron towards the sandbank in Broad Bay. The rain stayed off during the drive from Ness to Stornoway, but the wind had risen, and he saw it battering the Loganair Saab 340 as it flew in off the water. The turboprop lurched alarmingly from side to side as it descended towards the runway, then stabilised just before touchdown.

'Jesus Christ, that flight never gets any better,' Professor Wilson exclaimed when he saw Fin hovering in the arrivals hall next to the carousel. In many ways the pathologist had barely changed in all the years Fin had known him. A tall man, lean, with a cadaverous face lurking somewhere behind the prodigious beard that concealed most of it. Fin had heard him described once as having a face like a burst mattress. The one-time ginger horsehair that escaped it, however, had turned mostly silver now, interspersed with just the occasional strand of copper. 'Godforsaken bloody place,' he boomed, drawing glares from locals. 'Only compensation is that curry house on Church Street. The one with all the virulently coloured sauces. Is it still there?'

'As far as I know,' Fin said, and held out a hand.

Professor Wilson's big bony grip almost crushed it, strength developed during decades of cutting through human ribcages. 'Good to see you, Fin,' he said, and pulled his chequered cap down over an almost bald head. 'Nearly lost my bunnet out there! Now where's my bloody luggage?'

As they walked towards the sliding doors, the pathologist wheeling his case behind him, he glanced at Fin. 'You're not here in any kind of official capacity, are you?'

'No, Angus. Father of the accused is my only standing in this whole mess.'

The professor sucked on his gums and shook his head. 'Aye, I heard that Fionnlagh had been arrested.'

'Charged now,' Fin said.

Professor Wilson cocked an eyebrow. 'That's a bit premature, is it not? I haven't even done the PM yet.'

'Apparently the CIO thinks he has enough evidence without it.'

'Oh, does he? Which makes my trip out here a waste of fucking time? Who is he?'

'DCI Douglas Maclaren.'

The pathologist snorted.

'You know him?'

'Oh, aye, I know him alright. Snotty little shit.' He smirked. 'And I know a thing or two about him that I'm sure he wishes I didn't.' The doors slid open and they stepped out into a wind carrying the odd icy spit of rain. Professor Wilson raised his eyes to the sky. 'Does the sun *ever* shine here?'

'You just missed about five weeks of it.'

'Hah! Trust my luck.' And he turned his gaze on Fin. 'What *are* you doing here, Fin? You know I can't discuss the case with you, or anything I might find during autopsy.'

'I know that, Angus. And I wouldn't ask.'

'Good.'

'Just thought I'd give an old friend a lift into town. Taxis might be few and far between in this weather.'

The pathologist patted his back. 'Good man. Let's do it, shall we?'

CHAPTER TWENTY-THREE

Nearly three hours had passed since the alarm was raised, and the beach now resembled a war zone. The more than forty volunteers who had rushed to Ness from all over the island worked among those whales that were still alive.

Blankets and sheets and towels were laid across the stranded creatures, kept wet by buckets of seawater passed along lines of rescue workers to pour over them. The muted bugle calls issuing from blowholes were weaker now, and barely discernible above the wind and the waves.

Groups of helpers in red, orange and yellow waterproofs, some wearing hard hats, dug frantically in the sand, hoping to channel seawater from the incoming tide to those whales nearest the water. Marsaili worked among them, feeling the futility of it. A lost cause, she thought. How could so few people hope to divert the overwhelming power of nature with a handful of shovels? And yet, no one wanted to give up. Marsaili least of all.

Onlookers stood in silhouette all along the clifftop looking down on the carnage below. The two police officers who had arrived to secure the scene and cordon off the car park had abandoned their duties to lend weight to a small group attempting to refloat one of the biggest whales close to the edge of the wash. Trouser legs rolled up, they were knee-deep in the water, uniforms soaked through as they tried desperately to get the creature back out into the bay. Marsaili was one of those who had spent nearly an hour digging away the sand to allow for that possibility. And she stood back exhausted now as a small cheer rose above the sound of the wind. The whale had been lifted suddenly by a tidal surge and drawn back out into the bay. A sprinkling of applause came from onlookers on the cliff. Marsaili held her breath as the beast flapped its tail fin and exhaled loudly through its blowhole, before inexplicably turning to let itself be carried on the edge of an incoming wave that washed it straight back on to the beach.

The dismay among those who had worked so hard to refloat it was palpable.

Marsaili felt a touch on her arm and turned to find the coastguard at her side. He looked on grimly at the freshly re-beached whale and sighed his despair. Pàdraig had been at school with Marsaili and Fin and Artair. He said, 'I heard it was you that found them, Marsaili.'

'It was. First thing this morning, Pàdraig. But Fin and I were on the beach last night, and I think we heard them then. Though we didn't know it. A strange kind of crackling noise, and what sounded like gulls calling from somewhere far out at sea.'

Pàdraig nodded. 'Aye, that would be what they call the echolocation. Clicks and whistles and pulses that they use to communicate with each other.'

Marsaili shook her head. 'What I can't understand is how so many of them came to be beached like this.'

'It's a whole family, Marsaili. Fifty plus whales. Males, females, juveniles. A pod is what they call it. A very bonded social group. If one of them is in trouble, they'll all pitch in to help.' He took her arm and started walking her along the beach. She saw Donna and Eilidh still working to keep a group of whales near the rocks hydrated. Pàdraig pointed back along the beach. 'You see the woman with the blue hat and the green jacket?'

Marsaili turned and saw her directing operations at another group attempting a refloat.

'She's the strandings coordinator for an organization called SMASS. The Scottish Marine Animal Stranding Scheme.' He chuckled. 'I think someone must have worked pretty hard to get that acronym to work.' His smile quickly faded. 'Anyway, they deal with events like this all the time. As luck would have it, she was on the island. Birdwatching, would you believe? So she was here pretty fast. She figures one of the females got into trouble giving birth. A prolapsed horn of its uterus. It tried for some reason to come ashore, and the rest followed her in. The whole family sacrificing itself for one of their own.'

Marsaili followed his eyeline as he glanced towards the onlookers on the cliffs. 'We've got quite an audience,' she said.

PETER MAY

He shook his head. 'We put out a radio alert, asking people not to come. But it's a double-edged sword, because it also alerted people to the fact that it was happening. The roads department have sent men to set up diversions on the road into the port so that emergency vehicles can get through.' He sighed. 'The SMASS truck is already on its way from Inverness.'

'What will they be able to do?'

'Nothing, Marsaili. Nearly forty of these poor things are dead already, and the ones who are still alive are probably not going to last long. So by the time SMASS get here, all they'll be doing is necropsies. Cutting them up, every single one of them, trying to figure out how this all happened.'

They passed one of the biggest of the whales, covered in wet sheets and lying on its side. Big cow eyes stared up at them, a silent plea for help. Its mouth lay partially open, revealing rows of tiny sharp teeth.

Marsaili said, 'Realistically, what are the chances of getting the live ones refloated?'

'Next to zero,' Pàdraig said. 'I've alerted the vet. He's on his way.'

She nodded, absorbing the significance of this, and depression settled on her like the fine spray blown in off the bay by the wind. 'Who is the vet these days?'

'Duncan Macgowan.'

She looked up sharply at Pàdraig, as if seeking confirmation that she had heard right, then felt the colour rise high on her cheeks.

He cocked his head to one side. 'You know him?'

And she turned her gaze out towards the Minch and the mist of rain that obscured the mainland. 'I used to,' she said.

Marsaili trudged back up the slope from the cliff edge, legs heavy with exertion and fatigue. If anything, the crowds lining the cliffs had grown. Looking to the north, she could see orange lights flashing on the road where council workers had erected a barrier, and were directing traffic up through Crobost. There were vehicles parked on the verge all the way up the hill, and a constant stream of cars on the road.

Her mood was low. Despite their best efforts, another whale had died, and they had failed to refloat even one.

Nearing the road, and realizing she now had a signal again, she checked her phone. But there was no word from Fin, and her despair extended once more to the slow disintegration of her own family.

Donna and Eilidh were still on the beach with the other volunteers. A reality check, Marsaili thought, for her grand-daughter. An encounter first-hand with death. Tragedy on an unimaginable scale. Life in the raw. If nothing else, she would learn just how tenuous a hold any of them had on it, and how easily it could be lost or squandered.

Marsaili had volunteered to return to the house to make flasks of tea and coffee for the helpers. She also needed a break. She had been out since dawn. Working in the wind and the wet, the cold penetrated your soul, and there were folk on the beach who would not be able to carry on for much longer. Marsaili was one of them. She promised to be no more than half an hour. Climbing wearily up the steps to the kitchen, she felt the residual warmth of the house as soon as she stepped inside. She immediately set a kettle going, and found a spare under the sink. Rinsed and filled, she plugged it in, before turning her attentions to the coffeemaker.

She decided then to strip off her wet clothes and change into something dry. She and Fin had come equipped only for a few days, having had no idea of how long they might stay, and she realized she was going to run out of clothes very quickly.

She caught sight of herself in the mirror and was, as always, disappointed by what she saw. Long gone was the slender young girl who had embarked at eighteen on the adventure of a lifetime. Student accommodation in Glasgow, the prospect of three, maybe four years of university. A whole lifetime ahead of her filled with limitless possibility. A young woman confident in her mind and her body. Indefatigable and, she knew now, filled with foolish optimism.

It occurred to her that she had been exactly the same age then as poor Caitlin. And, disappointed as she was in herself and the way her life had unravelled, she was at least still alive.

She quickly averted eyes from her own reflection, and they fell on the laptop sitting open on the dresser, a screensaver scrawling a never-ending pattern of changing colours across its monitor. On an impulse, she sat on the stool in front of it and swiped the trackpad. The screen cleared to reveal her browser searches on Niall Black, and she was reminded that she had found something yesterday that might interest Fin. She would try to remember to tell him.

But that wasn't the impulse that had drawn her to sit down in front of it.

At the age of eleven, she had started to keep a diary. Around the time that Fin jilted her for the qually dance. A prelude to teenage angst. But it had become a habit, and one that she continued to this day. About ten years ago, Fin had introduced her to a piece of OCR software that could recognize handwriting and convert it to digital text, and she had spent six months filling in empty hours by digitizing all her old diaries. She had already begun posting her entries on the laptop, and now she had a digital record of very nearly her whole life before then. Something her grandchildren might one day read, wondering at the sad life of the grey-haired old lady they had called Granny, who lay buried in the machair at Crobost cemetery.

The purpose of these diaries was, and always had been, a purging of emotions, and she had never felt any need to reread them, even during the process of digitization. But hearing Duncan Macgowan's name on the beach had brought back a long-buried memory, and she felt inexplicably drawn now to reread her diary account of it. A crossroads that might have taken her life in a very different direction.

CHAPTER TWENTY-FOUR

The entries were arranged by year, in separate folders, and by month within those. She scrolled down until she found the year that she and Fin had left for university, opened the folder and ran her cursor down the list of months to select November. Even just the simple act of opening it brought memories flooding back.

November 3rd

I don't know why I go to these parties. Fin always wants to go and we set off together, then we get there and he heads off on his own. More often than not I've had enough, and I'm ready to come back long before he wants to. So I make my way back home by myself. Like tonight. And he'll turn up later, and no doubt want to have sex.

It's not what I pictured. I thought coming to uni and sharing a room and a bed with Fin, spending every day, every night with him, was all I wanted. Now I don't know.

He spent all night, tonight, with a blonde. She's in the drama department, dressed like she was ready for the Moulin Rouge. He was getting her drinks, laughing too hard at her jokes. He knew I could see them.

Did he want to hurt me?

What does he want?

Or did he even think about me at all? He was so focused on giving her all of his island charm.

Speaking of which, I actually got chatted up myself tonight. Duncan Macgowan. He asked me out once when we were in 3rd year at the Nicolson. He always seemed a bit too . . . 'nice'. So I turned him down. He appeared out of nowhere at the party, suddenly at my elbow, and introduced himself like I wouldn't remember who he was. I pretended to 'vaguely recall' him, but I knew fine. He's still 'nice'. In fact, pretty good-looking now that he's grown up a bit. Maybe a bit old-fashioned. His jeans had a crease in them. How is that even possible? He's at the vet school – so part of the uni. I'm amazed our paths haven't crossed before now. First thing he did was notice I didn't have a drink and went and got me one. Like I said . . . nice! Why is it I never fall for the nice ones?

Over the music, I heard Fin speaking Gaelic to Miss Student Theatre Group. She'd no idea what he was saying. She was all wide-eyed wonder. I said to Duncan, 'You don't speak Gaelic, do you?' And he said his folks came from Inverness, and that he was ten when he came to Stornoway, so he never learned. I've heard it said that it's different to make love in Gaelic! I wouldn't know, cos that's what I speak. But I figured it was probably what Fin was telling that lassie right now.

I think Duncan could see what was going on. He asked if I

was still with Fin. I said yes, we were sharing a room in a flat in Highburgh Road. And that's when he took out a wee notebook, with a fiddly wee pen in its spine. He wrote something on a page and tore it out. 'Here,' he said. 'If ever you need it. There's a spare room in the flat where I'm staying. The others are all vets of course.' And he laughed. 'But nobody's perfect!'

I said, 'Thanks. I'm happy where I am.'

He said, 'Are you?'

And there was something in his voice. Something in that moment. Something in the way he looked at me. He slipped the wee page out of the notebook into my hand and folded my fingers over it. And held my hand closed around it. It felt a bit awkward. That's when I decided it was time to leave.

And Duncan, the perfect gentleman, helped me find my coat among the pile in the bedroom, and offered to walk me back home. Like I said, nice guy. Too nice for me. I thanked him for the offer and left.

Marsaili scrolled through the diary to find what she knew was the awful denouement to this.

November 16th

I'm on the train to Inverness. I'm done with Glasgow. I'm done with Fin. I'm done with uni. I'm done with pretending this is what I wanted. I don't want it. I'm sick of it all. I feel physically sick. Although that might have more to do with the couple of bottles of wine and God knows how many joints I got through last night.

Oh, my God!

Where do I even start?

That flat in Highburgh Road. Art nouveau stained glass, high ceilings, huge rooms. It seemed magical, pure class, when Fin and I first moved in. Who knew it would play host to cheap sex and tawdry betrayals. But maybe if you throw eight random teenagers together in four bedrooms, side by side, all those hormones are going to stir something up.

That Anita. The one with the legs. She's been throwing herself at Fin since the start of term. I couldn't even bear to be in the same room as her. I knew she was trouble.

Oh, that's it. The train's moving. We're leaving. It's still dark out there. The carriage only has a few other passengers.

So . . . that's definitely it. It's done now. I'll never be back.

What happened?

Well, the snow was beginning to fall. It was dark already. And freezing cold. I got back to the flat after a tutorial on Paradise Lost, *looking forward to a cup of instant hot chocolate. Anyway, the hall was gloomy, and the door to Anita's room was lying half open. I went to our room and opened the door, and even in the half-light, before I could see anything, the sounds of voices and movement sent a chill through me.*

The two of them were there. Fin and that Anita, having sex in our bed. He was whispering to her in Gaelic. She didn't understand a word of it, of course. Stupid stuff, full of fake emotion. I think that's what hurt more than anything, because he stopped speaking Gaelic to me weeks ago, as if he's embarrassed by it.

But there he was. With her. And her long legs and silky blond hair. Making love to her in our language. The one thing we shared that I thought made us special.

He saw me before she did. He seemed shocked that he'd been caught.

She didn't even hear me come in. She's going, 'What is it, Fin, what's wrong?' And then she saw me.

I just said, 'Why don't you pick up your clothes and get out.' I thought for a minute she wasn't going to.

She just froze and looked at Fin. Fin looked sheepish. He nodded towards the door. I don't think she was impressed. She threw back the covers, gathered up her stuff and flounced out. She was so proud of herself in all her nakedness. I think she wanted to show off how much more sophisticated than me she was.

And if she wanted to make me feel inadequate, well, she succeeded.

I heard her door slamming on the other side of the hall.

I closed the door to our room very gently.

I didn't have the energy for anger. I had no desire to scream or shout. Fighting would have made it seem like you had something to fight for. And if you want to fight for something, then it would have to be worth it.

Maybe you do prepare yourself for the worst. Maybe I did see this coming. I really didn't have to think about what to do next. I got my suitcase, and started filling it. I left all the books and papers and folders. Why would I need those? I packed my clothes and personal stuff.

Fin watched me in silence. I don't know how much dope he had smoked or beer he had drunk. His eyes were dilated. He tried to focus on me and asked, 'Where are you going?'

'Home,' I said.

Even in his stupor he knew I couldn't go straight to the island. He asked where I was going to stay the night.

I had absolutely no idea. I just told him it wasn't any of his concern. All I knew was, I had to get out of there.

He was shivering, naked, sitting on the edge of the bed watching me pack my stuff. He made one pathetic attempt to speak. 'Marsaili—'

I cut him off abruptly. 'Don't, Fin!' Then more softly, 'Just don't.' I didn't want to hear it. We'd gone way beyond the point where it was something we could talk about.

I got my case and wheeled it out of the room. Out of the flat. I didn't look back. Just shut the door. And knew I was shutting it on almost the whole of my life up until then.

Maybe that's what he wanted all along. Rid of me. And didn't know how to do it? Didn't have the courage to tell me it was over? Well, it's over now.

He didn't exactly fight to stop me from leaving. I could feel his eyes on me as I walked down the road. Watching me from the window. But I didn't look to check. I just walked as confidently as I could towards the traffic lights at Byres Road. I'm done with him. I'm done with all of it.

Thing is, you make the grand gesture, then you get to live with the consequences.

I turned the corner and it wasn't till I found myself outside the Iceland supermarket, beside the entrance to the subway, that I stopped to think about where the hell I was going.

I couldn't get the train to Inverness till the morning. I couldn't afford a hotel. The snow was falling. And that's when I stuffed my hands in my pockets and found that wee bit of paper that Duncan had folded my fingers around. Do things happen for a reason? Is there such a thing as fate?

Duncan Macgowan. And his phone number. And his spare room.

Such a nice boy. Surely he would come to the aid of a girl in trouble.

I certainly must have looked like someone in trouble when he opened the door to me. Bedraggled. Wet snow melting in my hair, dripping from my coat on to his 'welcome' mat. He just stood and stared at me in shock.

So I had to take the initiative and suggested, 'Can I come in?'

And he jumped back, opening the door wide. 'Of course, of course. Here, let me take your case.'

I walked into the hall. There were four doors leading off it. 'So, you've still got that spare room?'

'Ah . . .' He pulled a face.

And I knew there was no spare room.

'I've got a spare bed,' he said. 'There's an extra bed settee in my room.'

To be honest, at that point I was past caring. I just wanted somewhere that wasn't in the cold and wet, where I could hunker down till I could get a train out of there. 'Fine,' I said. 'Lead me to it.'

He took me into a big room with a gas fire burning. Pictures of what I assumed were his family stood in frames on the mantelpiece.

The fire made the room stuffy, and there was a vague hint of feet and dirty laundry lingering in the air. Unwashed clothes overflowed from a basket in the corner. But there he stood in his pressed jeans and open-necked shirt with the flap over the breast pocket, all neatly ironed. Someone your mum would approve of. Someone you could feel safe with. He looked at me with such concern in his eyes. When he asked me what had happened, I just fell apart.

Floods of tears.

The poor guy didn't know what to do. He took my wet coat off and walked me over to the settee. He hung my coat up to dry. And said, 'You could do with a glass of something.' He disappeared off to the kitchen and came back with a bottle of wine and a couple of glasses.

He said, 'No pressure, if you don't want to talk about it . . .'

But I did want to talk. I've not really faced up to any of this. Something about Duncan not being directly involved made it easier for me to admit the truth.

I told him about Fin and Anita.

I told him I was going back to the island.

Of course he didn't think I should give up uni, my education, my future, just because a relationship had gone wrong. But when I talked it all through with him, I couldn't help feeling the whole uni thing had been a mistake.

Coming to Glasgow has been nothing like I expected. I only applied for uni to be with Fin. I thought it would cement our relationship.

But everything changed during the summer on An Sgeir during the guga hunt. Artair's dad dying and Fin being injured was just a part of it. Fin changed. He never really recovered. It's like he's not the person I fell in love with. But you can't abandon someone when they've been through terrible stuff. I felt I had an obligation to stand by him and see him through it.

Duncan said, 'There's only so much abuse a person can take.'

And I thought, really? Am I one of those women that gets abused and just comes back for more? What kind of idiot am I? And I felt exhausted by it all. I don't know if it was because I had finally let it all out and expressed my frustration, and admitted how unhappy I've been. I don't know if it was the wine, which had slipped down all too easily while I was telling him my story. But when Duncan put his arm round me, it felt awfully good to bury my head in his shoulder and feel the comfort and warmth of his support.

He held me like that for a while. Then he broke away and leaned forward to pick up a Golden Virginia tobacco tin from the coffee table. I was surprised, when he opened it, to see it contained half a dozen very neatly rolled joints.

Duncan was not as strait-laced as I thought. He told me to trust him, he was a doctor – nearly – and he recommended these for stress.

So we drank. And smoked. And relaxed.

He talked. He told me all about himself. About arriving in Stornoway and being appalled by all the restrictions of the Lewis Sabbath. His dad had come to run the veterinary practice. And Duncan had always known he wanted to be a vet, too. He seems to love vet school. Apparently Glasgow has some of the best professors around. Eccentric geniuses, he called them. World leaders in their fields. It was energizing to see his enthusiasm.

Being with Fin just seemed to suck the energy out of me.

Duncan was embracing life. He knows what he's doing. He knows where he's going.

Fin's drowning and I'm in danger of going down with him.

Duncan held me close to him and said that he'd always wanted to get to know me. I told him he'd only be disappointed if he did. He laughed. He didn't know I was being serious.

'You were always at the centre of the fun,' he said. 'You knew how to enjoy life! You were in the in-crowd. You and Donald, and Fin. I was on the outside. You would never have been interested in me.'

'Maybe I would have been interested if I'd got a chance to get to know you,' I told him. And I meant it.

'Well, you've got a chance, now,' he said.

And we started kissing.

To be honest, with the wine, and what we smoked, the rest is a bit of a blur.

I woke up early this morning, just after 6 a.m., with a mouth as dry as sandpaper. Feeling decidedly nauseous. Duncan lying wrapped in a tangle of sheets next to me. Both of us naked.

There was a discarded condom on the floor next to the bed. At least we'd had that much sense.

I gathered up my clothes and put them on. I felt terrible when I looked at Duncan lying sleeping. Did I really just use him to get back at Fin because of Anita? I know I don't have any future with him. He's such a lovely guy. But way too nice for me.

I leaned over and kissed him softly on the forehead. He was dead to the world and didn't wake up, thank goodness.

I got my coat and my case and got out of there.

So here I am now on the train. The sky is leaden. The snow's falling on this frozen city as we leave it. And I'm going back to the island.

Marsaili sat reading with a sense of guilt and shame. Anger as well. At Fin, and how he had treated her. Though she knew now, why. She had made that long trip home, and fallen straight into the arms of Artair. And the die of her life to come had been cast.

She had never seen nor heard from Duncan again. Not even really thought about him. Until now, and the mention of his name by Pàdraig. She supposed that an encounter with him down on the beach, among the dead and dying whales, was unavoidable. And she wondered how she would be with him, how her life might have turned out had she not left him sleeping in the dark that cold November morning so long ago.

CHAPTER TWENTY-FIVE

The house at Tobson was almost lost in the smirr, standing full-square on the clifftop, stubbornly facing down the cloud that drove in from the west. A stark contrast with the fine weather that had bathed it in sunlight just two days earlier. Tears of rain wept down its floor-to-ceiling windows in mourning for a summer that already felt long gone.

The unexpected warmth with which Ailsa received him left Fin feeling slightly uncomfortable. Their first encounter two days earlier had begun, initially, somewhere in the deep freeze. Before loneliness and grief, and perhaps doubt about Fionnlagh's guilt, had led to a slight thawing of the ice. Now she seemed almost pleased to see him, and he noticed how she unconsciously adjusted her hair in the reflections she cast in those huge sliding glass doors.

Bella danced excitedly around him, barking, as Ailsa led him into the living room. Oscar, anxious to join the fun, warned them to *mind the gap*. A reminder that Caitlin was only a few days gone.

Fin noticed the half-full glass of red wine on the coffee

table. Or was it half-empty? Early in the day, he thought, to be drinking. She was dressed in the same jeans and man's baggy shirt that she had worn the other day. Or perhaps, like Steve Jobs, she had a wardrobe full of both. Though somehow he doubted it.

'Can I get you something?' she said.

'No thanks, Ailsa.'

'Well, sit down.'

He dropped into the reclining armchair he had occupied during his previous visit, and she folded her legs beneath herself on the settee and reached for her wine.

'I'm just drowning my sorrows. Lost child, lost summer, lost everything.' Her smile was brittle and self-pitying.

Fin made no judgement. He knew what it was to lose a child.

'So have you found my daughter's killer yet, or do you think Fionnlagh did it after all? I hear they've charged him.'

He kept his voice level and calm. 'Ailsa, why didn't you tell me that Caitlin wasn't Niall's daughter?'

If he had slapped her face, she could hardly have been more startled. But her surprise grew immediately defensive. 'Who told you that?'

'You must have known that Caitlin knew, Ailsa. She told Iseabail.'

The defiance that flared briefly subsided just as quickly, and there was a sense that her whole body had just sunk deeper into the cushions of the settee, as if she were trying to make some kind of escape from the moment. She took a long

273

drink of her wine, gazing through the rain-streaked windows as though composing a considered response. In the end, she failed to find inspiration in a view obscured by the weather. Fuaigh Mòr, Bhàcasaigh and Pabaigh Mòr were pale shadows in a mist of sea spray and rain. The beach at Reef and the distant mountains of Uig and Harris had vanished as completely as if they never existed. 'I spent a lifetime trying to make sure she never found out.' Ailsa's voice was hushed, as though she were still trying to keep the secret.

'Are you going to tell me about it?'

She looked at him. 'I suppose it'll become common knowledge.'

Fin shrugged. 'Not necessarily. Not if it has no bearing on her murder.'

Her face was flushed now, and she was taking deep breaths to retain her calm. 'Have you any idea what it is to be lonely, Fin? I mean really lonely?'

Fin took the question to be rhetorical and made no attempt to respond. He did not want to interrupt her flow before it had even begun.

'When the person you love – supposedly – and who's supposed to love you is never there. Not just for a day, or two. Or a couple of weeks. Even a couple of months. But months on end. And you're left to raise a young boy on your own, a kid who wonders why his daddy is never around.' She drained her glass and stood to cross to the kitchen island, where she refilled it from an open bottle. 'Children are no company. Not like dogs. Children demand your attention every waking minute of every day, and, when there's no one to share the load, you find yourself just counting the hours until it's bedtime. And then you sit on your own with a bottle of wine, staring at your reflection in the windows of the house that Niall built, but didn't want to live in. Apparently. Or maybe it was me he didn't want to live *with*.'

She came back to the settee, a full glass in her hand, and dropped heavily into the seat. Wine splashed over the rim of it and on to the legs of her jeans, but she appeared not to notice.

'You spend all those hours looking at your own reflection, physically, metaphorically. You pick out all your faults, and end up hating yourself.' She sipped pensively from her glass, and Fin saw that it wasn't the view that drew her eyes, but the reflection of herself that she had spent all those years watching in the glass. 'The thing that came out of it all was the bond between me and Eòghann. I was mum *and* dad. His whole world through all his formative years.' Her tiny laugh was laced with bitterness. 'But while for Eòghann I was maybe an acceptable substitute for Niall, Eòghann could never be that for me.' She turned eyes towards Fin that appealed for understanding. 'I had needs, Fin.'

'So who was it that fulfilled those needs, Ailsa?'

She shook her head slowly and her smile was scornful. 'You don't really want to hear my story, do you?'

Bella had settled herself, as before, at Fin's feet, and he leaned forward to ruffle the ears of the red setter. When he looked at Ailsa, he thought how she appeared to have aged, even just in the last two days. 'I do, Ailsa, really. And I'm guessing it would probably do you good, too, to get it off your chest.'

She smiled. 'Oh, you're smooth, Fin. You always were.' She sipped her wine and stretched back in her seat, as if releasing the constraints that had held her story locked inside for all of this time. 'I was teaching Gaelic at the Nicolson. Part time, because Eòghann was still at primary school, and I needed to be there for him when he got home. And this new English teacher arrived.' She half smiled, remembering. 'A guy I'd known from school. He'd always been sniffing around me back then. Like a dog. But I'd never been interested.' The look she gave him was so direct he almost felt the need to look away. But forced himself to maintain eye contact.

She drank more wine and drew breath to continue her tale.

'So anyway, here's this same guy. Ten years on. Single. Still interested. And I am so lonely. My confidence shot to pieces. You've no idea how good it makes you feel that someone thinks you're still worth the trouble.' She drifted off in a dwam, an escape into private recollection. 'But it wasn't until I met him at a party in town one night that it all began. I was a bit the worse for wear and he offered to drive me home.' She smiled. 'And that's a long drive, as you well know.'

She finished her glass and returned it to the coffee table, standing then to wander across to the window. She was too close now to see her reflection and the view beyond was still obscured by the weather. She was, instead, it seemed to Fin, lost in a world of memories she had never shared, wondering how on earth to convey them to this stranger who had once been her obsession, and whose son was accused of murdering her daughter.

'It was a Friday night. Eòghann was sleeping over at a friend's house. So we had the place to ourselves. I asked him in. Offered him coffee, but he wanted something stronger. So I joined him. And we talked and drank, and drank and talked. Then there was no way he could drive home, and . . .' she half turned towards Fin without looking at him, 'I'm sure you can guess what happened next. I made certain he was gone early the next day, before Eòghann got back.'

Fin said, 'How long did it last?'

'Oh, not long. There was no future in it, you see. Then, when I got pregnant, I knew I had to put an end to it. And a few months after that, Caitlin arrived on the scene.'

'And Niall found out?'

'Not immediately, no. Though I figure he always had his suspicions.' She turned away finally from the window. 'He was too busy making his millions to lose sleep over it. It wasn't until Caitlin was about four that it all blew up. We had a fight. Nothing unusual about that. All we ever did was fight when he was home. I don't even remember now what it was about. And I suppose I had probably been drinking. Anyway, I kind of threw it at him. Something to hurt him with. God knows, he was the one with all the hurting things in his locker. There was only one in mine. And I could have bitten my tongue out the moment I used it. Because that was it. The end of everything. Niall's nothing if not a proud man. Maybe he could deal with the suspicion, but he couldn't live with the knowledge.'

She returned to the coffee table to recover her glass and headed for the nearly empty bottle on the counter.

'He moved out that night. In some ways, I think he had probably always been looking for an excuse. And I just handed it to him on a plate. He filed for divorce within the week. And, shit, it was going to get messy.' The last of the wine filled her glass, and she turned to face the room, leaning back against the kitchen island. Fin swivelled in his chair to look at her. 'He fights dirty, does our Niall. Held a big financial stick over me. After all, I had nothing. And he threatened to make my infidelity public if I didn't play ball.' She shrugged. 'Though I have to admit, he made a generous offer.' She waved her free hand around the room. 'The house and everything in it. A monthly allowance amounting to more than most people make in a year.' She paused. 'But there was a catch.'

Fin said, 'Let me guess. He wanted custody of Eòghann.'

Ailsa stared into her glass, holding it in both hands now. 'He didn't care about Caitlin. Why should he? She wasn't his, and they had never bonded. But he wanted that boy. He knew – God he knew – how close we were. Me and Eòghann. I had brought him up like a single mother, Fin. And he barely knew his father. But those were Niall's terms. Accept, and Caitlin and I would live out the rest of our lives in comfort, without any financial worries. He would set up a trust fund to pay for her education, and beyond. Security for Caitlin in exchange for losing Eòghann.' She looked up now and Fin saw silent tears glistening on her cheeks. 'Asking me to play God with the lives of our children. I knew that to accept would secure the future for them both. But if I fought it, there was a good chance I would lose Eòghann anyway, along with the house and any financial security for Caitlin. What do they say about rocks and hard places?'

She pushed herself away from the island and wandered back across the room. Fin had the sense that she was no longer talking to him, but to herself, replaying a two-way dilemma in which neither choice had been acceptable.

'In the end I chose the security of my children above everything else.'

As well as her own security, Fin thought uncharitably, and immediately regretted it.

'Biggest mistake I ever made, Fin. But that's Niall for you. Always boxing you into a corner, forcing you to make decisions that in the end benefit only him.' Her hand was trembling as she drank from her glass. 'Caitlin was my daughter, yes. But Eòghann was my boy. And there was no way that Caitlin could ever substitute for that.' Tears that had begun as a trickle flowed freely now. 'The look of betrayal on his face when we told him. That'll live with me, Fin, till my dying day.'

She finished her glass and set it down on the coffee table so hard Fin thought it would break. She slumped down on to the edge of the settee and dropped her face into her hands. Silent sobs racked her body. Fin could think of nothing to say, and was loath to offer comfort that might be misconstrued. So he sat and waited in a room filled with tension and sadness. Until finally she drew a long breath, wiping the tears from her face, and looked up at him, attempting a grotesque parody of a smile. 'Sorry,' she said.

Outside, on the loch, a sudden break in the clouds sent shafts of sunshine, like spotlights, playing around the surface of the water, and the whole world lit up. For the first time that morning, the islands stood in sharp relief against the beach beyond, and a strong double rainbow spanned and framed the distant mountains.

Ailsa said, 'That's God trying to cheer me up. Tested me and I failed. Took away my children. But rainbows are a poor substitute.'

Fin saw Bella staring up at him, wide-eyed, as if prompting him to ask the question he had held back until her story was told. He said, 'Who was Caitlin's father, Ailsa?'

The look she gave him suggested that the answer would only leave him disappointed in her. She shook her head, perhaps disappointed in herself. 'Alasdair Fraser.'

'Ally Ruadh?' Fin could scarcely believe it. The freckle-faced red-haired boy who had been with them at the cages the night that Iain drowned. The boy that no one trusted. At least it explained the rich red in Caitlin's mane of chestnut hair.

'I know.' Ailsa's smile was pained and rueful. 'What was I thinking?'

Fin shook his head. 'I haven't seen Alasdair since before university. He didn't come to Glasgow.'

'No, he went to Aberdeen.'

'Is he still teaching at the Nicolson?'

'No, Fin. After I broke it off with him, he went to teach at a school in Edinburgh. He met someone there and got married. Then . . .' she shook her head in disbelief, 'the next thing I heard, he'd started training part time at the Edinburgh Theological Seminary on the Mound.'

'Alasdair?' Fin could not keep the incredulity out of his voice.

It made her smile. 'I know. But it gets worse. He quit teaching to train as a minister.'

'Well, where is he now?'

'So you haven't heard, then,' she said.

'Heard what?'

'He came back to the island to fill the vacancy as minister of the Free Church at Crobost after the death of Donald Murray.'

It had stopped raining, clouds shredded by the wind shedding light in shifting patches all around the island. Ailsa and Fin stepped from the back door of the house out into the court-yard. The wind had a cold edge to it, and Ailsa folded her arms in a vain attempt to conserve some of her body warmth. Bella pranced around them as they walked to Fin's car. Fin stood with the door open, feeling the wind drag his curls back from a hairline that had begun to recede more than just a little in the last years.

Ailsa said, 'You never answered my question, Fin.'

'What question was that?'

'Do you still think Fionnlagh didn't do it?'

He took a moment to consider his response. 'It's something I have to believe, Ailsa. Until someone else can prove me wrong.'

'I suppose if I was you, I'd have to believe it, too.'

Fin was about to get into the car, but paused. 'Ailsa, how did Caitlin find out that Niall wasn't her father?'

She exhaled her frustration. 'Stupid, really. My fault. When I broke it off with Alasdair, I didn't have the courage to face him with it, even though I saw him every day at school. So I sent him an email. It sparked off a whole exchange. He tried to change my mind. Persuade me to leave Niall. Said he would take care of Eòghann as his own.' Ailsa scoffed. 'As if Niall would ever have let that happen. Not that I could ever have contemplated a life with Alasdair anyway. It was just a thing, you know. He provided something I needed in the moment. But it would never have lasted. They say if you make your bed, you have to lie in it. Alasdair is not a bed I would ever have made, Fin.'

'And Caitlin found the emails?'

'I don't know why I kept them. Maybe to remind me that there was at least one man in this world who wanted me. I saved them into a folder that I stupidly called Alasdair. And, you know, with the cloud and everything, nothing is ever lost any more, unless you choose to lose it.'

She gazed off across the water and Fin saw that she was shivering now with the cold.

'Caitlin was using my computer a few months back. She must have gone exploring. Anyway, she came upon the Alasdair folder. I guess it came as a helluva shock to her to read those mails. Though she was cool when she confronted me about them. Wanted to know if Alasdair Fraser really was her father.' Ailsa shrugged. 'I could hardly deny it. The evidence was there in black and white. Like those politicians with their incriminating WhatsApp messages, I should have deleted it all years ago. But I didn't. And boy, did I pay the price.'

Perhaps, Fin thought, Caitlin did, too. And he reflected on Ailsa's almost endless capacity for self-destruction.

CHAPTER TWENTY-SIX

I.

You could tell the males from the females. At around six and a half metres in length, the males were a good metre longer than the females, Pàdraig had told Marsaili. There were more females in the pod, but even so, the presence of so many whales on the beach made it feel crowded, the sheer size of them dwarfing their setting.

There was one final attempt under way to try to refloat one of the surviving males, which was less than a yard from the water. Groups of volunteers had taken it in turns to dig away the sand, allowing the brisk tidal surge of the Minch to flow in and around the stranded creature.

There were fewer volunteers now, as one by one the cold and the sheer energy-sapping effort of it all had forced them to give up, and there were perhaps only a dozen of them trying to move the creature. Pàdraig was shoulder to shoulder with Marsaili as they leaned into the solid black of the whale's flank.

But try as they might, there simply wasn't enough incoming water to lift the weight of the beast free of the sand.

Pàdraig stood back, shaking his head despondently. 'We'll never do it,' he said. 'At least, not until the tide comes further in, by which time it'll likely be too late. This thing probably weighs about two and a half tons. All that weight bearing down on it, crushing the internal organs.'

Marsaili could have wept. When she had first found them on the beach this morning, she'd believed that somehow, some way, they would get the live ones back in the water. But they had failed spectacularly. Almost as if the whales themselves wanted to die here on this remotest of beaches on the edge of Europe, the few that remained sacrificing themselves for family members already gone.

One big sad eye looked up at her, as if it were somehow her fault that they were all dying.

She caught sight of the spectators lining the cliffs. Many more of them now than there had been earlier. Like crowds at a bullfight, she thought, or the rabble that cheered the glad-iator as he entered the ring to kill the lion. Eager consumers of the spectacle of death. And she wanted to shout at them. To ask if they were satisfied. But, of course, they weren't cheering, or satisfied. They stood silent and sobered by the sight of so many deaths on a beach they knew well.

'Hello, Marsaili.'

She turned, startled, at the sound of the voice. A voice that even after all these years still carried familiarity. Like a good wine, Duncan had aged well. A tall, handsome man in his fifties, steel-grey hair swept back from a lined brow. That same brown-eyed gaze framed now by a tanned face that had seen things, learned things, the wisdom of experience etched in all the fine lines around his mouth and eyes. He wore jeans, unpressed, and wellingtons, and a green parka jacket. Her hand went involuntarily to her hair, sweeping it back from her face.

She remembered lying with him naked on a cold, snowy night in Glasgow. Skin on skin. And how she had left early without waking him. Her stomach flipped over. 'Hello, Duncan.'

'It's been a while,' he said.

'It has,' she agreed.

He smiled. 'And you never said goodbye.'

II.

As Fin approached the port, he saw the roadblock and the orange flashing lights, and followed diversion signs that took him round past the cemetery. Beyond the gravestones that bristled on the slope of the machair, he saw the Atlantic breaking white all along the shore, and on a whim pulled into the visitors' car park. Sand, like snow, had blown in drifts to pile up around the edges of the asphalt. He felt the icy blast of the wind as he stepped from the car to unlatch the gate. And the machair, softened now by the rain, was spongy underfoot.

It was a long time since he had been here. The older he got, the more aware he became of his own mortality, and the final journey that would lead him, in all probability, to this same place where his parents, and grandfather, and aunt were laid to rest before him. Donald, too. And Artair. And Mr Macinnes.

And Iain. At only eighteen. A future lifetime squandered by the folly of teenage stupidity.

He found Iain's grave quickly enough and tried to recall some moment, some happy memory that might define him. And all he could think of was that fleeting glimpse, by the light of a streetlamp, of his bright-eyed wonder at Fin and Artair hearing a corncrake in the middle of the night. Something he never got to hear for himself. And here his teenage bones had lain in the ground for more than thirty years, while for Fin and the others, life had gone on into middle age.

On the brow of the hill, his parents were laid side by side. John Macleod, loving husband of Eilidh, father of Fionnlagh. His parents' car had left the road, apparently turning over several times before bursting into flames. But what shocked him most was how young they had been. Both still in their thirties. Fin had outlived them by more than fifteen years.

He crouched down and kissed the top of his mother's headstone, and laid a hand on the cold stone they had placed over his father. He thought of how they would have done anything for him. Made any sacrifice. And he wondered if they would have been proud or disappointed by the life he had lived.

When he got stiffly once more to his feet, he walked the half-dozen paces to the grave of his mother's sister. The aunt who had raised him in that cheerless house, a duty she had borne, not for him, he supposed, but for her sister. A familial obligation. And so he moved on.

It was spitting rain by the time he got back to the car, and he looped around to cut across the main Stornoway road and climb the hill towards Crobost. Cars were parked the whole way along the left side of the road, making it almost impossible for two oncoming vehicles to pass. He could see crowds still lining the top of the cliffs, but his view of the beach itself was obscured. Whatever had happened down there in the course of the last few hours was still unravelling.

Fin turned off and crossed the cattle grid into the car park of Crobost Church. It was very nearly full, though none of those who had parked here had come to worship. He found himself one of the last remaining spaces and walked back through the pedestrian gate, across the road and down over the machair to join the watching crowds.

The scene on the beach below was extraordinary. Golden sands littered with the blue-black and grey carcasses of more whales than he could count at a glance. Moving among them, still, were volunteers in waterproofs, tipping buckets of seawater over blankets and towels laid like ill-fitting shrouds across the few surviving members of the pod.

He ran his eyes over the figures in the sand, looking for Marsaili. And found her, finally, walking side by side with a tall man in a green parka, deep in conversation. Fin strained to focus on the man's face through the rain. There was something familiar about him. But he couldn't come up with a name. Until suddenly it dawned. Duncan Macgowan. He had been in Fin's biology class at the Nicolson. Came top in all of his science and maths subjects. A prefect with silver piping on his blazer. Old-fashioned, self-righteous, conservative, dull. Marsaili told Fin that he had asked her out once, and then teased him by saying she was still thinking about it.

A sudden image came back to him. Of Marsaili and Duncan sitting together on a settee at some party in Glasgow, drinking beer and laughing. He had recognized him then, in spite of the drink and the dope and the bad lighting. Fin had been chatting up a girl he'd met earlier, but still it had annoyed him to see Marsaili with someone else, and he'd found himself all evening stealing glances at the two of them across the room.

For some inconceivable reason, that same green-eyed monster came sneaking up again now to catch him completely off-guard. He watched Marsaili put a hand on Duncan's arm, and there was such an easy intimacy in it that he found himself turning away to stride back up the hill to the road.

III.

Fin passed once again through the gate to the church car park and looked up at the dark, forbidding silhouette the church itself cast against the greyest of skies. Tall arched windows, unadorned by stained glass that might, God forbid, have lent some colour to dull lives. A bell tower reached for the heavens, flanked by two small turrets. No bells hung in it, or ever had. The peal of bells could be misconstrued. Something joyful that smacked, perhaps, of papism.

For Fin it was a place redolent of an unhappy childhood. Sundays spent squirming on hard wooden benches, the minister thundering from the pulpit, the unaccompanied choral chanting of psalms, led by the single wavering voice of a precentor, like some tribal incantation that reached back across generations of his ancestors. The memory of which still raised the hair on Fin's neck.

The manse sat proud on a hill to the left of the church and was reached by a flight of steps set into the hillside. It offered an unrivalled view across the north of the island, from the port to the lighthouse and beyond. From here, the weather God willed for the island could be seen coming, allowing time for the minister to compose an appropriate prayer. At one time, that minister had been his childhood friend, Donald Murray. And Donald's own father before him.

Now it was Alasdair Fraser. *Ally Ruadh*. A boy Fin had never trusted. A boy who, with the rest of them, had participated in the theft of salmon from the cages of Niall Dubh's father, and later pursued an adulterous relationship with Niall's wife, fathering an illegitimate child. The word *hypocrisy* played unspoken around Fin's lips, banished by guilt at the behaviour of his own son.

He climbed the steps to the manse with heavy legs, and a heavy heart. At the door he rang the bell and turned to look out across the view. The orange lights of the roadblock twinkled in the poor light of the early afternoon. The odd scrap of sunlight all too briefly lit up the waters of the Minch before being swallowed by fresh rolling waves of black cloud. The wind spat big fat raindrops in his face.

He turned as the door opened, and found himself confronted by a middle-aged woman wearing sensible black shoes and a grey woollen jumper over a Harris tweed skirt. She had a round, smooth-skinned face softened by the dyed brown curls of the perm that framed it. She smiled pleasantly. 'Hello. Can I help you?'

Fin nodded acknowledgement. 'I was hoping to see the Reverend Fraser.'

'He's writing tomorrow's sermon, Mr eh . . .? '

'Macleod. Fin Macleod.'

The mere speaking of his name cast a shadow on her smile. She became flustered. 'I, er, I don't usually like to disturb him.'

'It won't take long . . . Mrs Fraser, is it?'

'Yes.'

'I'm an old friend. We were at school together.'

Very reluctantly, she stood aside, holding the door open for him. 'You'd better come in.'

She showed him into the living room. 'I'll just let him know you're here.'

Fin stood uncomfortably and looked around. The last time he had been in this room, he and Donald finished a bottle of whisky between them, burying old animosities, rediscovering, at least in part, the friendship they had shared in childhood. For by then they also shared a granddaughter, and it was important to put differences aside in the interests of family.

Everything about the room had changed. The wallpaper, the carpet, the furniture. All physical traces of Donald erased along with his memory. Fin felt inestimably sad.

From somewhere deep in the house he could hear voices. Hers raised, slightly shrill. The softer tones of a calming male voice. There were no words discernible, but the timbre spoke of anxiety, and conflict.

Fin waited a long time before Alasdair's wife finally returned, colour high on her cheeks. 'He can give you a few minutes,' she said.

He followed her through a darkened hallway to a door that opened off it to the right, opposite the foot of the staircase. A brightly lit room with a window that looked out across the moor behind the village. Wooden bookcases lined the walls, the spines of countless books lending muted colour to an austere space where the word of God was interpreted for his parishioners by a self-righteous incumbent.

Alasdair sat behind an enormous leather-tooled wooden desk littered with papers and a laptop computer, and a very large open copy of the Gaelic Bible. As Fin recalled, Alasdair's Gaelic had never been particularly good, and he thought that his sermons probably required a great deal of work. He spotted Malcolm Maclennan's etymological dictionary of the Gaelic language standing handily among the books on the shelf behind him.

Alasdair himself was almost unrecognizable. Most of his hair had gone, and the little that remained had lost its vibrant red, lying in wisps and whorls around a narrow, freckle-spattered head. Lines had formed in deep creases on either side of a mouth that was as mean and untrustworthy as it had been when they were teenagers.

He attempted a smile that never quite reached his pale green eyes, and made no attempt to stand or shake Fin's hand. 'Well,' he said. 'You haven't changed.' An echo of Niall's greeting.

Fin refrained from comment. 'It's been a while, Alasdair.'

'It has.' He waved a hand towards a vacant captain's chair on the other side of his desk. 'To what do I owe the pleasure?'

Fin lowered himself into the captain's chair and said, 'I'm not sure pleasure is how either of us might feel about this meeting.' And he saw the colour rise on Alasdair's cheeks, translucent skin betraying an increased blood flow to the face. 'You know my son has been charged with murder.'

Alasdair looked acutely uncomfortable. 'I had heard, yes.'

'Caitlin is the name of the victim. An eighteen-year-old lassie who lived down in Great Bernera. With her mother. Ailsa Black. You remember Ailsa, Alasdair? Used to be married to Niall.'

Alasdair's face set itself in stone, and he glared back at Fin with naked dislike.

'Until he found out that Caitlin wasn't his daughter. Did he ever confront you about that? Or maybe he never knew that you were the father.'

'What do you want, Fin?'

Fin leaned back in his chair and looked around the room. 'You know, never in a million years would I have put money on you succeeding Donald in this job. Never saw you as minister material, Alasdair. Though, to be fair, I could have said the same thing of Donald. Funny, isn't it, how a misspent youth so often leads to middle-aged piety. Why do you think that is, Alasdair? An attempt to get into God's good books again as passage to the next life approaches?'

'I don't think I like your tone, Fin.'

'Oh, my tone? You don't like my tone? I'm sorry about that. I thought we were friends. After all, you didn't seem to mind my company when we were stealing fish together down on Loch Roag.'

The colour on Alasdair's cheeks darkened.

'But I'm sure your God's a forgiving one, Alasdair. I mean, where's the harm in stealing a few salmon? They're all God's creatures, after all. Though I do seem to remember that thou shalt not steal was among the commandments that Moses brought down from Mount Sinai. You'll be familiar with those, of course.'

Alasdair stood up. 'I think you should go.'

Fin ignored him. 'Adultery. Now, that's altogether something different, wouldn't you say? Fucking your friend's wife.'

'For God's sake, Fin, keep your voice down.'

'For God's sake or yours, Alasdair?'

Alasdair sat down again, abruptly.

'Now, maybe you think you've made amends with your God, and a few more years of pious worship will wipe the slate clean, but I'm not quite so sure how forgiving your own congregation might be. Adulterer. Thief. Liar. Because, let's face it, you were as complicit in covering up Iain's death as any of us.'

Alasdair leaned his forearms on the desk in front of him and glowered up at Fin from beneath gathered brows. 'What do you want?'

Fin said, 'It wouldn't surprise me at all that a young girl would want to know who her real father was. Probably came as quite a shock to learn that she was illegitimate. But *she* had nothing to feel guilty about. Nothing to hide. After all, it was hardly her fault.' He paused. 'Did she contact you, Alasdair?' He could read Alasdair's thought processes as clearly as if they were printed on his forehead, and saw him arrive at the realization that there was no point in denying it.

'What if she did?'

'Did she come and see you? An encounter with the father she'd never known?'

Alasdair said nothing.

Fin pressed on. 'What did she want? Acknowledgement, perhaps? For the world to know who her real father was?'

'No!' Alasdair almost shouted his denial.

'Then tell me.'

Alasdair sat back, releasing a long, troubled sigh. 'She just wanted to meet me, that was all.'

'I'm figuring you didn't want her to come here.'

'We met on the beach at Dalbeg in the early spring. Before the tourists arrived.'

Fin knew the tiny beach well, almost entirely enclosed by rocks that ringed the bay. It could be reached only by a long drive down a single-track road. 'Frightened to be seen with her?'

'I was being discreet. For both our sakes.'

Fin let that one slide. 'And?'

'All she wanted to do was meet. Talk.' He seemed to be replaying the moment in his memory. 'It was . . .' he searched for the right word to describe the encounter, 'awkward.'

'I bet it was.'

Alasdair glared at him with an intense dislike. 'You've no cause to be so smug, Fin Macleod. After all, wasn't Fionnlagh sixteen or seventeen before you discovered that he was yours? And wasn't he having sexual relations with my girl, one of his own pupils?'

But Fin wasn't going to be diverted by his embarrassment. 'So what did you talk about? What did she say?'

'Not much. What was there *to* say? She was my biological daughter, yes. But she'd have been a different person if I'd brought her up.'

'You didn't hit it off, then?'

Alasdair interlocked his hands on the desk before him and gazed at them as if he might find inspiration in their white-knuckled clasp. 'I got the sense . . .' and he clearly found it difficult to say, 'that she was disappointed by me.'

'Well, there's a surprise.'

There was unadulterated hatred now in the green eyes that Alasdair turned on Fin.

'And maybe you thought that your reputation might be safer if she wasn't around any more. After all, you were already three commandments down. Why not a fourth?'

Alasdair stood up so suddenly that his chair spun away on its castors to crash into the bookcase behind him. All colour had left his face now. 'Get out!'

Fin stood up slowly and Alasdair stared at him with a malevolent intensity.

'You can't deflect from the sins of your son by accusing others of committing them.'

Fin said, 'I'd do anything to protect my boy, Alasdair. But only with the truth. I never knew Caitlin, but if she'd been my daughter, I'd have done everything in my power to protect her, too. It's a pity you didn't feel the same way.'

Outside on the top step, Fin paused to draw breath. If anything it was colder now. The rain had stopped, but he could see it still falling far out in the Minch. The wind filled out his waterproof jacket and flattened his trousers against his legs.

His encounter with Alasdair had left him depressed. A weak man, deceitful, self-serving. Hiding behind a religion Fin found it hard to believe he had truly embraced. And yet incapable, he thought, of killing his own daughter. What kind of monster would that have made him?

Poor Caitlin. The more he learned about her, the more tragic the life revealed by her death. Everyone had loved her, except the people she needed to. The man she had always believed to be her father, who wasn't interested; her real father, too scared of risking his reputation even to acknowledge her; the mother who thought her a poor substitute for her son; the friend who had persuaded her to swim out to the cages so she could ingratiate herself with Colm Hendry.

No matter how wrong Fionnlagh's relationship with Caitlin, perhaps his son was the only one who had really loved her.

He pulled up his collar and started down the steps. As he reached the car park, he heard the patter of footsteps on the stairs behind him, and turned to find Alasdair's wife hugging an unbuttoned coat around herself, the belt flapping in the wind. Something snatched quickly from the peg as she hurried out of the house after Fin.

She stood on the step above him, which placed their faces on the same level. Hers was bloodless and bleached, wet lips almost blue. 'Don't you dare come into my house accusing my husband of things your son has done.'

'Mrs Fraser—'

But she wasn't prepared to listen. 'I've always known about Caitlin. Alasdair told me when we first met. There have never been any secrets between us. Everyone makes mistakes, Mr Macleod. And those who regret them acknowledge them and try to atone.'

The stress of confronting Fin had made her breathless, and she took a moment to collect herself.

'Alasdair was devastated by Caitlin's death. Devastated! I found him in tears in his study the day the news broke. And destroying my Alasdair's reputation will do nothing to change the fact that it was your son that killed that girl. Why else would they have charged him?'

Fin stood in silence until she had finished her piece. She was halfway up the steps when he called after her. 'Mrs Fraser . . .'

She turned, tears wet on her face. 'What?'

He had been going to suggest she ask Alasdair about Iain Murray and what happened at the fish farm when they were all just eighteen. One secret, he was certain, that Alasdair would not have shared with her. But the thought stalled. After all, none of this was her fault.

Instead, he said, 'I'm sorry.' And turned away to cross the car park.

He slumped into the driver's seat and saw that his hands were shaking.

CHAPTER TWENTY-SEVEN

I.

Some time had passed since Marsaili persuaded Donna to take Eilidh back to the house. Both had spent hours trying to keep whales alive in deteriorating weather conditions. Both were close to hypothermia by the time they left the sand, and both in tears of frustration at their failure to save the animals.

Someone had been handing out silver and gold tinfoil rescue blankets, and many of the volunteers were wandering around with them wrapped around their shoulders, sipping on fresh coffee, gathering in disconsolate groups to share their disappointment.

Marsaili, with Duncan and several others, was endeavouring to right one of the few creatures left alive. It was half in the water, but resolutely refusing to move. Marsaili was numb with the cold, but determined to see it out to the end. An escape, perhaps, from the situation awaiting her at home, of grief and uncertainty, and a growing sense of apprehension.

The burgeoning fear, which she couldn't allow herself for one moment to admit, that Fionnlagh had, after all, murdered Caitlin.

'Can I help here?'

She and Duncan looked round to find Niall Dubh hovering next to the group gathered around the whale. He was swaddled in a thick waterproof jacket, stamping his feet and rubbing his hands briskly to keep warm.

'Niall?' Marsaili was taken aback. 'What are you doing here?'

Niall nodded towards the big white house on the cliffs above the harbour. 'Just got back from the fish farm,' he said. 'Thought I'd better lend a hand.'

He and Duncan exchanged nods and Marsaili glanced from one to the other. 'You know each other?'

Duncan said, 'Vets and fish farmers usually do.'

'What are we trying to do here?' Niall asked. 'Refloat it?'

But Duncan shook his head. 'Too late for that, Niall. Just trying to keep her blowhole out of the surf so she doesn't drown. Really, all we can do at this stage is try to make them all as comfortable as possible, making sure the pectoral fins are tucked underneath the body and not splayed out.'

Niall nodded. 'Because that would be excruciatingly painful.'

'You know about whales, then?' Marsaili was surprised.

Niall's smile was bleak. 'My degree was in aquaculture, Marsaili. I know that once one of these animals is stranded on the beach, it kicks off a cascade of pathology that'll kill it in the end, even if it is totally healthy when it comes ashore.' He cast his eyes along the length of the beach and shook his head. Then turned to Duncan. 'They're all going to die, aren't they?'

Duncan nodded. 'I'm afraid they are.'

Marsaili's despair lifted her voice above the wind. 'For God's sake, is there not *anything* we can do?'

Duncan said, 'Whales lose their ability to carry their body weight when they're not being supported by the water, Marsaili. So when they're left high and dry, certain things start to happen immediately. They begin crushing their tissue. So that, even if they are finally refloated, they'll have suffered the kind of injuries you see in humans who've been in road traffic accidents, where their legs get crushed by the car.'

Niall said, 'And you end up with a whole load of metabolic toxins being released into the body, essentially killing the person or the animal.'

'Reperfusion injuries,' Duncan said.

A final, collective heave half righted the whale, moving the blowhole well clear of the water. They all stood back, then, and Niall said, 'I'll see if I can lend a hand further along the beach.' He nodded and headed off along the sand. Marsaili and Duncan watched him go, sea spray and fine-grained sand whipped around his legs by the wind.

Marsaili stole a glance at the vet. He looked troubled, sad. She said, 'When did you come back to the island?'

'About ten years ago.' He cast a sad smile in her direction. 'You had already left. It didn't take me long to find that out.' His lips set in a hard line. 'And that you were back with Fin again.'

She felt the heat of the blood rising on her cheeks and quickly changed the subject. 'Where had you been all the years in between?'

He tilted his head back to gaze up at the sky. 'Where hadn't I been, Marsaili?' They started walking towards the far end of the beach, following in Niall's footsteps. 'I spent a few years in North Yorkshire. James Herriot country. You went into a barn at three in the morning and lit a lamp. No electricity. Stone floors, hissing Tilley lamps and the smell of burning paraffin.' He raised his nose slightly as if smelling it all again. 'And the heat off them.' He looked at Marsaili. 'It was something magical to be able to experience that.'

Marsaili could neither imagine it, nor understand what might be magical about it. But she saw that he was transported by the memory.

'I went out east after that. Indonesia. China. Before coming home.' He chuckled. 'When I was a student coming back to the island for the holidays, folk were still cutting hay by hand with a scythe. I can remember coming across the Minch on the ferry. It was the *Suilven* back then. And halfway across, with a westerly in your face, you could smell the peat smoke. And by the time you got to Stornoway, it was dead fish and diesel.' He turned towards her. 'That had all changed by the time I came back to take over the veterinary practice.'

They walked slowly in silence then, between the dead and dying whales, the wind whistling all around them.

'Married?' she asked.

He avoided her eye. 'Very happily. For the last twenty-five years.'

'And kids?'

'Two. Boy and a girl. Both grown up now.'

She saw him almost visibly retreat into some dark place in his thoughts.

'Sally's been taken by early-onset Alzheimer's.' He closed his eyes. 'Jesus, Marsaili, she's not even fifty. She was taken into care in Stornoway after I stopped being able to cope with her at home. I visit her most days, but she hasn't known who I am for a while now.'

They stopped and Marsaili took both of his hands in hers. 'Oh, Duncan, I'm so sorry. I do know what that's like. My father had dementia. He spent several years in a home in South Uist, cared for by someone who loved him, who'd known him all his life. He didn't know who I was, though.' She dropped her head a little. 'He died a couple of years back.'

When she lifted her head again, she saw that Duncan was gazing off towards the cliffs. She turned to see what he was looking at and saw Fin approaching across the sand. Almost as if they had burned her, she quickly dropped Duncan's hands, and wondered why she felt guilty.

Fin's face was set and grim as he reached them. He took Marsaili's elbow and kissed her cheek. 'How are things?'

'Not good, Fin. We couldn't get any of them refloated. Most of them are dead. Just a few still hanging on.'

Fin cast sad eyes around the beach.

Marsaili said, 'You remember Duncan? Duncan Macgowan? He was at the Nicolson at the same time as we were.'

Fin turned cold eyes on Duncan. 'Yes,' he said. 'I remember.'

'He's the vet now.'

Duncan thrust out a hand, and Fin felt obliged to take it. 'Good to see you again, Fin,' he said.

Fin looked at Marsaili and spread his arms. 'What happened here? How come so many of them beached at the same time?'

'Pàdraig said that one of them got into trouble giving birth, and the rest followed her in.'

'The pods are like extended families, Fin,' Duncan said. 'They hunt together, stay together their whole lives. Sometimes as many as a hundred of them. They're like packs. Loyalty is absolute.' He looked despondently about the beach. 'Even to the extent of sacrificing themselves like this when one of them gets into difficulty.' With a shake of his head, he said, 'There's an annual summer event in the Faroe Islands, where pods of pilot whales are enticed into a suitable bay. The Grind, they call it. Get one, and the rest follow like lambs to the slaughter. The Faroese wade out with big hooks that they slash into the whales. They drag them into shallow water, then cut their throats to let them bleed to death. The sea turns crimson with their blood.'

Marsaili said, 'That's awful! Why would they do that?'

'For food, they say.' Duncan shrugged. 'I've seen video of it. Looks more like bloodlust to me. They describe it as being like an outdoor slaughterhouse. The worst thing was watching children playing around the dead and bleeding carcasses. Jumping over them as if it was some kind of a game.'

Fin said, 'My grandfather used to hunt whales in the South Atlantic when he was young. Spent the rest of his life regretting it.'

Duncan nodded. 'There were quite a few men from Ness who used to go to the whaling back in the day. The fifties and sixties. When I came back to the island, there were one or two of them still alive. I used to go and ask their advice if we had a stranding. I mean, I understand the scientific physiology of these creatures quite well. But these guys understood it better, because they had hacked them up for a living.' He pursed his lips. 'They're all gone now.'

He released a long breath of resignation and glanced at his watch.

'I need to go and talk to the coastguard,' he said. 'It's approaching decision time, I'm afraid.'

He nodded and left them to weave his way among the whales, back towards the port. Fin watched him go, thoughtfully, then turned to find Marsaili watching him.

She said, 'Are we any nearer to resolving things with Fionnlagh?'

Fin lowered his head. 'Afraid not. I'm going to go back to Stornoway. The post-mortem on the girl will be over by now. No one's going to tell me anything, but I want to be around if there are any developments.'

There was a hint of desperation in Marsaili's voice. 'And you learned nothing else? All day?'

He said, 'I learned that Caitlin was the illegitimate daughter of Alasdair Fraser. Remember him?'

She frowned. 'Red-haired boy? Freckles? Bit of a clype.'

'In a nutshell. Hard to believe, but he's now the minister of Crobost Free Church.'

'Alasdair?' Her mouth fell open in disbelief.

'I know.'

'Have you spoken to him?'

'I have.'

'And?'

Fin shook his head. 'He was pretty hostile, Marsaili. But I don't think he killed his own daughter.'

II.

When Fin had gone, Marsaili sat shivering on the rocks at the far end of the beach. Was it really only last night that they had lain among them and made love? It had been unnaturally warm, the sea dark and placid as they splashed into the water. The calm before an unanticipated storm.

She thought of the sounds they had heard, carried on the water in the still of the night. The distant clicks and wailing. The whales, she knew now, communicating their distress, signalling the disaster to come.

She cast troubled eyes across the beach at the stricken

beasts, lying singly and in random groups, dead or dying. Only a handful of hardy volunteers remained, still with sheets and blankets and buckets of water, trying to keep the surviving creatures comfortable.

She thought about why she was even here. How only three days ago she had been in Glasgow. Disillusioned with life, wondering how the years had managed to wash her up and leave her stranded there, like any one of the whales lying on the beach today. Fin, stressed by a job he detested. Remote, withdrawn, somehow beyond the reach of arms that had only ever wanted to hold him. Both unaware, beyond their self-absorption, that their son's marriage was falling apart. That he was sleeping with a girl little more than half his age. A girl he would be accused of raping and murdering.

Gradually, as her thoughts dispersed, she became aware of Duncan striding purposefully across the sand towards her. He stopped in front of her, and when she looked up into his face, she saw that it was taut with tension. Almost grey. He said, 'I've talked to Pàdraig.' He swallowed, barely able to get the words out. 'We're not going to get any of these poor things back in the water. Even if we could, it's too late now. And they're only going to die a slow, painful death here on the beach.'

'How many left alive?'

'Nine.'

'You're going to put them down?'

He nodded.

'How will you do that? Injection?'

He shook his head. 'Not with animals this size.' He sighed. 'I'm going to have to shoot them.'

CHAPTER TWENTY-EIGHT

I.

Police cells, even when heated, somehow always felt cold. All that concrete and steel, Fin supposed. Hard, unforgiving surfaces that retained no heat. Only anger and regret. And fear.

He had sat on an unyielding plastic seat in reception for some time, with the patience of a man who would rather the wait continued than come to an end. The officer behind the glass cast curious eyes in his direction, but Fin barely noticed.

With each mile on the drive from Ness to Stornoway, he had sunk deeper into depression. In two days he had made no headway in casting doubt on Fionnlagh's guilt. And the fear of losing his son was only compounded now by a sense that he might be losing Marsaili, too. All the unhappiness of these past months crystallizing into guilt and regret. His unhappiness blinding him to hers. Both oblivious to the catastrophic failure of their son's marriage. All of which had led him to this place in time and space, sitting in a cold and draughty public reception area in Stornoway police station, waiting for permission to see the son he feared was guilty of murder.

The swing door creaked open and a uniformed sergeant beckoned him in. Fin followed him along to the charge bar, where the sergeant drew out keys to unlock the gate to the cells. He let Fin into the corridor before opening the door to Fionnlagh's cell.

Fionnlagh was sitting on the concrete plinth as before, legs folded and splayed out in front of him. He was leaning forward with his forearms on his knees, head bowed, staring at the floor. He barely looked up as Fin stepped in.

Fin waited until the door had closed behind him and he heard the key turning in the lock before leaning his back against the wall and sliding slowly down it until he sat on the floor. For the longest time he remained like that, looking at the boy he had rescued from the cliffs on An Sgeir. Remembering the pain of Fionnlagh's uncertainty about his real father. And the DNA results that confirmed him as Fin's son. There was so much he wanted to say, and yet no words came.

The longer they sat in silence, the more agitated Fionnlagh became. In the end he couldn't contain himself any further. 'What?' he demanded.

Fin just shrugged. 'You tell me, son.'

'What do you want to hear?'

'The truth.'

In his best Jack Nicholson voice, Fionnlagh said, 'You can't handle the truth.'

A Few Good Men was a movie they had watched together several times, and it brought reluctant smiles to both their faces, in spite of everything. But the smiles faded quickly, and the silence grew once more between them.

Regarding his son, Fin thought he had lost weight. Even just in the few days he had been here. His face was the colour of putty, like someone who hadn't seen the sun in years, and the skin around his eyes was panda-dark.

Finally Fionnlagh said, 'No, really. What do you want from me, Dad?'

Fin's head shake was despairing. 'I'm running out of ideas, son.'

'Then stop this. You're wasting your time.'

Fin said, 'Did you know that Caitlin was the illegitimate daughter of the minister at Crobost?'

Fionnlagh's eyes opened wide. 'No, I didn't.' He frowned. 'Is that true?'

Fin nodded.

'She never told me. I mean, I knew there was something off about her relationship with her father, but . . .'

'Not that it makes any difference now.'

'I suppose not.' But Fionnlagh was still clearly shocked.

Fin braced himself. 'They carried out the post-mortem today.'

Breath escaped Fionnlagh's lips in a muted sigh. 'Oh, Jesus.' And Fin knew he was picturing the girl he loved lying butchered on a cold stainless steel table. When the young man had brought his emotions under control again, he looked up and said, 'What did they find?'

'I don't know. Obviously, they're not going to tell me.' Fin shrugged, staring at the floor, and without any certainty, said, 'If we're lucky, it might have thrown some new light on how she died, who might have killed her.'

When he looked up, he was shocked to see tears shining on his son's face. 'Don't get your hopes up, Dad.'

'Why not?'

Fionnlagh looked at him more directly than at any time during Fin's previous visits, and uttered the words his father had never wanted to hear. 'Because I killed her.'

II.

Uniformed officers were clearing the beach. And up on the cliffs, the watching crowds were being turned away from their viewpoint. Execution was not a spectator sport.

Marsaili was among the last to leave the bay. It was a desolate scene. The bodies of nearly fifty pilot whales lay scattered about the beach as the cloud thickened over the Minch, dark and ominous and reducing visibility to a few hundred yards. She watched as Duncan came down the steps from the port and began the weary trek to the far end of the beach to start the killing. He clutched a large rifle to his chest and looked for all the world like a soldier advancing on the enemy.

But as he drew close, she saw the tension in his face, dilated pupils turning his eyes black. His knuckles glowed white in the afternoon gloom. The nine whales to be shot were spread out across the sands. Marsaili stood close to the farthest away, which was the nearest to the path she would take back up the cliffs to the bungalow. She felt helpless to offer any real comfort, but thought she should stay to the last.

When he reached her, she said, 'You've used that before?'

'I have.' He hefted it in his hands, feeling its weight. 'It's a high-powered 30-06 Springfield. An old American military calibre that they used in both wars. And still probably the most popular for hunting. It takes a big, big cartridge, which I hand-load myself. And nowadays, with modern powders, you get incredible performance. Which is what we need.' He paused. 'Got to be careful, though. You have to load slowly, incrementally. Don't want to blow your hands off.'

Marsaili had the sense that he was talking to keep from thinking. Staying professional to stop from becoming emotional. In a tiny voice, she asked, 'Where do you shoot them?'

'Find the blowhole, then angle back about forty-five degrees. The problem is that the whales are not always lying square. Then there's the different shape of the older ones. Lots of things you have to take into account.'

'That all seems so cold,' she said.

'It is. Right now I can't afford to be anything else. That way I'll do the job right, and the animals won't suffer.' He drew a long, deep breath. 'You shouldn't be here, Marsaili.'

'I know. I'm sorry. I'm gone.' And on an impulse she reached out and squeezed the hand that gripped the stock, before turning to run away across the sand towards the cliffs. Not looking back as she scrambled on to the path, beginning the long climb to the top. She was almost there when the first thunderous, heart-stopping bang echoed around the bay, and she closed her eyes.

III.

The silence in the cell was broken only by Fionnlagh's soft sobbing, and the wind outside that found its way in through every crack and crevice, a soulful mourning for the dead.

Fin felt as if someone had nailed him to the floor. He sat against the wall, unable to move, unable to think clearly. Unable to speak. It was a long time before he could summon any kind of a voice to ask, 'What happened?' It came out as little more than a breath.

The tears on Fionnlagh's face reflected the harsh overhead lighting. He gazed at the floor, unable to meet his father's eye. There was a crack in his voice when finally he spoke.

'We'd been meeting at that house on the Black Loch for a couple of months. Two or three times a week. Iseabail—'

'I know. She gave you the key.'

He flicked a look of surprise towards his father.

'I know everything, Fionnlagh. Except what happened that night.'

Fionnlagh lowered his eyes to stare once more at the floor.

'It's hard to explain this, Dad . . . I knew that what we were doing was wrong. Not because what we felt for each other was wrong. But because I was married. Had a beautiful little daughter – and, when I think about it, just six years younger than Caitlin.' He closed his eyes. 'But it was so . . . so exciting. I suppose in part because, well, because of the adrenalin rush. The risk we were running. Every time we met, it was all so charged. High-octane. Addictive. And I'd never felt like that about anyone. Not even Donna.' He corrected himself. 'Never that way about Donna.' He looked up suddenly at his father, as if appealing for understanding. 'We were so young, Donna and I. Just children. She was only sixteen. Not old enough to drive. Or drink. Even if no one ever did bother to ask our age at the Social. Not old enough to be trusted with a vote. But old enough to have a baby. What did either of us know about anything? Least of all one another.'

'You don't have to explain yourself to me, Fionnlagh. There are many things in my life I'm not proud of. We are who we are, we've done what we've done, and in the end you have to embrace that or regret it. And regret is such a corrosive thing.'

Fionnlagh nodded. 'I know. I regret the hurt I've caused. To Donna, to Eilidh. To you and Mum. And Caitlin . . . God help her.' He drew breath. 'She'd still be alive if it wasn't for me.'

'What happened?'

For a long time he appeared lost in painful recollection. 'She was kind of hyper that night,' he said at last. 'Passionate. All over me. We had sex . . .' The stolen glance at his father betrayed his embarrassment. 'She could be wild. You know? Uninhibited. She was on the pill, so we never had to take precautions. Which is why I never thought she could get pregnant.'

And the reason, Fin thought, that they had been able to recover Fionnlagh's sperm.

'Afterwards . . . well, afterwards, we would lie in bed and just talk. And drink wine. She was so ambitious. Saw so much ahead for herself in life. University. Campaign work – animal rights, climate change. It used to frighten me. Because I would wonder where I was going to fit into all this. She could project herself so easily into the future, but somehow never saw *us* beyond the moment. I don't know what she imagined our future might be. But I could see it all too clearly. At least, for me. Divorce. Losing Eilidh. My job. And if I followed her to Glasgow, what then? Her days would be spent with people her own age. How would she feel about coming home to this old man?' His tiny self-deprecating laugh. 'Even though I was barely out of my twenties. And how would I ever be able to keep pace with all that energy?'

'In other words, you knew there was no future in it.' Fin could see it all too clearly.

'Totally head in the sand. I never wanted to think beyond the next time we would meet, the next time we would have sex. I didn't want to spoil all that. Ruining the present by worrying about the future.' He looked up. 'I was in love. Really. I mean, for the first time in my life, I knew what that felt like.

I wanted to embrace it, hold it close, keep it precious, because somewhere, deep down, I knew I was going to lose it.'

'So after you'd had sex . . .?' Fin prompted him, and saw a shadow cross his son's face.

'She kept checking her watch. Said she couldn't stay. But wouldn't tell me why. And I got pissed off. You know? I was the one taking all the risks. Making excuses to Donna so that I could be there. Knowing that if we were caught, I would lose my job. Everything. And she always made light of that. As if it was nothing.' Suddenly his voice filled the cell. 'Fuck!' He stamped both feet on the floor and clasped his hands tightly in front of him. 'I wish to God I'd just said okay, see you next time.'

'Why did you *think* she wanted to leave early?'

'Oh, she and Iseabail had cooked up something clandestine with that fucking activist. I knew that without asking. But it didn't stop me. And in the end, she admitted it. She and Iseabail were swimming out to the cages again. But it was the last time, she said. That would be an end to it. But I knew it wouldn't and I told her I wasn't going to let her go.' He swung his head slowly from side to side. 'Stupid! You don't tell someone as headstrong as Caitlin that you forbid them to do anything. She kind of flew off the handle. Told me it was none of my business, and that there was nothing I could do to stop her.' He looked up. 'Oh, God, Dad. We had the most terrible fight. First time ever. And for me, I suppose, as much as any-thing, it was the realization that there *was* no us. Only Caitlin. And I was just along for the ride. Sacrificing everything. I'm not sure she ever really understood that. Not her fault. I was the one old enough to know better.'

He stood up then, animated, agitated, spooling through it all again in his mind's eye, pacing the tiny cell.

'She was in tears. Red-faced. Shouting. And I guess I must have been shouting back. Anyway, she ran out of the house, and I could hear her sobbing as she headed out on the path along the cliffs towards the headland. Of course, I went after her. It wasn't dark yet, but the light was going. I could see her twenty, thirty yards ahead of me. She was fast. But I was faster. When I caught up, I grabbed her elbow and she spun around, breathless. Her eyes on fire. I don't even remember now what it was we said. But we stood shouting at each other. Until she hit me. Never even saw it coming. The flat of her hand swinging out of the fading light to catch me full on the side of the head.'

He stood with his back to his father, staring up at the cubes of light that fell from the window high in the wall.

'I've never in my life hit a woman, Dad. God forgive me. I didn't even think about it. I was so angry, and the shock of that slap in the face. I . . . I just reacted.'

'You hit her?' Fin was shocked.

'Far too hard.' He turned to face Fin and screwed up his eyes. 'She was so startled. I could see it in her eyes. Disappointment. Disillusion. That I was not the person she'd thought I was. She took several steps back, staggering, caught her heel on a rock half buried in the turf. We were so close to the edge of the cliff.

319

She just went over. I tried to catch her, I really did. Fingertips touching her sleeve as she fell.' He shook his head. 'She must have fallen twenty, thirty feet. Without a word. I didn't see her hit the water, but I heard it. Even above the surf.'

Fin closed his eyes and pictured his son's description of then sprinting back along the path to the house, and down the road to the tiny beach below. Fin had followed that same route himself, just yesterday.

'When I got on to the beach, I ran into the water, splashing out as far as I could go. It's east-facing, so there was very little light. The cliffs and the rocks around the bay just seemed black. When I got out of my depth, I started swimming, as far out as I could go. But there was no sign of her. Nothing. The tide was on the way out. I could feel the undertow trying to take me with it. My wet clothes dragging me under. And I figured if Caitlin had struck her head on the way down, she was probably unconscious when she hit the water. Otherwise she would have swum back in.'

Fin opened his eyes to see the despair on his son's face as he relived the moment.

'It must have carried her right out into the bay. I didn't give up, though. Honest to God, I tried everything to find her. Until my arms and legs started to cramp up, and I knew I needed to get back to the shore or the tide would carry me away, too. I staggered out of the water and just collapsed on to the beach, and sat weeping for God knows how long. Till I'd cried every tear it was possible to cry. And then some.'

He raised both hands to cover his face. 'I killed her, Dad. Took her life, her promise, her future. And my love for her with it. Destroyed it all in one stupid, mindless moment.' He took his hands away from his face and stared, wild-eyed, at his father. 'Whatever they do to me, I deserve it.'

Fin was awash with mixed emotions. Anger, sympathy, frustration, helplessness, and a deep hollowing sadness. Fionnlagh slumped back on to the concrete plinth, wrapping his blanket around his shoulders, and burying his face once again in his hands.

Fin fought hard to clear his thoughts. 'What did you do then?'

Fionnlagh looked up, puzzled by the question. 'Nothing. What could I do? I'd just killed Caitlin. I didn't mean to, but I had. I have never felt so utterly devastated as I did in that moment. My legs would hardly support me as I tried to stand up. I must have stood there for . . . I don't know how long. Because I had no idea what to do. It was like my life had ended, too. But I was still there, haunting myself. In the end I went back up to the house, got into my car and drove home. I can't remember a single thing about that drive. I blinked and I was heading up the road to Crobost. By the time I got to the house, I had more or less dried off. But I must have presented a hell of a sight. Donna knew immediately that something awful had happened. But I wouldn't even speak to her. Just locked myself in one of the spare rooms. And when I sat on the edge of that bed, with Donna banging on the door screaming at me to talk to her, I knew that my life was over. That I had dragged my wife and my daughter down with me. Through no fault of theirs. I had taken a life and ruined another two, and if I could have exchanged all that for mine, I'd have done it in a heartbeat.'

CHAPTER TWENTY-NINE

I.

The wind was gusting through the narrow back streets of the town as Fin plunged, head down, out into the fading light. He was consumed by a numbness like nothing he had ever experienced. He felt nothing, saw nothing, heard nothing. It was as if he, too, had died.

He'd had no words of wisdom or consolation for his son. Nothing that could mitigate the awful truth. Fionnlagh had admitted killing that poor girl. He hadn't meant to, and he certainly hadn't raped her, Fin believed that, but it didn't mean he wasn't going to spend the best part of the rest of his life in prison. Fin knew that, whatever else, he had to stand by him.

He thought about Donna. As good as widowed. And poor Eilidh, bearing the stigma of a convicted killer for a father, something that would pursue her for the rest of her days. There was no way either of them could remain on the island.

His mind was seething with thoughts that came randomly,

without logic or order. He and Marsaili would take Donna and Eilidh back to Glasgow with them. Fionnlagh would be accompanied to Inverness on Monday and placed on remand until the trial. Fin would have to secure the services of the best lawyer he could afford, even if it bankrupted him. He was so lost in his internal turmoil that he did not at first hear the voice shouting his name. It was only the second or third calling of it that broke into his consciousness.

He looked up, surprised. He had walked several hundred yards along Kenneth Street, past garages and lock-ups, the Masonic lodge with its freshly sandblasted sandstone frontage, and barely noticed. He had left his car parked in the street outside the rear entrance to the Royal Hotel, opposite a private car park belonging to a firm of chartered accountants. He turned to see three figures striding towards him from the direction of Church Street. They must, he figured, have been waiting for him and were hurrying now to catch him up.

'Hey, orphan boy, fucking pay attention!'

Fin's heart sank. Murdo Macritchie. Another Ruadh whose hair was no longer red, but an indeterminate and thinning grey that he hid beneath a chequered bunnet. Murdo and his brother Angel had been the school bullies in Fin's day, terrorizing and brutalizing the boys, leering at the girls with crude sexual innuendo and frequent groping. The last time Fin had seen Angel he was lying cut open on an autopsy table, following his murder at the port. And his last encounter with Murdo had been in McNeil's pub, when a fight initiated by

Ruadh had spilled out into The Narrows, along with most of the clientele and enough beer to drown an army.

Twelve years of torment at the hands of the Macritchies had also spilled out of Fin. No longer the skinny orphan boy, Fin had broken Murdo's nose, taken out most of his front teeth and pummelled his beer belly until he puked all over the pavement. He might have killed him if George Gunn had not intervened to pull him away in time, steering him off into the night before the uniforms arrived, saving him from almost certain arrest. Which would have put a premature end to his career as a police officer.

Murdo looked in even worse shape twelve years on, though his ugly smile revealed a new set of incongruously white front teeth. He was flanked by another equally bulky Niseach, who seemed vaguely familiar to Fin, and a skinny man with a pock-marked face wearing overalls and mud-caked wellies. They looked like extras chosen by central casting for a soap opera on crofting. They were of a generation, and no doubt all members of the Macritchie clique from school. The three men formed a loose semicircle around Fin on the road, and the smell of alcohol blew about them in the wind.

Murdo would almost certainly have avoided confrontation with Fin had he been on his own. But he had backup, and so the bully's confidence of old had returned. 'Did you not hear us shouting?'

'I had things on my mind, Murdo.' Fin took a wary step back.

'Aye, like that fucking son of yours killing yon lassie.'

325

'What do you want?'

'I want you . . .' and Murdo jabbed a stubby finger into Fin's chest, 'to stay away from my minister.'

'*Your* minister?'

'Aye. *Our* minister.' Murdo took a quick glance at his fellow congregationalists. 'Me and Jock and Anndra here are all elders of the Crobost church.'

Fin snorted. 'God must be desperate if he's reduced to recruiting the likes of you. From recollection, drunkenness and bullying aren't in the job description.'

'Now, see,' Murdo said, 'that's just the kind of shit that's going to get you in fucking trouble, orphan boy. Alasdair – the Reverend Fraser to you – doesn't take kindly to folk interfering in his private life.'

And all became clear to Fin. Alasdair had recruited some unsavoury characters from his flock to warn Fin off. Favours owed, or maybe debt extended. Perhaps he didn't trust Fin to keep the secrets they shared, though he doubted that Alasdair would have imparted the nature of those secrets to these way-ward elders. In the end, all it did was confirm for Fin that Ally Ruadh wasn't fit to walk in Donald Murray's footsteps.

He didn't see the first blow coming. A fist that flew out of left field and caught him high on the cheekbone. Anndra, the skinny one. But he had knuckles of steel, and Fin's knees buckled beneath him. Even as he went down, he knew that this was not what Alasdair had envisaged. This was Macritchie's revenge.

He felt the full weight of that retribution as Murdo's boot sank itself into his midriff, and he curled up, arms crooked over his head, trying to protect himself from the kicks that began raining in from all sides. But still, one caught him full in the face, and he felt his mouth fill with blood.

A voice like thunder broke suddenly through the circle of violence. A voice that rang familiar, though somehow very far off, like a storm on the horizon. He rolled over and saw George Gunn squaring up to Fin's three attackers. He stood, legs slightly apart, feet planted firmly on the tarmac, the wind catching his oiled black hair and lifting it up into a cockscomb. Fin spat out blood and raised himself on to one elbow, trying to clear his head.

Without taking his eyes off the other three, George leaned over to give Fin a hand back to his feet. 'Alright,' he said. 'Now it's two against three. Though I doubt if Mr Macleod's in any fit state after being kicked half to death by a bunch of cowards. So it's just me and you.' He smoothed down his cockscomb. 'But let me tell you, the first one that comes within reach of my fist will not be getting up again any time soon. And when he comes to, he'll be in a police cell charged with assaulting a police officer. Enough to see him sent to Inverness for a good few months. If not longer.'

All three men, breathless from their exertions, looked at him uncertainly.

'So, which one of you is going to be first?'

Anndra tugged on Murdo's arm as he turned away. 'Time to go, Ruadh.'

Jock glanced at Murdo, waiting to take his lead. Murdo spat on the pavement and turned a foul look in Fin's direction. 'Next time, orphan boy.'

And he turned to follow after Anndra down the hill towards Bayhead, Jock waddling hurriedly in his wake.

George looked at Fin and shook his head. 'Just like the last time, eh, Mr Macleod? Only then I was saving you from yourself.' He tutted. 'We'd better get you cleaned up, and a wee something to take the taste of blood out of your mouth.'

II.

McNeil's was doing brisk business. Picnic tables outside it, which had been popular with tourists during the long spell of fine summer weather, were deserted. A folding chalkboard struggled to keep its feet in the wind swirling around The Narrows. *Coves & Blones, open from 7 p.m., Thu, Fri, Sat, Upstairs Bar.* Another, advertising *Live Music, Open Mic with Bugsy,* had fared less well and was flattened up against the wall of the pharmacy opposite. An ashtray on a stand had spilled its contents all over the street.

Inside, it was noisy and warm and smelled of whisky and stale beer. Gunn had found them a spot in the far corner, and he arrived at their table with a dram and a half-pint for each of them, slipping into his seat and looking speculatively at the damage to Fin's face. It was bruised and swelling below the right eye. Miraculously all of his teeth had survived. The blood in his mouth had come from biting his tongue. 'How are you feeling now?'

'Like I've been run over by a steamroller.' Fin had slunged his face with cold water in the toilets and rinsed out his mouth. But no amount of water could wash away his depression or overwhelming sadness. He knew he shouldn't discuss it with Gunn, but he had to talk to someone, and Marsaili was a long drive away. He took a mouthful of whisky and hung his head. 'Fionnlagh's confessed,' he said.

Gunn stiffened. 'I don't think you should be telling me this, Mr Macleod.'

Fin ignored him. 'It was an accident, George. They had a fight. She slapped him. He slapped her back. She fell. Manslaughter. There was no intent.' He looked into Gunn's stony face. 'He didn't mean to do it.'

'With all due respect, Mr Macleod, rape is no accident.'

'He didn't rape her, George!' Fin's voice was raised. He immediately glanced around self-consciously and lowered it again. 'He absolutely denies that. They'd been having sex for months. And they'd slept together that night before the argument.'

Gunn was acutely uncomfortable. 'You realize, sir, I'm going to have to report this conversation.'

But Fin had no chance to respond before a familiar voice crashed into their conversation.

'Well, this is a nice cosy wee corner.' Professor Wilson placed his pint carefully on the table and cocked his head, examining Fin's face. 'I hope you're just drunk, Macleod, and had an argument with a lamppost. Because you're far too fucking old to be getting into fights.' He sat down and took a sip of his foaming IPA, then leaned forward to take a closer look. 'Nasty contusion, that. You should get yourself checked for signs of concussion.' He looked at the glass of amber in Fin's hand. 'Shouldn't be drinking either.'

Gunn said, 'He's just had some bad news, Professor.'

The pathologist lifted an eyebrow. 'Oh? What's that?'

Fin took another sip of whisky for Dutch courage. 'Fionnlagh's confessed to killing Caitlin.'

'An accident,' Gunn filled in the rest for him. 'But claims he didn't rape her.'

Professor Wilson snorted. 'Well, I could have told you that.' He took a long pull at his pint, and left a line of white foam clinging to his abundantly whiskered upper lip. 'The girl wasn't raped at all.'

Gunn caught the pathologist's eye, pointing a finger at his own upper lip, and the professor wiped away the foam from his with the back of his hand.

He glanced at Fin and said, 'Silly of me. Shouldn't have said anything in the presence of the father of the accused.' He raised an eyebrow. 'You didn't hear that, did you?'

'Hear what, Angus?' Fin felt the first tiny stirrings of optimism.

'Of course,' the pathologist said, 'I have no problem in briefing DS Gunn here on my findings, as long as you turn a deaf ear, Fin.'

'Hear no evil, see no evil,' Fin said.

Professor Wilson directed his gaze towards Gunn. 'The thing is, Detective Sergeant, rape is always notoriously hard to determine. But in this case, someone inflicted vaginal damage post-mortem to make it look like the poor lassie had been. The presence of semen in itself is not an indication of either rape or consent. But the girl was dead by the time the mutilation was carried out. A clumsy effort, I have to say. And in no way indicative of non-consensual sex.'

Gunn frowned and glanced at Finn. 'So someone else killed her.'

'That's not for me to say, Mr Gunn. But it is clear that she didn't drown in that little bay on the Black Loch.'

Fin felt a cloud of silence descend on him, muting the voices raised in laughter at neighbouring tables, and all the social interaction around them. His focus on what Professor Wilson had just told them was intense. But still it made no sense.

Gunn gave voice to Fin's confusion. 'How's that possible, sir?'

'Well, drowning is very hard to establish as a cause of death at the best of times, Detective Sergeant, unless there are absolutely no other obvious causes.'

'And there weren't?'

'There were several head injuries and contusions to the body, none of which would have been sufficient to kill her. So . . .'

'You think she drowned.'

'I'm pretty sure she did. But here's the thing, Mr Gunn. The water in her lungs was full of sea lice. In a far greater concentration than would ever occur naturally in the open sea, or in a sea loch like An Loch Dubh.'

Fin interrupted, everything he had learned in the last hour suddenly turned on its head. 'The cages! She was drowned out in the cages. She must have been. It's the only place you would find sea lice in any kind of concentration.'

Professor Wilson sat back and took a long swallow of his beer.

Gunn's mouth fell open. 'So someone else *did* kill her?' he said.

'Again, Detective Sergeant, that's not for me to say.'

Gunn's eyes flickered back and forth across the table in front of him, as if he might find some plausible explanation among the beer mats and spillages that masked its scarred surface. 'If she was drowned out at the cages, then someone must have brought her body back to dump it on the beach at the Black Loch.'

As if a pause button had been released, all of Fin's senses were suddenly assailed once more by the world crashing in around him, noise, light, movement, bringing the realization that Fionnlagh's account of what happened that night was only half the story. 'Fionnlagh didn't kill her,' he said, barely able to trust his own voice. 'Either by design or by accident. Even if he thought he had.'

All three were startled by the voice that cut through the

hubbub in McNeil's, and the shadow that fell across their table. 'For fuck's sake!'

All three faces turned up to find DCI Maclaren glaring down at them, a large whisky in his hand. His smooth face beneath the undercut hairstyle favoured by Premier League footballers was pink with indignation. A colour that almost matched his shirt.

'I come in here,' he said, 'at the end of a long day, for a civilized dram. And what do I find? My pathologist and my DS colluding with the father of the man I've just charged with murder.' His fury was evident in the clenching of his jaw. He inclined his head slightly and looked at Gunn. 'I'm of a mind to suspend you with immediate effect, Gunn.' Then swung his anger in the direction of the pathologist. 'And you can rest assured, sir, that I will be reporting you to your superiors first thing on Monday.'

Professor Wilson leaned back in his seat, languid and relaxed. 'Is that so, sonny?' He took another draught of beer. 'First thing I need to correct. I'm not *your* pathologist. And I'm wondering exactly what it is you'll be reporting to my superiors. That I was having a quiet drink in McNeil's on a Saturday night with two old friends? Because let me tell you, I've known Fin Macleod since he was a young DC, and you were still flunking your eleven plus – if they even have such a thing any more. And I've been acquainted with DS Gunn since he turned green at my first island autopsy twelve years ago. Unlike a certain wet-behind-the-ears university graduate who managed to throw up all over my autopsy table, George actually succeeded in keeping the contents of his stomach where they belong.'

Another mouthful of beer sharpened his sarcasm.

'Now, I'm quite sure that the young man involved would rather word of his digestive sensibilities did not gain common currency among his fellow officers, and I am always happy to remain discreet in such matters. But for your information, Detective Chief Inspector Maclaren, Fin Macleod has not asked me one single thing about this case, and so I have not had to embarrass either him, or myself, by telling him that anything discovered during post-mortem is strictly confidential.'

Having had the legs cut away from under him, the CIO hovered uncertainly. Humiliated in front of a junior officer and the father of the accused. Withdrawal with any kind of dignity seemed impossible. But Professor Wilson offered him an olive branch.

'Well, Mr Maclaren, now that we've cleared that up, are you going to join us for a drink, or not?'

Maclaren stood for a long moment, weighing his options, before taking a chair from an adjoining table and pulling it in to join them. He folded his hands on the table in front of him. 'So,' he said. 'Who's buying?'

CHAPTER THIRTY

The house was empty, and cold. Donna had taken Eilidh to her other grandmother's. An escape from the shooting of the whales, and the overwhelming weight of Fionnlagh's impending transfer to remand in Inverness.

Marsaili had turned on the heating, but it would be a while before it took the chill off the air, and she crouched in front of the fireplace to light the peats in the grate. When the flames licked up between the chunks of dried turf, and the toasted scent of burning peat began to permeate the room, she got to her feet and smiled awkwardly at Duncan.

He stood looking a little lost in the middle of the room, the butt of his Springfield tucked under his arm, the barrel pointed towards the floor.

'I'm sorry. It's through here,' Marsaili said. And she brushed past him to open the door to Artair's father's old study. 'Mr Macinnes used to hunt deer out on the moor, and after . . . well, after he was gone, we got rid of his rifle, but never thought to take out the old lock safe gun cabinet.' She led him into the room where she knew that terrible things had happened all those years before. It was a room in which she never spent time, a room that felt haunted by all those memories, even though none of them were hers.

The cabinet stood against the far wall. Polished oak, which looked for all the world like any household cabinet. But it was fixed securely to the brick, and when she unlocked the door, revealed itself to have a steel lining. A felt-lined base was designed to accommodate the stocks of half a dozen rifles. Above it, a notched shelf held the barrels. Cartridge drawers were tucked in underneath.

'He only had the one gun,' she said, 'and I don't know where he got the cabinet. It might have been handed down through the family. But he was very proud of it, from all accounts.'

She stood back and watched as Duncan slipped his rifle into one of the slots, and emptied his remaining cartridges into a drawer. Then she locked it and handed him the key. 'You'd better hang on to this until you go.'

He closed his hand around it, but still stood uncertainly in front of the cabinet. 'I don't know that I should stay over, Marsaili.'

'Duncan, you're traumatized. I can't let you go home to an empty house.'

'I go home to an empty house every night.'

'Not after shooting nine whales in cold blood.' She turned back to the living room. 'Come on, I'll get you a drink.'

He followed her through, and she poured them each a stiff

whisky. As he took the glass from her, she saw that his hand was trembling. 'Was it really awful?' she said.

He stared into the rich amber of the island malt and nodded. 'In a way it's like what we do when we're putting dogs down. Some of them I've treated since they were puppies. Others have played regularly with my own dogs. You focus on putting a needle in a vein.' He took a slow, pensive sip, and she thought that maybe he was holding the glass against his lips to stop it from shaking. 'It was the same with the whales. Just concentrating on what I was trying to do.' He looked at her. 'Which is put a bullet in the brainstem as cleanly and efficiently as possible.' He took a larger, swifter mouthful. 'You have to divorce yourself from it, Marsaili. If you stood back and looked at what you were doing . . . you couldn't do it. At least, I couldn't.'

He sat down on the arm of the settee and she stood in front of the fire, sipping her whisky, feeling the sensation of warmth slowly return to her body. This wasn't the Duncan she had known as a teenager, crass and unsophisticated, and hoping to seduce her with drink and dope. Here was a human being who had just taken nine sentient lives and was suffering for it.

He said, 'I mean, I'm someone who'll happily harvest a deer for the table. You're killing a wild animal who doesn't even know you're there. For the meat. It's totally different.' His eyes dipped away again from hers to seek solace in the liquid gold he held in his hand. 'What I did today. It was like an execution. You have to be able to separate the action from the emotion. But when it's done, the dam bursts, and all that emotion you've been holding back nearly bloody drowns you.' He drained his glass, and looked at her with troubled eyes. 'You'd think it would get easier as you get older.' A slight shake of the head was all he could muster. 'It doesn't. If anything, it gets worse. The closer you get to death yourself, the more precious life becomes. All life.'

His eyes were blurred by the tears he held back, determined not to let them spill in front of her. She set her glass on the mantelpiece and took his to place on the coffee table. Then she made him stand and put her arms around him. There were no words of solace, just the passing of warmth and comfort from one human being to another. They stood holding each other for what felt like a very long time. Until the sound of the kitchen door opening startled them apart.

When Fin came into the sitting room from the kitchen, he had the sense of having interrupted something. He wondered what Duncan was doing there, and took in the two whisky glasses. One on the mantel, the other on the coffee table. Marsaili's face was flushed. She gasped when she saw him. 'What happened to your face?'

'An accident,' was all he said, his unasked question evident in the look he gave her.

Self-consciously, she said, 'Duncan had to put down the remaining whales.'

Fin cast a quick glance towards Duncan and caught the look

in his eyes. Something somewhere between guilt and grief. And he felt an instant empathy. 'That must have been tough.'

Duncan nodded acknowledgement.

Marsaili said, 'I told him he could stay over. His wife has Alzheimer's. She's in care in Stornoway. I didn't want him going back to an empty house.'

Fin nodded. 'Of course not.'

'And Mr Macinnes's old lock safe gun cabinet is still in the study, so . . .'

Fin frowned and turned his eyes back to Duncan. 'You shot them?'

'Creatures that size, Fin, there's no other way.'

'Jesus, Duncan. I'm sorry.'

Duncan inclined his head in resignation. 'Thanks.'

An awkward silence hovered among them before Marsaili asked, more in hope than expectation, 'Any word?'

Fin managed a smile of reassurance. 'Good news and bad,' he said. 'The bad news is that Fionnlagh confessed to killing Caitlin. By accident.'

Marsaili's hand flew to her chest, and a sound like pain escaped her lips.

'The good news is that the autopsy shows he didn't. He only thought he had.'

Marsaili's face was creased with consternation. 'I don't understand.'

And Fin explained about the sea lice and the pathologist's conclusion that neither had she been drowned in the Black

Loch, nor been raped, though someone had made a very clumsy effort to make it seem as though she had.

'So who did kill her?' Duncan asked.

Fin shook his head. 'No idea.'

Marsaili sat down heavily on the edge of the settee and dropped her face into her hands, overcome with relief. 'Thank God, thank God,' she said, over and over. When she looked up, her face was wet with tears.

Fin wanted to take her in his arms, but felt uncomfortable in Duncan's presence, and both he and the vet stood in uneasy silence as Marsaili wept.

She said, 'And all this time he thought he'd killed her and couldn't tell us. God, what kind of hell must he have gone through?'

Fin said, 'The same hell he put us through, Marsaili, until he finally told me the whole sad story this afternoon.'

Marsaili wiped away her tears with the palms of her hands and stood up. 'I need a drink.' She crossed to the bottle and refilled her glass and Duncan's, before finding a third for Fin. All three raised and clinked their glasses in silent toast before drinking from them. Fin felt the whisky burning all the way down. Marsaili took a step towards him and ran fingertips lightly over his bruising. 'What kind of accident?' she said, concerned.

But Fin wasn't about to go into it. His smile was rueful. 'It's a long story, Marsaili. For another time.'

Duncan laid down his glass. 'I really should be going.'

Marsaili put a hand on his arm. 'No. Stay, Duncan. You shouldn't be driving after drinking whisky anyway.' She caught Fin looking at her hand on his arm and took it quickly away. And as if to deflect from her embarrassment, she said, 'There's something I've been meaning to show you since yesterday, Fin. Just forgot about it with the whales and everything.'

'Forgot about what?'

'Come and I'll show you.' She bustled out of the room into the hall. And over her shoulder, said, 'It's something I found when I was doing those internet searches on Niall Black.'

Fin and Duncan followed her into the bedroom, where the laptop still sat on the dresser. Marsaili was momentarily distracted by the unmade bed, and quickly dragged the quilt over sheets and pillows that betrayed a troubled sleep. She turned to the computer and swiped away the screensaver to reveal a screenful of open windows, the digital tracks left by her search. Her cursor jumped about from window to window until she found the one she was looking for.

'There's a ton of stuff out there in the ether about Niall and Bradan Mor. But this was almost buried, and I only asked Google to do a translation from the Greek on a whim, because of the photograph.'

She zoomed into the image, and they saw it was a newspaper cutting. The photograph was a split image. Niall on the left, an attractive, dark-haired young woman on the right. Marsaili clicked on another window, which had converted the article into text that Google had been able to translate.

The headline read LIFE FOR GARDENER WHO CONFESSED TO MURDER OF MILLIONAIRE'S NANNY. Both Fin and Duncan leaned in to read it. The story came from coverage of a court case in Nicosia. It had ended in the conviction and sentencing of a gardener for the rape and murder, at Niall Black's lavish Cypriot villa, of Eòghann Black's long-time nanny, a young Greek Cypriot woman who had been with the family for five years. The sentence was life. She had been twenty-eight years of age, and the young Eòghann just fifteen at the time. So, it had all happened nearly ten years ago.

Fin reached for the trackpad and clicked back to the original newspaper clipping. There was a grainy black and white photograph at the foot of it, of the fifteen-year-old Eòghann, and you could see that even then he had been a good-looking boy.

'What's the significance?' Duncan said.

Marsaili shrugged. 'There isn't any, really. I just thought it was interesting. You know, the parallels with Caitlin's rape and murder.' She sighed. 'Only, as it turns out, she wasn't raped after all. Thank God.'

Fin ran the cursor over several other open windows, clicking on them one after the other, bringing them to the foreground. He stopped on a more recent set of photographs of Eòghann, now in his twenties and living the high life of the glamorous playboy heir to a fortune. Photographed on the arms of beautiful young women, he was dressed always in designer suits and shirts, never a hair out of place, his tan flawless. And Fin thought how unlikely it was that he would ever follow in his father's footsteps.

Marsaili said, 'He has an Instagram account. He posts pictures of himself on it all the time.'

She took over the trackpad from Fin to pull up Eòghann's Instagram, and scrolled through endless photographs of him at parties and other social events, as well as countless selfies, taken often in bad light, smirking at his smartphone in a mirror. He was bare-chested in a remarkable number of those, showing off the sculpted torso of which he was clearly so proud.

'Stop!' Fin's voice filled the room suddenly, like the report of a rifle. And Marsaili's hand shot up from the trackpad as if it had burned her fingers.

Fin took over, and with thumb and forefinger, expanded an image of Eòghann leering bare-chested at the camera. His eyes looked glazed, unfocused, as though he was either drunk or high on some other substance.

'Look,' he said.

Marsaili and Duncan stepped closer to peer at the image. 'What are we looking at?' Duncan said.

Fin expanded the photograph further and stabbed a finger at Eòghann's chest. Marsaili's eyes opened wide suddenly, and her voice was hushed. 'Oh my God!'

CHAPTER THIRTY-ONE

Fin drove up the gentle slope from the village to the house on the cliffs, the wind buffeting his car. With the cloud cover, it was almost dark now. But there was enough light to see the carcasses of the whales littering the beach below. Hulking dark shapes lying lifeless in sand that somehow retained a little of the day's light, waves breaking in luminescence all along the tideline.

He parked on the road outside the walled garden, and cast his gaze across the sad scene below. At the far end of the beach, there were two figures walking side by side, back towards the port. Ghouls, he thought, come to survey the carnage, or perhaps simply tourists passing in sadness among the dead. Or maybe even animal health officers from the council's environmental department, trying to work out how to dispose of the bodies. Though there would be no attempt to do that until Monday. To bury the dead on a Sunday would be a violation of the Sabbath.

The three vehicles that had been there during Fin's first visit stood side by side in the parking area beyond the gates. The dark green Range Rover driven by Dempsey when he dropped in on Colm Hendry's base of operations. The Mercedes that Niall had used to drive Fin to and from Great Bernera. And the Nissan pickup. A security lamp, triggered by his movement, bathed Fin with light as he walked between the Mercedes and the Range Rover towards the sliding glass doors of the rear extension.

There were no lights on in the house itself, and Fin cupped his hands around his face, pressing it against the glass to see inside beyond the reflections. The dark silhouettes of furniture stood in silent groupings around the room. Fin looked for a doorbell but couldn't find one. Finally he tried the glass door and it slid smoothly open. The house breathed its stillness into his face.

'Hello?' he called. Then again. Louder. 'Hello?' The house responded with a silence so thick it felt as though he could touch it. He hesitated for only a moment before stepping inside.

Marsaili had urged him to call the police. But Fin knew he could expect nothing from Maclaren without something more substantive to offer. Now, for the first time, he began to entertain second thoughts.

Still, he pressed on into the house, calling again. Once more he received no response. He retraced the footsteps of his previous visit, through the house to the large lounge that opened on to the wraparound conservatory at the front. As before, it stood in darkness, except for the flickering light of Eòghann's large flat-screen TV, casting the illumination of its ghostly, ever-changing images of war around the room. Shadows shifting among the furniture.

Eòghann was spreadeagled in the same armchair, playing the same mindless video game. He wore jeans and a hooded sweatshirt, and his earbuds deafened him to Fin's presence. Fin stepped into Eòghann's line of sight and startled him to his feet.

'Jesus Christ! You just about scared the shit out of me.' He ripped out the earbuds, paused his game and peered at Fin in the gloom. 'What the fuck are you doing here?' And when Fin said nothing, he grew less sure of himself. 'Dad's with Dempsey. They're about somewhere. Not sure where exactly. They might have gone down to the beach.'

'That's okay,' Fin said. 'I'm not looking for your dad.'

A little of Eòghann's bravado returned, and he jutted his jaw towards Fin. 'Who are you looking for, then?'

'You.'

'What would you want with me?'

Fin reached into his back pocket and drew out a folded photocopy of the photograph from Eòghann's Instagram. Carefully, he unfolded it and held it out towards the younger man.

Eòghann stared at him uncertainly for a moment before taking it. He absorbed the photograph at a glance. 'What, you got the hots for me, or something?' And he looked up with a sick little smile on his face.

'Look again,' Fin said, and Eòghann lowered his eyes once more to the sheet of paper in his hand.

'What?'

'That pendant you're wearing. Expensive piece. Solid gold. And that's a sapphire at the centre of it. Giving it the appearance of an eye. Which is probably why the jeweller named it "the Evil Eye". The same piece, attached to a broken chain, that was found tangled in your sister's hair when she washed up on that beach at the Black Loch.'

Eòghann looked up sharply. 'She was *not* my sister!'

Fin cocked an eyebrow. 'Your half-sister, Eòghann. Still your blood.'

The boy thought about it for a moment, then smiled. 'Whatever. Doesn't matter anyway. The one they found on Caitlin isn't mine. I've still got it.'

'Is that right?'

'It is. I'll show you it, if you want.'

'Why don't you do that?'

'It's up in the bedroom.' Eòghann pushed brusquely past him and into a square hallway with stairs leading to the upper floor. He paused at the foot of the steps. 'Well, come on,' he said. 'I'm not going to bring it down to you.'

Reluctantly, Fin followed him up the stairs, two steps behind him, and noticed a thin red contusion around the back of Eòghann's neck, almost hidden by his hood. They emerged from the stairway on to a narrow landing. Eòghann opened a door off it that led to a large bedroom at the front of the house. Bay windows presented a spectacular view out over the harbour below and the beach beyond. A king-sized bed was pushed against the window-facing wall, black silk sheets thrown carelessly aside, unmade since the morning. A faint musty odour of unwashed clothes was masked by the almost overpowering scent of some designer aftershave.

Eòghann crossed the room to a red lacquer Chinese cabinet and switched on a reading light that sat next to a large wooden jewellery box inlaid with mother-of-pearl. Fin stood in the doorway watching as he opened the lid and began rummaging among its contents. Finally he turned around to face the older man.

'What do you know?' he said. 'I can't find it.'

Fin inclined his head a little to one side. 'You surprise me.'

'Someone must have taken it.'

Fin stared at him with such unvarnished dislike that Eòghann almost recoiled. 'You killed her, didn't you?

Eòghann appeared to be running any number of possible responses through his head until finally he decided on dumb insolence.

But Fin was running out of patience. 'Didn't you?' His raised voice bounced from wall to wall in the confined space, and Eòghann winced as if struck, before his face contorted itself into a sneer.

'That bitch!' he growled. 'Not content with stealing my mother, she was about to destroy my father, too.'

348

'So you knew that she and Iseabail were swimming out to the cages to get footage for Colm Hendry's documentary?'

'Of course we fucking knew!'

'Is that the royal we, or did your father know, too?'

But Eòghann knew better than to implicate his father. 'I got Dempsey to attach a little tracking device to the wheel arch of the bitch's car. We could track her all round the island. Knew where she was at any given time we chose to check. I stood myself one clear, moonlit night out on the headland that looks directly across to the fish farm, and watched those two stupid girls swimming out to the cages, floating a canoe between them.'

'And the night she was killed?'

Eòghann turned around and slammed the jewellery box shut. He stood with his back to Fin for what seemed an inordinate length of time. Then, as if reaching a decision, he turned to face down his interrogator.

'I was watching her the night she and your boy met at that house above the Black Loch. I saw him chasing her out on to the headland, till he caught up with her. And they just stood there, facing off, shouting at each other. Until she let him have it. Open slap, full in the face. I could almost hear it from the other side of the bay. Then he hit her back. I could have cheered.' He grinned. 'No more than the bitch deserved. Then, oh dear, she staggers back and manages to fall off the fucking cliff. Brilliant. Just brilliant.' Eòghann was enjoying himself now, reliving the moment. 'Course, your lad panicked.

Ran all the way down to the beach, then into the water. Must have spent a full fifteen minutes floundering around, trying to find her. But she was gone. And he was in a state, because he thought he'd killed her.'

He moved into a shaft of light from a streetlamp that fell in at an angle through the window, and Fin could see the pleasure shining on his face.

'He just sat there on the beach, for one hell of a long time. Looked to me like he was crying. Must have figured he'd just fucked up the rest of his life.'

'Or perhaps he was grieving for the girl he loved.'

'Caitlin? Give me a break. He was in it for the sex, your boy. She was a good-looking girl, my *half*-sister. I'd have given her one myself, if only there'd been some way to stop her talking. Real passion killer when she opened her mouth.'

'So what happened?'

'Eventually Fionnlagh got up and went back to the house. Just got into his car and drove off. I was about to do the same thing when lo-and-fucking-behold the bitch comes swimming in from the bay and crawls up on to the beach.' He laughed. 'I mean, she must have been hiding from him or something. Somewhere out there among the rocks. Teaching him a lesson. Have to say, though, I was a bit disappointed.'

'So you went down and confronted her?'

'Damn right I did. Told her I knew exactly what she'd been up to. Swimming out to the cages for that bastard, Hendry. And screwing your boy up in that empty house. Told her a lot of people were going to be interested to learn about both those things.' He chuckled. 'And fuck me if she doesn't try the same slap trick she did with your boy. Only I saw it coming and punched her right in the face. She went down like a sack of potatoes. Cracked her head on those rocks that break the surface of the sand there. For a minute I thought I'd killed her. But no such luck. She was just groggy. Then I had this great idea—'

Fin stole his glory. 'To take her out to the cages and drown her there. People would think she'd been trying to get footage for Hendry's documentary, got into trouble and . . .'

'Exactly right. Once I got her into the back of the pickup, it was five minutes round to the harbour at Baile na Mara, another ten out to the cages in one of the RBBs. It was dark by then. Not a soul around. Easy. Just held her under till she stopped kicking. Strong, that girl, but no match for this boy.'

'So why on earth did you take her back round to the Black Loch?' It made no sense to Fin.

Eòghann sighed and shook his head in frustrated recollection. 'I was just about to get her all tangled up in the nets, to make it look like she'd got caught. Which was when I remembered. Her fucking car was still sitting up at that house. Then I had an even better idea. In fact, a brilliant bloody idea. Why not take her back round there? Leave her on the beach. Everyone would think your boy had killed her.' He smirked. 'And the best part of all, he'd believe it himself.' He held out open palms, self-congratulatory, almost as if seeking Fin's acknowledgement of his brilliance. 'It was a risk, yeah, but one worth taking.'

'Only, you just couldn't resist gilding the lily, could you? Trying to make it look like she'd been raped as well. I mean, that wouldn't make any sense, would it? Two people who'd been having sex for months.'

Eòghann shrugged. 'Yeah, well, that was probably a mistake. But you know, who cares? No one's ever going to know anything about it.'

His eyes strayed beyond Fin to the dark of the hall behind him. Fin sensed a presence and half turned. As something hard and unyielding struck his head, filling it first with light. And then with darkness.

CHAPTER THIRTY-TWO

The first thing Fin became aware of was the thrum of a motor vibrating painfully through his head. He was lying face down in an inch or more of water and couldn't move. His mouth was filled with the taste of salt and diesel.

He opened his eyes to the same darkness from which he had just emerged and blinked several times, before shadows cast by a light somewhere behind him began to take shape. As consciousness returned fully, he realized why he couldn't move. His hands were tied behind his back. Not rope. But something soft and restraining. His ankles were bound likewise. A rhythmic slap-slapping from below brought the realization that he was in a boat of some kind skimming over choppy water.

With a great effort, he managed to roll over on to his side, and saw a figure in the light standing at the helm near the rear of the boat. Somehow he had expected it to be Dempsey, but was shocked to see Niall standing there, his entire focus directed somewhere in the darkness ahead of them.

'Niall!' he shouted at the top of his voice, fighting to make it heard above the roar of the motor. But it didn't penetrate until the third shout, and Niall looked down to see him lying on his side in the bottom of the RBB. His face was tight with tension. He pulled back on the throttle, and the boat slowed, the noise of the engine retreating to a purr. But the wind still howled around them, and without the forward drive of its inboard, the boat rocked violently on the swell.

'Jesus Christ, Niall! What are you doing?' Fin was struggling to reconcile his situation with a friendship that went back to childhood.

Niall swung his head slowly from side to side in sad resignation. 'I'd have had it end any other way but this, Fin.' He sighed. 'But you just wouldn't let it go, would you?'

With a great effort, Fin managed to turn on to his back and pull himself into a half-sitting position. 'You knew all along!' The realization struck him like a blow to his midriff.

Niall nodded and sat down behind the wheel. 'From the moment I saw that pendant in the newspaper.'

'And it wasn't the first time, was it?'

Niall frowned. 'What are you talking about?'

'Eòghann's nanny.'

And darkness crossed Niall's face like a shadow. He was lost in momentary contemplation before returning to the boat and the wind and Fin lying helpless in the hull of his RBB. 'That's the beauty of having so much money, Fin. You can make anything go away.'

'Even murder?'

'Everyone has a price, and a sacrifice they are willing to

make. Even a lifetime in prison. In return for the guarantee of security for a whole family.' There was no humour in his smile. 'It was a drop in my financial ocean.'

Fin felt sick. 'All so that your boy could kill again.'

Niall bared his teeth in suppressed fury. 'That was *not* supposed to happen.'

'So how much did you know? And when?'

'Eòghann told me everything when I confronted him about the pendant. There have never been any secrets between us. I protected the boy from himself once, I can do it again.'

'He's a psychopath!' Fin shouted, and Niall cast him a dangerous look. 'For God's sake, Niall, you can't go killing people to cover up for him.'

'You do whatever it takes, Fin. Make whatever sacrifice is required of you for your family. Like that gardener in Cyprus. Like those pilot whales that came ashore today and died because one of their females was miscarrying.' He looked very directly at his old friend. 'Even you, Fin. Look how hard you've been working to prove your son innocent, even when you probably thought he wasn't.' He reached for the throttle, and Fin began to panic.

'What are you going to do?' he shouted. 'For God's sake, Niall!'

Niall's shoulders slumped and he released the throttle again. A shake of his head reflected genuine remorse. 'It's all coming full circle, isn't it? Iain's body found drowned in one of my dad's cages. You found drowned in one of mine.'

Fin felt his stomach lurch. 'Jesus, Niall!'

'I'm sorry, Fin. I really am. It's going to look like you came out searching for some kind of evidence to prove your son's innocence.' He shrugged hopelessly. 'Fell in. Got tangled up in the nets. Couldn't get out. Tragic.' His sigh seemed heartfelt. 'A tragedy compounded by Fionnlagh being found guilty of Caitlin's murder. I mean, I don't have much sympathy for him. Fucking a kid who's twelve years younger. Bloody child abuse! It's Marsaili I feel for. Really. She doesn't deserve any of this. I'll do what I can for her, Fin. I promise.'

Fin felt his final minutes slipping away. Never in all his wildest dreams had he imagined that it could all end like this. Drowned by a childhood friend in the same water from which they had stolen Hamish Black's salmon all those years ago. He said, 'You killed that ghillie, didn't you? Coinneach Smith. When he threatened to expose us.'

But Niall just shook his head. 'No, Fin. You've got that wrong.'

'So who did kill him, then?'

Niall lifted his eyes to the folds of low, black cloud scudding across the island. 'After they found Iain's body in one of the cages, my dad was out there examining it for damage. And guess what he found bobbing about in the water? Something that no one had paid the least attention to, even if they had seen it.'

Fin had no idea.

'A little blue plastic and silver inhaler. One of Artair's puffers.

356

Artair had been at the house often enough that my dad had seen him using it. So he knew immediately.' He sighed. 'Trust bloody Artair to drop us all in the shit.'

And Fin thought that, even all these years after his death, Artair was somehow still managing to exact his revenge.

'My dad confronted me.' Niall threw his hands out to either side. 'What was I going to do? Couldn't deny it. So I told him the whole sordid story, including Coinneach's threats to grass on us. Next thing I know, Coinneach's found dead at the foot of a cliff, and it all goes away.'

'Your dad killed him?' Fin was incredulous.

'Couldn't say for sure, Fin. But I'm pretty certain he went to confront him. Some kind of a scuffle, maybe. I don't know. Maybe it was an accident. Maybe it wasn't. All I know is that my father did what he had to do to protect his boy. Just like I've done for mine.'

This time he stood up and pulled back hard on the throttle, and the RBB lurched forward in the water, gaining speed as it scliffed across the loch, its lights reflecting in momentary licks of silver on black. His focus moved away from Fin towards the cages somewhere up ahead.

Fin's panic rose from his stomach and into his mouth like bile. He twisted frantically in the water in the bottom of the boat, trying in vain to free his hands and feet. His bindings felt harsher now, cutting into him as he fought in desperation against them. The boat lurched and banked into the swell, throwing him from one side to the other. Then suddenly the sound of the motor retreated and the boat's speed decreased rapidly. Niall swung the RBB side on, and Fin felt it bump up against the walkway of one of the cages.

Now he cut the motor, and jumped off with a rope to secure it. Fin thrashed about, desperately trying to break free.

Niall's silhouette loomed over him. 'Come on, Fin. Don't make this any harder than it needs to be. It's going to happen. Accept it.' He bent over, trying to loop his arms under Fin's oxters. But Fin kicked and bucked, so that Niall lost his balance and toppled over.

'For fuck's sake!' Fin heard him curse under his breath. Niall scrambled to his feet, staggering to the back of the boat, before returning with something clutched in his hand. The RBB lurched dangerously as he raised it above his head. A short length of pole, or pipe. He swung it viciously at Fin's head, and Fin managed to squirm to one side so that he took the brunt of the blow on his shoulder. He cried out involuntarily from the pain of it, and saw Niall raise the weapon again. This time it struck him on the left temple. He heard it, a sickening hollow sound, and thought it must have cracked his skull. All consciousness of the world around him was displaced by pain. And he felt his limbs, his whole body go limp.

He was not unconscious, but had no conscious power of movement over any part of himself. He was only vaguely aware of Niall leaning over him, legs apart to brace himself against the violent movement of the boat. He seemed to be untying Fin's hands and feet, but Fin was unable to move them. Neither was he able to resist as Niall heaved him bodily out of the boat and on to the walkway. His face smashed hard on to the metal grille as the other man dropped him.

He lay there, unable to move. Aware that the end of his life was now only moments away, and there was nothing he could do to stop it. As his head rolled back, he saw Niall standing above him, releasing part of the net that covered the cage from its securing rings on the handrail. Then Niall had his arms through Fin's, pulling him to his feet, and for a moment they staggered towards the rail together, locked in embrace, as if performing some grotesque dance of death. Before Fin felt the handrail slam into his back, and the pain of it made him gasp. Niall stooped and lifted his feet to tip him over, and Fin fell backwards into the cage.

The cold shock of the water restored something like consciousness, and as he sank beneath it, Fin found that he could move his arms and his legs. The cage was alive with Hendry's zombie fish. Washed-out salmon with staring eyes, white flesh half eaten away by lice. He saw bubbles of air escape his own lips and rise swiftly to break the surface above.

It was pure panic that propelled him up after them, fish scattering all around, as finally he too broke the surface, gasping for air. He saw Niall looking down on him, watching from the walkway, a long pole with a boathook on the end of it held across his chest.

Fin grabbed for the walkway, and found his fingers closing around a loop of rope. Before he felt the curve of the boathook pressing into his chest, and the violence of the thrust that broke his grip on the rope and pushed him back under.

This time he swallowed water as he tried to fill his lungs with air before going down, and he started choking and vomiting as the pressure on his chest held him below the surface. He grabbed for the pole, managing to force it to one side before losing his grip on it. A kick of his feet brought him back to the surface, head tipped back, sucking air into distressed lungs. Incongruously he became aware of a break in the clouds almost directly overhead, and the scattering of careless moonlight tossed by the night across the troubled surface of the water. And then there it was again. The pressure of the boathook in his chest, all of Niall's strength driving him back down. Down, down, down into the loch. Fin felt his own strength waning. Lungs, exhausted now of oxygen, bursting, desperate for air. He tried so hard to resist the reflex to breathe. Until he couldn't.

His whole life spooled before him then at breakneck speed. His first day at school. Marsaili's coy little smile, pigtails falling across her shoulders. His aunt taking him back to that cold, lonely house above the harbour the day after the death of his parents. Artair sucking on his puffer, and cursing him on the cliffs of An Sgeir before he went over. Robbie laughing and kicking a football in the garden. Mona's tears when she told Fin his son was dead. Whistler lying bleeding on the floor of his crofthouse. Donald falling as the gunshot rang out from the rooftops opposite. Fionnlagh weeping for his lost love in a police cell. And Marsaili again. Always Marsaili. Marsaili.

Fin felt the water rush in to fill his lungs, stealing away strength, and light, and finally consciousness.

CHAPTER THIRTY-THREE

The slow tick of the clock on the wall thundered in the silence of the kitchen. Marsaili sat on the edge of a chair at the table, wringing her hands in front of her.

'Something's happened, Duncan. I know it. That's more than an hour and a half now.'

Duncan turned away from the window that gave on to the road above. 'Do you want me to go down to the port to see if his car's still at Niall Dubh's place?'

'No. No. If we go down there, we should go together.'

'Isn't there anyone we can phone for help?'

The headlights of a car turning into the parking area above the bungalow raked across the window and off into the night. Followed by darkness.

Marsaili was on her feet in an instant, hurrying to the window to peer into the dark, before the security lamp came on and flooded the path with light. Donna and Eilidh made their way down from the car to the steps leading up to the kitchen, and Marsaili turned away in disappointment.

Donna sensed the tension in the house the moment she

opened the door. She glanced from Marsaili to Duncan and then back again. 'What's happened?'

Marsaili drew a deep breath. 'Donna, Fionnlagh didn't kill that girl. We think it was Niall Dubh's son, Eòghann. Fin went down to confront them ages ago, but he's not come back.'

The blood drained from Donna's face, and she dropped into a kitchen chair, barely able to absorb what her mother-in-law had just told her. Eilidh said, 'Does that mean my dad's innocent?'

Marsaili nodded. 'It does, Eilidh.' And the child ran to her, burying her face in her grandmother's chest and clinging on as if her life depended upon it. Marsaili looked at Donna over the girl's head. 'I don't know what to do about Fin. I'm scared for him, Donna.'

Donna stood up abruptly, as if suddenly she was the grown-up in the room. 'What about George Gunn? We could call George.'

Duncan said, 'That's a good idea.'

Marsaili released Eilidh from her arms. 'I think Fin's got a home number for him in our contacts app.' She hurried out into the hall and through to the bedroom. The screensaver filled the room with its ghostly light. Marsaili banished it and ran her cursor along the dock to open the contacts file she shared with Fin. When she turned, she saw Donna standing at the door waiting with her phone. 'Got it,' she said.

CHAPTER THIRTY-FOUR

Pain was the first of his senses to return. An all-consuming, wholly disabling pain, his entire body in spasm, expelling foaming brine from his mouth to splash across the unforgiving metal grille. He was on his side, retching uncontrollably.

Then strong hands rolled him on to his back, and soft lips met his, breathing life back into dead lungs. As the lips moved away, he coughed and gasped and drew the first stuttering breath. He opened his eyes wide, blind for a moment, before the concern on the face of his saviour came slowly into focus.

Iseabail ran a hand across his forehead. 'Thank God,' she said. 'Thank God.'

Another face floated into view. Pierced and unshaven, but equally concerned. 'Are you alright, man? Jesus, we thought you were dead. Thought we were too late.'

Fin had a thousand questions and none, as he concentrated on breathing. Gulping down cold, sweet air to send oxygen coursing once more through his veins. The very act of which was normally unconscious. Breathing. The thing that kept you alive that you never thought about until you couldn't do it.

'Here.' Hendry reached round to slip his backpack from his shoulders, and took out a plastic container filled with orange juice. He held the mouthpiece to Fin's lips and Fin gulped down two mouthfuls, before turning suddenly aside to vomit into the loch.

Hendry forced a grin. 'It might have been a day or two past its sell-by, but I didn't think it was that bad.'

Fin grasped his hand and guided the mouthpiece to his lips again. This time he kept down the cloying sweetness of the juice, citric acid burning his mouth and throat. He pulled himself up on to one elbow and lay breathing stertorously for several long minutes. Finally the question reached lips that were able, at last, to form it. 'How?'

Iseabail said, 'We came out in Colm's dinghy. I'd never have been able to swim across in this weather. And anyway it would have been too dangerous on my own.' She glanced at Hendry.

'It was our last chance, Mr Macleod, to get the footage I need for the documentary. That big bastard Dempsey threatened that if I wasn't off the island by tomorrow, he'd do me physical harm.' He glanced at Iseabail. 'And said that if Iseabail wasn't careful, she'd go the same way as her friend.'

Fin felt his voice scraping in his throat. 'Well, I'm glad you ignored him.'

'We were already here when we saw the light of Niall Dubh's boat,' Iseabail said. 'We paddled round to the far side of the feed silo and hid there as he tied up the RBB. We saw him hitting someone, then dragging them out of the boat on to the walkway. It was only then we realized it was you.'

Hendry said, 'Jesus, Mr Macleod, I thought he was your friend.'

'*Was*,' Fin said.

'Couldn't believe it,' Iseabail said, 'when we saw him push you into the cage and hold you under.'

'No point in trying to intervene at that stage,' Hendry said. 'He's a big fella, that. Who knows, even with two of us, if we could have taken him down.'

'By which time you'd have been dead.'

Fin felt Iseabail's fingers on his face, and was almost overcome by a rush of gratitude.

'He didn't hang about,' she said. 'As soon as he headed off, we came round and pulled you out.'

Hendry looked at him in wonder. 'You were gone, man. And you wouldn't be here now if it hadn't been for Iseabail. She pumped and pumped your chest until I thought she would break your ribs. Water gouting from your mouth. You must have swallowed half the bloody loch.'

Fin gazed up into her warm brown eyes and reached for her hand. He squeezed it in both of his. 'Thank you,' he whispered. Then, 'Help me up.' The two of them lifted him to his feet, and he stood on shaking legs clutching the handrail. 'I need to get back to Ness.'

*

The throaty rasp of the outboard motor on Colm Hendry's inflatable was almost lost in the roar of the wind as they turned into Loch Riosaigh. The Irishman drove it straight up on to the shingle in front of the abandoned crofthouse, lifting the outboard clear of the water at the last moment and stalling it. They jerked to an abrupt stop on the slope of the finely pebbled shore, and Iseabail and Hendry helped Fin out and over the broken concrete to the house, Iseabail scanning a flashlight on the ground ahead of them.

Fin's clothes were still soaking, and he was shivering almost uncontrollably from the cold. He heard his own teeth chattering, almost disembodied, as if the sound of it were coming from somewhere else. They sat him on a broken chair and, as Iseabail lit candles, Hendry fetched a couple of blankets, which he wrapped around Fin's shoulders. Iseabail handed him a beaker full of cold water and he gulped it down with the thirst of a man who had spent days in the desert. He said, 'Anyone got a phone?'

Hendry shrugged helplessly. 'No signal here, mate.'

Their shadows danced around the walls of the room in the flickering candlelight, and Fin took a moment to recover his breath. 'Can I borrow your Land Rover?'

'Sure.'

Iseabail was alarmed. 'You're not going back to face Niall Dubh on your own.'

'I don't have much choice, Iseabail. I know who killed Caitlin.'

'So do we, mate,' Hendry said. 'The fella that tried to kill you.'

But Fin shook his head. 'No. Not Niall. But we're dealing with very dangerous people here. They've got to be stopped.'

Hendry scoffed. 'By you? You're in no state to do anything about it, mate.'

'I'll be fine. Is there enough petrol in the Land Rover?'

Hendry nodded. 'And the heater works well. She'll have you warm and well dried by the time you get there. But take my advice, fella. Much as I hate to ask them for anything, I'd call the police as soon as you can. And, remember, you've got a couple of reliable witnesses here to attempted murder.'

Even with his foot to the floor, the old Land Rover wouldn't kick past fifty miles an hour, and it lumbered painfully all the way up the west coast to Barvas.

Several times Fin tried to call the police. But his phone had not survived the drowning as he had. At the Barvas crossroads he hesitated for a good thirty seconds. A right turn would lead him across the moor to Stornoway. But it would take a good twenty minutes to get there. In that same time he could almost be at Ness. He turned left, wiping the condensation from the side window with his sleeve. Hendry was right. The heater worked well, and his clothes were almost dry already. But all his windows were steamed up, and he opened them now to let fresh air flood in.

He had stopped shivering, though every part of him still

ached. His head felt as though it were in the grip of a vice. But that didn't stop the clear thought and anger that filled it. One of his oldest friends had just tried to kill him. To murder him in cold blood. Force him below the water and watch him drown. All to save a son who had murdered his sister then tried to blame it on Fionnlagh.

He had absolutely no doubt that Dempsey would be tasked with getting Eòghann off the island as soon as possible. And that in all probability Niall would join them. The early morning ferry from Stornoway. Or the 9 a.m. departure from Tarbert to Skye. Earliest flight was at 8.40, but then they would be without wheels. Though it wasn't beyond the bounds of possibility that Niall would have a helicopter come pick them up.

Fin had no idea what time it was. His watch had stopped working, and there was no clock in the Land Rover. But he thought it must be late. Niall would figure that Fin's body wouldn't be found until the morning, so he'd have a few hours' grace to get his boy off the island. Better for him not to be around when the shit hit the fan.

Fin was determined to stop him.

369

CHAPTER THIRTY-FIVE

Fin cut the motor and extinguished the lights of the Land Rover to freewheel into the village. Even as he reached the Breakwater, he could see that there were no lights breaching the darkness at the house on the cliff. He turned into the parking area in front of the restaurant. The Breakwater itself was long shut and stood in shadow, but the single track up to the house shimmered beneath orange streetlights, and far below, the incoming tide rushed into the harbour, breaking white all along the retaining wall.

Fin eased himself out of the vehicle and found a toolkit strapped to the inside of the rear door. He selected a sturdy wheel brace around eighteen inches long, and felt the weight of it in his hand, closing his fingers around the grip. He was determined that the anger that suffused him would simmer slowly and not tempt him into anything rash. He began walking up the road towards the house.

The wind filled out clothes that remained only a little damp, and it swirled around his mouth as he breathed. Off to his right, the beach was doused in darkness, the darker shapes of the dead whales that littered it barely visible. Before a sudden break in the cloud washed it with unexpected moonlight, and the full extent of the carnage revealed itself to the night.

Fin returned his focus to the house. As he approached the gates, there was no sign of life inside or out. He stepped cautiously into the parking area. There was only one vehicle there now. Niall's Mercedes.

The security lamp snapped on, flooding the rear of the property with light. Fin stood fully exposed on the asphalt and realized that anyone inside would know now that he was there. He tried the sliding glass doors. But they were locked. He crossed towards the original extension and turned the handle on the back door. It opened into a kitchen bathed in light from the streetlamp immediately outside the far window. Marble worktops, slate-grey cabinets. A modern peat-fired range. Pinpoints of red light winking on an array of electronic devices. A digital clock in the darkness revealed the time to be 23:35.

Fin hefted the wheel brace in his hand and stepped carefully through the kitchen and into the hallway, listening for any tiny sound that might betray the presence of another human being.

A movement at the foot of the stairs registered in his peripheral vision, and his heart pushed up into his mouth as a black cat streaked through the shadows, between his legs and out through the kitchen. Fin fought hard to control breathing that sounded inordinately loud in the still of the house.

The door to the lounge where Eòghann played his video games stood open. Someone had forgotten to turn off the TV, and it had reverted to a screensaver taking the viewer on a journey through outer space. Past planets and stars and cosmic clouds. None of which radiated more than the feeblest flicker of light around a room otherwise simmering in darkness.

Fin stood for a long time in the doorway, undecided. Before calling out Niall's name. When there was no response, he tried again. Then, 'Eòghann?'

He moved forward into the room, and saw a figure approaching. A familiar figure, but not Niall or Eòghann. A figure filled with tension and clutching a weapon in his right hand. Fin smothered a small cry as he realized it was his own reflection in a tall, wall-mounted mirror. He released his tension in a long breath as a shadow flew at him out of the dark. Fin saw it in brief silhouette against the TV screen, before it was on him. And the two men fell to the floor, breath exploding from each as they landed heavily.

The other man's face was inches from Fin's, and, as the screensaver on the TV opposite flew them slowly around the rings of Saturn, he saw that it was Niall, his face contorted and ugly. The wheel brace had been knocked from Fin's grasp as he hit the floor, and skidded away across the carpet. There was incredulity in Niall's eyes. 'What the fuck, Fin?' he hissed at him. 'I killed you!'

But Fin swung a hand balled into a fist, and struck Niall's face twice, the second blow bursting his nose. Fin felt the spray of warm blood on his face, and heard Niall's cry of pain. With an effort, he pushed the other man aside, and scrambling to his feet, staggered across the room in search of the wheel brace. He found it by the light of the Milky Way as its space fog filled the screen, and he turned to repel a second attack.

But Niall was gone. Sprinting through the kitchen and out into the night. If, momentarily, he had entertained the idea of trying to get away in the Mercedes, he must quickly have realized there was no time to get into the vehicle.

Fin found a bank of light switches by the door, and threw them all on. The house lit up like a Christmas tree, inside and out, and as he stepped into the parking area, he saw Niall running down the road towards the village.

Fin drew a deep breath and started after him. He was lighter and fitter than Niall and knew that, if he paced himself, sooner or later Niall would start to lose momentum. And he would catch him. Realizing that when he did, it would take a great effort of will not to beat him to a pulp with the wheel brace.

He loped down the single track to the village, conserving his own energy, keeping a careful eye on Niall in the distance as he veered off the road beyond the Breakwater. There were steps there, Fin knew, that wound down to the road that led to the boat shed where, all those years before, Angel Macritchie had been found on the eve of the Sabbath, hanging from the rafters, buck naked, disembowelled and bleeding out on the concrete floor.

Ironic, Fin thought, that on this night, too, the Sabbath was only minutes away.

He jogged down the steps to the road and saw Niall jump from the wall on to the sand, a hundred yards ahead of him. Just as the wind tore the clouds apart and let the moon spill its light across the killing beach with all its dead.

By the time Fin got down to it himself, he could see that Niall was flagging, the sand sapping strength from his legs with each step. Fin was amazed at his own reserves of stamina. For a man who had been dead for what must have been minutes, he found that he was still able to draw on unsuspected reserves. Fuelled, perhaps, by anger. Or maybe revenge.

Niall staggered from dead whale to dead whale, weaving his way between them, his gait increasingly erratic. Whale blood soaked black into the sand in the moonlight, and not even the wind could carry off the stench of death.

Fin slowed to a walk and knew that he would catch him.

Finally, Niall's legs gave way beneath him and he toppled into the soft, fine grains. He dragged himself up into a half-sitting position, leaning back against the carcass of a whale, and watched Fin approach.

'You're not going to get my boy, Fin!' he shouted at him, spittle gathering in a creamy froth about his lips. 'He's long gone.'

Fin watched as his own moonlight shadow fell across the other man. He stopped in the sand in front of him and tightened his grip on the wheel brace. One swift blow would probably kill him. And yet, somehow, that seemed too easy.

Niall spat in the sand and looked up at him. 'Why are you not dead? I drowned you.'

'You did.'

'Jesus, Fin, you're like a fucking cockroach. Impossible to kill!'

'Until now.' The voice came from behind him, and Fin turned, startled, to find Dempsey standing a few paces away, the butt of a sawn-off shotgun tucked under his arm. The big man was breathing heavily. But at this range he couldn't miss. He said, 'The thing about cockroaches is that they're really quite easy to kill. Soapy water will do it.' He leered at Fin. 'As for the human variety, a shotgun will do nicely.'

He swung the gun into both hands, holding it at hip height to level at Fin.

The sound of the shot filled the night air, brutal and deafening, like a clap of thunder rising above the roar of the wind and the sea. Fin gasped, bracing for its impact, and was stunned to see Dempsey spinning off into the darkness, his shotgun discharging harmlessly into the air. His blood sprayed dark in the moonlight, and as he landed heavily in the sand, Fin saw that his right arm was hanging on by a thread at the shoulder.

A cry of anguish rose above the wind, and Marsaili ran out of the night and into his arms, sobbing uncontrollably as he held her close, trembling and wondering how it was that he was still alive. Then beyond her he saw the pale, traumatized face of Duncan Macgowan, the barrel of his 30-06 Springfield pointing harmlessly now at the sand. From behind him the burly figure of George Gunn emerged breathless from the darkness. He took the gun from Duncan, glanced at Dempsey, then at Fin. 'Well, this is another right bloody mess, Mr Macleod,' he said.

CHAPTER THIRTY-SIX

The wind was still blowing, but the cloud cover was broken, allowing sunlight to seep through in fits and starts, peppering the purple of the land with ever-shifting shades of yellow.

Breakers still rolled in off the Minch, surging foamy and white at high tide among the carcasses of the whales.

The mood in the bungalow was solemn. Fin had barely slept, despite the medic's diagnosis the previous night of concussion and the need to rest, both physically and mentally. Each time he felt himself drift away, he was back in the cage, Niall's boathook in his chest forcing him under, and he was startled awake. And each time, he felt Marsaili's fingers on his face, softly stroking, gentle and reassuring.

He had no appetite for breakfast, and stood by the window in the kitchen watching the road expectantly. Marsaili sat at the table, toying with a piece of toast she had managed to burn. The smell of it, along with fresh ground coffee, filled the room.

Earlier, not long after they had slipped from their bed, the newsreader on Radio nan Gael had announced that police had picked up Eòghann Black in a green Range Rover trying to board the ferry at Tarbert. Jack Dempsey had been airlifted to Inverness, where, according to latest reports, surgeons were trying to save his arm. And perhaps his life.

A line of churchgoers in black passed along the road above the bungalow, clutching hats and Bibles, coats flapping in the wind. On their way, Fin thought, to listen to the sanctimonious preaching of the hypocrite they called their minister. A man without honour or merit, an unworthy successor to Donald Murray.

He heard the motor of a car straining up the hill, and a few moments later a blue and white police vehicle pulled into the gravel parking area at the top of the drive.

'Is that him?' Marsaili joined him at the window.

'Looks like it.'

After a moment, the rear door opened and a pale, fragile-looking Fionnlagh, clutching an overnight bag, stepped out into a wind that seemed like it might blow him away. He stood there for a long moment as the police vehicle drove off, head raised a little, breathing in the sweet air of freedom.

Fin said, 'Where's Donna?'

Marsaili sighed. 'In her bedroom. I'm not sure she's going to come out.'

They turned at the sound of the outside door opening behind them, and saw Eilidh rushing out on to the steps. From the window they watched her run up the path to bury her face in her father's chest. Fionnlagh dropped his bag, encircling her

378

with his arms, kissing the top of her head and cupping it in his hand, eyes tight shut.

Marsaili took Fin's arm. 'We should leave the three of them to it.'

They met Fionnlagh and Eilidh halfway up the path. Eilidh stood aside to watch as Fionnlagh held his mother, smothering her sobs, his own face wet and shining in the morning sun. When finally they broke apart, he and Fin looked at each other, almost warily. For a moment it seemed as if they would shake hands, and then at the last, they fell into a father–son hug that required no words. Standing there on the path, battered by the wind, Eilidh and Marsaili looking on and smiling through silent tears.

When they parted, Fionnlagh took Eilidh's hand and stood a moment, regarding the house that had been his home, and weighing up the reckoning he couldn't avoid.

Fin grasped his arm. 'The present used to be the unimaginable future, son,' he said. 'You and Donna still have each other for now. Try to imagine a future where you don't.' He paused. 'Fix your mistakes before you make them. Because there is so much you do that can't be undone.'

Fionnlagh's face was full of pain and regret. He nodded. And he and Eilidh set off down the path towards that unimaginable future.

If anything, the wind had stiffened by the time Fin and Marsaili reached the top end of Crobost, tugging at their clothes and filling their mouths as they spoke. And they stood staring out over the bay and the arc of shingle beach below. Boats rocked gently with each successive gust on the slipway above the tiny Crobost harbour, and behind them Fin's aunt's old house stood proud against a broken sky. They watched clouds chase one another across the Minch, dodging patches of sunlight that lay like pools of molten silver on the surface of the ocean.

Marsaili held Fin's right arm with both of hers, leaning into him, head resting against his shoulder. 'What are we going to do, Fin?'

He inclined his head to look at her. 'What do you mean?'

'If that CIO is right, you're not going to have a job to go back to.'

'Well, if I'm honest,' Fin said, 'that would be a relief.' He shook his head. 'Somewhere along the way I took a wrong turn, Marsaili. We both did.' He felt her gentle nod of acknowledgement. 'We can't undo the past, but we can still make the future. Maybe this is where we should have been all along.'

She looked up at him. 'You mean the island?'

'Maybe we should never have left. Maybe this is where we belong.' He was lost in thought as his eyes drifted along the far horizon. And from nowhere, he said, 'You told me once that Duncan Macgowan asked if you would go out with him when you were at the Nicolson.'

'He did.'

'So why didn't you?'

She shrugged. 'I had my eye on someone else.'

'Oh? Who was that?'

She punched him playfully in the ribs and he winced. She laughed. 'Sorry.'

'So what if you had gone out with him? I saw you with him at a party once in Glasgow.'

'Who knows?' She smiled. 'The unimaginable future.'

But still Fin could see the way she had put her hand on his arm. The odd sense of intimacy in it. He said, 'Did you ever sleep with him?'

He felt her stiffen at his side, and there was a long silence, before she said in a small voice, 'I did.'

He turned, prompted by a sudden stab of jealousy, and said, 'When?'

'Remember the night I came home to the flat in Highburgh Road and found you in our bed with that girl?'

Fin closed his eyes. It was something they had never discussed. The lowest point of their time together in Glasgow. The guilt still pained him. 'You didn't sleep with him *that* night?'

'Where did you think I was going to go, Fin? In the dark. In the snow. With nowhere to sleep and no trains till the morning. I don't think I could even have afforded a hotel room. And if I could, I wouldn't have had the train fare home.'

He knew he had no right to be jealous. But that green-eyed monster had its claws in him again.

'But don't worry, it was pure revenge,' she said. 'Too much wine and too much dope, and an overwhelming desire to hurt you back. Even if you didn't know it.'

They stood for a very long time then, swaying slightly in the wind, hoping it might blow away the ashes of the past.

Before she said, 'Of course, it was a mistake. Another of those things you do that can't be undone. But Fin . . .' She turned her face towards him. 'Imagine I hadn't slept with him that night. We probably wouldn't have connected again on the beach yesterday. And Duncan wouldn't have been at the house last night.'

Fin finished for her. 'And if he hadn't been, there would have been nothing to stop Dempsey from killing me.'

It was a sobering thought. They started walking, arm in arm, down the slipway to the harbour where a small boat tethered to a rusted metal ring rose and fell on the swell, its fenders rasping as they scraped up against the harbour wall.

Marsaili said, 'If we sold up in Glasgow, we could buy a place down at Uig. Imagine something with a view over that beach. And the mountains rising up behind the lodge.'

'We could fly kites on windy days,' Fin said.

Marsaili laughed. 'Every day, you mean?'

He grinned. 'The imaginable future.' Then his smile faded. 'What would we do for a living?'

Her shrug was careless, and lost in the wind. 'We'll figure it out.'

He leaned over to kiss her, and remembered that little girl with the pigtails who had walked him up the road from school to Crobost Stores, giving him the nickname that had stuck for the rest of his life. 'Sure,' he said. 'We'll figure it out.'

GAELIC PRONUNCIATIONS

CHARACTER NAMES

Fionnlagh – Fj (as in fjord) oonlagh, soft gh ending

Iseabail – Eeshuhbal

Marsaili – Marsahlee

Niall – Nyeeall – The ny is similar to that in Enya

Eòghann – Yo-inn

Coinneach – Cawnyach – as in ny above

Artair – Arstur

Mac a'Ghobhainn – Mac uh-Ghowing – gh as in above

Nic Ille Dhuibh – Neek Ilyu Ghooch – ch as in Ich in German

Nic a'Phearsain – Neek uh – Ferrsan

Eilidh – Ay as in hay followed by lee, Aylee

PLACE NAMES

Loch a Tuath – Tuath has a soft dental T, followed by ooh-uh

Rubha Robhanais – Roouh Rowanish

Tràigh Mhòr – Soft T again, as above, then rah-j (as in fjord)
   Vore

Bernera Beag – Bernarah Beg

Loch Ceann Hùlabhaig – Loch Kjaawn – that j again as above, Hoolahvig

Fuaigh Mòr – Foo-uh-j (same j) Vore

Bhàcasaigh – Vackasayj

Pabaigh Mòr – Pahbahj More

Eilean Beag – Aylan Beg

Baile na Mara – Baluh nuh Mara

Rudha Linsiadair – Roouh Leenshadar

Rudha Glas – Roouh Glass

Dùn Èistean – Doon Aysh-chen

Loch Riosaigh – Loch Reesahj

Aird Mhòr – Ard Vore

Breascleit – Bree-ass-klaych (ch as in chair)

Breacleit – Bree-ah-klaych

Loch Geal – Loch Gyaal

GENERAL

Eilean Fraoch – Aylan Frao (as the i in in – but elongated – IIIIIn) then hard ch as in loch

Seanair – Shenaar

Shen – As written

Dubh – Dental Doo

Ruadh – Roo-ugh

Canùdh agus Cuan – Canoe ughas Coo-aan

Comunn Eachdraidh Nis – Co-mun-j (as in fjord again) ech (as
   in echt) dree

Ràc an fheòir – Rack unjawr

Comhairle nan Eilean Siar – Koo-urr luh nun Aylan Sheer

Radio nan Gàidheal – Radio nun Gyjail

Geodha – Gyjawe-uh

An Taigh Cèilidh – Un Tayj Kaylee

Pronunciations kindly provided by Rhoda Macdonald

ACKNOWLEDGEMENTS

I would like to offer my grateful thanks to the following for their generous help in my researches for *The Black Loch*.

Dr Steven Campman MD, medical examiner, San Diego, California, as always for his invaluable advice on forensic pathology; Ewan Kennedy, retired solicitor and campaigner against industrial aquaculture in Scotland, for guiding me through my initial researches on fish farming; Dr Andrew Brownlow, director of SMASS (Scottish Marine Animal Stranding Scheme), for his expertise on the mass stranding of whales; Kenny Macleod, animal health inspector at Comhairle nan Eilean Siar (Western Isles Council), for his advice on the processes involved in dealing with stranded whales; Hector Low, veterinary surgeon, Isle of Lewis, for his compelling account of euthanizing stranded whales; Detective Constable Louise Henderson, Stornoway Police, for her insights into police procedures on the Isle of Lewis; Alasdair Fraser, owner of the Stornoway Smokehouse, for his wisdom on early fish farming on the Isle of Lewis; Callum Macaulay, director of the Great Bernera Community Development Trust, for his

extensive knowledge of the history of fish farming on Loch
Roag, Isle of Lewis; Don Staniford, director of $camon $cotland,
and campaigner against industrial aquaculture; Corin Smith,
photographer and anti-fish farm activist; Rhoda Macdonald
and Derek 'Pluto' Murray, for their invaluable advice on Scots
Gaelic; Jenny Wilson, of Jenny Wilson Art, Great Bernera, Isle
of Lewis, for her help with island locations and her wonderful
photograph and painting of the fictitious Black Loch; Janice
Hally May, my wife, best friend and confidante, for being my
fiercest critic in the most constructive way; Jon Riley, for being
the best editor any writer could hope for.

ISLE
OF
LEWIS

Cages

Tobson

Great
Bernera
Baile na Mara

Bridge over
the Atlantic

Mangersta

Scarp